CLOSING TIME

A STONECHILD AND ROULEAU MYSTERY

CLOSING TIME

BRENDA CHAPMAN

DUNDURN
TORONTO

Publisher: Scott Fraser | Editor: Shannon Whibbs
Cover designer: Laura Boyle
Cover image: shutterstock.com/istock.com/Ugreen
Printer: Marquis Book Printing Inc.

Library and Archives Canada Cataloguing in Publication

Title: Closing time / Brenda Chapman
Names: Chapman, Brenda, 1955- author.
Description: Series statement: A Stonechild and Rouleau mystery
Identifiers: Canadiana (print) 2019018437X | Canadiana (ebook) 20190184388 | ISBN 9781459745339 (softcover) | ISBN 9781459745346 (PDF) | ISBN 9781459745353 (EPUB) Classification: LCC PS8605.H36 C56 2020 | DDC C813/.6—dc23

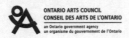

We acknowledge the support of the Canada Council for the Arts and the Ontario Arts Council for our publishing program. We also acknowledge the financial support of the Government of Ontario, through the Ontario Book Publishing Tax Credit and Ontario Creates, and the Government of Canada.

VISIT US AT

 dundurn.com | @dundurnpress | dundurnpress | dundurnpress

Dundurn
3 Church Street, Suite 500
Toronto, Ontario, Canada
M5E 1M2

For Ted

All extremes of feeling are allied with madness.
— Virginia Woolf, *Orlando*

There will be time, there will be time
To prepare a face to meet the faces that you meet;
There will be time to murder and create.
— T.S. Eliot, "The Love Song of
J. Alfred Prufrock"

CHAPTER ONE

The jagged line of pine and balsam trees cast spindly black fingers onto the beach. Rachel knew that the shadows would stretch into a solid line of darkness within the hour. She turned her face away from the path through the woods where he would come and looked out across the lake. She was cold. The mist had seeped under her skin and dampened her hair so that it hung lank and heavy down her back. The chill had worked its way up her spine and into her limbs from the rock she'd been sitting on for the past hour. She knew that she should give up and go home, but the light would hold another fifteen minutes or so. After that, she'd have no choice but to leave. The woods were too thick and eerie to stumble through in complete darkness. As it was, her mother would be pacing and working herself into a lather wondering why she was so late.

The lies were getting harder to pull off.

He'd promised to meet her. Rubbed the knuckles of his hand up and down her cheek when he'd said it. She'd let her eyes drop deliberately, slowly, suggestively to his groin, and he'd laughed when he cupped her chin and lifted her face upwards. "Don't start what we can't finish," he'd said. Rachel shivered, remembering the huskiness in his voice. She'd stared up into his eyes, unblinking, unreadable, and she'd felt powerful at being able to unleash this animal passion in him. They were like characters in a romance novel, only for real.

Sometimes she didn't recognize herself. She'd turned inside out to please him and this need to see him was with her all the time. It was as if she were thirsty and only getting sips that made her thirstier. He was like a drug she'd die without. She had moments of self-reflection when she wondered if she should have ever started down this road, but every time they were together, the doubts disappeared.

Her eyes scanned the western horizon. The sun was a glowing half-circle seeming to sink into the sea. She knew this to be an optical illusion. The earth's daily rotation around the sun was causing the shades of peach and golden light that radiated across the still water, soon to be swallowed up by mauve and the darkest shade of purple. She'd studied the planets the year before in grade ten science class. The days were getting shorter by two minutes every day and the nights were cooler than even a week ago.

She closed her eyes and remembered the morning he'd put both hands on the wall, one on either side of her head, before leaning in to kiss her. Her heart had been pounding so hard in her chest she'd wondered if she was having a heart attack. He knew that she had a boyfriend named Darryl Kelly, but he hadn't cared. After they made love for the first time, she hadn't cared about Darryl Kelly either. The funny thing was that Darryl still was waiting around like an annoying lovesick puppy while she could barely remember why she'd gone out with him in the first place.

There was a lull in the wind, and she sensed him behind her before she heard his feet leaping across the rocks. He was a tall, dark shape coming toward her but his eyes glinted in the half-gloom. She stood to meet him, arms wrapped around herself for warmth. He jumped from the rock below, straightened from a crouch less than a foot away from her, and then she was enclosed in his strong arms, their bodies pressed tightly against each other as if they belonged together.

"I'd almost given up on you," she said before his mouth was on hers, cutting off her breath in a deep kiss that would have brought her to her knees if he hadn't kept a firm hand at her waist.

"Let's get out of here," he said when they broke apart. "Out of the cold at least."

He didn't tell her why he was late. She knew better than to ask and put pressure on him. Instinctively, she sensed that he kept coming back to her because she made no demands. She let him lead her away from the rocks and sea. The wind whipped her damp hair and blew through her woollen sweater. She stumbled when her foot touched the hard-packed sand. She thought she saw a movement in the trees and strained her eyes to peer into the shadows. Her hand tugged on his arm. "Is someone there?" she asked.

He stopped and looked in the direction of her finger. His voice sounded irritated, as if she was making up obstacles to put off his pleasure. "Who'd be out here this time of day? I don't see anything."

"I guess I imagined it." *Surely I'm not being followed, too?*

She set aside the uneasy feeling and sagged against him as they crossed the stretch of beach and entered the wood. Her desire flamed once they were in the shelter of the trees. She wanted to announce her love for him to the world. She'd suggested going away together the last time they'd met, thinking he wanted the same. He'd caressed her cheek and said it was too soon. She had two more years of high school and had only just turned sixteen. Her parents would need time to come around, to give their blessing. They might force her to give him up. He had a lot to lose, too. He'd argued for secrecy and she'd promised to stay silent until they agreed to take the next step.

She stopped beside a pine tree and pulled on his arm. He turned and she twisted her fingers through his hair. He pushed her back against the tree and his hand snaked under her shirt to grab her breast.

"Are you sure?" he asked, lifting his face from hers to look her in the eyes. "This isn't the most comfortable of places."

Her voice came out a panting command, "Don't stop."

"Good answer."

She could see his smile before he leaned in to kiss her. She whispered "I love you" as his lips reached hers and felt him hesitate momentarily before his hand was pulling down her zipper and wrenching her jeans and underwear down her legs until she could kick them off. She bit back a yelp of pain when the weight of him pushed her hard against the tree, the rough bark scraping her back. He eased off and she adjusted her back into a better position, pulling him closer to her until they were one. He liked her to close her eyes when he was inside her, but this time she kept them open. His eyes were shut tight and his breath came in pants and grunts as he slid in and out of her. She couldn't mistake the emotion on his face. He wanted this ... he needed her. He couldn't live without her either. She only had to be patient and give him the space to realize they didn't have to wait any longer to start their lives together in a new town. She'd have enough money soon to get them started while he looked for another job. It would work. There really could be a happily ever after.

All she had to do was close her eyes and dream.

CHAPTER TWO

Tanya Morrison put away her cellphone and crossed the street to where Kala Stonechild was chatting to a uniformed officer. The afternoon had warmed up while they were inside speaking with the owner of the Chinese restaurant who'd been beaten and robbed the night before. He was shaken up, but in good enough shape to be out of the hospital. She'd flinched at the sight of his face, a crisscross of swollen bruises and cuts that made him look like a prizefighter on the losing end of a long bout. His right eye was turning purple and had swollen completely shut.

She waited until Stonechild finished speaking before nudging her with an elbow. "That was Rouleau. He wants us to check out an assault since it's nearby. Do you have time or should I go alone? I know you're on leave after this shift." She held her breath. Averted her gaze.

Stonechild began walking in the direction of her truck. "No, I'll come with you and will head home from there if you don't mind briefing Rouleau and following up."

"Works for me. Thanks." Her breath released in a slow exhale. As predicted, Stonechild couldn't turn down a case.

Stonechild pulled out her truck keys and spun around to face her. "Where to, exactly?"

"The Delta parking garage on Johnson Street. An officer is with the victim now and waiting for us to get her statement."

"Okay. I'll meet you there."

Tanya saluted and crossed the street, doubling back to her car. She followed Stonechild's truck the length of Princess Street toward the waterfront. She passed a couple of teenage boys and her son's latest acting out episode at school intruded into her thoughts. Her ex-husband wouldn't agree to ground him when the kids were staying at his place, leaving her holding the bag once again. His refusal to be a parent was grinding her down. Even his latest bimbette, Shona, had looked at him oddly when he told Tanya to loosen up. Somehow she'd force herself to put all that aside for this evening. Put on the happy face.

She passed the Merchant pub and turned right onto Ontario Street where Princess fed into the Holiday Inn. The Delta was a few blocks down on the lakeside of the street with the parking garage east of the hotel. She pulled up behind Stonechild's truck as they waited for oncoming traffic to pass and they both made the left turn onto hotel property and another sharp left to go past the front entrance into the parking garage.

The doorman motioned to Stonechild, and she stopped her truck next to him. Her passenger window slid open. He leaned in to speak with her, then straightened and motioned to Tanya to follow the truck into side-by-side parking spots. She had to hurry to park and catch up to Stonechild, who'd leapt out of her truck and was striding back toward the entrance.

Stonechild glanced behind her as she stepped inside the hotel lobby. "The victim is with security. They've taken her to a meeting room on the second floor."

"Was she staying at the hotel?"

"Doorman says no."

The elevator was waiting for them at ground level and they were the only occupants. "I hope this goes quickly," said Stonechild when she punched the button to the second floor. "I haven't even packed yet and was hoping for an early start in the morning." She shot Tanya a sideways grin. "So with my luck we'll be here half the night."

Tanya folded her arms across her chest and looked away. With effort she kept her face still.

The door to the meeting room was closed. Stonechild tapped lightly before pushing the door open. She stood frozen for a moment.

"Gotcha," said Tanya into her ear.

"Surprise!" The room echoed with the yell of a week-long secret conspiracy released.

The room was muted: gray walls and charcoal carpet — a bland canvas for the row of tall picture windows framing the harbour and the fading daylight. The staff had set up a long table, covered it in white linen, and arranged dinner settings for eleven. The group gathered around Stonechild. Someone gave her a drink and she had a moment to recover her composure. Dawn hugged her aunt and Tanya saw Stonechild meet Gundersund's eyes above her head. They smiled at each other, the intimate connection between them evident. The rest of the team was present: Andrew Bennett, Zach Woodhouse, Jacques Rouleau, Bedouin. Marci Stokes hung back with Henri Rouleau and Vera — everyone there to wish Dawn and Kala a good holiday and perhaps to remind them that they had ample reason to return.

Tanya knew she wasn't the only one who'd seen the restlessness in Stonechild. Sometimes Tanya caught her staring into the distance when she should have been working, her mind far away, her fingers still on the keyboard. Gundersund would watch her, too, with an intentness in his eyes that disappeared when Stonechild's gaze fell on him. They kept their relationship out of the office, but Tanya knew that they were spending most of their free time together. Gundersund had all but moved in with Kala and Dawn.

Dinner was a noisy affair. Four courses picked and paid for by Rouleau, a chance to thank the team for the overtime and high conviction rate for the cases that had landed in Major Crimes over the past year: creamy mushroom soup, Caesar salad laced with garlic and anchovies, prime rib with roasted potatoes and lightly grilled asparagus, dessert an airy concoction of egg white, sugar, and lemon that melted on the tongue. Rouleau stood as coffee was being poured and toasted those in the room.

"I want to thank each of you on the team for all your hard work. For the many weekends and late nights that you've put in without complaint — well, with the exception of Woodhouse who can't help himself —" he waited for the laughter to die down "— and all those hours of grunt work that have resulted in our high conviction rate. You've earned some time off ... but not all at once, *please*. To get the vacations started, please join me in wishing Kala and Dawn a restful and happy time on their northern adventure."

They coaxed Stonechild to her feet. "Thanks for surprising the heck out of me," she said to a round of laughter, "and for being such a terrific team of colleagues and friends. Dawn and I truly value each and every one of you."

"How long are you planning to be away?" Vera asked.

Everyone looked at Stonechild, studying her face for signs of whatever struggle was going on inside. Watching for any clue as to what was troubling her. Stonechild's eyes rose above their heads to stare out the window.

"I'm not sure. A few weeks. Maybe longer. Dawn can catch up easily enough if she misses a bit of school. We'll see how she does in the northern woods. We have a week booked at Pine Hollow Lodge and then will relocate somewhere closer to Lake Superior."

Tanya glanced over at Gundersund. He was watching Stonechild and she thought he must be looking for hidden meaning in her words. *Is this the end of their relationship?* she wondered. Was the footloose Kala Stonechild easing out of their lives? She'd moved south from the Red Rock–Dryden OPP detachment and her roots were in smaller northern communities. She owned property in Kingston, but she could easily sell it and make a tidy profit.

"We'll be waiting for your return," said Rouleau, as if reading Tanya's mind. "Don't stay away too long."

Dawn went into the house to pack for the next day. Gundersund stretched out next to Stonechild on the steps that led up to the deck. She'd lit candles and left the back door light off. They sat in silence, watching the hazy moon above the trees at the far end of her property.

"Would you like to come in?" she asked. Her face was half in shadow. "I have some packing to do, but you can spend the night if you want."

"No, you need your rest and I have a full work-day ahead tomorrow." The words weren't what he wanted to say, but he knew she needed this time to pack without being distracted. He needed to get used to them being gone.

"You could come visit us on your days off. Algoma's only a nine-hour drive." Her voice was wistful as if she'd already been gone a long time and was wondering when she'd see him next.

"Depends on how the month goes." She was leaning against him. He lifted his arm and pulled her closer. "You both need this time," he said into her hair.

"We're taking Fisher's ashes. We're going to find the perfect fishing spot, and Dawn will set her dad's spirit free." Stonechild tilted her head to look at him. "Dawn is sad that you're not coming with us."

"Are you planning to spend the entire time at the cottage you rented?"

"For the week, yeah. After that, I'm hoping to bring Dawn into the wilderness if she can handle roughing it. I'm bringing my tent as well as the canoe. This cottage, which northerners refer to as a camp, is on the edge of some decent rivers ..." Her voice trailed off. She seemed to realize that he wouldn't be able to follow them when she took Dawn away from Pine Hollow Lodge for an extended canoe trip.

"I'll be here when you get back. Someone has to be waiting to hear your stories." He kissed her for a long time before pushing up from the steps. "I'll be off so you can get ready for the morning. Stay safe and enjoy your time away."

He was almost at the corner of the house when he heard her say, "I miss you already." He nearly turned around to go to her but knew it would be a mistake. She needed this time to figure out what she wanted, and he had no choice but to wait and pray she came back to him ready to commit to their life together.

CHAPTER THREE

Martha Lorring snapped the sheet toward the ceiling and let the fabric float gently onto the bed. She tucked in the ends and plumped the pillows before putting on fresh bedspreads. The cabin was damp and musty, but she'd turned up the heat when she entered, and it would be toasty warm when the new guests arrived. She took a moment to look out the window. The glass framed a view of the birches in the foreground with the pines, aspen, and elms thick on the ridge. She closed her eyes and pictured the view of the lake from the living-room window. The treed land sloped down to a small beach and a wooden dock that stretched into the deep, cold water. She'd go for a swim at her strip of beach later once the air warmed. The water still held on to summer's heat even though the late August nights were getting cooler. The *Farmers' Almanac* predicted an early winter this year and she feared it might be right.

She walked down the short hall into the living room and her critical eye surveyed the space. Glen

Cottage was one of their larger cabins with two spacious bedrooms. It was also the most private. Neal had removed the wall separating the kitchen from the common area the summer before. A floor-to-ceiling fieldstone fireplace filled most of the back wall with a full basket of logs and kindling ready to lay a fire. Guests had lit one three nights earlier and the smell of woodsmoke lingered. Shiny stuffed fish and moose paintings decorated the knotty pine walls and gave the place the rustic feel that guests seemed to expect. She'd bought striped woven rugs for the floors and painted the kitchen walls a cheery yellow after the renovation. The couches and easy chairs were old but reupholstered as well — green plaid on the couch and tan leather on the chairs. The place was spotless. She was satisfied; the cottage was ready.

Neal met her on the path. "I finished cleaning Bluebird and Climbing Rose," he said. He gave a grimace like he always did when he used the names she'd given the cottages. He wiped his forehead with the back of his hand. She could see beads of sweat glistening in his black beard. "I came to see if you need help with anything."

So he'd decided to act as if their argument from the night before was over. She was grateful for the reprieve but knew the angry feelings would simmer and boil over another time. Nothing had been settled between them. "I'm finished. I was coming back to get some lunch."

"I'll walk with you."

The path carved through the woods was wide enough for them to walk side by side, but he followed a few steps behind her. Neither of them spoke. Martha tried to clear her head of the million-and-one things left to do and simply enjoy the late-summer smell of the woods and the trace of a breeze on her cheeks. She tried not to think about how distant Neal had been since her last miscarriage earlier in the spring.

She'd give anything to make things right between them, but she seemed incapable these days. Losing another fetus had plunged her into despair. She'd been vulnerable and made mistakes, but she was coming through the fog. Neal had to see that. The shadows on the path thickened. She sensed a movement in the underbrush to her right and a brown hare hopped across the path two feet in front of her. It took a few moments for her heartbeat to return to its normal rhythm. She was getting as jumpy as a jackrabbit.

"Shane's back from town," Neal said when he pulled open the screen door for her. "Petra went on her own, but she's not back yet."

"Shane said he'd be here in time to get supper started. I'll give him a hand and meet you in the cabin for lunch. I made a casserole last night." She paused before stepping across the threshold and studied him to see if his casual remark about Petra meant anything. "Is Rachel on site yet?"

"Haven't seen her, but that doesn't mean she isn't. I've been working in the cabins."

"Of course."

Martha crossed through the restaurant and pushed the door open into the back room. Shane didn't notice her at first, and she stood in the doorway watching him chop onions with his back to her.

He was wearing a short-sleeved white T-shirt and she liked watching his arm muscles flex and relax as he worked the knife. He sensed her presence and turned. His eyes were watery from the onions.

"Good day, is it?" he asked as he slid the onions into a large pot.

She wrapped an apron around her waist and moved next to him. He had on a cologne that smelled strongly of lemons and spice. She took a step toward the fridge. "The woman and her kid should be arriving soon." She ignored his question. What would be the point of saying today was the same as every other day? Continual work from the moment she got out of bed. She usually enjoyed the labour but was looking forward to closing down the lodge after school started the first week of September. Only one week to go. She and Neal would return to Cobourg for the winter and maybe take a trip to Arizona in late January. They'd be back here soon enough at the end of March to open the cabins. Bookings had already been coming in steadily for the spring season. Neal would have spent the winter here if she'd agreed, but the one year they had done that she almost went crazy.

"Petra went into the Soo for the day," he said.

Martha grabbed the bag of carrots from the lower bin and straightened. "She's been spending a lot of time in town," she said as she ripped the bag open. She dumped the carrots in a heap on the cutting board and got a knife and peeler from the drawer. She glanced over at Shane. "We're already late getting this stew in the oven."

"I'll get a chicken roasting after lunch. The scalloped potatoes are prepped and in the fridge. No worries. Everything will fall into place. What's the guest total?"

"Ian Kruger and Blaine Rogers are paid up for this week and next. Thomas Faraday, of course, and the new woman and her daughter in Glen Cottage." Martha was adding up potential dinner customers in her head. The rental price came with breakfast and supper included. She took reservations for supper from other cottagers on the lake and from Searchmont. "Bluebell's empty this week. Four town couples are booked for supper."

"Sounds like thirteen plus us. There's those who might say thirteen guests is a bad number." He grinned. "A bad omen, if you will."

Martha stood still with the knife suspended in the air. She turned her face toward him and his smile evaporated. "What is it, Martha? You look as if you've seen a ghost."

She took a second to shake the fear that had paralyzed her limbs. She breathed deeply and calmed the fluttering in her chest before giving him a shaky smile. "I don't know what's going on with me today. I haven't been sleeping well." She gave a sharp laugh. "Do you ever get that bad feeling that you can't shake?"

"Only if I have a reason."

Martha set the knife on the counter and rubbed her hands on the apron. "Do you think you could finish making the stew? I promised Neal I'd meet him for lunch at the cabin."

Shane nodded. His eyes were concerned. He touched her arm as she walked past him, but she pretended not to notice.

Martha had trouble getting herself in gear and entered the restaurant well into the supper hour. She breathed a sigh of relief to see Rachel setting down plates of chicken and scalloped potatoes on the table in front of Ian Kruger and Blaine Rogers, the Ontario Hydro linesmen who'd rented the cottage for the summer while they upgraded service in the backcountry. They wouldn't be returning in the spring, which was a shame. They'd been easy guests and the rent money had been reliable. Her eyes scanned the room and rested for a moment on the new renters: an Indigenous woman named Kala Stonechild and a girl who looked to be fourteen or fifteen years old. They'd started into their meal and had both ordered the stew. As she watched, Rachel walked over to them and asked if they needed anything more. She was pleased to see that Rachel had tied her long hair back securely as she'd requested the day before.

The door opened with a gust of cold air and she turned. Thomas Faraday stood behind her, running a hand through his white hair while his brilliant blue eyes darted around the room. He frowned when he saw the woman and girl at his usual table, but let his mouth return to a straight line when he saw Martha staring at him.

"New blood," he said before stepping past her to take the table closest to the picture window. He nodded a hello to Ian and Blaine as he sat down. Three couples from town arrived a few moments later: the Catholic priest Alec Vila and his sister, Sara; Phil and Greta Bocock, both teachers at the regional high school; and Reeve Judd Neilson and his wife, Elena, who let Martha know that the fourth couple booked for supper wouldn't be able to make it. *So not an unlucky number of guests for dinner after all.* The new movers and shakers in town. All young and each in a position of authority. There was talk that they were joining forces to get provincial grants for tourism. The little community could do with an infusion of money, but residents were divided on the ways and means. The six of them asked to sit together and Martha settled them at the longer table against the back wall. She motioned for Rachel to come over and pour water for the group while she took care of Faraday.

The room was alive with chatter and clinking dishes and someone, probably Shane, had turned on the stereo system. He liked music from the fifties and sixties and Perry Como's voice crooned like gooey syrup through the speakers. Martha relayed Faraday's order to the kitchen and took a moment to stop by the newcomers' table.

"I'm Martha Lorring, the owner of Pine Hollow Lodge," she said. "Sorry that I didn't greet you on arrival. I hope everything is to your liking."

The Indigenous woman glanced at the young girl. "No complaints. Our cottage is comfortable and this meal is delicious. My name is Kala and this is my niece, Dawn."

"I'm so pleased you've decided to spend your holidays with us. We're a rustic retreat and a chance to get away from the city. We don't have Wi-Fi and cellphone usage can be sporadic … well, pretty much non-existent, but that's all part of our charm." She smiled while watching their faces to see if this was a problem. Neither gave anything away. "Town is just over five kilometres south of here and you can get Wi-Fi in any of the shops and restaurants," she added.

"How many people live in Searchmont?" asked Kala.

"Three hundred or so. We go farther southwest to the Soo, that's Sault Ste. Marie, when we want to shop for anything more exciting than coffee."

"Suits us. We plan to get in some canoeing and hiking."

"Well, you couldn't have come to a better spot. We have inland lakes and rivers with some challenging white water if that's your thing. Shane's our resident canoeist if you want some direction about routes. He's also our cook, but I know he'll be happy to speak with you when the rush is over."

"I'd appreciate that."

Martha glanced at the girl. She had her head lowered and was moving the stew around on her plate with a fork. She looked morose and Martha wondered if she'd been dragged here against her will. She knew that teenagers could be tricky. She directed her last words to the woman. "If you need anything don't be shy to ask. Welcome to Pine Hollow Lodge."

She left them and walked to the kitchen. Rachel was inside talking to Shane, and she turned when

Martha pushed the door open. Her face was flushed as if she'd been standing over a steaming pot at the stove. Tendrils of red hair had escaped the elastic. The smile on her face vanished as soon as she saw Martha. "So, I'll come back for Thomas's stew order in ten minutes," Rachel said before manoeuvring her way around her and through the door.

"Don't forget to offer the new people pie," said Martha before it swung shut. "I'll look after the people from town." She stared at Shane, who was working at the stove with his back to her. "Did Petra make it home okay?" she asked.

He half-turned. "She hasn't checked in with me. Any idea where Neal is?"

"He got the new people settled and then went fishing."

"Looks like our spouses are enjoying themselves while we hold down the fort." Shane smiled, but Martha didn't see any humour in his eyes. "Of course, you'd know all about Petra's talent for getting others to avoid their responsibilities."

"It's over," she said softly. "We need to move on."

"I know we'd all like to think so." He turned back to the stove, his shoulders hunched in, head lowered over the pot.

Martha knew better than to say anything further on the subject of Petra. Some stones were best left unturned. She pushed the door to the outer room open and heard Neal's laughter before she saw him. His eyes lifted and met hers where he stood with Rachel. The late-day fishing had added a sheen to his already brown face and he looked more relaxed than when they'd parted after sharing her casserole. Lunch had been strained and he'd avoided being lured back into the argument of the night before. She'd tried to provoke him into a reaction only because she hadn't liked his indifference. He'd refused to engage.

Rachel turned toward Martha while lifting a piece of pie from the counter. She said something to Neal and smiled at him before starting on her way across the room.

Martha lifted a hand to brush a strand of hair from her face as she watched Rachel take the pie to Thomas Faraday's table. She sensed someone's eyes on her and her gaze shifted slightly to her right. The woman was sitting motionless, her searching black eyes, as dark as ink, focused squarely on Martha's face.

You don't miss much, thought Martha. She took a step toward Neal before pivoting and walking into the kitchen. She didn't trust herself not to snap at him and it would be a mistake to air their dirty laundry in front of the new lodger.

CHAPTER FOUR

Kala and Dawn left the restaurant in the main lodge and walked the dirt path through the woods to their cabin. A thick line of birch and evergreen trees hid the building from view until they broke into the clearing.

Dawn ran ahead down the incline that sloped to the sand beach in front of their cottage. The sun was setting and streaks of pink and orange flamed across the horizon and rippled over the lake. "Why isn't it dark yet?" she asked when Kala reached her.

"We're farther north. The sun sets closer to nine o'clock in September."

"Then we can stay up later."

"A bit, but we'll get a good night's sleep tonight and put the canoe in the water once the sun's up." Kala felt the familiar peace that filled her at the thought of being back on the water. "I'll go get Taiku and will join you in a sec."

Taiku was waiting at the door and raced ahead of her to where Dawn stood on a rounded rock staring out at the water. Dawn squatted and wrapped an arm around his neck. Kala lowered herself onto the rock next to them. The warmth penetrated through the cotton fabric of her pants. "What do you think of the big outdoors?" she asked. She kept her voice light to hide her uncertainty. Dawn had never spent any time out of the city. She might very well hate being away from her friends and everything familiar.

"It's so quiet." Dawn leaned her head back. "And ... the sky is endless."

"No city lights to get in the way of the stars."

Dawn had sidestepped her question, but Kala didn't press. She was bound to feel out of her element. She needed a chance to settle in, to feel part of this.

Dawn looked at her with accusing eyes. "I wish Gundersund was here. Taiku misses Minny."

And I miss Gundersund. She closed off the feeling. "We'll see them soon enough."

"I thought we'd be able to Skype him tonight, except there's no Wi-Fi. Did you know that before we came?"

"I remembered reading about it, but only after Martha told us. We'll go into town and call Gundersund from there. Maybe tomorrow evening after supper."

Dawn's expression lightened. "I can tell him about our cabin."

Taiku was sniffing around the brush growing close to the shore. A fish jumped in the lake, sending concentric circles across the still water. Reeds swayed below the surface to the left of the rocks they were sitting on, the water opaque a few metres out. A stretch of sand beach and a dock were farther to their right. They'd be able to launch the canoe easily from there. A bird's deep-throated call travelled across the lake.

"Look," said Kala, pointing to a dark spot bobbing on the water. "A loon. That's its lonely song you're hearing."

They listened without talking and darkness began to eat up the fading light. Blackflies found them and Kala reluctantly called to Taiku. "Time to head in," she said to Dawn. "Before we're nothing but a mass of bug bites." They jogged up the incline through the trees to the cottage, swatting at flies as they went. "Tomorrow we load up on bug spray before the sun sets," she promised. "Luckily, I brought a few bottles."

Kala lay awake long after Dawn and Taiku had settled in the adjoining bedroom. Dawn's wish to have Gundersund and his dog Minny here was the most emotion she'd showed in months, but her desire to have them with her could simply be that she felt out of place. She'd been closed off since her ordeal in the spring and the death of her father. She hadn't asked to visit her mother in Joliette pen and had said she was too busy with schoolwork when Kala suggested they go for the day. Kala knew she wasn't imagining Dawn's detachment. Even her therapist, Dr. Lyman, was concerned. She'd called Kala in to discuss her inability to break through the wall Dawn had built up around herself. Dr. Lyman said that all the progress they'd made since she first started treating Dawn had fallen away.

Kala had left the bedroom doors and windows open after checking for holes in the mesh screens that would let in the bugs, and a cool cross breeze snapped the white curtains like billowing sails into the room. The chirping crickets and the late-summer air perfumed by fireweed, goldenrod, and clover lulled her into half-sleep. Her mind drowsily relived the day and the people she'd met. She'd instinctively filed away first impressions and the interactions she observed.

These people are not what they appear.

The thought came unbidden and momentarily jolted her from sleep, much like the feeling of falling just before slumber. She'd sensed an undercurrent in the dining room from the moment she and Dawn sat down at their table. The feeling had intensified as the meal wore on. She'd watched the interactions of the people from this small, isolated community and tried to pinpoint her unease without success.

She rolled onto her side and watched the shadows on the wall before her eyes fluttered closed.

But we don't have to engage, she thought as she let go of the day. *Dawn and I are here to reconnect, not make friends. I'm not going to get involved in their business, and I hope they leave us alone. I need this time and distance from Gundersund to figure out what I'm going to do next.*

Rachel stared down the dirt road in the gathering darkness looking for her father's truck. He'd insisted on picking her up, saying that she shouldn't be roaming around the countryside after dark even though she'd ridden her bike home most nights over the summer, always making it close to town before the sun set. If it was raining, one of the Hydro guys, Ian or Blaine, always offered to drive her and she'd leave her bike at the lodge. "The days are getting shorter," her dad had said at breakfast. "I'll come get you when your shift is done." She'd tried to talk him out of his offer. Was happy now that she hadn't. She had no desire to make small talk with anybody.

The kitchen had been closed a good hour and the wind had gotten stronger while she waited, chilling her in the thin sweater she'd tucked into her bag that morning. She'd tried calling her dad, but the reception was terrible and she hadn't gotten a signal … as usual. Martha said she didn't bother getting Wi-Fi in order to keep the lodge a rustic getaway, but Rachel had heard that the lodge was situated in a dead zone — a valley surrounded by rock cliffs that kept out the signal. She could walk over to Martha and Neal's cabin to use the landline in Martha's office but didn't feel like making the effort. *I don't want to talk to them. I'll begin walking*, she thought. *I'm bound to meet Dad on my way.*

She started toward town on the narrow, unpaved road that allowed cars to pass with little room to spare. The road abutted onto culverts in places and sloping rock cuts in others. Spruce, balsam, and pine stretched along both sides creating a claustrophobic feeling magnified by the swaying branches and long evening shadows. The lonely road suited her mood. She was glad she could stop working at Pine Hollow in a week when it closed. Her dad had never understood why she chose a summer at the lodge anyway when she could have worked for his outfitting business. He'd be happy to hear that she never intended on going back.

Rachel picked up her pace the farther she got from the lodge. Her house on the edge of town was five kilometres away and would take her an hour walking at a good clip. She checked over her shoulder periodically and listened for the sound of a car coming from either direction. The wind that was whistling around the cottages off the lake was muffled inland, making her feel even more cocooned and removed from civilization. Darkness was settling around her like fine silt as she walked, gradually blurring her view of the road ahead. A black, knee-high form darted out of the underbrush and ran across the road three feet ahead of her. She stopped dead and clutched at her heart until she was certain the fox or wolverine or whatever it was would not be returning to attack her. A distraught sob escaped her lips. *I'm going crazy*, she thought. *Where the hell are you, Daddy?*

She began humming loudly as she walked to ward off wild animals and to keep herself from losing it, because she'd always had an irrational fear of being alone in the dark. Twice she pulled out her cellphone and tried to call her father, but both times the signal didn't hold. She was shivering now, the cold having worked its way through the light sweater and short-sleeved T-shirt. She stumbled on a furrow in the packed dirt and rolled over on her ankle, catching herself before she went down on her knee.

Oh no. She straightened and gingerly put weight on the foot. *Nothing broken.* Relief flooded through her. The pain was bearable and she wouldn't be sitting by the side of the road until morning. She took a few steps and slowed her pace to keep from falling since the darkness was now almost complete.

She cursed her father as she walked, storing up the angry words she was going to say to him when he finally pulled up. She was no longer the mature woman with a secret lover, but the frightened little girl that she'd thought she'd long outgrown. All she wanted was to be home in bed snuggled up with her pain and her teddy bear and a cup of herbal tea. She shuddered, thinking of how far her belief in herself had fallen in the last few hours. Part of her thought that maybe she deserved what she was getting. She'd gotten involved in things that she now regretted. The universe was making her pay for her sins.

At first, her lover's nearness in the restaurant made the evening exciting, but she played it cool even as she relived all the intimate ways he'd touched her the night before. She knew he couldn't acknowledge her and she kept her part of the bargain, pretending not to notice him more than anybody else. Their secret life was a turn-on. She served meals and cleared tables all the while feeling a heat in her chest and between her legs. She chanced to glance his way once and found him watching her. She'd started to smile but bit her bottom lip when she saw his eyes. They were cold. *Cold as ice, staring straight at me.* An embarrassed blush heated her cheeks and she looked away flustered, blinking back tears that stung her eyes.

He's been using me, she thought. *He never meant for us to last.*

She'd wanted to throw down her tray and run from the restaurant. When she turned back he was walking away from her. A shiver rippled up her spine. She hadn't imagined what she saw in his eyes. His mask had dropped … long enough. If she was honest with herself, she'd sensed something off with him for a while, but she wasn't ready before now to accept that he was manipulating her. She had still believed in the power of romance novels. She'd been such a fool.

If you could hide your true self from me when we were alone together, what else are you capable of hiding?

She moved to the edge of the road as she heard a car engine growing louder. She thought it was coming from the direction of the resort, but it could as easily be coming from town. The darkness disoriented her and the revving sound of the engine echoed off the rockface. The headlights were on high and they blinded her as the car rounded the corner in the road. She lifted an arm across her eyes while waving her other arm to get the driver's attention. The lights swerved and she thought in that split horrifying second that the car was coming toward her. She took two steps to the right, bending at the knees as she prepared to throw herself into the culvert, but the car braked and stopped several metres away, the headlights still pointed at her so that she felt like an actress on stage.

Oh my god. Oh my god. Oh my god. She grabbed her chest. The driver's door swung open. Anger replaced her fear. "You scared the crap out of me!" she yelled. She stomped her foot. "What the hell were you thinking?"

She couldn't make out who was getting out of the car and squinted through the dazzling light that made miniature explosions sparkle in the darkness. She cupped a hand over her eyes but still couldn't see who was standing next to the open car door. The figure took a running step toward her, picking up speed until it was charging at her like a mad bull. She instinctively cowered backwards a step. "Don't come any closer!" she yelled, but the black shape covered the distance between them without pause until it loomed over her, blocking out the glare from the car's headlights. She closed her eyes to clear the blurriness that clouded her vision from the blinding lights and the panicky tears that seeped from under her lids. The whoosh of something swinging through the air startled then terrified her. She ducked and lifted both arms over her head but she was a split second too late. *This is insane*, she thought. *Help me, Daddy!* She opened her mouth to scream the words but a loud crack split the silence and the world exploded into a flash of stars and pain as her eyes widened in horror and she crumpled into the blackness. She lay motionless on the dirt road, unaware of the successive blows to her head or the hands rolling her ... rolling her ... over the edge and down the steep incline into the culvert where she breathed her last on a flattened bed of goldenrod and purple fireweed.

CHAPTER FIVE

Shane was sitting in the chair facing the door when Petra's key rattled in the lock. He could pretend to be asleep, but he wanted her to know that he'd been waiting up for her. She opened the door and stepped inside. For a moment she was illuminated by the outside light before she turned and silently eased the door shut. He could see her standing motionless in the entranceway while her eyes grew accustomed to the darkness. His breath still caught in his chest at the sight of her. Soft blond hair to her shoulders, five foot five and all curves, but slender at the same time. Her eyes, he knew, were large and blue as cornflowers. Thirty-five and he'd been in love with her more than half their lives.

She bent and took off her shoes, setting them on the rack before she walked on stockinged feet to the kitchen. He saw the light from the fridge and her leaning over the door looking inside. She pulled the half-eaten apple pie out and gently closed the fridge. He heard the rattle of a plate and the drawer open as she found a fork, then the scrape of the stool as she settled in at the counter to eat.

He walked as quietly as she had into the kitchen, and she gasped when he turned on the lights. The forkful of pie was halfway to her lips and she set it back onto the plate. She stared at him without speaking.

"Where've you been?" he asked.

"I got waylaid." She smiled as if she'd said something amusing. Then she lifted the fork to her mouth and bit into the pie.

"If by *waylaid* you mean laid, I'm not impressed with your wordplay. I expected you home hours ago."

She chewed slowly and swallowed without taking her eyes from his. She ran her tongue slowly across her top lip, then the bottom. "Sorry, I didn't mean you to think I was having it off with someone."

Her smile said otherwise, but he decided to let it go. "How was traffic?"

"No more than usual. I just needed some time away from here. I shopped and had supper and went to a movie. I left the Soo later than I planned. I'm sorry if you were worried."

He tried to detect a false note in her words, but she'd gotten so good at lying ... hell, they'd gotten so good at lying to each other ... that he had no choice but to accept her story. He was too weary to get into their marriage this late at night. Wasn't even sure he wanted to go there again because thinking about her with others drove him crazy. But she always came back and he'd learned to live with what he couldn't change. "I'm going to bed," he said.

"Then I won't be far behind."

* * *

A light rain started an hour before dawn. White mist hung suspended over the lake when the sun finally rose above the thick grey cloud cover.

"The weather report says drizzle until early afternoon when the storm moves in," called Kala from the kitchen. She turned off the radio. "Are you still game to go for a paddle?" She crossed the cold floor to the bedroom in the semi-gloom. Dawn had chosen the bottom bunk and was lying on her side, facing the door, wrapped in a blanket. Taiku was stretched out on the floor next to her on an area rug. His tail thumped against the bed frame.

"I guess."

"I know it's not ideal for your first time in a canoe, but we have rain gear and I'll make a Thermos of hot chocolate."

"I'll be fine, Aunt Kala."

"It's just that I don't want to wait."

They dressed and ate a quick breakfast before carrying the canoe from the truck to the dock. Kala left Taiku indoors rather than have him wet and miserable in the boat, even though he'd liked past excursions on the water. They put life jackets on over their raincoats and launched from the dock, Dawn in the front and Kala steering from the back. Dawn picked up the basic stroke after a quick lesson and they moved into deeper water, keeping the shore in sight through the heavy mist. The sound was muffled as the rain pattered on the lake all around them.

"I feel like we're alone in a world all our own," said Dawn. She dipped her paddle and turned to look at Kala. "Am I doing this right?"

"You're doing beautifully. A natural paddler."

Kala settled into the rhythm of their strokes, steering the canoe around the bend into a wider expanse of water. The white haze thinned and she could make out sheer cliffs dense with trees. The air smelled of fish and pine. They cut a path through a bay of reeds and water lilies, and Dawn pointed to a turtle lying on a rock protruding from the water near the shore. She rested her oar across the canoe and leaned forward to get a better look.

This is going to work out, thought Kala when Dawn turned to smile at her. The tightness in her chest had been loosening with every stroke. *Dawn hasn't disappeared where I can't find her.*

Martha lay in bed and listened for the slam of the front door to let her know Neal was on his way to deal with breakfast for the guests. Shane would do the cooking and Neal would serve. Her morning to lie in. She rolled over and looked out the window toward the lake. A rainy, grey Sunday. She was glad now that they'd put Shane and Petra in the cabin up the road instead of inviting them to stay in this one. How awkward and cramped that would have been in hindsight. How difficult to carry on. It meant giving up one cabin as a rental, but they could absorb the lost income without much problem.

She got out of bed and sat in a scented bath for half an hour, reading this month's *Architectural Digest* magazine, clearing her mind, letting the stress seep from her limbs. She climbed out of the tub when the water cooled and dressed in jeans and a red-and-white checked shirt before throwing a load of laundry into the washer. The kitchen clock read seven forty when she put on a pot of coffee and toasted two pieces of brown bread. She didn't feel up to facing the lodgers this morning and wasn't hungry anyway. Instead, she took her coffee to the screened-in veranda where she could watch the mist lift from the lake. This was her favourite time of day, even if today's weather was dreadful.

She heard the crunch of tires on the gravel in the side yard as she was getting up to refill her coffee mug and opened the back door before her visitor had a chance to knock.

Rachel's father, Owen Eglan, stood with his back to her, but he turned as the door opened. "Martha, I'm looking for Rachel. Has she shown up here this morning? Her bed hasn't been slept in." He looked rumpled in a tan corduroy jacket and wrinkled T-shirt. Rachel had inherited her thick red hair from him, although his hairline had receded somewhat. He'd also passed along his tendency to blush at the slightest provocation.

"Rachel went home after her shift ended last night and isn't expected back until this afternoon. I thought she said that you were picking her up?" She kept her voice light, the judgment unspoken. How could he not have begun the search for her earlier if she hadn't made it home the night before?

"I know we seem negligent," he said, appearing to pick up on her tone, "but I had an unexpected trip into the backwoods and left Rachel a voicemail that she'd have to get home on her own." His voice trailed off. A rosy stain crept into his cheeks.

Martha didn't insult him with a reminder that Rachel's cellphone wouldn't have worked at the lodge. She knew that he knew. Customers liked to get away from technology and this was one of the lodge's marketing strategies. Owen had stood her up and guilt was written all over his face. "Have you checked with her friends? Maybe she had impromptu plans after work."

"Isabelle is calling them now. I thought I'd check with you on the off chance."

"I'm sorry. I really have no idea where she went after work."

Martha leaned on the door and watched him get into his truck. Owen and Isabelle had never been friendly, but she felt a twinge at what they must be going through. Having a teenage daughter out all night would be a worry for any parent. She ignored the rain and ran across the yard, waving at him to roll down his window. "Rachel is due here at two, so I'll make sure we get word to you when she arrives."

"I'd appreciate that. Sometimes she can be thoughtless."

"Sixteen is a conflicted age." Martha smiled in sympathy before she ran to the back door. She shook the rain from her hair and stood for a moment watching Owen drive away before she crossed to the counter for a second mug of coffee. Instead of returning to the veranda, she took out the sheaf of bills and her laptop and sat down at the kitchen table. Paperwork would take her mind off Rachel. She opened the laptop and stared at the screensaver: a photo of her and Neal at the waterfront in Cobourg. A jogger had stopped and offered to take the picture with Martha's phone even though Neal had first refused. He wasn't smiling but he'd finally put his arm around her waist and she was leaning into him.

That's how it was with Neal. Never up for spontaneity or displays of affection. He'd rather sit quietly in the room than be part of the party. Their fight, which had started two days before, seemed over in his mind, but not hers. He'd left the restaurant after she saw him talking with Rachel and had not returned to their cabin until she was lying in their double bed, pretending to be asleep. They hadn't spoken this morning, and she would put off their next encounter as long as she could.

He needed space to cool off. He needed time to forget that he'd told her he wanted a separation.

CHAPTER SIX

OPP officer Clark Harrison got the call just after eleven Sunday morning. A sixteen-year-old girl named Rachel Eglan hadn't made it home from her shift at a restaurant at Pine Hollow Lodge the night before and her parents were worried. "Can you drive up and have a talk with them?" the dispatcher asked.

"Could you repeat the address?" Clark asked. "Okay, just punched it in. The drive should take about an hour." *Or longer if the rain picks up.*

He pulled a U-turn and stopped at the side of the road to call his wife, Valerie. She answered on the fourth ring as his heart was beginning to pound with trepidation.

"Hey," he said. "Were you busy?"

"Lying down. The baby kicked all night and kept me awake."

"Not much longer."

"Three weeks and two days, but who's counting?"

"I got a call and have to head out of town for the afternoon. You'll be okay?"

"Yeah, I'll sleep the day away."

"I'll check in with you once I know what's going on with the call."

"Don't worry about waking me up."

"Sleep tight, babe."

He tucked the phone back into his pocket and drove until he reached Great Northern Road, which fed into Highway 17. The road split at Heydon and he kept right, taking the 556 East for a ways before it angled north and became the 532, which took him the last leg of the route into Searchmont. The trip took three-quarters of an hour with the constant rain drumming on the windshield to keep him company. Puddles filled the hollows and gullies and spread across the road. Searchmont was a ski and snowmobile destination in the winter and kept itself alive in the summer by outfitting vacationers for water ventures. The sawmill had once been the mainstay of the town, but its closure had depleted the population to handfuls with their houses spread out amongst the trees and along the river. Some went so far as to call Searchmont a ghost town. Clark had visited the Searchmont recreation centre once as part of a community policing presentation, but he'd not taken any calls since. Crime was not an issue in this neck of the woods.

The Eglans lived in a log cabin painted chocolate brown across the road from Garden Lake, which was also the name of their street. Manicured lawn spread from the front yard around the house to the water. The nearest neighbour was half a kilometre down a road thickly lined with conifer trees.

A stressed-looking woman in her early fifties opened the door and introduced herself as Isabelle Eglan. She invited him into the living room. He took the easy chair and looked out the windows at the storm clouds over the lake while she went in search of her husband who was outside working in the garage. The room was comfortable: log walls in honey brown and well-worn furniture. The pictures on the wall were framed photos of the landscape around Searchmont. A wooden cross hung above the dining-room table.

Clark heard the back door creak open and slam shut. He stood and shook hands with Owen Eglan after he'd clumped across the floor in his work boots. He was a stocky man with red hair and beard and a ruddy complexion that looked to have been recently wind-burned. They sat facing each other and Isabelle offered coffee, which Clark gratefully accepted. The woodstove wasn't lit and dampness from the day's rain had seeped into the house.

"Can you tell me about your daughter, Mr. Eglan?" he asked, taking out his notebook and pen. He settled back in the chair and rested the notepad on his crossed leg.

Owen took a moment to organize his thoughts before speaking. "Rachel is sixteen and our third child. Her brothers are both away working at summer jobs in the oil patch in Alberta. Rachel took a position at Pine Hollow Lodge for the summer and went missing after her shift last night. I was supposed to pick her up but got called into work last minute. I left her a voicemail but can't be sure she got it. I'd

forgotten how sporadic the reception is at the lodge."
He glanced over at his wife, who was pouring coffee
at the counter, and Clark could tell they'd had words
before he arrived. Owen added, as if trying to ratio-
nalize his mistake, "I wasn't all that worried, though,
because she'd gotten home on her own steam all
summer. She usually had her bike or got a lift from
one of the lodgers if the weather was bad."

"But she wouldn't have taken her bike if you
said you were picking her up," said Isabelle.

"I suppose not." Owen dropped his eyes to stare
at his hands folded in his lap.

Isabelle set a full mug of coffee on the end table
at his elbow and sat on the couch next to him. She
added, "Rachel is responsible. She always tells me
when she's going to be late. This is not like her at
all."

Clark kept his voice even although Isabelle's
statement gave him pause. "When was your last contact with her?"

"Yesterday before she went to the lodge. It was
just after lunch."

"And I hadn't seen her since the night before.
She was still in bed when I left for work yesterday
morning." Owen rubbed a hand across his eyes.
"I went up to the lodge this morning, but Martha
Lorring said Rachel had gone home after her shift
the evening before as far as she knew. I drove the
route Rachel would have taken home last night
around midnight and again this morning and didn't
see any sign of her."

"Does she have a boyfriend?" asked Clark.

"Yes," said Isabelle. "His name is Darryl Kelly and he's in her class at school. He said that he hadn't seen her all week. Rachel seemed lukewarm about him lately, so I wasn't surprised by that. I called everyone else I could think of and nobody saw her yesterday. We have no idea where she's gotten to."

Clark took a drink of coffee while he thought. "I'll take a run out to the lodge. Maybe she spoke to somebody about her plans after work."

"I could come with you," said Owen. "I can introduce you to Martha and her husband Neal. They're the owners."

"I'll come too," said Isabelle, starting to rise from the couch.

Clark nodded at Owen, but said to Isabelle, "I think it best you wait here, ma'am, in case someone calls with information. Owen will be able to give me the lay of the land."

"If you insist. Make sure you come straight back, Owen. I'll be waiting for news." She stooped over the table and began clearing the coffee mugs.

Clark realized that her anger directed at Owen was a defence that was keeping her from losing control. "I'll be in touch as soon as we have anything. Try not to worry," he said, and followed Owen to the front door and into the pouring rain.

The distance to Pine Hollow Lodge was between four and five kilometres, but the road was unpaved and wound through forest and rock cuts. Add in the pouring rain and mud and the drive took ten minutes longer than it should have. The lodge consisted of a string of cabins stretched out along the lakeshore with a larger building and parking lot off the main road. He pulled into the parking area and they sat for a moment with the rain pattering onto the roof of the police car.

"Lights are on in the restaurant," said Owen. "It's that bigger building through the trees."

"Should we start there?" asked Clark.

"Good a place as any."

The front door was unlocked and they stood on the welcome mat shaking off rainwater from their clothes before following the music from a radio into the kitchen. The building was constructed with wooden beams and pine log walls, roughly hewn but sturdy. There was nothing fancy about the decor, but Clark felt that the buildings suited the wilderness setting. Visitors who wanted the spa treatment would have to go elsewhere.

A dark-haired man had his back to them, chopping vegetables and singing along to "Magic Carpet Ride." He had a decent voice and was good enough for a career in music, thought Clark. The idea was reinforced when the man turned. He had the good looks that sell concert tickets. Lean, but broad-shouldered, sandy hair tied back in a ponytail, dark bedroom eyes and stubble on his cheeks. He saw them and turned down the radio. "Can I help you?" he asked.

"Shane, it's Owen Eglan. We met a few times when I came to get Rachel. This is Officer Harrison who's helping us find her. Officer, this is Shane Patterson, cousin of the lodge's owner."

Shane stared at Owen. "What, is Rachel missing?"

"She didn't make it home last night after her shift. We have no idea where she is."

"Christ. How can I help?"

Clark stepped forward. "Did Rachel say if she planned to go anywhere after work? Did somebody pick her up?"

"I have no idea. We were busy and it took me a while to clean up. Three town couples and the new woman and her daughter in Glen Cottage, plus the three long-term renters, Ian, Blaine, and Thomas."

"Did they leave at the same time?"

"Like I said, I was working in the kitchen and didn't see all the comings and goings." Shane appeared to be thinking. "Rachel left shortly before I did and told me that you were coming to get her, Owen. I went out the back door and she was waiting out front." His eyes darted over to Owen and back to Clark.

"What time was that?"

"Just after eight. The other customers had all vacated sometime earlier. I dished up the last meal at seven. Martha was also serving, but she left before me and Rachel, I think around seven-thirty. Rachel had a bite to eat with me in the kitchen before she cleared the last tables and went outside to wait for her ride. I have no idea where Neal was. Somebody said he was by, but I was in the back." He gave a sharp laugh. "I sound as if all I do is keep track of people."

The front door opened and a moment later another man entered the kitchen. He was as tall as Shane and lean with black hair cut short, a full beard, and hazel eyes. "What's this about?" he asked looking at Shane.

"Speak of the devil — this is Neal Lorring," Shane said to Clark. He looked at Neal. "Rachel didn't make it home after her shift last night."

"You're kidding."

"I wish I was."

Clark couldn't read into the look the two men exchanged. He said, "Did Rachel say anything to you about where she might be going?"

Neal shook his head. "I hardly spoke to her. She was getting pie at the counter for the new renters when I came into the room and we only chatted for a moment."

Clark took out his notepad. "The names of the new renters?"

"Stonechild. The woman has an unusual name. Not Carla ..."

"Kala," said Shane. "Not all that unusual."

Clark lifted his head. Surely there couldn't be two Kala Stonechilds? "I should speak with her. Which cabin is she in?"

"You won't find her there. She and the girl went canoeing first thing this morning. I saw them paddling around the bend." Shane turned to Neal. "Where's Martha? She should know about this."

"I talked to her early this morning," said Owen. "She has no idea where Rachel could be."

Clark was getting a bad feeling but didn't think he should push the panic button yet. Sixteen-year-old girls were unpredictable by all accounts. She might have met up with a friend and gone off to a party. Gotten drunk or stoned and lost track of time.

"I'll buy a cup of coffee if you have a pot on," he said to Shane. "May as well wait around a bit and have a word with Kala Stonechild. I can't imagine she'll be out on the water much longer with the storm front moving in."

CHAPTER SEVEN

Clark was on the dock when Kala Stonechild angled the blue, canvas-covered cedar-strip canoe alongside. The rain had let up slightly, but he knew the reprieve wouldn't last long. He knelt and grabbed on to the front end, steadying the boat while Stonechild and the girl stepped onto the dock. They both wore green poncho raincoats under their life jackets, but their faces were slick with rain.

"Thanks," said Kala. She looked him over before saying to the girl, "Run inside and I'll be right there."

The girl hesitated, her wide black eyes studying him, but Kala nodded and she started toward the cabin.

"I never expected to see you again," Stonechild said. Her voice was mild, neither friendly nor antagonistic, and he took this as a good sign. She turned and bent to hold on to the front of the canoe. She dragged it through the water from the dock until she'd pulled it up on the shore. He followed behind her and grabbed the back end. They flipped it over and carried it to a protected spot resting on a layer of pine needles under the shelter of tree boughs. The canoe must have weighed all of thirty-five pounds — lightweight and easy enough to handle alone.

"I gather this isn't a social call," she said, nodding at his uniform. "Let's get inside where it's dry."

She was as fit as he remembered, but leaner, her cheekbones more pronounced and her eyes larger. Her beauty was intriguing and ageless. She greeted the dog, kicked off her boots, and hung the raincoat on the hook next to the door. "Coffee?" she asked as she walked barefoot to the kitchen. She still had that animal grace — like a gazelle, leggy and sure-footed.

He didn't need another cup but wanted to make this meeting as relaxed as possible, to prolong his time with her. "Sure, one cream and one sugar." He slipped out of his wet boots and joined her at the kitchen island. The girl was reading a book on the couch and ignoring them. Taiku stretched out on the floor next to her. Clark remembered seeing Stonechild with the same dog after shifts when they worked together in the northern detachment.

"When did you leave Red Rock?" Stonechild asked, scooping coffee into the top of the coffee machine.

"I transferred to the Sault detachment two years ago." He could have let her work her way into asking about his brother, but he wasn't one to play games. "Jordan moved to Thunder Bay just before that. He and Miriam split up so he decided to start his own electrical business. It's doing well and he's been able to hire a couple of guys. He gets the kids every other weekend and holidays."

"Kids?"

"Two. A boy and a girl. They're still pretty young and need their mother. He didn't fight her on that. He misses you. I guess I can say that because I know he'd like to tell you in person."

He wasn't sure if he'd made a mistake being so open, but his brother had never hidden his feelings for her. Jordan would still be with her if she hadn't left town and refused to speak to him. He'd gone back to his wife and they'd tried to make another go of their marriage. The daughter was proof of that, but bottom line — the two of them were incompatible.

"I'm with someone," she said. She turned her back to pour the coffee into mugs and busied herself getting cream out of the fridge. When she finally joined him at the island her mouth was set in a tight line and he could see by the rigid set of her shoulders that she wasn't going to talk about his brother.

He looked toward the girl in the living room. "She can't be your daughter. You haven't been gone from Red Rock that long."

"No. I think of Dawn as my niece. Her mother's in Joliette. We've been like sisters since we met up in foster care."

They each sipped from their mugs. He knew her well enough to know that she wouldn't be more forthcoming about her relationships, and he wouldn't make this strained situation even more awkward by asking the obvious follow-up questions. He was about to change the subject, but she beat him to it.

"Why are you here?" she asked, lowering her cup of coffee. Her face was closed off, her hands gripped around the mug.

"A sixteen-year-old girl named Rachel Eglan served you supper last evening."

"Yes, although I didn't know her last name."

"Did she tell you where she was going after her shift?"

"No. Is there a problem?"

"Rachel didn't make it home last night and her parents have no idea where she is."

He could see Stonechild's brain running through possibilities. "Did they call her friends?"

He nodded.

"Boyfriend?"

"Yup. Nothing."

"Has she done something like this before? Gone off and not told them?"

"They say not."

"How was she supposed to get home from the lodge after her shift? She did tell us that she lives in Searchmont."

"Her father was going to pick her up, but he got called in to work. He's an outfitter. He left a voicemail but forgot about the connectivity problem at Pine Hollow, or that's his story anyway. His wife is some pissed off at him. Rachel likely walked, but maybe someone picked her up."

Stonechild called to the girl in the living room, "Dawn, did Rachel, our server last night, tell you anything about her plans after work?"

Dawn raised her eyes from her book. "No."

Stonechild looked from her to Clark. "I'm sorry. We really have nothing to offer."

Clark gulped the last of his coffee. "I know it was a long shot. I'm running out of ideas."

"She'll show up. Girls of this age can be unpredictable."

"I'm right here," sang Dawn from the couch, the first sign she was listening in.

"I didn't mean you, big ears," Stonechild said. She smiled fondly in Dawn's direction.

Clark pushed himself off the stool. "I'll be going, then. Here's my card in case you overhear anything that would help me locate her."

Stonechild stood as well. "You're heading back to the Soo?"

"I'll canvas the route she likely walked one more time. Then it's home for the day. The drive's about an hour." He crossed to the front door and stooped to put on his boots before stopping with his hand on the knob. "Can I tell Jordan that I saw you and you're doing well next time I speak to him on the phone?"

"If you like. Tell him … tell him that I hope everything works out for him in Thunder Bay."

"I will, and I know that he would wish the same for you."

Kala watched Clark walk through the wet grass to the path opening until the trees and brush swallowed him up. She could tell that he was worried about Rachel even while he'd been downplaying her disappearance. She clearly remembered the girl from the night before. She was slender with long red hair tied back and a dusting of freckles on her nose and cheeks — not classically pretty, but attractive with creamy skin, dancing blue eyes, and a wide smile. She'd been eager to please and friendly. While she served their dessert, she'd talked about the town with Dawn and the lack of things to do there. Nothing in her interactions with them had seemed out of the ordinary.

Kala turned from the window. Dawn was in the kitchen making sandwiches as they'd agreed in the canoe on their way to shore. They'd eat and drive into town around suppertime to Skype with Gundersund. Already the afternoon was slipping away. Kala sat on the stool vacated by Clark, set her elbow on the counter, and cupped her chin in the palm of her hand. She watched Dawn slice the bread and put the kettle on for tea, her thoughts turning back to her life in the two neighbouring towns of Red Rock and Dryden in northwestern Ontario and the man she'd wanted to spend her life with. She hadn't thought about Jordan in a long time.

Their affair took place over the year that he was separated from Miriam while Kala was living in a cabin in the woods outside Nipigon. On Miriam's invitation, he'd dropped by their old house one evening to speak with her about a divorce. She'd brought out the Scotch, defences had dropped away, and she'd ended up pregnant. Jordan swore he could barely remember how it happened and it meant nothing. Kala would have forgiven him, but she couldn't let him turn his back on the child. She wouldn't let herself have any regrets. Not now.

"Just peanut butter for me," she said. "If you want jam, there's a jar of blueberry in the fridge."

"Okay." Dawn was at the cupboard, taking out mugs. "We can check out the ski resort when we go into town. I was looking online and it has a cafeteria."

"Might be a good place to drink hot chocolate and use the Wi-Fi."

"Exactly."

After they ate, Dawn took Taiku for a walk up the road while Kala tidied the kitchen. When she was done, she hung up the dishcloth and walked to the front of the cabin to look out the window. Dawn should be returning any minute. The rain appeared to be letting up, although the sky was still grey and bloated with clouds. A strong wind made the treetops sway in intermittent gusts, the weather having worsened since their canoe ride. Kala strained to look up the path into the woods, searching for Dawn and Taiku. She couldn't see them but knew they wouldn't be much longer. She returned to the kitchen to top up Taiku's water bowl and to grab her phone. She heard a knock at the door as she was taking her raincoat down from the hook.

The dark-haired man who'd first greeted them when they arrived was standing on the bottom step. She was relieved to see Dawn and Taiku over his shoulder exiting from the woods.

"Neal," she said remembering his name at the last second. "Can I help you?"

"We found Rachel partway toward Searchmont. She must have been hit by a car on her way home.

They just left her there to die in the culvert." His face was ashen and his mouth seemed to be having difficulty forming the words.

"Oh no. I'm so sorry. Does Clark want me to come with you?"

Neal nodded. "He asked if you minded."

Kala was already putting on her raincoat. "Of course not. Let me tell Dawn where I'm going and I'll be right with you. I'll follow you in my truck."

She bent to put on her boots. *Not here*, she thought, angry at whatever fates had let death pursue them to this isolated retreat. *Can't you even give us a few weeks' peace?* She straightened and took a moment to breathe deeply and to centre herself before stepping outside to meet Dawn and Taiku and to break the news that their trip into town would have to wait.

CHAPTER EIGHT

K ala stood on the edge of the road next to Clark's OPP cruiser. The rain had slowed to a drizzle, but the wind was building in strength to compensate. She let it buffet her without seeking shelter, liking the feeling of being outdoors in the full-blown wildness of nature. Clark finished talking into his car radio's speakerphone and exited the car to join her. He'd sent Neal back to the lodge after he led her to this spot. They both looked down to the bottom of the gully where Rachel's body lay under a makeshift tarp that Clark had fastened with stakes. He'd driven the metal posts into the dirt amassed at the sides of the culvert in an attempt to preserve any evidence. A sheered rock face jutted above the road some ten feet back on either side. The path had been blasted through the Canadian Shield to make way for the dirt road that connected the Pine Hollow Lake to town.

"Ambulance and coroner are on their way," he said. "I called this in to the Sault about forty minutes ago so they'll be here within the half hour, hopefully. Searchmont has a volunteer fire-paramedic service, but they're of no use to us this time with her already dead."

"Does her father know?" Kala asked.

"No, I'd driven him home to be with Isabelle before I started the search. Neal was with me as a second set of eyes. He was actually the one who spotted her. As you can see, Rachel didn't get that far from the lodge before she was struck. Would you like to have a look at her body?" He gave her a sideways glance.

Kala knew that accepting would mean she was agreeing to help him. She hesitated. "Are you going to be lead on this case?"

"Looks that way. I was just speaking to my sergeant, and while serious, a hit and run won't be top on the list of priorities. We've had two homicides that our Major Crimes team is handling while also juggling a detective on maternity leave and another out on long-term disability in the Sault detachment. I mentioned you were staying in Pine Hollow Lodge and suggested you might be amenable to helping out. We can make a formal request to your detachment if required."

"Your headquarters is in North Bay."

"Correct."

"I've taken an assignment with the Kingston force."

"You're still OPP, though?"

"Well, officially maybe. The paperwork for a formal transfer is in progress."

"Works for now then." He grinned and for a moment she saw Jordan in his face. Her heart caught and she scuffed at the ground with her foot.

"Dawn and I are here on vacation."

"I get it." He took a step away and looked back at her. "Do you want to have a look anyway?"

She could tell he was tired and remembered how dogged he'd been when they worked together. He'd taken the less-pleasant shifts to give her time off. "May as well," she said.

He got her a pair of white boot covers from the trunk of his car. She put them on and they scrambled down the culvert some distance away from the tarp and walked carefully through the tall wildflowers growing in the shallow soil toward Rachel's body. Kala followed in Clark's footsteps so as not to disturb the scene more than necessary. Out of the wind, the rain was a white mist that lingered like wisps of hazy smoke. The culvert felt eerie and she had to fight back the claustrophobic urge to get back in her truck and drive away.

Clark squatted and carefully lifted back the tarp with gloved hands. Kala crouched down next to him. She took a deep breath, looked up at the grey clouds and steadied herself. This broken girl was only a year older than Dawn. She'd served them dinner the night she died. Kala's heartbeat slowed and she looked down at Rachel's face, pale as alabaster with her eyes bulging and staring straight ahead at nothing. The blood that must have pooled around her had all but washed away. Her face was shiny, and her red hair was plastered to her head from a day and night in the rain, her jacket and pants soaked through. The right side of Rachel's face was bruised and concave from where she'd been struck or thrown against the ground. Kala closed her eyes and said a silent prayer for her spirit to soar free. Clark waited silently beside her.

"Did you take photos?" she asked.

"I did."

"You haven't turned her over?"

"I thought it best to wait."

They retraced their steps. The culvert was steep and it took an effort to climb back onto the road. A car drove past as they stood on the shoulder, but the driver didn't give them more than a passing glance. "We could wait in my car out of the wind if you like," said Clark.

"I am a bit chilled."

They got inside and Clark turned on the engine and jacked the heat up before answering a call on his radio. "The team is passing through Searchmont now," he said. "Are you warm enough?"

"Yes, thanks."

"I have to make a call to my wife, Valerie. She's due in a few weeks with our first and jumpy as a cat where I'm concerned. She thinks something bad is going to happen to me on the job. Normal paranoia, her obstetrician tells me."

"I could wait outside."

"Don't even think about it."

After the call Clark shifted positions so that he was looking directly at her. "You seem different."

"Oh, how so?" Her heart had picked up speed, but she kept her hands and body still.

"I can't put my finger on it. Are you happy?"

"Happy enough. I own property outside Kingston on the water. I have friends and a good job." *And I'm thinking about throwing it all away.*

"I never thought you'd really put down roots, but I'm glad that you have. You deserve to be happy." He checked his watch. "I know this is a lot to ask, but would you come with me to tell Rachel's parents? You can follow me in your truck."

She could have said no, but she didn't want to say goodbye to him yet. He was a link to her past and to the time she'd loved his brother. She had to let all that go again, but a few more hours of reliving old attachments before putting them away wouldn't do any harm. She swivelled her head to smile at him. "Of course I'll come with you."

Telling parents that their child would no longer be coming home never got easier. Kala supposed that if it did, she should give up policing. They were in the front entrance when Clark broke the news because Isabelle had refused to invite them farther into the house until they said their piece. The news hit both parents like blows to the stomach, as if they'd been holding on to hope since the night before even while expecting the worst. Afterward, Kala put an arm around Isabelle's waist and led her into the living room. She heard Owen's fist smash the wall behind her and then the murmur of Clark's voice calming him down. The front door creaked open. The two men went outside and the door slammed behind them.

"Who would do this?" Isabelle's face was a

shocked mask that could crumple like shattered glass at any moment. Her eyes beseeched Kala. "Who would hit her with their car and just drive off without trying to save her?"

"Perhaps the driver didn't realize they'd struck a person. We have to locate them to find out what happened that night."

Isabelle jolted up from the chair. "I want to see her. I need to see her."

Kala stood and put a hand on her shoulder. "She's being taken to the Soo and Officer Clark is going to drive you both to her when he gets word that she's arrived."

Isabelle flopped back in the chair. She looked straight ahead.

"Let me make some tea," said Kala bending and rubbing Isabelle's two hands in hers. "Can I call anybody to be with you?"

"No. My boys will have to know, but I'll call them later. My church ... Father Vila. His number is by the phone."

"Would you like him to come here now?"

"No. No. I'll call him when we get back from seeing her. We'll have to make arrangements for burial." She sobbed but quickly gathered herself. "My faith will keep me going."

Kala made a strong cup of tea and brought it to her. She sat on the edge of the couch with their knees almost touching. "Would it help you to talk about Rachel?"

Isabelle sobbed and recovered. Her voice wavered before gaining strength. "Rachel came later in our lives. I'd all but stopped believing we could have another child. She was such a shining light in my life right from the start. God's gift to us. She loved being in the woods with her father and helping out at home. We often cooked supper together and she'd tell me about her day. She was introverted but smart. Always a book on the go and a dreamer. You know? From the time she was a little girl she liked to imagine — played dolls and dress-up all the time and never lost the magic of that. I don't know if she went to church to humour me, but we'd go most Sunday mornings. She liked to help with the younger kids. She said that she wanted four of her own someday." Isabelle's voice cracked on the last words and she took a sip of tea. "Owen wanted her to join him in his outfitting business and I think she would have after this summer at the lodge. She was good in the outdoors. Owen used to take her canoeing and camping. He's going to miss her so much. She was his favourite, although we're not supposed to think that way."

Kala stayed with her another half hour until Clark re-entered the house and motioned for her to leave Isabelle and come with him into the kitchen.

"I'll be right back," she said and joined him. "What is it?" she asked.

He kept his voice low and turned his back to the living room. "I got a call a minute ago. Rachel wasn't hit by a car. Somebody took a solid object to her back and head. The coroner thinks a tire iron."

"So not a hit and run."

"No. She was beaten to death. I'm not sure how to break this to her parents."

"Where's Owen?"

"He went for a walk but said he won't be longer than ten minutes. He wanted to clear his head." Clark gave her a rueful smile. "Wait until I refill it with this news."

Clark had always hated this part of the job. Kala had been the one to tell the families when a son had been in a car accident or a daughter raped. She knew her matter-of-fact demeanour was better than his stilted attempts to explain the unexplainable. She took pity on him. "We'll tell them together when he gets back."

"Thanks, Stonechild. I know this isn't what you envisioned in your holiday plans." The Jordan-grin was back on his face. "I wonder if I could ask one more favour of you?"

She steeled herself not to feel anything. Not to let the past unbalance her. "What do you need?"

"I have to take them to see Rachel's body, but now this is a murder investigation. Could you return to the lodge and be my eyes and ears? Don't correct the idea that Rachel was the victim of a hit and run. Let them believe that for now. Only the killer will know the truth. They might slip up."

"It could be somebody from town. There were several at Pine Hollow Lodge for supper the last night she served. Her mother also said that Rachel had a boyfriend." She caught herself getting caught up in the investigation while Clark waited for her to run through possibilities. They both knew this was the moment when she'd commit to helping officially or not. She stared at him, the cop she'd known and liked when they were on the same team. *Jordan's brother.* "Dawn is waiting for me to go into town."

"You could take her tomorrow. It's getting late in the day."

She took her time answering. "I'm not agreeing to do more than this, you understand, Clark?"

"Of course. I know that what I'm asking of you is above and beyond."

They locked eyes. The front door opened and Owen stomped into the hall. She nodded even while knowing that she was going to live to regret her decision.

"This is it, then," said Clark. "Time to break more devastating news. Thanks again, Stonechild. I know you won't be sorry for giving me a hand. It'll be like old times."

Chapter Nine

Martha heard Neal enter their house late afternoon. She was putting the last pan of bran muffins into the oven for the next morning's breakfast and stayed in the kitchen to let him come to her. *It feels as if I'm waiting for the other shoe to drop*, she thought.

"I have some terrible news," he said from the doorway. He'd taken the good bottle of Glenlivet from the sideboard in the dining room and held it with both hands. His face was sickly pale and sweat beaded on his forehead. "Rachel's been found dead at the roadside on the way to Searchmont. She must have been hit by a car and left in the ditch last night on her way home."

Martha put a hand on her chest. "Oh, dear God, no. Are you sure?"

"I saw her."

The raw pain in his voice made her open her arms and cross the floor to him. They clutched each other for a moment until Neal pulled away. He turned from her and took two glasses out of the cupboard.

With his back to her he poured them each a healthy slug. "I can't believe this," he said when he turned and handed her the glass.

Martha took it with a trembling hand and swallowed a long, burning mouthful. She held the lip of the glass against her chin and said, "The poor girl."

Neal lowered himself onto a chair. "I can't believe she won't be in the restaurant when we go over for supper. This is so unbelievably horrible."

Martha watched him closely through tearful eyes. She slid into the seat kitty-corner to his. "Is there any ... are the police involved?"

He glanced over, but his eyes returned to stare into the glass he clutched in one hand. "An officer named Clark Harrison came up from the Soo to help look for her. I was outside when he and Owen Eglan were walking back to his police car, and the cop asked if I had time to help with a search along the route into town. He was driving Owen home to be with his wife before he started looking and wanted another set of eyes. We drove and walked the road at different spots. I'm not sure if the cop had a gut feeling or not, but it was a blessing that Rachel's father wasn't with us when we found her. I saw Rachel's body down the gully amongst the flowers on that long, curved section of road about halfway to town. Harrison wouldn't let me any closer, but I recognized her jacket and ... her red hair. He asked me to walk back to the lodge and ask that Stonechild woman to go meet him at the site. I found her in her cabin and then got my car and led her to the site in her truck." Neal raised his eyes. "Did you know she's a cop?" He gulped at the drink as if he had a thirst to quench.

Martha took another sip from her glass before setting it carefully on the table. "No, I didn't know. Have you told anybody else about Rachel?"

"Shane. He's probably told Petra by now. Thank goodness it's the end of the season because this has killed any desire I had left to be here."

Her heart felt as if a vice were tightening around it until she could hardly breathe. She grabbed on to his forearm. "Please, Neal, let's take some time and get our bearings again. I don't want us to separate. I know that I'm to blame for ... for all that's gone wrong. I'll do anything you want to make things right between us."

He didn't shake off her hand, which she supposed was progress. She couldn't read the expression in his eyes before he drained the last of the Scotch. He set his glass next to hers. "I need to get back to the restaurant and think you should, too. The other guests will need to be told."

You haven't shut the door completely. Martha kept the hope from her voice. "I'll change my clothes and will be right behind you. We'll get through our grief." She wanted to say "together," but wouldn't push her luck.

"Do we have a choice?"

She waited at the table and listened to him put on his coat and boots and clomp out of the house. He had a heavy tread, but she'd gotten used to the sound. She supposed she'd hear him walking around the house in her dreams if he ever left her for good.

Word had travelled through the lodge like a brush fire because everyone was gathered together when Martha stepped inside the restaurant. All, that is, except for Kala Stonechild and her niece. Petra and Shane were standing slightly apart from the others, but Neal was talking to the lodgers — Ian, Blaine, and Thomas.

"We cancelled the dinner reservations from town," she heard Shane say before he saw her standing in the doorway.

She crossed the floor to stand next to him. "This is unbelievable," she said. Everyone looked stricken, but Thomas Faraday appeared the most distraught. He'd run his hand through his white hair so often that it was sticking on end. She added, "I don't know how this could have happened."

"One of us should have driven her home," said Blaine. "Ian or I often do, but last night she said that she had a ride coming. We should have checked back with her."

"You couldn't have known," said Neal.

The door opened and they all turned. Martha shivered in the sudden blast of air that brought Kala Stonechild into the room. The girl Dawn was behind her, body language closed off and face sullen. Their entrance was a reminder of the investigation to come. Everyone broke apart as if caught in a guilty act and moved toward their tables while Martha stepped forward to greet them.

"This has been a terrible day," she said. "I'm sorry that you've come to visit us at such a time."

"You couldn't have known."

"No, but just the same — this is so horrible. We're reeling and it's going to take a bit of time to recover from this devastating news. We all loved Rachel." Martha had to remember that these were first-time lodge guests and had no connection to Rachel or to the other people here. She forced her voice to lighten. "Come take a seat. We're serving lasagna tonight, or leftover stew." She led them to the table they'd sat at the night before. She remarked, "I had no idea you were with the police."

The Stonechild woman's gaze sharpened. "There was no need to tell you. I'm here on vacation."

"Of course. I know this hasn't been the most pleasant day. We're all in a bit of shock, but we don't want this tragic accident to interfere with your holiday. Please let me know if we can do anything to make your stay more pleasant." She felt the blood drain from her face as she realized how odd her comment was given the circumstances. She added, "Although I know that sounds out of place at the moment." She turned and stifled the urge to slap herself on the forehead for letting herself get so flustered.

Petra was waiting for her outside the door to the kitchen. Her face was pale and her eyes glassy. She'd tied her hair into a sloppy ponytail that cascaded in messy strands to her shoulders. Martha grabbed her by the arm and led her into the hallway to the washroom. "You can't carry on here. What have you taken?"

"Nothing too strong. I'm fine. What happened to Rachel? Shane wouldn't tell me anything except that she's dead."

"We heard that she was struck by a car and left at the side of the road on her way home from work."

"When?"

"Last night, sometime after closing."

Petra closed her eyes and sagged against the wall.

"You don't know anything about it, do you?" asked Martha.

Petra shook her head and her hair swung side to side like a child's. She opened her eyes. "I was late getting home last night ... I don't remember the drive. What if I hit her and didn't know it?"

Martha wanted to shake her. "That's crazy. You'd have felt something strike the car."

Petra straightened and pushed herself from the wall. Her face was inches from Martha's and Martha stepped back. She could smell Petra's trademark scent: musky damask rose. The perfume left on many a pillow after she got out of whatever bed she'd leapt into. Petra's voice dropped to a hiss. "I never liked her. Always lurking around doors and listening. I won't pretend sorrow when I feel none." Her breath smelled like peppermint and wine. Her wide blue eyes sparkled in the harsh overhead lighting.

"You can't mean that."

Petra's thoughts jumped again. "Shane told me to go home and rest. I'm going to do as my husband ordered. I hope you can get through the night without me here."

"We'll manage." Martha thought of the cop Stonechild sitting steps away, watching and weighing every nuance, every comment, every bit of body language. "Sleep this off," she said more gently than she felt. "I'll see you tomorrow."

Petra saluted and hit Martha's cheek with her fingers as she lowered her hand, sliding her fingertips down Martha's face. "Try not to look so worried. I'll leave by the back entrance so I don't get the lodgers talking. God forbid I make a scene."

Kala refused a coffee refill from Neal and studied his slow walk back to the counter. The other lodgers had watched her and Dawn enter and take their seats. Neal had come right over with glasses of water and pointed them to the night's menu written on the chalkboard near the door. While they waited for their meals, Kala searched the faces of the others seated nearby, looking for guilt. Dawn squirmed in the seat across from her and she shifted her gaze. "Everything okay?" she asked.

"Was Gundersund waiting for us to call him?"

"Maybe. We can go to town in the morning and try him at work." If Dawn wanted her to feel bad she was succeeding. "We've only been gone two days."

Dawn looked around and lowered her voice. "You're checking them out, aren't you?"

Kala's default reaction was not to answer but she owed Dawn the truth. "Officer Harrison wants me to be a set of eyes and ears. It's possible someone in the lodge was responsible for Rachel's death."

"Why would he ask you?"

"They don't have a police force in Searchmont, and Clark and I used to work together. He trusts me, I guess." Dawn's eyes signalled that someone was coming up behind her and Kala stopped talking.

"Mind if I join you for a minute?" The older man she remembered was named Thomas stood at her elbow.

"Please," said Kala, pointing to the vacant space at the table between her and Dawn.

He dragged over a chair from the next table and set his beer down. "I like to welcome new guests. I'm the resident old codger, Thomas Faraday. Good canoe ride this morning?"

"It was." Kala remembered there were no secrets in small communities. He likely already knew she was a cop. "How long have you been staying here?" she asked.

"Third summer. I go out shooting most days." He laughed at the look of disgust on Dawn's face. "I should clarify. Shooting with my camera. I'm an amateur wildlife photographer in my retirement, although my photos have been bought for calendars and tourism campaigns. A couple even made some of my pictures into a book. I used to have my own portrait business on King West in Toronto." He put both hands around the beer stein. "I guess you know about the death of our young server, Rachel. We're all devastated by the news. She worked here all summer and was well-liked. A most pleasant young lady." He dropped his eyes to the table before taking a drink from his glass.

"We only met her when she served our meal yesterday. We're so sorry for your loss. Was she close to anybody here?" Kala tried not to meet Dawn's eyes, which fixed steadily on her face.

"Rachel was everyone's favourite. She wasn't talkative lest you got her one on one. She confided in me once that her mother curtailed her freedom so she took employment at the lodge to get out from under her." He laughed. "She liked that we had no internet or cellphone service so her mother couldn't keep tabs on her every movement." He grimaced as if remembering that this was not a time to make light.

"You spent a lot of time talking to her?"

"Not overly. Only during mealtime. She also chatted with our resident Hydro workers." He looked over at the two young men sitting at the table by the window. "Ian, the taller, good-looking one with the dark brown hair and five o'clock shadow, is getting married at Christmastime when he goes home to Thunder Bay, which is slated to happen next week. Blaine hails from Marathon. They met at trade school in Thunder Bay and got hired by the same company."

Kala followed his gaze. Both men wore checked bush jackets, jeans, and Kodiak boots. Their hair had grown shaggy over the summer and their faces had tanned to a deep shade of brown. However, in comparison to Ian's dark good looks, Blaine was plainer: clean-shaven, dirty-blond hair, hooked nose, and stocky build. "They seem to be good friends."

"One would assume. They spend a lot of time together, although Ian of late has taken up fishing in the evenings, making me think that they've had their fill of being constantly in each other's pocket."

"The lodge owners seem nice," she said to get his reaction. Lobbing out softballs. She realized that this was a man who liked to watch and judge those around him. He got off on feeling superior to the others. Spoke in affected language.

"They are intriguing beyond a doubt. I believe Martha and Shane are cousins of some variety. Second or third. Perhaps even first. He got into a spot of financial trouble and she gave him a job here for the summer." He bit his bottom lip and smiled as if leaving some malicious tidbit unsaid. "Shane's wife, Petra, is something of an ... oddity." Thomas waved a hand at Neal, who approached the table with their dinners.

"Your meal is served," Neal said pointedly to Thomas as he set plates of lasagna and garlic bread in front of Dawn and Kala. "Shall I bring another beer to your table?"

Thomas stood and bowed his head toward Kala. "I'll leave you to it, then. I trust our paths will cross again."

Neal stayed standing in place until Thomas was back at his table. His voice was apologetic but annoyed. "I hope Thomas wasn't bothering you. Impolite as this sounds, he likes to have his nose in everyone's business."

"No, he was fine," said Kala. "It's a difficult day for everyone."

Neal nodded. "We're just trying to understand how it could have happened."

"Rachel sounds like she was a good kid."

"I keep expecting to see her coming out of the kitchen with a tray of food and then remember what happened. The only saving grace is that we're closing for the season in another week. It's tough being here right now."

Dawn had begun eating with her head down. After Neal left, she didn't break the silence and Kala let her be. She took a bite of lasagna and debated asking to have it reheated. She decided she was too hungry to wait and tucked in. As she scraped up the last of the tomato sauce she lifted her eyes and found Dawn watching her.

"You're going to take on this case, aren't you?" Dawn asked.

"If it were you this had happened to, I'd move heaven and earth to find out who did it and make them face the consequences, but no, I'm not doing more than this little bit of assessment." Kala softened her voice. "I'm helping Clark today and that's it. Tomorrow you and I and Taiku are going for a long canoe ride to find the perfect place to scatter your dad's ashes. We'll only do it when you feel we're in the right spot."

"And we can talk to Gundersund tomorrow?"

"Yes, I promise." Kala smiled. "I miss him, too."

Shane had made a Boston cream pie for dessert, and Martha insisted they each have a piece. By the time they were ready to head back to their cabin, Ian and Blaine were gone. Kala had wanted to speak with them and would have to waylay them in the morning, hopefully while Dawn was still asleep. After she talked to them, she'd stop helping Clark altogether and could spend the rest of their vacation with a clear conscience.

CHAPTER TEN

Jacques Rouleau checked his watch before turning his attention back to the PowerPoint presentation on youth gangs. The information was interesting enough but not particularly pertinent to his current job. He'd had to set aside the stack of paperwork he faced every Monday morning to come downtown to the conference centre and wasn't convinced he'd made the best decision. Kingston had its share of youth problems, but nothing like they had in the larger urban centres like Ottawa and Toronto. Sometimes smaller really was better.

The workshop wrapped up before noon and he texted Marci that he was on his way. The August sun was still strong enough to counter the cool wind off the lake and he left his jacket in the car after parking and backtracking to Chez Piggy on Princess Street. Marci was waiting for him in the courtyard, a pitcher of sangria on the table. She stood and embraced him before he took the seat facing her.

"Good day so far?" she asked, pouring him a glass.

"It's been informative but not all that exciting. I might be late leaving work tonight since the paperwork will have piled up on my desk all morning. Are you expecting company? Because I have to get back to HQ." He pointed to the pitcher and smiled.

"I'm taking the afternoon off and plan to sit here and read the news and sip from my glass until I walk to your dad's for supper."

"That's right. He's slow-cooking a prime rib this afternoon."

"With roast potatoes and gravy." Marci raised her glass. "A toast to your dad and to this end-of-summer day."

"To Dad and summer." Rouleau clinked his glass with hers and drank. "Has something good happened at your work?"

"Well, now that you ask ..." she set down her glass and rested her arms on the table. She was wearing a kelly green turtleneck sweater that complemented her auburn hair. "I've been made an offer that I wanted to talk over with you."

She appeared hesitant and he braced himself for whatever she was going to say. "I'm listening."

"There's an overseas opening at the *New York Times* in Paris. It's a great opportunity to live in Europe and travel. You've spoken about retiring and this could be a wonderful time to hand in your notice and come with me. We could bring your dad and rent a house or apartments in the same building. I'm excited thinking about what a great adventure we'll have." She reached across the table and entwined her fingers with his. "I know this is a big change, but I'm really hoping you'll take some time to consider it."

Rouleau let her words sink in. He'd spoken about retiring, but in an abstract way, and not for another five years. "Will you take the job if I don't go with you?"

She bit her bottom lip and shook her head, but he could see the truth in her eyes. "I hope you'll say yes and that won't be an issue. Will you promise me that you'll think about this move seriously, Jacques?"

"I will." He squeezed her hand before releasing and picking up his glass. "At the very least we should toast your success."

"It never hurts to keep doors open," she said, laughing, and clinking his glass with hers. "That way wonderful surprises can arrive out of the blue."

He was late returning to headquarters but had kept an eye on his messages, and nothing pressing arrived that needed his attention. Marci's news had him distracted and he thought over the possibility of chucking everything and going with her to Paris. He wasn't certain Henri would want to come along. Perhaps he was up for an adventure — you could never tell with his father. Then Rouleau reminded himself that Henri had lived in Kingston for fifty years and was a creature of habit. He still kept an office at the university and his research was ongoing. The odds of him giving up this town were slim.

He parked in the lot and took the stairs to the second floor. Gundersund followed him into his office and took a seat in the visitor chair while Rouleau turned on the desk lamp. "Any word from Stonechild?" he asked as he sat down. She'd been gone three days but it felt longer.

"I thought they'd call yesterday once they settled in, but no word yet." Gundersund's foot tapped on the floor while his fingers played a drumbeat on his leg. "Minny keeps searching the house looking for Taiku. It's amazing how quickly the two dogs became attached."

Rouleau knew he wasn't speaking only about the dogs. "They'll be back. It's only for a few weeks."

"I know we'd like to believe that."

The phone rang and Rouleau reached for it, holding up a finger to Gundersund. "Caller ID says North Bay OPP. I'd better take this."

"Should I wait?"

"I'll signal if it's going to be a long call." He picked up and identified himself. He watched Gundersund while he listened to the North Bay sergeant ask to have Kala Stonechild work a murder case out of the Sault detachment. "She's agreed to this?" he asked when there was an opening in the conversation.

"She's already been helping out unofficially. She has a unique perspective from staying at the lodge where the victim worked. She's been developing relationships that could lead us to the killer. This is a highly unusual request I know, but she and the investigating officer Clark Harrison worked together previously. He's sung her praises and wants her on the file."

Gundersund had stopped fidgeting and was staring at him. Rouleau knew what Stonechild would want him to say. "You have my okay as long as it's what she's agreed to do. I expect there'll be paperwork?"

"I'll have it sent after we hang up."

Rouleau recited his email address before ending the call.

"Stonechild?" asked Gundersund.

"She's gotten herself involved in a murder case that happened up the road from where she and Dawn are staying. A high-school girl who worked at the lodge."

"This was supposed to be her time to unwind and reconnect with Dawn." Gundersund shook his head and was silent for a moment. He stood. "We both know that she won't be able to pass up the chance to work on a murder case. Everyone in her life takes second place once she's on the trail." He shot Rouleau a half smile. "At least now I know why she didn't call yesterday." He started toward the door and said over his shoulder, "See you later. I have some documents to review before I testify in court this afternoon."

Rouleau stood after Gundersund was gone and crossed to the window, his favourite thinking spot. He watched frothy cumulus clouds scudding into view. He'd felt a change in the wind walking from the restaurant to his car and predicted a rainstorm on the horizon. They were due, he supposed. The good weather they'd had the last two weeks had to come to an end. The August heat was inching down into cooler temperatures overnight. Ontario meteorologists were calling for an early winter across the province with higher snowfall than usual. Climate change, he supposed. More bad weather to dominate the news.

Rouleau's mind circled back to the idea of moving with Marci to Paris. He enjoyed being with her and didn't want to think about her being gone from Kingston. Yet he also couldn't envision leaving his father at this stage in his life or ending his policing career. He liked where he was in the department. He had a good team and satisfying work. He felt at home in this city. Yet Paris could be the kickstart his life needed — to take chances and to embrace being alive.

Loud voices in the outer office made him turn. Woodhouse and Bennett were having a heated discussion, but Woodhouse shut it down quickly by crossing the room and stepping into the hall. Everyone on the Major Crimes team seemed out of sorts since Stonechild's departure. They'd be even less settled when they found out that she'd taken an assignment with the OPP. He didn't know what Gundersund would do if she didn't come back. Would he follow her north?

The times they are a-changin', Rouleau thought. *The trick will be making sure that nobody gets left behind.*

CHAPTER ELEVEN

Kala looked in on Dawn, still sound asleep, and called softly for Taiku to come. He rose stiffly from the carpet next to Dawn's bed and stretched each of his legs on his way across the floor to her. She stooped to rub his ears. She'd dressed in leggings, a T-shirt, and a windbreaker, and bent to lace up her running shoes at the door. Five thirty, and the sun wouldn't fully rise for another hour, but twilight had brightened the sky enough so that they could safely make their way through the woods.

She walked the shadowy path to the road with Taiku darting in and out of the underbrush ahead of her, constantly stopping and turning his head to make sure she was following. They reached the main road and Kala broke into a jog. Taiku fell in beside her and kept pace for twenty minutes until she slowed to a walk and reversed direction. The sky had brightened above the treeline as they ran and had transposed into the muted pastel colours of an Impressionist painting by the time they returned to sit on the rock down the incline from their cabin.

Kala hugged her knees with one arm and pulled Taiku close with the other. She rested her head on his. Bands of orange and pink bled into a cover of indigo cloud with the lake a mirror image of colour. The trees on the distant shore were stark black shapes reflected in the still, pink water. "I could stay right here with you forever," she whispered into Taiku's ear and his tail thumped hard against the rock.

They returned to the cabin and she filled his food bowl after checking that Dawn was still asleep. Satisfied that Dawn wouldn't be up anytime soon, she left the cabin and walked the path to the dining room in the main lodge. It was nearing seven o'clock. The lights were on and the door was unlocked. Blaine was sitting alone at the same table as the evening before, eating a plate of bacon and eggs. He looked up at her in the entrance and back down at his plate. He hadn't shaven and stubble roughened his face.

"Guess we're the only ones up. Mind if I join you?" she asked.

"Sure. Pull up a seat." His words belied the uneasy look he'd given her when he saw her in the doorway.

Shane came out of the kitchen with a pot of herbal tea that he set down in front of her. He'd already figured out that she preferred herbal tea to coffee. Not that she honestly preferred herbal tea but she knew the drink was healthier. "How would you like your eggs?" he asked.

"Scrambled, with bacon and brown toast if you have it," she said.

"Coming right up."

When he'd returned to the kitchen, Kala turned her attention back to Blaine. She remembered that Ian, the much handsomer of the two, was the one getting married in Thunder Bay when the summer ended. "Is your partner sleeping in?" she asked.

"Ian already ate. I'm the slow one today. Sorry if I'm wolfing this down. We meant to be on the road by now, but I caught an extra hour of shuteye trying to get rid of a headache. I had a migraine last night."

"That's rough. How're you feeling now?"

"Well enough to climb up and down Hydro poles."

His skin did have a greyish pallor and black circles rimmed his eyes. "Do you get these headaches often?" she asked, sipping her tea. She had to admit that the chamomile brew was refreshing after the morning run.

"First one this summer."

"I guess Rachel's death is stressful for everybody," she said, leaning back in the chair and keeping her eyes on him.

"I'm gutted. She was just a kid." Blaine took a bite of toast. He chewed and swallowed it with a sip of coffee. He set the cup down and wiped his mouth with the back of his hand. "You're a cop ... has the OPP shared anything about who hit her?"

"I'm a Kingston cop on vacation." She ignored his question. "I imagine you'll be happy to get home after the summer away. Where is home?"

"I've got an apartment in Thunder Bay across from the marina."

"Did you sublet for the summer?"

"No."

She waited a beat. "When's the last time you saw Rachel?"

"Ian and I left the restaurant together and she was serving you pie, as I recall. I didn't see her after that."

"Did she ever confide in you about her life?" Kala gave a self-deprecating smile. "I guess I can't seem to shake sounding like a cop even on vacation."

"No worries. We talked, sure, but she never got too personal. It's not like we had anything in common. She was just a high-school kid, after all."

"Did you and Ian go straight back to your cabin after supper last night?"

"Yeah." He gave her a sideways glance. "Look, I gotta go." He pushed back his chair and stood. He turned his face toward the kitchen and raised his voice. "Thanks, Shane." He grabbed his jacket from the back of the chair and nodded at her. "Catch you later."

Kala sipped from her mug and stared out the window at the lake after he'd gone. The sun was fully up, the sky a pale blue with no rainclouds in sight. A good day to be out on the water. The need to be away from the lodge was like a fever making her slightly nauseous. The disquiet that swirled around the restaurant the night before was getting stronger with every conversation. These people had secrets, she had no doubt. She closed her eyes, a sudden wave of fatigue washing over her so that she wanted to weep. What kind of person would kill that young girl and steal her life so cruelly? What possible reason could they have to justify her murder in their own mind? Rachel had been only a year older than Dawn.

The times she had faced a truly evil person were few. Most killers had a reason — perhaps a crazy reason understandable only to themselves — but a reason all the same for what they did. The nature of Rachel's murder, beaten with an object on a country road in the middle of nowhere under the cover of darkness and left to die in the culvert, pointed to a crime of passion or opportunity or both. For all intents and purposes, this was a small, closed community, the road travelled mainly by locals as the summer season wound down.

Kala opened her eyes. *This was not a random killing*. Rachel's murderer had targeted her. Rachel had angered or threatened someone desperate to keep her quiet, and this knowledge led to a second truth: Rachel's death would haunt Kala forever if she turned her back and walked away.

Dawn helped to carry the canoe to the water and took her place in the front with the ease of an experienced paddler. Kala held the canoe steady while Taiku got in and settled in the middle. He'd been her companion over numerous canoe trips since he was a pup and knew to lie quietly at her feet. Kala steered the boat in the opposite direction from the day before. They passed Pine Hollow tucked in on the rocky shore and settled into a comfortable rhythm, Kala matching her strokes to Dawn's. The cabins set back from the water's edge tapered away into jagged unbroken forest. A thick line of black spruce, Jack pine, and balsam guarded the deeper wilderness inhabited by northern wildlife: moose, deer, bear, beaver, fox, and wolf. Clumps of white pine topped rocky outcroppings with hemlock and cedar filling lower-lying boggy valleys. Sunlight glinted off the layers of rock — granite laced through with pinkish quartz and glinting black silica. In the distance, as far as the eye could see, were steep, rounded hills dark with thick stands of conifer trees. Away from shore the mosquitoes and deer flies were bothersome, but manageable since Kala had thought to spray them both with insect repellant before setting out.

After three hours of steady paddling, when she could see that Dawn was tiring, they pulled the canoe onto a sandy curve of shoreline nestled in a wide bay. Driftwood, bleached bone-white by the sun, lay scattered across the sand. They separated and collected enough wood to build a fire that would keep away the flies while Taiku inspected the shoreline and darted in and out of the woods. Fire built, Kala and Dawn sat side by side on a log smoothed by time and tides. They ate the sandwiches Dawn had made before setting out, washing them down with bottles of water and topping them off with apples and the molasses cookies that Kala had packed in Kingston. Worn out, Taiku snoozed after eating his bowl of dog food.

"It's so quiet out here," Dawn said. "We could be the only two people left in the world."

Kala slid into the sand, her legs stretched out in front of her and her back resting against the log. A dragonfly landed next to her but darted away when Taiku lifted his head. She poked at the fire with a stick, and orange sparks crackled into the air. The lake was grey-blue, and a soft wind ruffled the surface. "Are you glad we came?" she asked. Dawn hadn't said more than a couple of words since she'd lit the fire.

Dawn was quiet a moment longer. "I didn't think I would be, but I am." She pulled her sketch pad and pencils from her bag and the urn that held her father's ashes. "I want to capture this place. Fisher will be at peace here."

Kala looked up at her adopted niece. "You're sure? We have lots of time to look further."

Dawn nodded her face lifted to the sun, eyes closed. "I'm sure. Before we leave."

"Then this is the place."

Kala drowsed in the sun's warmth along with Taiku while Dawn sketched. When the sun was still at its peak Dawn took the urn containing Fisher's ashes and they waded into the lake together. She looked at Kala. "Would it be wrong to say something?"

"Say whatever you feel in your heart."

"Okay." Dawn opened the lid of the urn. "I didn't know you for long, Dad, but I always knew you ... inside. Your heart was good and your spirit will journey with me. I'll love you forever." She tipped the urn and let Fisher's ashes float on the wind and fall into the water. "You're home now."

Kala said a silent prayer and put an arm around Dawn's shoulders. "This is a good place," she said. "Your father's returned to the wilderness, where he was happiest."

"He's been coming to me in dreams. Now his soul can rest."

They returned to shore hand in hand and Kala tamped out the fire, burying the ashes under the sand. They collected their belongings and walked to the water's edge where they'd turned the canoe on its side. They righted it and Taiku took his place in the centre. Dawn got in next and Kala pushed the boat into deeper water before climbing in. They started back the way they'd come. When they rounded the bend, Dawn lifted her paddle and rested it across her lap. She turned half sideways to look at Kala. Kala let her paddle rest in the water and the canoe bobbed in the swell. She waited, not sure what Dawn was going to say.

"You have to help find who killed Rachel. You're the only one who can." Dawn's eyes were dark and earnest.

"There are others."

"But I know you'll be the one. I'd want you to find my killer if … if that ever happened to me." Dawn smiled and squared back around. She picked up the paddle and resumed pulling it through the water in long, even strokes without looking back.

A shiver travelled up Kala's spine despite the warmth of the day. Was this a premonition or left-over worry from Dawn's recent ordeal in the spring when she'd come close to being killed? Should Kala pack up their things and take Dawn back to the safety of Kingston? But even home hadn't proven safe in the end.

She'd fought so hard against the fears of her childhood, to face the world head-on. She wouldn't let fear determine her actions now. Dawn was strong, too. Stronger than she'd been at the same age. Kala drew her paddle through the water and stilled the worry in her mind. Dawn had given her blessing to proceed with the investigation and that is what she would do. Track Rachel's killer and make them pay for what they'd done. Stop whoever was responsible before they killed again.

CHAPTER TWELVE

Clark was once again standing on Stonechild's dock when her canoe rounded the point. He watched its steady progress toward shore and thought about how best to approach her. They'd worked together three years out of the Nipigon–Red Rock detachment and most of that time on solo shifts. She liked working alone; he knew that much. Didn't look back once she moved on. Jordan was still pining after her even though he hadn't heard from her in three years. Last time they got together, Clark had told Jordan he was an idiot and to get on with his life, but he'd replied that there was something about Kala Stonechild he couldn't shake.

Clark crouched on the dock and guided the canoe alongside, holding the boat while the girl and the dog climbed out. Dawn gave him a quick smile before she and the dog started toward the cabin. Stonechild manoeuvred the canoe onto the sand and stepped into the water. Her feet were bare and her torn jeans rolled up to the knees. With her long black hair loose and brown face glowing from the sun, she looked more rested than the day before. He could admit that he'd been attracted to her once, before she got tangled up with his brother, and before Valerie. He still might be if things were different, but that was a thought best left alone. She tossed a bag onto the ground and grabbed the bow of the canoe.

"I've come to plead my case," he said, grabbing the other end. They lifted the canoe and started walking up the hill toward the trees.

"I've decided to help you," she said, without breaking stride.

He'd been preparing to counter her refusal and was momentarily at a loss for words. They reached the pines and rolled the canoe over. He straightened. "Do you mind if I ask what changed your mind?"

"You can ask, but I don't have to tell you." She shot him a quick grin and picked up the paddles. "Coffee?"

"Yeah. That'd be good."

He followed her into the cabin and took a stool at the kitchen counter. Stonechild filled him in on her meetings with the other lodgers while she waited for the coffee to brew. She filled one mug and slid it across the counter in his direction as she took a seat across from him. She'd poured a glass of water for herself. "So what's our plan?" she asked. "By the way, you might need my staff sergeant to approve this."

"About that. My sergeant already got Jacques Rouleau's approval. I have papers in the car for you to sign."

She scowled. "Shit. You really thought you could work me, didn't you?"

"No, I honestly didn't know if you'd come around." He grinned and raised his palms to the ceiling. "But a man could hope."

She glared at him but after a brief silence said, "I have to still be here for Dawn so I'm not going to spend every waking moment on the case. You can run stuff past me and I can do research and help with interviews."

"Fair enough. The autopsy's scheduled for tomorrow morning in North Bay, but I can go alone and report back to you. It's a five-hour trip each way so I won't return to the Soo much before suppertime."

"That should work. I know you're thorough."

"Try to be." He drank from the mug. "You off coffee?"

"I'm using this vacation as a health break."

"Fair enough. Do you keep in touch with Shannon?"

"A couple of times a year. She's busy with her life." Stonechild's face got the closed-off look that told him he'd better tread carefully. He knew for a fact that she'd stopped initiating any contact with the woman who used to be her best friend in Dryden. He wasn't surprised when she pointedly changed the subject. "How's your wife doing?"

"She's tired and ready to shove the baby out into the world, although the doctor says another three weeks is likely. Sleeps a lot when she's not eating. Has this craving for peanut butter, horseradish, and onion sandwiches, which turns my stomach, so not sure how the baby's handling it."

"Might come out needing some Alka-Seltzer."

Clark laughed. "Or its stomach pumped. I'm nervous about having a kid, considering all the crap I see in this job. I know you said Dawn's mother is in Joliette. What's she in for?"

"Armed robbery. She has seven years left on her sentence."

"She got ten?"

"Yeah, so she comes up for parole next year. She's been a model inmate."

"Kid must miss her."

"She does, although there's a lot of anger mixed in. I'm hoping Rose comes to stay with me when she gets out."

"She's lucky to have you." He gulped the last of the coffee. Stonechild had taken on someone else's kid and seemed to be sticking with it. Maybe there was hope for her yet. He slid the mug across the counter. "I'm going to head out. Back to the Soo for supper and North Bay first thing tomorrow. I'll check in after the autopsy."

Stonechild's forehead furrowed. "We need to talk to the other people at the restaurant that night. Three couples. Rachel also has that boyfriend in town we should interview. Why don't I type up what I've got so far from people and make a list of those we need to follow up with?"

"*That* would be an enormous help."

"Anything else you want me to do tomorrow morning?"

"Forensics has Rachel's cellphone and laptop, but I haven't gone through her bedroom yet. Her parents said they'd stay out of it until I give the green light."

"Okay, I'll get on it."

"Now I remember why I liked working with you so much. You take initiative." He smiled again. "Walk out with me and sign that release paper before you change your mind."

"Are we getting any more resources?"

"Only when the need arises. You and I are alone in the field for now."

"Is that usual?"

"Not unusual. Remember we're stretched thin this month. The team will help track down information as needed back at HQ, and of course the forensics team is in play. Not like working on a big-city force."

"Although even city forces have resource issues and priority files that push other cases aside."

"I still think of you as a northern cop. Can't quite picture you in the overpopulated south."

She didn't say anything and he wondered if he'd struck a nerve. He hadn't yet decided about phoning Jordan and telling him that Stonechild had surfaced and was working this case with him. He'd wait to see how the next week unfolded before making up his mind. Might be best to keep things professional and steer away from the past. He was leaning that way by the time he reached the outskirts of the Soo. The sight of his brother's truck in his driveway ten minutes later came as a shock.

"Shit," he muttered under his breath as he pulled in behind it. *This could get weird in a real hurry.*

"I'll try his number again," said Dawn. She typed and sat back to wait while Skype tried unsuccessfully to connect with Gundersund's computer. "Where could he be?" she asked.

"He's probably working. Emergencies can arise out of nowhere, as I'm sure you remember from all my late nights."

"He's going to think we've forgotten him."

Kala laughed. "I very much doubt that. We've only been gone four days."

"Still." Dawn shut her laptop and crossed her arms across her chest. "I guess we can try again tomorrow."

"We can and we will." Kala picked up their empty plates and cutlery and set everything on the tray. "I was hoping to get some groceries, but we're going to have to go into the Soo since the only store in Searchmont burned to the ground several years ago."

"Who told you that?"

"The woman behind the counter when you went to the washroom."

"We have enough bread and milk for another day."

"As roughing it goes, we don't have it too bad. A forty-mile drive to restock isn't much of a hardship." Kala thought she could fit the trip in midafternoon if she got the search of Rachel's room done in the morning.

"How do these people stand having to go so far for everything?"

"They'll have learned to take the good with the bad. Living close to nature always comes with some concessions."

"Would you want to live this far away from a city?"

Kala decided to leave her answer open-ended. "I've lived with Taiku in a cabin outside a town in northwestern Ontario and it suited me. I also like where we live now, in a community near a city. I can adapt to either."

"But which do you prefer, Aunt Kala? Where do you want to be if you have a choice?"

She's intuitively landed on the crux of it. Can I stay rooted in one place with the same people for the foreseeable future or is this yearning in me to get in my truck with Taiku and hit the open road going to win out? If I go back, my life is going to change big time. And the truth of it is, I don't know if I'm built for the responsibility. This ache in me is only getting stronger. I don't know if I'm wired to be with one person forever. I don't know if I'm capable of making Gundersund happy.

Kala picked up the tray and stood, looking down at Dawn. "I'm where I need to be for now," she said. "I'm not going to worry about the future today and neither should you."

Kala woke up early the next morning and checked outside before she put on her running gear and bug spray. Rain might be on the horizon, but for now the sky was transitioning from black to indigo with silver streams of moonlight bathing the trees and shimmering across the lake. The beauty of this place, the isolation and the calm were a balm for her soul. She called to Taiku and they walked through the woods and past the restaurant to the road. She thought about Rachel while she ran and the best way to approach the interviews that lay ahead. Word would soon get around that the girl been murdered — her parents would tell somebody and, like oil spilled on water, the news would spread through the entire town. She didn't know if this would inspire people to come forward or make them retreat further behind the impenetrable wall that united small towns against outsiders.

Shane was alone in the restaurant after she settled Taiku back in the cabin. He heard her enter and appeared with a pot of tea as she took a seat near the window. He was wearing a white apron over jeans and a blue-and-white-checked flannel shirt, and had tied his brown hair back with an elastic band. He ran a hand over a few days' growth of stubble on his cheeks while his velvety black eyes levelled with hers. "Blaine and Ian have come and gone," he said. "I'm making cheese-and-onion omelettes this morning unless you'd like something else."

"An omelette would be great, but hold the onions. If you make a second with onions before I leave, I can bring it to Dawn in the cabin."

"No problem."

She watched the light strengthening across the lake until he returned. He set a fluffy, golden omelette with brown toast and hash browns on the table in front of her. "Please join me," she said.

He looked toward the door and back at her as if

weighing his desire to leave against the need to be polite. "I'll get a coffee and will be right back."

She was halfway through her meal when he finally returned and dropped into the seat across from her. "Sorry, I was getting a soup started for tonight. We've got a few reservations already."

"Were you a cook before you came here for the summer?"

"I worked at a couple of diners in Sudbury. The last one went under and I was out of work, so Martha bailed me out by asking me to work here. She used to do all the cooking and said she'd be happy for an easier summer."

"How do you know her?"

"Our mothers are first cousins."

"I haven't met your wife."

"Petra."

"She was here the other night, but I didn't get a chance to speak with her. How does she like living in the woods for the summer?"

Shane's gaze passed over hers and out the window. He drank from his mug. "Petra would rather be anywhere but here." He refocused on Kala and gave a tight smile. "She's managed to spend a lot of the summer in the Soo."

"Where will you go when the lodge closes?"

"Not sure. I have some job applications out in Sudbury and Toronto, although I prefer not to return to Sudbury. I'm thinking of heading farther west as well."

Kala took a final bite of hash browns and set down her fork. His use of the singular pronoun might be unintentional, but for now she wouldn't probe. She sensed he'd shut down if she went there. She rested her elbows on the table and leaned in. "I'm helping Officer Harrison look into Rachel's death. What can you tell me about her?"

"I thought you might be. I hear you worked with him before."

"That's right."

Shane scratched his cheek while he appeared to organize his thoughts. "Rachel was quiet, pleasant, a good worker. She melted into the background and you forgot she was even in the room. I got the feeling she was micro-managed at home by her mother."

"Was anything bothering her aside from her home situation?"

"I wouldn't know." He twirled his coffee mug before taking a drink. "She seemed happier as the summer went on. I thought it might be because she was away from her mother. She'd started talking more and joking around. Becoming more self-confident."

"Did you meet her mother, Isabelle?"

"Yeah, we've met." He gave a half smile. "She's a religious, self-righteous worrier from our few conversations. I wasn't impressed with how she interacted with Rachel."

"What do you mean?"

"Isabelle treated her like a child, and she was anything but. I figured Rachel had reason to act out."

"How was she with her father?"

"They seemed to have a looser relationship. He was into his outfitter business and often away overnight. She told me that he asked her to work for him this summer, but she wanted to try something different."

"So the last time you saw Rachel was at closing time Saturday evening."

"That's right. I locked up and she went out the front door to wait for her father. I asked her if she wanted a lift to town before she left but she said no and that he'd be there any minute. Like I said before, I exited by the back door and didn't see her again."

"Did Neal leave with you?"

"I didn't see him at the restaurant. I heard he came by, but I was working in the kitchen."

"You and Petra have one of the cabins?"

"We do. The one up the hill farthest from the lake. You might not have noticed it in the woods, which have gotten thicker up that stretch of land. Martha's father built our cabin first, and it was meant to be temporary while he spent more time and effort on the rentals. It's basic, which doesn't suit Petra, as you can imagine. I don't mind roughing it a bit."

"Where's Petra now?"

"Sleeping. You won't catch her up before noon. She's like a teenager that way." Shane lifted his mug and made as if to stand. "Well, if you've asked all your questions, I've got to get back in the kitchen and make that second omelette for your niece. I'll be around if you think of anything else needs answering."

"Thanks. I'll keep that in mind. I also want to pick your brain about the rivers and where to put in my canoe."

"Sure thing."

Kala returned to a still-sleeping Dawn and set the food in the fridge, leaving a note on the table telling her it was there and saying she'd be back by lunchtime hopefully, when they could go for a swim. She locked the cabin and drove her truck toward Searchmont. She passed the spot where Rachel's body had been found. A makeshift wooden cross and flowers had been placed on the shoulder of the road nearby. Kala parked a short distance farther on and backtracked. The cross was thigh-high. Rachel's name had been printed in capital letters on the horizontal piece of wood in black magic marker. A photo of her face was stapled below. Two bouquets of white lilies and pink roses were at the base in vases of water. Kala pulled out her phone and took photos, forwarding them to Clark with a short explanation. Likely not germane to the case but he should know, nonetheless. Ten minutes later she pulled into the Eglans' driveway and prepared herself for the morning search through Rachel's bedroom.

CHAPTER THIRTEEN

Clark was on the road by 4:00 a.m. as planned. The autopsy was scheduled at the North Bay Regional Health Centre for nine thirty, and with clear sailing on the highway he pulled into the hospital parking lot with ten minutes to spare. He signed in at the front desk before meeting the coroner and pathologist in the operating room. They'd already prepped for the autopsy and Rachel was lying naked on the metal table. He tried to remain detached even as overwhelming sadness filled him. She was so young and she'd had so much living ahead of her.

He watched the cutting and weighing and inspecting but let his mind wander to the night before. Jordan and Valerie were sitting in the kitchen when he'd entered the house. Jordan had jumped up to give him a bear hug, and Clark had gotten them both a beer after hugging his wife.

"I've ordered a pizza," she said. "I'm going to lie down for a bit, but save me a piece."

"Are you feeling okay?" he asked.

"I didn't sleep well last night, so I might be gone for a long nap." She eased herself out of the chair and lumbered past him, one hand supporting her back. "I'm sure you boys have lots of catching up to do." She gave Clark a meaningful look before disappearing from the room. He knew what she was referring to and regretted telling her about meeting Stonechild at Pine Hollow Lodge.

"What brings you to the Soo?" he asked Jordan.

"I had some time off. Thought I'd get in a bit of fishing and help you paint the baby's room. I'm guessing you haven't gotten around to it." Jordan grinned as he lifted the beer bottle to his lips.

"Still got three weeks." Clark hated the defensive note in his voice. Jordan knew him too well. His nickname in high school had been "Last Minute." He preferred to think of himself as methodical.

The front doorbell rang and Jordan jumped up. "This meal's on me," he said and playfully shoved Clark back into his seat on the way by. He returned with the pizza box and got a couple of plates from the cupboard and two more beers from the fridge before sitting down. Clark watched him serve up slices and thought about the time his brother had been going out with Stonechild. He'd been happier with her than anyone before or since, and that included his wife, Miriam, who'd had a nasty streak wider than a country mile. Clark had hated how Miriam controlled and manipulated anyone who got close to her. Two children later, his brother had had all he could take of sharing his life with her. Nobody in the family had tried to talk him out of his decision to split up for good.

Jordan appeared more at ease than the last time Clark had seen him the year before. He'd shed a few pounds and looked as if he'd been working out. Clark was taller than his brother by a couple of inches, coming in at six three with a stockier build. He'd been the football player in high school while Jordan had been a hockey star forward — quick and agile with a deadly slapshot. He'd met Miriam in grade ten and she'd snared the high-school heartthrob, even though Jordan never saw himself that way. He was self-effacing but with an easy-going confidence. A lot like Stonechild in the self-assured department, except she was a loner whereas Jordan was not; he liked being with family and friends and had trouble being separated from his kids. Stonechild had proven that she could walk away from everybody in her life without looking back.

"So what's new?" Clark had asked, hoping to keep the conversation away from his own work.

"Not a lot. Business is going well. I picked up a contract to rewire a bunch of stores in the Intercity Mall. The guys start next month. What about you? Val tells me you're working a big case."

"A sixteen-year-old girl was murdered a few nights ago on her way home from a server job at a lodge near Searchmont."

"That's awful. Any leads?"

Clark shifted uncomfortably in his seat. "I can't talk about an ongoing case, but we're looking at various angles. Getting statements. I'm leaving early in the morning for the autopsy in North Bay. Before sun-up."

"Are you alone in the field?"

And here it is. Decision time. "I've got a recruit at the lodge who's helping with the investigation."

"Well that's good. I guess you'll be wanting to hit the sack early if you're on the road before dawn. We can catch up tomorrow. Tell me, have you bought the paint for the bedroom yet?"

"I have. The cans and brushes are just inside the door of the room."

"I'll get the first coat on while you're working and I'll keep an eye on Valerie."

"Thanks bro. I'll rest a lot easier knowing you're here."

Clark watched the pathologist cut into Rachel's abdomen with his scalpel and winced before checking that nobody had noticed his reaction. He hated the sight of blood and had passed out once when he and Jordan were kids and Jordan ripped his leg open falling off his dirt bike. Since then he'd toughened up, but autopsies were the worst part of his job. That and car accidents. He kept watching the scalpel slicing through Rachel's skin and muscle and knew he had to think of something else if he was going to make it through to the end. He let his mind drift back again to the night before and his conversation with Valerie.

He'd eased into his side of the bed after finishing the beer and pizza. He was lying on his back, staring at the shadows on the ceiling when Valerie rolled onto her side to wrap an arm around his waist, nestling her face into his chest.

"Sorry," he said. "I tried not to wake you."

"It's okay. I'm so uncomfortable that I can't sleep for long."

"Just a few more weeks."

"Then neither of us will be getting much sleep if all the newborn stories are true."

"We might luck out and get a sound sleeper."

"That's called living in a fantasy world." She danced her fingers across his skin. "Did you tell him about Kala?" she asked.

"No."

"You're going to have to sooner or later."

"I'm not sure why. It's not like he ever has to find out."

"What if he does? Word is bound to get around, and someone who knows her will tell someone...."

He sighed. "Sometimes your common sense makes my life difficult."

"Better difficult now than regretful later."

He tilted his head and kissed her. "Let me sleep on it and I'll decide tomorrow. I need another day to make up my mind. I don't want to upset either one of them needlessly."

Clark checked his watch. The autopsy had been underway for well over an hour and would wrap up soon. The pathologist had taken scrapings from under Rachel's fingernails and fibres from her skin. Clark's job was to bear witness and testify later when required about each exhibit being removed. He was responsible for maintaining continuity of the evidence until the samples reached the lab. He'd feel like a kid released from detention when this was over and he could get back on the road. It would take a couple of beers and a shot of rye when he got home to relax him enough so that he could fall asleep. He'd share any revelations from the autopsy with Stonechild in the morning.

Owen Eglan opened the door before Kala had a chance to ring the doorbell. The lines in his face cut deeper than the last time she'd seen him, and his pale-blue eyes were exhausted. "You're helping then," he said flatly. He swung the door wide and waved her into the hallway. "Come in. Isabelle's at church. Rachel's death has given her a reason to get more religious, not that she needed one."

He rolled his eyes and Kala returned his sideways smile before she followed him down the hallway to the bottom of the stairs. "Officer Harrison asked me to go through Rachel's room. I understand that you've left it as it was before she died."

He turned. "We shut the door and haven't been inside except ... well, I found Isabelle lying on Rachel's bed that first night after we learned she was dead. She was holding on to Rachel's nightgown, rolling around on the blankets and crying. I don't imagine that will impact your search."

The same emotionless voice that only amplified the crushing pathos. "No, but thank you for telling me."

"I'll let you get to it then. I'll be outside in the yard if you need me."

She put a hand on his forearm. "How are *you* doing, Owen?"

He was still for a moment and his face began to crumple in on itself before he took a gulping breath and regained control. "Not great. I feel this guilt eating me up. If I'd turned down that job and gone to get her, she'd still be alive."

"The person who killed her holds all the blame. People get delayed or forget appointments all the time without anything like this happening. It is not your fault."

"I hope I come around to believing you, but I doubt I'll ever get out from under this. Isabelle blames me entirely."

"Well, she shouldn't. I don't."

He dropped his head and nodded once. His voice was gruff. "Thanks. Rachel's room is upstairs. First door on the right. I'll be outside."

She climbed the carpeted stairs to the landing. The hallway smelled of lemony cleaner and beeswax and she looked into the corners. Not a speck of dust; everywhere she looked was spotlessly clean. *Isabelle's doing*, she thought. *She's keeping the grief from pulling her under.* Kala opened the door to Rachel's bedroom and stood on the threshold, trying to get a feeling for the girl. She closed her eyes and breathed deeply, imagining she smelled the delicate scent of Rachel's perfume that surely would have faded, but perhaps not completely. She said a silent prayer for Rachel before opening her eyes and looking around.

The room was small and cramped. A single bed was pressed up against the lavender-painted wall with posters of popular male singers filling the entire space. Kala recognized Drake and Bieber but not the rest. She wondered if Dawn listened to any of them, not certain what played in her headphones when she was doing homework in her room.

A three-tier chest of drawers that served double duty as a bedside table was wedged beneath the window. A hooked oval throw rug filled the small space next to the bed with barely enough room for the straight-backed chair against the wall. The chair was loaded down with clothes, likely tossed there by Rachel after she'd worn them. Kala opened the closet door. The space was crammed with clothes on hangers and shoes stacked haphazardly on the floor. Yearbooks and shoeboxes were tucked on the shelf above. All would need to be gone through.

She returned to the chest of drawers and scanned the assortment of drugstore makeup and costume jewellery scattered across the top. A clock rested on top of six paperbacks and she moved them sideways to read the spines. Four Harlequin romances, Charlotte Brontë's *Jane Eyre*, and Daphne du Maurier's *Rebecca*. Two photos stood in silver frames: Rachel with two taller red-headed boys — Kala guessed they were her brothers — and another of Rachel with a boy her own age, most likely her boyfriend.

She picked up the picture with the boyfriend and lifted it closer to study the faces. The boy had his arm slung around Rachel's shoulders and he was grinning widely, while her smile looked forced, as if someone had instructed her to show some teeth for the camera. He was a tall, skinny kid in a blue suit a size too big. Big ears and brown hair cut spiky and greased with gel to stand up from his head. Blue eyes behind black-rimmed glasses. Not unattractive, but not a boy whom girls would spend nights dreaming about. Definitely not a Harlequin hunk.

She set the photo down and picked up a nearly empty purple glass bottle of perfume. Wonderstruck by Taylor Swift. She pulled off the top and sniffed. A mix of florals with a sandalwood base — the faint scent she'd detected when she opened the door. She set it back on the dresser and opened the top drawer. A jumble of underwear and socks sprung out and needed to be pushed down before closing. The second drawer held shirts and sweaters, most unfolded and wrinkled. Jeans and sweatpants packed the bottom drawer with no room to spare.

She stepped back and took one last look around, soaking in the overall picture before starting a thorough search. Rachel had been a typical teenager, with dreams for a bigger, more romantic life than the one she was living in Searchmont. Had she been as close to her mother as Isabelle claimed? Or had she been desperate to get out from under her mother's religious zeal and smothering concern, as Thomas Faraday had observed? Kala tempered the hope that she'd find the answers in the bedroom. A mother like Isabelle would have made any daughter secretive and careful about what she left lying around. Rachel would have known that not even her bedroom would be off limits from snooping done in the name of motherly love.

Three hours later Kala had made her way through the desk and closet. She'd been right about Rachel not leaving anything revealing where her mother could find it. She hadn't kept a diary, although she'd filled a couple of notebooks with her poetry. The poems had been surprisingly mature, the later ones written about a romantic relationship. Had she drawn from a vivid imagination or her own experiences? Likely the former since she was only sixteen, but Kala had no way of knowing at this point. She picked up the photo of Rachel with her boyfriend again. He didn't look like someone who'd inspire this kind of lust and longing, but sixteen was the age of out-of-control hormones.

Kala sat cross-legged on the floor, thinking and rereading the last haunting poem, dated only a week before Rachel's death. She'd written it with a purple pen in rounded cursive. The poem seemed a dire omen of what was to come.

> *The darkness sifts the light from day.*
> *I rest to see*
> *The blackness crawl in silence through the trees.*
> *The grass a sweep of armied sway*
> *That gives and bows as candle flames.*
>
> *The night will lead a road to you.*
> *We are the same.*
> *Like grass and wind we push and yield anew.*
> *I wait for dark to hide your eyes from mine*
> *I take the road toward the phantom sun*
> *I run and do not look behind.*

CHAPTER FOURTEEN

Martha woke, rolled over, and flung an arm across the other side of the bed only to come up empty. Neal was gone, the sheets cold. She lay still for a moment, listening for him in another room of the house, but all she heard was the furnace turn on and blow warm air through the vent. He must have left already, gone to the main lodge to help Shane with breakfast. She inspected his side of the bed and couldn't tell if he'd slept there at all.

She showered and dressed in jeans and a T-shirt before going into the kitchen. Neal hadn't put on the coffee, something he would have done when they were getting along. He never would have left in the morning without waking her or leaving a note to tell her where she could reach him. They'd had fights before, but nothing like this. The sick feeling in the pit of her stomach was always with her now. *Is this how it's going to be?* she asked her grim reflection in the window. *Hoping he finds his way back to me and dreading the worst?*

The coffee had brewed and she was reaching for a mug when the front door opened. She turned with a smile on her face, expecting Neal, but Petra flew into the kitchen instead. "Sorry for not knocking," she said, "but it was unlocked." She looked around. "Where's Neal?"

"I expect he's helping Shane with breakfast." Martha took down a second mug and filled both before sliding one across the island to Petra. "You're never up this early. What's going on?"

"I'm having trouble sleeping since Rachel died." She pulled out a stool and sat, then wrapped both hands around the mug. "I feel so on edge."

Martha took a closer look at Petra's face. The skin under her eyes was bluish against her too-pale complexion. She'd bitten down the nails on the hand that she lifted to push a long strand of hair behind her ear. Petra had never been particularly sensitive to the plight of other females, nor had she given Rachel the time of day. In fact, she'd said she didn't like Rachel upon learning of her death. This distress was out of character.

"You can't still believe that you hit Rachel with your car?"

"No." Petra's long blond hair tumbled back and forth across her face as she shook her head. "Shane heard a rumour from a credible source about her death that lets me off the hook."

Martha's stomach tightened. "What rumour?"

"Rachel wasn't hit by a car. Somebody murdered her."

Martha's body went cold. "Why would somebody do that?" she asked. She stared past Petra to look out the window while she struggled to keep herself together. "Rachel never caused any trouble."

"Oh, come off it. She was such a sly little thing. I never trusted her and maybe she threatened someone or ... I don't know, pissed them off?" Petra snorted. "She had her hooks into Neal, so I wouldn't have put it past her to be shagging every man in this town."

Martha stared. "I wish you'd stop saying that about my husband."

"We both know what went on between them meant nothing. A one-off to get back at you."

"I still don't like you talking about them." Martha lifted her coffee cup and drank.

Petra's eyes studied her. "How's it going with Neal? Has he recommitted to your marriage, or is he still being a cold, hypocritical prick?"

"We've been better."

Petra's voice softened. "I'm sorry I brought this pain on you both."

Martha closed her eyes. "I can't do this, Petra. Not now and not with you."

"I wish Neal were more accepting like Shane, and that's the last I'll say on the matter." Petra was silent until Martha looked at her again. "I told Shane I'm going to stay in Sudbury with friends until this place closes up, and he said that the police might want me here. How odd is it that the Indigenous woman is a cop? Shane said she's helping with the murder case."

"How does he know this?"

"He went to visit Owen Eglan at his house yesterday afternoon between shifts. I was surprised he did that, to be honest."

The queasiness returned and Martha abruptly stood, picking up her mug and turning her back on Petra. "I have to start cleaning the cabins. I'm already late."

She heard Petra push back her stool. "I'll see myself out then. I'd offer to help but know how you prefer to work solo these days."

Martha didn't dignify the comment with a response. She stood with her hands resting on the counter and head bowed until she heard the crack of the screen door snapping into place.

Clark arrived home shortly past six, greeted by the smell of fresh paint and his brother waiting in the kitchen with two cold beer bottles on the table. "I heard you pull up," Jordan said. "How'd it go?"

"Tiring but okay. Where's Valerie?"

"I sent her out for the day to be away from the paint. It's not toxic but best to hedge our bets. She's been at the spa, and we're to meet her in half an hour at Giovanni's for some good Italian cooking."

"You're a better husband than I am," said Clark, twisting the top off the bottle and taking a swig of beer. He tilted the bottle toward Jordan. "And a better brother. Thanks for getting that room painted. She swore she wasn't going to go into labour until I got that done."

"Not sure how she planned to keep the kid inside her womb until university, but you'd have saved a fortune in diapers."

"C'mon. Grade school. Give me some credit."

"I thought I was."

Clark dumped a bag of Old Dutch chips into a bowl and sat down at the table. "Hors d'oeuvres, northern style."

"The best kind." Jordan took a handful. "So, tell me as much as you're able about the case."

"A couple of days ago a sixteen-year-old girl turns up dead on the side of the road between Pine Hollow Lodge and her house on the outskirts of Searchmont. She'd finished a shift working in the lodge restaurant and her father never showed to pick her up as promised, so the assumption is that she started walking. Someone hit her with a hard object that we believe was a tire iron and rolled her into a culvert."

"Suspects?"

"Nobody and everybody. Had to be someone local."

"Is that another assumption?"

"Yeah, but it's such an out-of-the-way location I can't believe a stranger would happen to be there looking for somebody to kill. Doesn't add up."

"How big a team you got working on it?"

Clark shoved a handful of chips into his mouth to buy some time. Had Valerie already told him about Stonechild? He watched Jordan pick a chip from the bowl, but his face was free of guile. "I'm lead in the field. I have others I can call on if needed."

"What happens when Valerie goes into labour? You got a backup plan?"

Clark had no idea if he was doing the right thing but said, "I'm working with a cop who happens to be staying at the lodge. Kala Stonechild."

Jordan had the beer bottle halfway to his lips. He stopped as his body went still. He set the bottle on the table. "Kala. How is she?"

"Same as ever. Closed off. She's renting a cabin with her niece who looks to be about fourteen. They're living together in Kingston and here on a holiday."

"She married?"

Clark didn't like hurting his brother but figured false hope might be the worst kind of cruel. "No, but she told me that she's with somebody."

Jordan hesitated for a second before he picked up the beer bottle. He took a big mouthful, swallowed, and said, "Guess we should get moving or Valerie will be sitting at the restaurant all alone."

"Listen, Jordan. I didn't want to …"

"It's okay. I'm glad you told me, but let's not make a big deal of it. I'll find my coat and we can get a move on."

"I'll change my clothes and meet you out front."

Clark climbed the stairs to the bedroom, knowing he'd delivered a body blow to his brother. Jordan had avoided commitment after leaving his wife on the mistaken belief that Kala would find her way back to him. He had a suspicion that Jordan wasn't going to leave the Soo without making an attempt to see her — and there was no telling which way that reunion would go. Clark hoped he wasn't going to regret his decision, but at least Valerie wouldn't be hounding him any longer about keeping a secret that could destroy his close relationship with Jordan if it ever came out.

CHAPTER FIFTEEN

On Wednesday morning Kala left Dawn sleeping and took the canoe into the bay as the sun began to rise. Taiku lay at her feet, head resting on the gunnel to catch the breeze. The three of them had gotten in a late-day paddle the afternoon before when she returned from the Eglans' place, and she and Dawn had played Scrabble after supper. They turned in early, but she'd heard Dawn in the kitchen at 2:00 a.m. Another restless night. It would do her good to sleep in.

The air was cool and a white mist hung over the water so that sounds were muffled and the feeling was like being inside a globe of cotton batting. Even as she let the canoe drift, the sun began burning off the fog and warmed the dampness on her face. The pink and rose colours reflecting off the water faded. A lone loon called its haunting song near an outcropping of rocks farther down the shoreline, the sound echoing off the rock walls. She paddled toward the point using smooth, even J strokes. Dawn had progressed the few times they were out and their paddles had found a rhythm. Kala was eager to take her on a river run and would talk to Shane about one that wouldn't be too taxing. They'd work up to the rapids.

She expected a visit from Clark, and he arrived as she was finishing her second cup of chamomile tea in the main lodge. Shane had outdone himself this morning with thick French toast, blackberries, raspberries, whipped cream, and maple syrup with a side of bacon and sausage. She'd briefly thought about ordering seconds when asking for a plate to bring to Dawn.

Clark went into the kitchen and returned with a cup of coffee. "Smells so good in there," he said as he sat across from her. "Like cocoa and cinnamon and bacon grease. I hope you don't mind meeting here while I eat. I missed breakfast. Shane said he'd give me Dawn's meal and cook up a new one for her."

"No problem."

"How'd you do with Rachel's room?"

"She had a thing for music heartthrobs and romance novels. I'd say she was a typical boy-crazy teenager although she seemed more experienced than her parents appear to realize."

"What makes you say that?"

"She kept a book of poetry that she wrote over the past few years. The poems got progressively more physical- and love-themed this summer. She was either having sex with someone or had one terrific imagination."

"Do you have the notebook?"

"It's locked in my truck."

"Good. I'll give it a read, too."

They stopped talking as Shane crossed the room with Clark's food. He set down the plate and refilled his coffee mug. "Should I start Dawn's breakfast now, Kala?" he asked.

"Wait twenty minutes and that'll give Clark a chance to eat."

"You got it." He whistled as he walked back into the kitchen, letting the door swing shut behind him.

"Rachel spent a lot of time here," Kala said. "I wonder if one of the men was meeting up with her."

"Neal Lorring and Shane Patterson are married. Who are the others?"

"There are two Hydro workers named Ian Kruger and Blaine Rogers who're here for the summer, and an older retired photographer, Thomas Faraday." Kala paused. "But we can't assume her killer … and/or lover if there was one … came from the lodge. She had that boyfriend in town, and of course there are other men living in Searchmont whom we don't know."

"Are you good to come with me to interview those six people from town who were here for supper on her last shift?"

"I am after I get Dawn's breakfast to her."

Clark cut through the whipped cream and French toast. Before he took his first bite he said, "Then looks like we have an interesting day ahead."

Darryl Kelly's mother sent them down to the beach where they found him fishing off the end of the dock. He tossed a lit cigarette into the water at their approach.

"Your mom said we'd find you here," called Clark from the shore. "Do you mind coming over for a chat?"

Darryl shrugged but set down his rod and joined them on the scrubby piece of land where Clark had parked his police cruiser. He looked better than in his photo — his spiky was gelled hair longer now and he was sporting new wire-rimmed glasses that suited his face. He'd filled in from the time the photo was taken, although he was still on the skinny side. "You're here about Rachel," he said. "I can't believe somebody would do that to her."

"We're sorry to have to talk to you about her death." He nodded in Kala's direction. "I'm Officer Harrison from the Sault detachment and this is Officer Stonechild, who's helping me find out what happened to Rachel. I know it's not an easy time for you, Darryl. You were dating her, I understand."

Darryl hung his head and kicked at a clump of soil. "We hung out more than anything."

"What kinds of things would you do?"

"Ride our bikes. Go fishing. Swim in the river. Help out with the little kids at church." His voice petered away. "There's not much to do in this town."

"No, I imagine not. When's the last time you saw her?"

"Sunday morning at church. She was with her mother at the front but I was late and sat in the back pew."

"Did you talk to her after the service?"

"We went downstairs before the sermon started to help with the younger kids, so yeah, we talked about what we were going to do with them. She was in with the toddlers and I had the six-to-eight-year-olds. I asked if she wanted to hang out afterward, but she said she was busy."

"Do you know doing what?"

"No. I left before her and never saw her again."

Kala caught his eye. "It doesn't sound as if she was into being a couple."

He shrugged and pulled a face. "Maybe not."

"Had you ever been serious … or physical?"

"For a while. We kissed and stuff but she said it didn't interest her this summer."

"What's 'and stuff,' exactly?"

His face reddened and he dropped his head again. "You know."

"Intercourse?"

"I guess, yeah, but only a couple of times. She wasn't into it."

"But you were."

Eyes defiant. "I guess I'm normal, 'cause I liked it."

Clark looked at Kala and nodded. He waited a beat. "How did you feel when Rachel stopped wanting to be with you?"

"I dunno."

"Were you upset? Angry?"

"No."

Clark tilted his head from side to side as if thinking this over. "I would have been if I were you."

Darryl's shoulders pushed back, tight as drums. "A bit, maybe."

"Did you try to get her to go out with you again?" asked Kala.

"She told me to stop texting so I stopped." He kicked harder at the dirt. "I wouldn't hurt her."

"So you didn't see her Saturday night at all?"

"No."

"Where were you?"

"Home."

"All night?"

"Yes. My parents were home, too."

"This your car over on the side of the road?" Clark pointed to a rusty silver Honda Civic.

"Yeah."

"Mind if we have a look?"

"If you want."

Darryl stayed where he was while they walked over and looked in the windows. "We have to go carefully," said Kala, meeting Clark behind the trunk. "He wouldn't be stupid enough to leave the murder weapon covered in blood in plain view."

"Yeah, that'd be *way* too easy."

"We don't have enough for a search warrant either if his alibi checks out, which I'm betting it will." She glanced back at Darryl. He was watching them and his shoulders were slumped forward. No longer worried.

"I guess we can speak with his mom on our way to talk to the others."

"May as well cross the *t*."

CHAPTER SIXTEEN

Janet Kelly supported Darryl's story as expected, effectively making a search warrant request dead in the water unless they found evidence to contradict the alibi.

"It's highly probable that Darryl could have slipped out for an hour without his parents knowing. He must have been bothering Rachel if you read into her asking him to stop texting. He might have been stalking her." Stonechild buckled up her seat belt and stared at the Kelly house through dark sunglasses.

Clark agreed with her but knew they needed more than a gut feeling. "The Bococks live on the way to the church. Why don't we stop in and have a chat with Phil?"

"He was Rachel's English teacher." Stonechild appeared to be organizing the suspects in her mind.

"Greta taught her gym in grade nine and ten but not this year." He smiled at the look she shot him. "I had the team at HQ check into Rachel's background and do up some profiles of people who were at the restaurant the last night she worked there. I've printed them off for you since I'm not sure about the security of email."

"Which I might not get at the lodge anyway."

"That's right." He turned his head and pointed. "The info's in that blue file in the back seat. Sorry I didn't give it to you earlier. Slipped my mind, to be honest."

She reached around and took the folder without saying anything. She wasn't the kind of person who'd say his memory lapse didn't matter. The social niceties weren't her forte, as he recalled.

The Bococks had a small white home with a detached garage on a large property on Finn Road. A blanket of coniferous trees sloped upwards from the back of the house and clumps of pine ended at the road. The neighbour's house was visible across the road with rolling hills rising behind.

"Nice spot," said Clark pulling into the Bocock driveway behind a black Ford truck. He leaned into the front windshield and craned his neck skyward. "Those trees go on forever."

Phil greeted them on the front steps holding a full cup of coffee. He made eye contact as he shook each of their hands and invited them inside. The house had maple floors and red-pine wainscotting in every room. Phil poured them coffees while they took seats in front of a wood stove in the front living room. Someone had knocked out the wall separating this room from the kitchen and put in a wide island. The kitchen cupboards were made of the same red pine. Clark was too aware of Stonechild next to him, her black eyes observant, filing away details he was likely missing.

Phil handed them cups and sat down after returning to the kitchen to get his. "I wish Greta could join us but she's driven to the high school. She works with the girls' basketball team even during the summer. Now I assume you're here to talk about poor Rachel." Phil was the kind of man who'd be featured in a beer commercial. Six foot and solidly built with a boyish grin and straight brown hair that flopped over one dark-blue eye. He was not the English teacher Clark had conjured up in his mind before their arrival. No ascot or velvet reading jacket in sight.

"Was she a good student?" Clark asked.

"Rachel was a *brilliant* English student. I was encouraging her to go into a creative writing course at university or college, she was that good."

Stonechild straightened next to him on the couch. "Did you mentor her after school?"

Phil's gaze adjusted slightly to focus on her face. "Rachel wrote poetry and we'd meet to talk about it, so I suppose yes, I was a mentor of sorts."

Clark waited to make sure Stonechild didn't have a follow-up question before asking, "You and Greta were at Pine Hollow Lodge for supper the last shift Rachel worked there. Can you tell us what you remember about that night?"

Phil's eyes remained on Stonechild. "We arrived at the same time as Judd Neilson, the town reeve, and his wife, Elena; and Father Alec Vila and his sister, Sara, who was visiting from Sudbury. We decided on the spur of the moment to sit together for supper. I only spoke with Rachel briefly when

Greta was freshening up in the washroom. I asked her how the writing was progressing and she said that she'd have some new poems to show me once school started. She was excited about them. She waited on you and your daughter, as I recall, Officer Stonechild."

"Did you notice anyone acting oddly, or possibly paying attention to Rachel more than normal, or doing something out of the ordinary?" Clark asked. The question came out awkwardly and he inwardly groaned with Stonechild sitting silently next to him. She always had that effect on him. He felt this unsettling need to win her approval and he wasn't sure where that came from.

Phil had a half smile on his face, adding to Clark's discomfort. "I'm not convinced anyone was paying her more attention than warranted. We had a lively philosophical discussion at our table about the meaning of life and the existence of God, and after too much wine Greta promised Father Vila that we'd attend a church service. I'm a firm agnostic and believe she returned to being one as well once she sobered up on the drive home."

"Did Rachel interact with anybody else that you saw?"

"The kitchen staff. She chatted with the other customers." Phil opened his hands and shrugged. "I can't say that I noticed anything unusual, nor did I sense any tensions or animosity. I'm sorry, Officer. I haven't anything much to offer and truly wish I could help you. Rachel was a special girl and we're going to miss her."

Clark began to rise but relaxed into the seat cushion when Stonechild started talking again. "Did you and your wife go straight home from the restaurant?"

"We did." He hesitated. "I dropped Greta off at her mother's for a visit and I continued on home."

"So Greta was with her mother and you ... were alone?"

"You make it sound so suspicious, but yes, I was alone until Greta made it home a few hours later. I'd planned to pick her up, but her mother loaned her a car, which was not unusual. Greta then drove over in the morning to help her mother with chores. She's had MS for several years and has difficulty."

"That should do it for now." Stonechild snapped her notebook shut and stood abruptly. She left the room while Clark thanked Phil for his time and worked on a more graceful exit. Stonechild was sitting in the passenger seat checking her phone when he reached his cruiser.

"Did I miss something in there?" he asked as he buckled his seat belt.

"Why do you ask that?" Stonechild lifted her eyes and shifted in the seat to face him.

"You darted out of the house as if somebody lit a fire under your feet."

"He was done giving us anything. We need to dig elsewhere to confirm that his relationship with Rachel was platonic."

Clark turned his face sideways to look at her, his hand on the ignition key. "Are we going to suspect every man in her life of sleeping with her, married or no?"

Stonechild smiled. "I'd say that's a given. Where to next?"

"Reeve Neilson lives a street over. We may as well find out if he and Rachel were doing the dirty behind Elena's back."

"Now you're getting into the swing of it. We won't stop suspecting everyone until we find out who was having sex with Rachel and who had the most to lose."

"*If* she was having an affair. Remember, we have no proof except the poems, which could have been totally fabricated from her imagination."

"She'd experienced what she was writing — I'd bet my life on it. The depth of emotion is too intense." She pulled out her notepad and flipped through a few pages, then recited:

> *I yearn to feel the touch of your skin*
> *against my thighs*
> *our bodies one for this eternal moment*
> *my lips pressed soft*
> *as butterfly wings*
> *against your neck.*

Stonechild's eyes flashed as she snapped her notepad shut and tucked it back inside her jacket. "These are not the words of a sixteen-year-old girl daydreaming. The more times I read her poetry the more convinced I am that she lived this. Think about it, Harrison. The summer job had her out from under her mother's smothering watch and she was finally able to spread her wings. Somebody took advantage." Stonechild turned away from him and put on her sunglasses, her mouth set in a stubborn line. "And we can't forget that she upset somebody enough that they took a tire iron to the back of her head. That kind of emotion can't be faked either."

"I'm not disagreeing, but remember Stonechild, she was having sex with Darryl Kelly. She might have taken those first fumbling, unsatisfying efforts and used them as a launching-off point for her fertile imagination. She liked to read romance fiction. You said so yourself."

"Good to question, Harrison, but I think you should trust me on this one." She turned her head and gave him a quick half smile before looking back out the window.

He was silent as he pulled into the Neilsons' driveway, preparing himself to question the reeve. The house wasn't much bigger than the Bococks' but was in a more prime location with the grassy yard angling down to the water. Judd and Elena were both home and they settled into the back sunroom with a fresh pot of coffee and homemade cheese scones. Stonechild hadn't touched her coffee at the Bococks but she accepted another cup.

"Yes, we were at the restaurant that night," said Judd. "We left before the other people at our table because the sitter phoned that Robby was sick."

A boy picked that moment to walk into the room from the kitchen holding a Popsicle. He looked to be about four, but scrawny with a milky complexion. He had the same fair colouring and wide blue eyes as his mom.

"Come in, Robby," said Elena, holding out her hand toward him. She kept talking. "Judd drove Robby to the hospital in the Soo and stayed with him overnight. I was here with our twins. Cameron had a tummy ache and he was up half the night. Our punishment for going on a date." She smiled at Judd.

Robby backed into the kitchen and the television soon blared from wherever he'd disappeared to. Elena sighed. "Robby has cystic fibrosis and is going through a difficult patch."

"How old are your twins?" asked Stonechild.

"Two-and-a-half-year-old boys." Judd laughed. He ran a hand through his tight brown curls. He was fifty pounds overweight and his face was round and cherubic. "We're having trouble finding a sitter at the moment. Go figure."

"Thank the Lord that Judd is a hands-on dad, or I'd be in the loony bin by now," added Elena.

The two exchanged another fond smile. Judd looked across at Clark. "But you're here about Rachel, not our family trials and tribulations. To be honest, I can't say that I noticed her all that much on Saturday night. She didn't serve our table."

Elena interrupted. "She looks after the twins when I go to church. Judd wouldn't know that because he stays home with Robby and they have their bonding time. I thought she was terrific with the kids and always so friendly, although not outgoing. Yes, I'd say she was introverted."

"Did she have any other friends or close relationships that you know of?" asked Clark.

"She was friendly with Darryl Kelly, but I sensed he liked her more than she liked him. I didn't see her interact with anybody else except the kids and her mother and, of course, with Father Vila after mass. He'd come downstairs to his office and stop to chat to whoever was around."

"Did you see Rachel outside of church?" asked Stonechild.

They both shook their heads. "I tried to line her up to babysit, but she was always busy," Elena said.

"Such a loss," said Judd. "I'm going to see if anything needs to be done to make that stretch of road safer for pedestrians and bikers."

"It wasn't a hit and run," said Clark. "Somebody deliberately killed her. She was beaten and rolled into the culvert."

"Oh?" Judd's face drained of colour and Elena's gasp filled the silence. "This is the first we've heard," he said. "How could something so horrific happen in Searchmont? Who else knows?"

"Rachel's parents and a few people at Pine Hollow Lodge. We haven't made this information public knowledge, but as reeve, you should be aware."

"Of course." Judd looked across at his wife, who'd raised a hand to cover her mouth. "I'll need to get the town council together for a meeting tonight." He looked back at Clark. "You'll keep me informed?"

"I'll share as much as I can." He took out a business card and handed it over. "Call me if you hear anything of interest through your network. We'll follow up all leads."

"Certainly. This is going to take a while to absorb."

He was standing with an arm around Elena's shoulders when Clark and Stonechild left the house. She was leaning into him and he had his head bowed talking to her.

"I think we can rule them off the list. Agreed?" he said to Stonechild.

She watched them for a moment before opening the passenger door. "Yeah. You should still have your people check out the hospital alibi. She doesn't strike me as someone who'd leave the twins alone to go kill Rachel, so if he checks out, I think we're safe to put them in the *no* column."

"It's past lunchtime. You up for a cup of tea and a sandwich? We can stop in at the Mountainview Lodge before we go to the church in Goulais."

"Sounds like a good idea. We can review what we got this morning and prepare for the next interview. I'm hopeful that Father Vila will fill in some of the gaps about Rachel and her state of mind this summer."

Chapter Seventeen

Rouleau met Gundersund in the HQ parking lot after having lunch with Marci at Paradiso's on Division, where they'd shared a pizza. He was reluctantly returning to a desk filled with reports to read and paperwork that needed his signature. Gundersund was on his way to court to testify on a B and E. The thief had been followed to his apartment and a search warrant had led them to a room full of stolen laptops and televisions.

"Turning warm," said Rouleau, loosening his collar. "You may as well go home after you testify. Enjoy an early day while you can."

"Thanks, I'll do that. Gives me a chance to try to contact Kala and Dawn."

"No word from them yet?"

"None. I'd like to hear about the murder case she's working on." Gundersund's eyes were tired and his hair and beard were looking wilder than usual. He ran fingers through his blond curls. "The longer they're gone the less certain I am that Kingston is going to draw them back anytime soon."

"Stonechild has ties here — friends, her job, and a home she loves. She'll want to return to you most of all."

"Given time, but she's restless. I'm not convinced anyone will ever be able to hold her in one place for long."

"I don't know. I think you might be underestimating her."

Rouleau was still thinking about Gundersund's worried face as he walked into his office. He'd been doing double duty all summer. Acting chief and head of Major Crimes. Heath had officially resigned as chief at the beginning of July, and the police board had offered the job to him. He'd been mulling over the decision all month. The idea of declining the promotion and farming out the rest of his work so he could join Marci in Paris was tempting. Retire early and get out of policing altogether. Start fresh in a new country and be done with the endless paperwork.

But is that what I want?

He forced his mind to stop weighing the pros and cons and to focus on the job at hand, buckling down to review a report from the Drug Division. An undercover operation was reaching the half-way point and the classified update showed progress. The OxyContin problem was growing in the high schools and the team was infiltrating the supply chain. His desk phone rang and he reached for it without lifting his eyes from the page.

"Acting Chief Jacques Rouleau here. How can I help you?"

"*Allô*. My name is Lise Charlebois, calling from Joliette Prison. I've been trying to reach Officer Kala Stonechild without success. Can you tell me if she's *disponible* … available?" She spoke with a thick French accent, not unpleasant to the ear.

Rouleau set down the file. "Officer Stonechild is away on assignment and difficult to reach. Perhaps I could help you. I'm her staff sergeant."

"It's a personal matter."

"Officer Stonechild and I are good friends in addition to working together. Whatever you tell me will be in confidence, but I will pass it on to her if that is your wish."

A pause. "*Bien*, I suppose this will be our best option. She's fostering the daughter of her friend Rose Cook."

"I'm aware."

"Rose is in the hospital and is asking to see her daughter."

"Is her condition … serious?"

Another pause, longer this time. "She tried to take her own life yesterday. She's stable for now, but her doctors are worried about her mental health."

"I understand."

"The fact she's asked to see Dawn we believe is a good sign."

"Leave this with me and I'll see what can be done at our end."

"I would appreciate that."

Rouleau took down phone numbers for her cell and work and promised to call back within a day or two. He sat staring at the phone after he hung up and tried to think how best to handle reaching Stonechild and getting Dawn to Joliette as quickly as possible. Gundersund would be in court at this moment, but that was expected to be routine and should wrap up within the hour. Rouleau searched around his jacket pocket for his cellphone and sent Gundersund a text.

Something's come up. Merchant after court? Need to run idea past you.

He set his phone on the desk and waited for a return message. It wasn't long in coming. He had time to finish reading the report and send in his comments before driving downtown.

Gundersund was sitting at a table when he arrived at the Merchant with two beers in front of him. He pushed one across to Rouleau as he sat down. "Figured you could use this," he said. "Freshly poured."

"I knew I kept you around for a reason." Rouleau took a long drink and set the glass on the coaster. "How did court go?"

"Good. No surprises." Gundersund twirled his beer glass around in the moisture on the tabletop. "So, what was so urgent?"

"I got a call from Joliette. Dawn's mother's in the hospital after a suicide attempt. She's asked to see Dawn."

"Is she okay?"

"She's stable, but not in the best state of mind. What do you think about driving to Searchmont and picking up Dawn and taking her to see her mother? We can spare you for a week since we're not exactly swamped."

Gundersund didn't leap at the idea as Rouleau had thought he would. He seemed to be running possibilities through his head. "The thing is, if I show up unannounced Stonechild might not like it." He took a drink of beer, swallowed, then sighed. "But that's neither here nor there. The important thing is to get Dawn to see her mother. I'll leave first thing in the morning."

"I'll try to get in touch with Stonechild in the meantime. I can call the North Bay detachment and get a message to her that way. The staff sergeant sent a quick update two days ago that the investigation was going to take a while."

"Kala would want to take Dawn herself if she wasn't part of this case."

"Hopefully the staff sergeant was overly pessimistic and the investigation will wrap up soon so she can follow you."

Gundersund drained the last of his beer and set the glass on the table. He smiled at Rouleau and said, "Nice to dream, but I'm not counting on it."

The afternoon light was murky with late-day shadows stretching across the pavement when Clark drove into the church parking lot. The building was white clapboard, single-storey with an impressive steeple next to the highway into town. A sign out front told him that all children of God were welcome, a comforting idea but not one in which he held any stock. The parking lot was empty except for a green Toyota in the reserved spot near the door.

"Looks like we caught Father Vila at work," Stonechild said, unbuckling her seat belt.

"And he appears to be alone."

They followed a sign and arrows that took them down a flight of stairs and along a corridor that passed by a meeting room and daycare, both standing empty with the lights off. The hallway smelled musty like Clark's own basement at home. Nobody was working at the secretary's desk. Vila's office door was closed and Clark rapped sharply with his knuckles. Father Vila called for them to come in. He was working on his laptop on a worn couch and looked up at their entrance. He closed the laptop and invited them to sit. "You must be here about Rachel," he said.

Clark took the lead as he'd agreed with Stonechild before their arrival. "Thanks for seeing us, Father. I'm Officer Harrison from the Sault detachment and this is Officer Stonechild. We understand you were at the restaurant the night of Rachel Eglan's death." He moved into the room as he spoke with Stonechild behind him. They took the chairs facing Vila. He was dressed casually in jeans but with a black shirt and clerical collar. From the research, Clark knew him to be forty-one. Dark-haired, black-eyed, and olive-skinned, already sporting a five o'clock shadow on his cheeks. His face was solemn and his voice low and pleasing. Clark could imagine that voice holding a congregation spellbound during Sunday service.

"Please, call me Alec. I've been writing the sermon for Rachel's funeral, although Isabelle Eglan tells me that you haven't released her body yet. The community is devastated by her tragic loss and the ceremony will help to begin the healing." He stood and pointed toward a coffee machine next to his desk. "May I offer you a cup?"

"None for me," said Stonechild, but Clark nodded. They were silent until Vila returned with two mugs and settled himself again.

"Tell us about the last evening when you saw her at the restaurant," said Clark.

"She waited on other tables, but we exchanged pleasantries when we arrived and as we were leaving. I asked how her week was going and she said fine. My sister, Sara, was visiting from Sudbury and was leaving in the morning, so I was treating her to dinner. We sat with two other couples who happened to enter the restaurant at the same time as us."

Clark opened his notepad. "Phil and Greta Bocock and Judd and Elena Neilson."

"That's correct. Reeve Neilson and his wife got called home to tend to their son partway through the meal. We left shortly before the Bococks."

"We understand Rachel came to church with her mother and helped out with the children during service."

"Yes, Rachel came most Sundays. Her mother is devout, but Rachel less so. Still, she loved the kids and appeared happy enough to be here."

"Did Rachel ever confide in you about her life? Would she have told you if anything was troubling her?"

Father Vila closed his eyes for a moment as he considered the question. "Rachel was a private person. I would never have pushed her to confide in me if she wasn't willing. I can tell you, though, that she seemed happier than at the beginning of the summer. I put this down partly to her mother's loosening attentions. One might say that she was protective of Rachel to a fault." His gentle smile dimmed the rebuke implicit in his words.

Vila had effectively sidestepped his question. Stonechild glanced at Clark and he nodded for her to go ahead. She asked, "What can you tell us about Rachel's relationship with Darryl Kelly?"

"They dated at one time. He was more interested in Rachel than she was in him. They both worked with the children downstairs Sunday mornings."

"Was he upset by her disinterest?"

"Perhaps."

"Did she show interest in anyone else?"

"You mean as a boyfriend?"

"Yes."

He stared at her intently and took his time answering. "I couldn't say."

Clark posed the question they'd asked everyone. "After you left the restaurant, did you and Sara go straight home?"

"Yes. Sara was leaving on the morning bus so she wanted an early evening. She had a night shift at the hospital once she got home. I can give you her contact information if that helps." He seemed unruffled by the implication behind the question, and Clark glanced over at Stonechild to see if she had anything to add. Her eyes were on the priest but he couldn't read her face.

"Any more questions Officer Stonechild?" Clark asked.

"No, that does it for now." She closed her notebook and stood. "I think we can let Father Vila complete his sermon in peace."

They left him opening his laptop and followed the corridor to the steps leading to the outdoors. A wind had come up while they were in the church basement and swollen grey clouds were scudding in from the west. Stonechild squinted skyward and cursed. "I was going to take Dawn for a paddle before supper, but a storm's coming in."

"Do you have time to go over the interviews and plan next steps?"

She scowled. "I'd rather not. I've left Dawn alone all day." She took a few steps and stopped. "But I guess we should. Let's go back to Pine Hollow and we can do it there."

Clark thought about what he was asking of her and felt a twinge of guilt. She wasn't a person who could easily separate her work life from her personal commitments — when she got involved in a case she became a single-minded bulldog until it was solved. He could see the two forces pulling at her: her niece and their holiday versus the desire to immerse herself completely in solving Rachel's murder. She wouldn't thank him for putting her in this dilemma, not now; not later. He didn't dare throw his brother's presence into the mix no matter what Valerie's voice in his head was telling him to do. Informing Jordan about Stonechild was as far as he was prepared to get involved. If they happened to meet up, it would not be through his doing. The two of them were on their own.

Dawn woke a few times before she got out of bed at eleven. She couldn't figure out why she was so tired when she lay around all day, but liked not having to do anything. No school, no chores, and nowhere to be. She was even finding the lack of social media a relief, although she missed being in contact with a few people: Gundersund and Emily. Henri and Jacques Rouleau. Even Vanessa and Chelsea.

She rolled over and reached an arm over the side of the bed to scratch Taiku behind the ears. He followed her to the bathroom and waited outside the door until she emerged again. "Is Kala gone?" she asked him, but knew the answer before she checked the other bedroom and the front rooms. She didn't mind. Not really. She read the note propped up against the teapot and found her breakfast in the fridge. While it heated up in the microwave, she boiled the kettle and let the tea steep as she ate. The sky was blue but white clouds were creeping higher above the treeline. Fingers of shadow drifted across the window. She could hear wind rattling the windows and buffeting the cabin and knew a storm was making its way across the lake. It would be a few hours yet.

Kala's note had said that she'd be home late afternoon and they'd go out in the canoe then. The reminder not to go swimming alone was repeated, the worry implicit. Dawn cleaned up her dishes and took the mug of tea outside. Taiku led her down to the dock and she sat with her feet dangling over the side while sipping tea and looking into the dark water. She was leaning over to get a closer look at the fish wriggling past when Taiku leapt to his feet and stood at attention. Dawn turned her head and watched a blond woman in a red-and-white sundress and pink flip-flops emerge from the edge of the woods and start down the trail toward the dock.

"Hey, there!" The woman waved and smiled as she approached. She held a tall, blue glass. Ice cubes clinked against each other as she walked. She stopped at the end of the dock. "Permission to come aboard?" she asked.

"If you want." Dawn told Taiku to relax and held on to his collar as the woman dropped down next to her in a cloud of flowery-scented perfume. She held out her hand, "I'm Petra. My husband Shane's been cooking your meals all week." She laughed, showing perfect, white teeth, made brighter by her bronze tan. "And you're Dawn, right?"

"I am, and this is Taiku."

Petra reached a tentative hand and patted him on the head as if tapping on a tabletop. She looked toward the cabin and back at Dawn. "Are you here all alone?"

"My aunt Kala's helping the Soo police, but she'll be back soon." Dawn wasn't sure why she felt vulnerable alone on the dock with this stranger, but her inquisitiveness felt wrong.

Petra took off her flip-flops and set them next to her. She leaned back on her elbows. "What's your story then?" she asked.

"What do you mean?"

"Where do you come from and what brought you here?"

"Oh. We live in Kingston and my aunt likes the wilderness. I'm not sure why she picked this place."

"She's a cop?"

"In Major Crimes."

Petra chewed on her bottom lip and looked across the lake. "Quite a coincidence that she's here when we have a murder."

"She'd rather it didn't happen."

"Of course. Of course. I didn't mean …" Petra laughed again, but this time the lightness was gone. "Rachel's death has been hard on everyone. She's turned our lives upside down."

Dawn couldn't tell if Petra was sad for Rachel or upset that her death had tipped the equilibrium of her world. She stayed silent and watched the black shapes of the fish rippling past in the water.

"I want to go to Sudbury, but need to ask permission," Petra continued. "Unlike your aunt, I don't like the wilderness. I crave the city lights."

Dawn pulled her thoughts back. "Will your husband go, too?" Who would do the cooking if he left?

"That … I'm not sure." Petra reached for her flip-flops. "I'm going swimming later if you want to come. You can bring your dog."

"I think it's going to rain."

"We should go soon then. I'll meet you outside the main lodge in half an hour." She stood and stepped into her sandals. The scent of perfume rose with her. "The beach isn't far. It'll break up your day."

Dawn was going to refuse but Petra was already halfway down the dock before she found her voice. By then she thought that she might as well go for the swim, because there was no telling how long Kala was going to be gone now that she was tracking down a killer.

And perhaps I can find out something that will help Aunt Kala with her investigation, she thought. *Maybe Petra will let something slip if I play along and keep my ears open.*

CHAPTER EIGHTEEN

Kala called for Dawn and Taiku when she stepped through the cabin door. She bumped into Clark when she spun around to have a look outside. "Dawn isn't here," she said. "Where could she and Taiku have gotten to?"

"They've likely gone for a walk and will be back shortly. The storm isn't far off." Clark stepped aside and she walked around the property without seeing any sign of them. She even went to the end of the dock and scanned the water, which the wind was whipping into choppy waves, pewter-grey under the thickening cloud cover. Clark was sitting at the counter, typing on his laptop when she came inside.

"Any luck?" he asked, glancing at her as she put her hand on the teapot sitting on the table.

"Dawn's been gone a while if this cold pot is any indication."

"The dog is with her?"

"Yes." Kala tried to relax and let the bad energy go. *This isn't like the last time. Dawn is safe here.* But still the worry wouldn't leave her.

"So, we're keeping Darryl Kelly on the list of suspects," said Clark.

Kala tried to focus. "I'd like to know more about his interest in Rachel and what he did after she broke up with him."

"Noted." Clark typed and looked up. "The English teacher and his wife — the Bococks — had opportunity, too. Both had access to cars and they were alone during the time frame."

"Greta's alibi is that she was with her mother after supper, but she could have slipped out."

"I'll check with the mother anyway. I'll also call Father Vila's sister, Sara, to confirm his story so we can eliminate them." He typed another note. He let his hands rest on the keys.

"Somebody had to know Rachel was walking home alone on that dark and deserted road," Kala said. "Or was it mere chance that they came across her?"

"We haven't looked closely at the people in the lodge, but one of them seems more likely if we think the killer was aware she hadn't been picked up as planned. They might have seen her set out on her own and followed."

"We don't know if the killer was on foot or drove."

"You're right. I assumed they drove to the spot, but they could have gotten there on foot. The fact they used a tire iron could be a red herring." He gave a sideways smile. "So to speak."

Kala looked toward the front door. "I know I shouldn't worry, but I'd feel better knowing where Dawn and Taiku have gotten to. I can hear the wind picking up."

"Should we take a walk and look for them? I've got my notes done and we can talk about next steps while we stroll?"

"I'd appreciate that."

The door opened as they were walking toward it. Taiku bounded into the room with Dawn a few steps behind. Kala took in Dawn's wet hair and Taiku's muddy fur and her relief turned to anger. Dawn dropped her wet towel onto a chair. She took a look at Kala's face and her head drooped so that she was standing still, staring at the floor. Kala took a breath to calm the furious words that threatened to explode out of her. Dawn spoke first.

"I'm sorry, Aunt Kala. I should have left a note, but I thought I'd be home before you."

"You disobeyed me and went swimming alone." Kala's voice sounded dangerously flat even to her own ears.

Dawn raised frightened eyes. "No, I was swimming with Petra. She invited me to go to the beach, and I thought you wouldn't mind if I was with her."

"Petra?" Kala took a second to place the cook's wife and her anger dissipated as fast as it had come. She crossed the space between them and pulled Dawn into a hug. "I'm sorry," she whispered into her ear. "I was wrong to doubt you. It's just that I was so worried." She stepped back and held Dawn at arm's length, forcing a smile onto her face. "Did you have a good time?"

Dawn took a moment before returning her smile. "It was okay. We walked to a beach about a kilometre down the road and the water was sort of warm near shore, but the ground dropped off and it was really cold farther into the bay."

Clark made a noise behind them. "I'm going to be on my way. Why don't I come by tomorrow morning after I make the calls we talked about and we can interview the people at the lodge?"

Kala nodded. "Yeah, I think we've done enough for one day."

After he was gone, Kala made tea while Dawn showered. She chided herself for being so mistrusting when she was the one ruining their holiday with this case. She should have said no when she had the chance. She stood at the picture window looking through the trees across the stretch of property to the lake. It was four o'clock and the light was fading with the gathering storm so that the day had the feeling of dusk. A thunderclap made her jump and a ragged flash of lightning split the sky a few miles off to the east. Raindrops began plopping on the water and sliding down the windowpane in rivulets.

She was sitting at the counter on her second cup of tea when Dawn came out of her bedroom. "Feeling better?" she asked.

"Cleaner, anyhow." Dawn nodded as Kala held up the teapot before pouring. She sat next to Kala and accepted the brimming mug.

"I thought we could go into town and try Gundersund again, but this storm is giving me second thoughts. It feels like a good night to have supper at the lodge and stay in with a book."

"I'm okay trying him tomorrow … if you have time."

"I'll make time."

Dawn added sugar to her tea and said while stirring, "Petra had questions about the investigation."

"Oh?"

"She wants to leave here and move to Sudbury and was going to ask your permission."

"That will be up to Clark. We haven't interviewed her yet, though."

"She said she knew she couldn't leave before you spoke to her."

"Good. Did she say anything else about Rachel?"

"Just that Rachel was always listening at doors. It was as if Petra didn't trust her."

Kala knew Dawn wouldn't have said this unless she'd given the idea serious consideration. Another disquieting thought gave her pause. Was she compromising Dawn's safety by getting involved in this case? It was one thing for herself to be living near a killer, but Dawn might be unknowingly interacting with them. She needed to re-evaluate her involvement in the case, even if it meant letting down Clark.

They waited for the storm to ease up before walking the path to the restaurant. Everyone was at their usual table and Kala and Dawn sat at the one that appeared reserved for them. Martha poured glasses of water and took their order. Fresh pickerel, roast potatoes, and salad. "Neal was out fishing this morning and caught tonight's meal," she said. "You're in for a treat."

Thomas Faraday nodded at them but made no effort to engage. He had a section of the newspaper resting next to his plate and read while he ate.

Ian Kruger and Blaine Rogers were sitting together, still dressed in work clothes and looking grubby and tired. They finished eating and left ten minutes after Kala and Dawn ordered. Martha returned with their main course at the same time as two couples entered. "Cottagers," said Martha. "We have ten outsiders in total tonight. I believe curiosity is behind this sudden surge in dinner reservations." She asked if Kala and Dawn had everything they needed before moving away to greet the new guests.

They ate their food quickly and didn't bother with dessert. The wind blew the driving rain sideways as they ran back to the cottage. The storm held steady overhead throughout the night, not rumbling east until daybreak. Taiku slept fitfully on the floor between the two bedrooms, on guard against the noises and unease he sensed in the people he adored most. The people he would give his life defending if the threat ever found its way into their home.

The supper crowd gone, Shane shut off the lights and stepped outside. He locked the front door while the rain dripped down his back. He'd worn a light jacket when he walked from their cabin to the main lodge in the early afternoon, but it was no match for the wind and pelting rain. He was drenched through by the time he made it through the woods, relieved to see the porch light on and Petra's car in its parking spot under the giant fir.

The front door was unlocked. Petra was sitting with her back to him on the couch. She'd lit a dozen or more candles and placed them on surfaces around the room, several on a table in front of the picture window, the flames glowing golden against the dark, rain-streaked glass. Leonard Cohen's voice rumbled through the speakers and filled the room with haunting poetry. She turned her head sideways as if sensing him standing in the doorway.

"You're late," she said without looking at him. "I poured you a glass of red a half hour ago."

"I had to make beef stock for tomorrow. The wine's had a chance to breathe anyhow."

"Come sit."

He returned to the hallway and hung his jacket on the coat rack. His shirt was sticking damply to his back, but it would dry soon enough. He walked into the flickering light of the living room and picked up the glass of wine from the coffee table before lowering himself onto the couch next to Petra's feet. Her bare legs curved out to her side with the rest of her wrapped inside a Hudson's Bay blanket. One arm poking out from the blanket held a nearly empty wine glass. He noticed that the bottle had less than a quarter remaining. She'd placed a second uncorked bottle within arm's reach on the floor.

"Did you eat?" he asked.

"Cheese and crackers. Pâté. It filled me up. I didn't feel like seeing anybody." She stretched a leg so that her foot was resting against his thigh.

He was quiet. Thought about what she was after. Whether he wanted to fall into that abyss. A gust of wind knocked against the cabin and whistled through the gaps, rattling every loose window.

When the record paused between songs, he heard the rain pattering on the roof.

"I went to the beach with that cop's niece. Smart little thing. Swims like a fish. She wouldn't tell me a thing about the case."

"She might not know anything." He turned his face to study her. "Are you worried?"

"I want to get out of here. This bush camp is stifling. Promise me you won't sign on as cook next summer."

"Where would you like us to be instead?"

"I was thinking we could take one of those cruises and stay in Europe afterward. I adore Italian food. We could rent a villa in Tuscany and you could work in a bistro. I could be a hostess in a club like I did before we met."

"Neither of us speaks Italian."

"We can learn enough to get by. We both speak some French, so it won't take long." She bent forward and grabbed the nearly empty bottle by the neck. Her face was illuminated in the candlelight and her eyes glinted like a cat's in a dark alley. She filled her glass and took a drink before settling back. "I have this bad feeling. We need to leave and start our lives somewhere else."

"We can't go until Rachel's death has been solved."

"Do you believe one of us …"

"Killed her? For what reason? She was harmless."

"You'd like to think so." Petra took a drink, and Leonard Cohen's voice swelled to fill the silence. She kept her focus on the candle sitting in front of her on the table. "Rachel was sleeping with some-body and maybe wasn't limiting herself to one horny conquest. I'd bet my diamond earrings."

"She had a boyfriend."

"That kid from town?" Petra flicked her wrist. "Pfft. Not him. Somebody she was keeping secret."

Shane looked at the floor. He knew that she sus-pected him but would never ask because she wouldn't trust him to tell the truth. Secrecy had become a two-way street. "You could be imagining a relation-ship that wasn't there," he said.

"Plee-ease. I know somebody having sex when I see them." Petra raised both arms and the blanket dropped to her waist. Her breasts were bare and her skin glowed amber-gold in the light. She rubbed her foot higher on his thigh against his crotch. "But maybe I need a refresher," she said. "I could be get-ting rusty."

He doubted that but wasn't prepared to start a fight. He had no clue what was behind her behaviour tonight, but he could feel his need to know slipping away. She reached her free hand over and took his, drawing it to the curve of her breast. Her foot continued its relentless pressure, rubbing back and forth, back and forth until a moan escaped his lips. She pulled away and got to her feet. The blanket fell onto the floor and she stood naked before him.

"I can see you're in the mood to teach me a lesson," she said as she thrust a leg across his and straddled his lap. She ran her fingers through his hair as she leaned in to kiss him. "And I'm in the mood to learn."

Chapter Nineteen

Clark woke sometime around 4:00 a.m. and rolled onto his side to wrap an arm around Valerie, expecting to feel her soft roundness and finding nothing. He sat up. The sheets where she should have been sleeping were cold to his touch. He pushed himself off the mattress, still groggy, worry making him clumsy. He swore softly when his knee connected with the post at the end of the bed. He found her in the baby's room, sitting in the maple rocking chair they'd picked out two months earlier in the Soo. He could smell a faint trace of new paint, but the window was open and a clean breeze blew the curtains into the room like swooping birds. She took a moment to see him but smiled when she did. Her hair was silver in the light and loose around her face.

"The baby was playing soccer in my belly and I couldn't sleep."

He crossed the room to stand behind her. He massaged her shoulders through her cotton nightgown and kissed the top of her head. She was warm, her hair damp with sweat.

"Are you feeling okay? Would you like a glass of water or milk?"

She patted one of his hands while holding on to the heft of her stomach with the other. "I've had some contractions. Nothing serious. The doctor said to expect them about now. Braxton Hicks or something."

He moved so that he was in front of her and knelt, his hands on her knees. "I'll take the day off."

"Not yet. I'll need you soon, but it's still early. You've only started on finding that girl's killer. Besides, Jordan is here if I'm being too optimistic about the timing."

"You and the baby are my priorities. The case isn't going anywhere."

"Neither am I. The first baby usually takes its sweet time."

"Come back to bed. We can see how you feel once the sun's up."

She let him pull her out of the chair and he helped her into bed before carefully stretching out next to her. This time she kept a space between them but held his hand even after her breathing slowed and he knew she was asleep. He rolled onto his back and stared at the light playing on the ceiling. How could he bring a child into this world when a girl like Rachel could be murdered walking home from work on a summer evening? How could he keep his child safe when the world was so random? Isabelle Eglan had spent her life trying to keep her daughter from harm and the worst had happened anyway. There was no certainty that he and Valerie could do any better. There were no guarantees that their best would be good enough.

The thought kept him awake until the birds began their morning song at the first shimmers of dawn, when he pushed aside the covers and decided he might as well get an early start on the day.

He left Valerie still sleeping and had a quick shower in the basement bathroom, not wanting to wake her. Breakfast was a toasted bagel eaten while he waited for the coffee to brew. He filled his travel mug and left an almost-full pot for Jordan. Valerie was resigned to herbal tea to start her day until the baby was through breastfeeding. Another reason he was thankful that he couldn't give birth.

He made it into the office at ten after seven. Too early to make his list of follow-up phone calls, so he put on another pot of coffee and typed notes while he waited for the clock to strike nine. Anyone still in bed at that time shouldn't be.

Sara Vila answered on the third ring, panting as if she'd run a race. "I was in the basement hanging up laundry," she said without being asked. "What's this about, Officer?"

He realized she could read his name on call display. He risked redundancy and said, "I'm Officer Clark Harrison from the Sault detachment looking into the murder of Rachel Eglan."

"Who? I don't understand."

"Have you been speaking with your brother Alec this week?"

"No. I've been working nights at the hospital. I'm a nurse. I got home from a visit with Alec in Searchmont a few days ago and headed straight to work. I'm off today and start day shift tomorrow. I've had no time for anything except work and sleep. I've barely kept my house running. Who's this Rachel … Eglan was it?"

The woman was a talker, no doubt about that. Clark said, "Rachel was a high-school senior and was waitressing at Pine Hollow Lodge the night you and your brother were there for supper. She was killed walking home after her shift."

"Why that's horrible. In the dark? Was it a hit and run?"

"We thought maybe at first, but later found that she'd been beaten and left in the culvert."

"Good God."

The shock in her voice sounded genuine to Clark's ear, but he wished Stonechild was listening in to give a second opinion. She was intuitive and him less so. He asked, "Do you remember Rachel? She was sixteen and had red hair."

"I saw her, certainly. But she was so young." Sara's voice came out a wail. He could hear a sharp intake of breath and waited for her to gather herself. "The girl didn't wait on our table."

"No, although I understand she exchanged pleasantries with some of your group."

"I don't recall."

He thought he detected a change in her voice. A wariness. "You and your brother returned to his home after supper?"

"Yes. I went to bed soon after, and he retired to his study to finish a sermon for the following day."

"Can you confirm that he didn't leave the house?"

A pause. When she next spoke, her voice was quiet. Low and controlled. "Is this necessary?"

"I'm only checking alibis to cross people off the list. I have no agenda."

She again took her time answering. "I have no knowledge of him leaving the house. He was there when I went to bed and in his room when I woke up in the morning."

"Well, that's all I had to follow up on. Thank you for your time."

"That's it?"

He wondered if he'd missed something because he heard surprise and relief in her voice. Surely he was reading too much into her tone. "For now. Likely I won't bother you again."

"Well, that would be a welcome change."

She hung up and left him wondering what she meant. One phone call was not exactly harassment.

His second phone call took longer because he was transferred a few times up the chain of command until a hospital administrator confirmed that Reeve Judd Neilson had spent the night in question sleeping in his son Robby's room. Yes, all night. The staff were in and out several times and could attest to his presence if asked.

At least one family to check off the suspect list, Clark thought. He made one final call to let Valerie know that he was on the road to Searchmont as the clock struck ten before taking the stairs to get his car.

Clark found Stonechild and the girl returning from a morning paddle and once again reached for the canoe as it glided alongside the dock.

"Such a lovely morning," Stonechild said, and he heard regret in her voice, knowing his presence to be the cause. "Do you hang around our dock all morning, waiting for us to return?"

"Not exactly" — he steadied the canoe while she climbed out — "but they say timing is everything. If we get started now, we should be able to interview everyone by late afternoon and there'll be time for another paddle before supper."

"Can I hold you to that?"

"I'd like to get home at a decent hour, so I'm going to say yes."

They left Dawn and the dog at the cabin and walked through the woods to the main lodge. Tree boughs and leaves filtered the sun and the resulting dappled light kept the air cool. The tree stumps and rocks were lined in emerald-green moss and pine needles littered the path.

"How's your wife?" Stonechild asked from a few steps ahead of him. "Getting ready for the baby?"

"She's tired, but into the final few weeks." He laughed. "We're in for the change of our lives if what everyone says is true. What about you? Ever thought about having a kid, Stonechild?"

Her back straightened and she hesitated before taking her next step. She replied without turning around, "It's crossed my mind."

Clark kicked himself. He imagined she'd believed a few years ago that she and Jordan would start a family, too, once his brother divorced Miriam. But that was then. A lot had changed. He kept silent rather than add to his blunder.

Shane was working in the kitchen when they entered. Stonechild had told him they'd be carrying out interviews in the restaurant when she came for breakfast. He brought them a fresh pot of coffee and said they were welcome to use the room until supper hour.

"Do you have time for a chat now?" Clark asked.

"Give me two secs and I'll be right with you." Shane wiped his hands on the apron tied around his waist and pushed the kitchen door open with his hip.

Stonechild looked around. "We can set up over here," she said, walking toward a table for four in the corner away from the windows. "Might make people feel like they have a bit of privacy."

"Good thinking."

He poured two cups of coffee and handed one to her.

"I told the others we'd be coming to get them at some point today. The only two who aren't available until five o'clock are Ian Kruger and Blaine Rogers because they're working on the Hydro line. I couldn't see asking them to hang around all day."

"I guess I can stay and handle those alone if you want to go out on the water with Dawn."

"Let's play that by ear."

Shane joined them carrying a mug. He poured himself a cup of coffee and settled into the chair across the table from them. "Fire away," he said.

Clark took the lead. "Who hired Rachel to work here for the summer?"

"I did, since the job was working for me as a server for the most part. She also helped Martha clean cabins, but for that she only had to be good at taking direction. Martha met her after I interviewed her and didn't have any qualms. There weren't a lot of applications, to be honest."

"What can you tell us about Rachel?"

"A good kid. Always on time and worked hard. She was quiet until you got to know her." He took a sip of coffee and grinned. "I guess she was quiet even when you got to know her. I've been racking my brain trying to remember if she had a problem with anybody, but I can't think of an incident. She's the last person I'd pick to be murdered. I mean, for what?" He spread his hands and shook his head.

"Was she seeing someone romantically?"

"She mentioned a boyfriend Darryl — somebody from town — but I never met him."

"Anybody else? We believe she was hooking up with someone other than Darryl."

Shane rubbed his jaw. "Nobody that I'm aware of."

Stonechild put down her notebook. "Were you having sex with Rachel?"

"What, me?" His mouth curled in distaste. "Good God, no. She was a child."

Clark glanced at her and back at Shane. "That last evening Rachel's father was to come and get her. Were you aware he hadn't?"

Shane dragged his eyes back from staring at Stonechild. He took a second to answer. "She was still here when I locked up. I asked her if she needed a ride home and she said no. Her dad was supposed to pick her up. She seemed certain he'd be showing up soon, so I didn't think any more of it."

"And that's the last you saw of her?"

"Yes. I went home out the back way and fell asleep on the couch."

"Where was your wife?"

He hesitated. "Petra went shopping in the Soo for the day and got home late."

"How did Petra and Rachel get along?"

"Okay. Petra didn't have anything to do with the restaurant, so she only interacted with Rachel occasionally."

Stonechild leaned forward. "How was Rachel with the other lodgers? Was she friendlier with one over another?"

"I didn't see anything inappropriate going on, if that's what you're asking. Rachel came to the lodge midafternoon to set up. She took orders, served meals, and cleared tables. She helped with the dishes, scraping and putting them into the dishwasher. She set the tables for breakfast and then she went home. Usually she biked since it stays light until nine o'clock these evenings, closer to nine thirty in June and July, but she also had a light on her bike. Earlier in the summer, when we were busier, she'd come in the mornings to help clean cabins with Martha. We paid extra."

Clark looked at Stonechild. "Any more questions?"

"Not at the moment."

He said to Shane, "Then I guess that's it for now."

Shane stood. "I hear there's going to be a service at the Catholic church in Goulais River for Rachel tomorrow at one o'clock. Father Vila's officiating."

"Thanks for the information," said Clark.

Shane turned and started walking toward the kitchen. He stopped with a hand on the door and looked back over his shoulder. "I still can't believe she's dead," he said before he shoved it open.

"The information lines in these small towns are incredible," said Clark to Stonechild. "I imagine the entire town knows about the funeral through some freaky community osmosis. Frig, they know when someone sneezes before they reach for a tissue. I'll bet whatever led to Rachel's death is making the rumour round, but we're outsiders and not trusted."

"The gossip is the one thing I don't miss about living up here. I've grown to cherish anonymity." Stonechild looked out the window toward the lake. "The rest I miss like crazy."

CHAPTER TWENTY

Kala's first impression of Petra was that this was a woman who liked attention. Her cherry-red caftan flowed around her as she sauntered toward them in pink flip-flops that sparkled with rhinestones. She took off her small, round à-la-John-Lennon sunglasses as she slid into the seat and waved a bangled arm toward the kitchen. Her beautiful eyes were the sea shade of blue in which many a poet had drowned. "Shane told me you wanted a word?" she asked.

"Thanks for making time," said Clark. Kala couldn't tell if Petra's potent aura was having an effect on Clark, but he appeared to be working hard not to notice how she sucked the oxygen out of the room. Kala felt herself fading into the woodwork and thought how best to use the position to her advantage. She pushed her chair to the edge of the table out of Petra's direct line of vision. *Let's see how Clark deals with this overt bundle of sexual energy.*

"Soooo," said Clark, dragging out the word as if buying time to compose himself. "I understand you'd like to move back to Sudbury."

"Only if you give your approval, Officer." Petra bent forward so that she was closer to Clark. Her caftan gaped open. She was wearing a hot-pink bikini underneath that made her tanned breasts appear to glow. Clark blinked a few times before looking down at his notebook. Kala saw Petra's lips curve upward for a second before she settled back in the chair.

"We're early days in the investigation so we'd appreciate you staying here a bit longer."

Petra's face tightened but when she responded, her voice was light. "I'll remain until you give the okay, Offff … icer."

Kala clamped her lips shut to keep in a bark of laughter. Petra had effectively mocked Clark by mimicking him with one drawn-out syllable.

Clark showed no reaction. His voice was even. "Much appreciated. Can you tell me about Rachel?" He finally looked up at her. His face was calm, but Kala could sense his unease, like a man cooking a steak over a raging fire, scared of getting burned.

"Rachel appeared benign enough, but I didn't trust her." Petra's cutting observation was a throwaway, said without forethought.

Kala shifted her gaze to watch Petra, her head lowered. Petra's face was angry and Kala sensed that she'd spoken out of petulance at being told she had to stay at the lodge. This time she appeared to ponder her answer after Clark asked her to expand. Kala thought she might have regretted her previous impetuous answer.

"She was always watching, soaking up information about people. I caught her listening at doors a few times."

"Do you believe she had a reason for this behaviour?"

"None that was evident, but she liked the men, if you know what I mean. I thought she might be, how can I say? Slutting around. Getting it on with married men." Petra ran her tongue over her top lip. "Shane wouldn't confirm or deny my observations."

Clark's voice was puzzled. "Do you think Rachel was having an affair with your husband?"

"Goodness, no." Laughter trilled out of her. "Rachel was *not* his type … or old enough. Shane isn't *that* kind of man. No, what I'm trying to explain is that Rachel was more devious than people knew, and I believe she was seeing somebody on the sly. Not Shane, but somebody."

"Any idea who?"

"No." She'd said it quickly. Too quickly.

Kala thought that this woman would have had some experience with affairs. She had a knowing light in her eyes when she talked about men and the look she was sending Clark was practised. Kala considered his appearance: tall and solidly muscular, affable face, and coppery-coloured hair. Some women liked a man in uniform, and Clark wore his well. She began to wonder about the state of Petra and Shane's marriage and jotted a note to follow up.

"I never liked Thomas Faraday," Petra said, as if thinking out loud. She closed her mouth and bit her bottom lip.

"Did he interact with Rachel?"

"Well, yes. She was here all summer and so was he. I saw them together a few times outside the restaurant. I sometimes wondered ..."

Kala interrupted. "Did he do or say anything to make you dislike him?"

Petra glanced at her and back at Clark. "He's too interested in everyone. Smarmy. I don't trust the kind of man who's always complimenting and working to make you like him. Know what I mean, Officer?"

Clark nodded, but Kala could see he didn't have a clue what Petra was talking about. He wasn't a man who played games. She figured Petra was working to send them down a path that didn't lead to her husband. The reason why she was going to all this trouble made Kala curious.

Clark was working to shift the interview onto more comfortable footing. "You weren't at the lodge the evening Rachel was killed?"

"No, I was shopping in the Soo and ate supper with a friend. I drove home late evening."

"Did you see Rachel or anybody on the road?"

"No, I didn't see anybody. I wish I had."

Kala looked up from her notes. "Could you give us the name and contact information of your dinner companion?"

"Of course. Clare Summers. We ate at Gliss steakhouse on Bay. It was after ten when I started for home." Petra's focus swung over to Kala. She lifted a hand to cover a breast. "I hope you don't think of me as a suspect."

Kala returned her wide-eyed stare. "We're checking everybody."

Her hand dropped to her lap. Her words were a steely jab through pouted lips. "I'll bet you are."

The police authority was back in Clark's voice. "That'll do for now, Petra. Thanks for your time. If you could let Neal know we're ready for him."

She looked at him and seemed to sense that he wasn't going to play along any longer. Her voice hardened. "Sure. I'm hoping I can leave here by the end of the week, so please keep that in mind. I've had enough of roughing it in the bush." She adjusted the caftan so that the fabric draped lower over her shoulders and smiled at Clark before she took her leave.

Kala made a final note in her book and waited for Clark to speak first. He lifted the coffee pot. "Like a refill?"

She glanced at her mug. "No, I haven't touched this one yet."

He refilled his own. "I'm starting to think we've landed in Peyton Place."

"Just how old are you, Officer Harrison? Sixty-five?"

"So, I like the old shows. Point is she makes me think we're digging into a community with its fair share of shenanigans."

"By shenanigans do you mean sex?"

"I like my word better, but yeah, and sex that crosses boundaries. I'll follow up with the restaurant and her dinner mate, but not sure their confirmation will cross Petra or Shane off the suspect list."

"No. They were each alone for a period of time that night. She could have met Rachel by chance on the road and acted impulsively."

"The question would be why."

"Shane might have been more into Rachel than either is admitting."

Clark wiped the back of his hand across his mouth. "Petra's comments and attempts to distract and divert certainly takes one's suspicions into new places." He checked his watch. "Going on two. Not sure we'll be able to get to everyone today."

They both looked toward the entrance as Neal let the screen door slam behind him. "Sorry," he said, a sheepish look on his face as he crossed the room to take the seat vacated by Petra. He scratched at his beard, a nervous gesture that appeared to soothe him. He was wearing a black ball cap that he took off and set on the table in front of him. His black hair was thinning in the front, and Kala thought he'd be bald before long. He didn't seem like a man who'd let vanity bother him much.

"Thanks for coming," said Clark. "We're asking everyone about their interactions with Rachel."

"Yeah. Still having trouble believing she's gone." Neal kept his eyes on the ball cap. He inhaled loudly and let his breath out slowly. "What do you want to know?"

"What was your relationship like?"

"She was a sweet kid. Hard-working."

"Were you friends?"

"Friends?" For a moment he looked bewildered. "She was too young to be my friend, and she was an employee. I liked talking to her, though. She had a good sense of humour."

Kala hadn't heard this said about Rachel by anyone else, but she was beginning to understand that Rachel revealed different bits of herself to different people. She wasn't unusual in this regard. It was a rare person who consistently reacted the same to everyone — who let everyone inside.

Clark looked at Kala and she took the cue. "Were you romantically involved with her?" she asked.

Neal's face flushed crimson. "Has somebody suggested that?" he asked.

"Not you with Rachel, specifically, but we have to ask."

He muttered something under his breath. "No, I never had sex with that girl. I'm not the one who should be ashamed."

"What do you mean? Who should be ashamed?" Kala willed him to keep talking, but he'd clamped his lips together and refused to say anything more. The silence stretched uncomfortably until Clark broke the impasse.

"Can you tell us about the last night Rachel worked here?"

Neal's shoulders relaxed and Kala thought Clark might have let him off the hook too soon. "I was fishing all day with some tourists and got to the restaurant halfway through supper. You were there with your kid," he said to Kala. "I said hello to everyone, but didn't stay long. I was whacked from being outdoors all day. I turned in early."

"When did Martha get home?"

"That I couldn't tell you. I slept straight through."

"Did you hear her come to bed?"

He looked back at his ball cap. "No, I slept in the other room."

"Do you usually sleep in the other room?"

"Not always."

Clark stared at him a moment longer before beginning on a new tact. "Did Rachel spend time with anyone else at the lodge?"

"She talked to everyone. This isn't exactly a big city. She didn't argue or seem at odds with anyone though. I have no idea why somebody would kill her. Doesn't make sense."

Kala listened for a false note in his voice and couldn't be certain that he was being as forthright as he'd have them believe.

Clark waited a few more beats. "Okay, Neal. That'll do for the time being, unless you have something else to tell us about Rachel."

"Nothing I can think of right now."

"Well, when you do, we're ready to listen. Can you send Martha in for a chat?"

A troubled expression crossed Neal's face before he picked up his ball cap and swung it onto his head. "I'll let her know," he said. "She's probably finishing up in the cabins."

CHAPTER TWENTY-ONE

Martha set the basket of dirty sheets on the bottom step and rubbed her lower back. She took a moment's rest and turned around to soak in the view of the lake. The sky was a bowl of cloudless blue and the sun, while warm, had the late-summer hint of autumn. In a normal year, she and Neal would be getting the lodge ready to close for the season. Rachel's death had put everything up in the air. She was ready for the break but knew she'd miss being at the lodge by December. *What will happen next year?*

She doubted that Shane and Petra would return. Neal was another question mark. Her chest hurt at the thought of separating. Her head ached at the idea of being on her own. She heard him walking down the path before he came into view. He was wearing his favourite black ball cap and had his head down. He didn't see her at first and she drank in the sight of him like an addict long denied. When he raised his head he didn't smile, but he didn't look away either.

"The cops are ready for you in the main lodge," he said. He added after a pause, "They're on a fishing expedition."

"Okay. Thanks for the heads-up." She smiled at him, trying to find a softening in his armour, but he turned and started walking into the shadows cast by the trees along the path. The desperation she'd come to breathe in and out like oxygen filled her lungs. *We can't end like this. I know you still care for me.* For one confused moment she thought she'd screamed the words out loud, relieved to realize that she hadn't. The pain was still contained inside her. She tried to make out Neal's shape on the path, but the trees and shadows had swallowed him up.

She stooped to pick up the laundry basket and brought it inside. She drank a glass of cold water, washed her face, and retied her hair into a ponytail before her walk to the main lodge. The two officers were waiting inside at the table in the corner. The male officer pointed to a chair as Martha crossed the room toward them and she sat down.

Officer Harrison introduced himself and smiled at her. "Martha, thank you for talking with us. We know you're busy."

"No, this is important. We have to understand what happened to Rachel." She crossed one leg over her other knee and noticed a streak of dirt on her calf. She rubbed at it with the knuckles of one hand before seeing smears of dirt on her shorts. The sour smell of sweat rose from her T-shirt when she moved. She should have taken the time to change.

Harrison was talking again, and she pulled herself back. "You didn't hire Rachel, we understand. Shane chose her to help in the restaurant."

"That's right, but I gave my vote of approval after I met her."

"What did you think of her as the summer went on?"

Martha forced herself to look each of them in the eyes without wavering. "She was a good worker. Punctual. Went about things quietly and efficiently. She was smarter than she seemed at the beginning."

"Oh?"

Martha blushed. *Have I put my foot in it?* She wished she knew what the others had said before her. They'd had time to get their stories straight, but they weren't happy enough with one another to make the effort. "Sometimes she'd be reading a book at the beach between helping me with housekeeping and her night shift in the restaurant. She liked to read." *As if reading books made somebody smart.*

Kala Stonechild was staring at her, drawing her gaze into the officer's own inky-black pools. "Do you know if she was seeing anybody romantically at the lodge?"

Martha swallowed the moan that lodged at the base of her throat. "Rachel was a child." Her words came out a croak. She forced more air into her lungs and her voice gained strength. "I'd like to think the men at the lodge would respect that fact."

"You didn't find her precocious or mature for her age?"

"Not especially."

Stonechild looked at her notes. She raised her head and her black eyes again found Martha's. "We've had an observation from another person at the lodge that Rachel liked men. Would you agree?"

Martha took a moment to still the thoughts swirling in her head. Petra had opened her loose mouth and stirred the waters. What else had she told them? She spoke slowly and hoped she appeared thoughtful. "Rachel was sixteen, an age where most girls think men are worth pursuing. She had a town boyfriend, though, so she wasn't inexperienced." Martha stopped talking rather than say too much, happy to have Clark ask the next question and end her staring contest with the woman cop.

"The last day she worked here — how did she seem?"

"I didn't notice anything off. She served you, Officer Stonechild, and helped out with some other tables. I handled the customers from town. She was sitting down for some supper in the kitchen when I left at seven-thirty. She said that her dad planned to drive her home because it was getting dark earlier."

"How did she usually go to and from the lodge?"

"She rode her bike. Sometimes she walked. It's only an hour on foot. She told me that she planned to take driver's ed in the fall when she was back in school so she could get her own car next summer."

Stonechild broke in. "I can't figure out why she wouldn't have used the house phone to call her dad when he was late, or why she didn't ask somebody for a lift."

"I wondered that, too. She might not have wanted to bother me since the phone is in my office in our cabin. Perhaps she thought she'd meet her father along the way."

The officer didn't respond. Martha saw Shane push open the kitchen door and look over at her, but he didn't come into the room. He let the door shut quietly without the two cops seeing him. She wondered if he was giving her a signal but couldn't think what it could be.

Officer Harrison took over. "Did Rachel get along with the summer lodgers?"

"I'd say so, yes."

"Thomas Faraday?"

"She often served him supper. They chatted."

"Anything more than that?"

The suspicion inherent in the question had Petra written all over it. Martha shrugged and said, carefully, "I didn't follow Rachel around when she was on her own time so I can't say for certain. He's gone off in the woods with his camera, by the way. I saw him leave at around two o'clock."

The two cops exchanged a glance. "It's getting late in the day anyhow," said Officer Harrison.

Officer Stonechild tilted her head. Studied Martha. "How's business?" she asked.

She was changing the subject. Trying to lull her into a false confidence. "Decent. We've had a good year, what with the three men booked for the entire summer. Business is tailing off now, though."

"Where will you go when the lodge closes for the season?"

Martha tried to still the pain running through her gut and into her chest before it reached her face. "We have a place in Cobourg, but we like to spend part of the winter in Arizona."

Clark was watching her as closely as his partner. "Can you think of any reason that somebody would harm Rachel?" he asked.

"No," Martha responded. She shook her head. "I can't think of any reason at all."

Stonechild again. "Shane is your cousin, is this correct?"

"Distant cousin. Our mothers were first cousins. We knew each other growing up in Sudbury but grew apart once we started high school."

"Did you know Petra then?"

"I met her, but we didn't hang out."

"Would you say that Shane and Petra have a strong marriage?"

"Yes, they appear to be tight." Martha looked from her to Clark. "If you're all done asking about Rachel, I have work to do."

Officer Harrison checked his notepad one more time before saying, "That should do it for now. We'll be asking more questions though as this case progresses."

"I'll be here."

She felt their eyes on her as she started toward the front door. She'd have liked to go into the kitchen to see Shane and talk over their interviews, but she didn't dare. She'd have to wait until suppertime to speak to him. She wondered if he'd finally tell her about Neal betraying her with Rachel or if he'd lie to her as he'd surely lied to the cops. She straightened her spine and kept walking until she reached the edge of the woods where she broke into a run.

CHAPTER TWENTY-TWO

K ala said goodbye to Clark and hurried back to the cabin. She'd left Dawn too long and they had less than an hour before they had to return to the main lodge for supper. She'd suggest going into Searchmont to call Gundersund as a way of making up to her for another lost day. They could drive there and back in time.

She emerged from the woods and looked toward the lake. After the first moment of thinking that she had to be dreaming, her heart leapt skyward. She quickened her steps, never taking her gaze off the figures on the dock, not wanting to believe her own eyes until she was close enough to be certain. Gundersund turned his head as if sensing her there and said something to Dawn before pushing himself to his feet and starting to walk the length of the dock toward her. Kala drank in the sight of him, the desire to wrap herself around him a physical need. She started running and flung herself into his arms when she reached him. He kissed her mouth and held on to her, and she rested her head against his chest. She could hear the steady beating of his heart through his jacket.

"I'm so glad you came," she said before pulling back. She looked over his shoulder at Dawn and the good feeling evaporated. Dawn's head was bowed, her hair hanging across her face. Taiku had nestled against her leg, but Dawn wasn't reacting. Kala looked up at Gundersund with a question in her eyes. He shook his head enough for her to know that something was wrong.

"I've told Dawn that I've come to take her to see her mother. Rose is in the hospital."

"Oh no." Kala walked past him and crouched down next to Dawn. She put an arm around her shoulders and looked up at Gundersund who'd followed her onto the dock. "Is Rose okay?"

"She is, and asking to see Dawn." He paused. She saw regret in his glance. "I told Dawn that Rose tried to take her own life."

Kala rubbed Dawn's back. Gundersund had learned as she had that being forthright with Dawn was the only way. She knew that he could have waited and let her break the news, but that was not his way. He'd take the burden on himself. "This is hard," she said to Dawn. "I'm so sorry."

Dawn turned her face to Kala. Her cheeks were damp from crying. "How could she do it?" she asked.

"She must have lost hope ... for a moment."

"But she still has us. She still has me." Dawn's voice dropped to a whimper.

Kala wrapped both arms around Dawn so that her hands joined together at Dawn's shoulder. She leaned her head against hers. "You're stronger than your mom right now. She needs you."

Dawn stared across the lake. She sat silently for a long moment, but her sobs subsided and Kala could tell that she was calmer. "Okay," Dawn said. She swiped at her eyes. "When will we leave, Gundersund?"

"First thing in the morning."

"Will you be okay here alone, Aunt Kala?"

"I'll be following you home as soon as this case is over." Kala looked up at Gundersund, asking for understanding with her eyes. "The lead cop's wife is due with their first child any day, or I'd tell him to go this alone."

She couldn't read Gundersund's expression, but he nodded agreement. "I can look after this visit to Joliette, and you do what you have to do."

"Thank you."

They decided to drive in the opposite direction to Searchmont for supper at Mountainview Lodge. Kala wanted to envelop the three of them in a cocoon, to take them away from the people she was investigating at Pine Hollow Lodge. They each ordered the same comfort food: roast beef sandwiches with fries and gravy. They talked about inconsequential subjects, laughed a lot even though sadness tinged the quiet moments. When Dawn excused herself to go to the washroom, Kala reached over to hold on to Gundersund's hand.

"I've missed you," she said.

"I've missed you, too." He lifted her fingers to his lips and kissed them. "I'm sorry I brought bad news."

"I think it's a blessing in a way to have her depart from this place. I didn't like leaving her alone all day, even with Taiku. The girl who died was a year older than Dawn." She didn't need to tell him about the growing worry she'd felt, not sure if it came from the horror when Dawn was missing earlier that year, or if her concern was valid. His face showed her that he knew.

"She told me that she likes being in the woods."

"Did she? She hasn't let on one way or the other and I was scared to ask. Her canoeing skills have improved exponentially."

"Do you want me to bring her back after she sees Rose?"

Kala thought for a moment before saying no. "I'm not sure the danger here. Can she stay with you until this is over?"

"If that's what you'd both like." He was about to say something else but stopped when Dawn returned and slid into her seat.

"Can we order dessert?" she asked.

"I think that's a given," said Gundersund.

They lingered over tea and blueberry pie. Kala couldn't shake the trepidation that made her want to leave this restaurant and get in the truck and drive through the night with Dawn and Gundersund — to put distance between them and Searchmont — but she didn't protest when it came time to pay the bill and go back to Pine Hollow Lodge. She wouldn't give voice to the vague anxiety that filled her.

She helped Dawn pack when they returned to the cabin while Gundersund lit a fire in the pit near the beach. They joined him and sat close to one another, watching the flames crackle and spark into the moon-lit sky with the lake a backdrop sloshing against the shore. A wide shaft of light glistened off the dark water. Stars punctuated the black cover overhead like sequins nestled into black velvet. Kala smelled woodsmoke from the fire and cedar in the late summer breeze off the lake. She'd brought marshmallows from home and they roasted them with sticks, savouring the sweet, sticky gooiness that reminded her of childhood. Not every foster home memory was bad.

The fire died down to glowing orange embers when Dawn hugged them and walked up to the cabin with Taiku to read before falling asleep. Kala leaned against the solid strength of Gundersund and he wrapped an arm around her.

"I wish I could come with you."

He was silent but his hand rubbed up and down her arm.

"Let Rose know that I'll come to see her as soon as I can."

"I will." He poked at the fire with his marsh-mallow stick. "Tell me more about this case you're working on. Who's the officer you're helping?"

"The victim is a sixteen-year-old girl named Rachel Eglan, and she was working here the night we arrived. She served us supper, in fact. Her father was supposed to pick her up, but he got called in to work and didn't manage to let Rachel know. She waited a while and then set out for home on foot. My guess is that she thought she'd meet her dad along the way. It's about an hour walk and it wasn't dark when she set out. Someone took a tire iron to the side of her head and across her back when she was about halfway home and rolled her into the culvert. She was found the next day."

"Christ."

"Officer Clark Harrison used to work with me out of the Nipigon detachment. He's lead on the case now, working out of the Soo, although his headquarters is in North Bay. They have a staff shortage and asked if I'd back him up."

"Not that it matters to me, but were you involved with him outside of work?"

"No." She thought about telling him that she'd dated Clark's brother, but couldn't see the point. Jordan's name hadn't even come up. "I have to see this through, Gundersund. I keep thinking about the girl. Her parents won't be able to get over this without answers."

"I know. You do what you need to do, and I'll manage with Dawn. Have you got any leads?"

"The suspect list is long and wide open at the moment." She nuzzled her face into the curve of his neck just below his chin. "You smell so good. Like spicy summer heat."

He laughed. "More like sweat from a day driving."

She moved her lips higher and kissed lightly across his cheek and the top of his nose. She pulled her head back and looked into his eyes. "How's everyone back home? Rouleau?"

"He's at loose ends. Rumour is Marci is taking an overseas assignment and asked him to go with her."

Kala felt a familiar drop in her stomach. *Nobody ever stuck around forever.* "When will they be leaving?"

"Marci's departure is any day. Rouleau hasn't said when he plans to follow or even if he's going. The team is waiting on tenterhooks for his decision." He cupped her face in his hand and searched her eyes as if trying to see inside her mind. He rubbed his knuckles up her cheek and ran his fingers through her hair. "Are you ready for bed, Officer Stonechild?" he asked softly.

"Only if you are planning to share it with me."

He smiled. "Then I'd say you're ready for bed."

Gundersund and Dawn left at first light. Kala walked back through the woods to the cabin after seeing them off with Taiku at her side, his tail down, letting her know that he wasn't happy to be losing the rest of his family. "I know, boy," she said, bending over to give him a scratch behind his ear. "I'm going to miss them, too."

Clark arrived as she was finishing a second glass of orange juice in the main lodge. He seemed preoccupied when he joined her at the table with a full mug of coffee. Blood had dried on his chin where he'd cut himself shaving and exhaustion lines radiated outward from his eyes. He looked around the room and back at her. "Dawn still sleeping?"

"No. My partner arrived last night and took her to see her mother, who's in the hospital near Montreal."

He gave her a weak grin. "And you stayed to help me with this case. I appreciate that."

"I won't say I wasn't tempted to go with them. It's not in me to give up on a murder case, though."

"Fortunate for me."

"Single-mindedness is not, however, the best quality for maintaining healthy personal relationships."

"I think people worth having in your life understand."

"It's my turn to say 'fortunate for me.'"

Clark blew on his coffee before taking a sip. "So, the two Hydro guys first up?"

"No, they're working in the area and will come for their interviews at eleven. Faraday should be here within fifteen minutes."

"Great. The research crew sent me this last evening." He slid his phone over to her and drummed his fingers on the table while she read.

She raised her eyes. "Interesting. Warrant?"

"In the works."

She pushed the phone back toward him. "Our first decent lead, so that's something." She studied him. "You seem on edge today. Everything okay at home?"

"About-to-become-a-new-father jitters, I guess. Valerie's having those pre-contractions, but tells me we've got days to go before labour starts for real. I'm the one having trouble sleeping. Can't believe how nonchalant she is about the whole birthing thing." He picked up the coffee mug again. "I'm also frustrated by this case. Worried Faraday won't pan out."

"Women have been having babies a long time, Harrison. Valerie's got this. As for the case, don't lose heart. We're laying the groundwork. If it's not

Faraday, he'll be one more crossed off." Kala knew this was the hardest time in any investigation — the initial hope for a quick solution was over and the grunt work looked to be leading nowhere. Now was the time to dig deeper and to start organizing the puzzle pieces.

"You always did like the hunt."

"I won't deny it, although my real satisfaction comes in saving more people from becoming victims … and getting justice for the dead."

"Aaand you always were more patient than me."

"You could take a lesson or two from your wife."

"So she keeps telling me."

Thomas Faraday arrived ten minutes late, carrying his Nikon camera with one hand while the other held a metal tripod. A black bag filled with lenses and attachments was slung over his shoulder. "I had to leave my morning vigil but here I am as promised," he said. He set everything down on a table near the door and pivoted to face them. "Let me fetch a cup of delectable brew from the kitchen and I'll return anon."

Kala didn't dare meet Clark's eyes. He muttered, "Patience, patience," under his breath.

Faraday returned and sat across from them, leaning back in the chair and crossing his legs. He rested the coffee mug on his knee. He was wearing hunter-green Bermuda shorts and a black T-shirt under a burgundy wool cardigan, and tan dock shoes with leather laces. His white hair had flopped across one eye and he pushed the stray lock back into place with a fluid motion. "Query away," he said, his ice-blue stare going from Kala to Clark and back again.

Clark took a moment to pull his eyes away from Faraday. He checked his notes and cleared his throat. "I understand you owned a photography business on King West in Toronto until five years ago."

Faraday hesitated a fraction of a second before responding but spoke in the same jovial voice he'd used so far. "A most successful enterprise. I was a fixture on the street and snapped the portraits of the important theatre thespians and literary *intelligentsia*. Anybody who was anybody."

Clark kept his tone mildly inquisitive. "Can you tell us why you left such a thriving business? You weren't quite retirement age."

"Ah, I needed a change. Wildlife photography was a creative new challenge that I'd taken to like a duck to water." His generous smile included them both. "My subjects now have no vanity or feel the need to strike poses. Most refreshing, I assure you."

"Our researchers uncovered information about the closing of your studio."

"Oh? Do tell." Faraday's voice was still amiable, but his expression had darkened.

"You were forced to retire, or charges were going to be laid."

"Pish! Allegations only. Nothing was ever proven."

"Doesn't mean you weren't taking pornographic photos of children."

Faraday waved a hand in the air. "Hearsay."

"Do you deny that you were taking pornographic pictures of underage youth?"

"There's nothing to deny. I was never charged."

Kala could see that Faraday was feigning indignation. He was nervous underneath the bravado. She motioned to Clark under the table where Faraday couldn't see and Clark remained silent. "Did you take any photos of Rachel?" she asked.

His brilliant-blue eyes blinked. "She might have wandered into the frame in a few. Nothing illegal, I assure you."

"Then you won't mind if our team goes through your camera and computer."

"I'm afraid I would. Those are private."

Clark said, "I asked for a warrant last night. One of the officers from the Soo is on his way to pick up your equipment."

"This is an outrage. I'm being railroaded."

"If you're innocent you have nothing to fear."

"I've heard that malarkey before." He stood and pushed back the chair. "I'll be taking my leave."

"Sit down," said Clark without raising his voice. "We're not done."

Faraday sputtered, reminding Kala of a kettle on the verge of boiling, but he slowly lowered himself back into the chair.

"Did you spend time alone with Rachel?" she asked.

"We occasionally enjoyed each other's company when she was between shifts."

"Did you have sex with her?"

"Absolutely not. No. Never." He shook his mane of white hair. "Photographs are not foreplay, Officer. This is what those outside the art world do not understand. One can appreciate beauty without needing to possess it and appreciate the innocence of a child without the desire to corrupt one."

The front door opened, and two uniformed officers stepped into the restaurant. The taller one carried a warrant that he handed to Clark.

"They're going to collect your equipment and will look through your photographs," Clark said to Faraday. He pointed to Faraday's camera. "We'll start with that. Then we'll make a trip together to your cabin to sort through the rest of your artwork."

Kala wasn't needed for the search and used the break to take Taiku for a walk. They set off through the woods on a path that took them along the waterfront and around the bend to a cove surrounded by cliffs of stone capped by thick forest that blocked the sun. Kala scrambled across boulders strewn by a glacier thousands of years earlier until she came to a flat grey rock that overlooked the stretch of sand beach. Taiku took his time reaching her, following smells in the woods before stepping gingerly across the rocks. The wind was calm in the bay and the waves were gentle swells that lapped the edge of the shore. The water reflected green and gold with water lilies bobbing splotches of white next to moss-covered logs that lay half submerged near shore. The growl of a motorboat drew her eyes outward from the bay toward the open water. A couple of men with fishing rods were heading somewhere in a hurry. Seagulls swooped and screeched overhead on their relentless forage for food.

I could load my canoe on the truck when this is over and disappear farther north. The idea sent a shiver of excitement through her. Dawn was in good hands with Gundersund and they could survive a few months without her. Take a respite from caring for anybody and let her body decide the future. She'd buy a tent and some supplies and a warmer coat. Get an extra big bag of dog food for Taiku. It'd been a long time since they were alone sleeping under the stars, miles from a town. The ache in her to get away was growing into something unbearable. This restlessness, the craving to be free of entanglements and others' expectations — she didn't understand herself. She knew Gundersund sensed her disquiet. She couldn't find the words to explain this need inside her, the changes she could not stop or ignore much longer, no matter the questioning in his eyes.

Taiku jumped to his feet and growled deep in his throat. He was staring, laser-focused, back the way they'd come, and Kala twisted around to follow the direction of his eyes. She thought she saw a flash of blue disappearing into the trees. She stood and called out as Taiku started across the rocks, his progress slow and careful. He leapt off the last boulder and bounded toward the edge of the wood ahead of her where he sniffed the path's entrance, looking back at her and waiting for a command. "Stay," she said, and checked the ground for signs that someone had been there watching her. The earth was trampled but she couldn't tell if the footprints were new. None were distinct in any case. She jogged down the path with Taiku leading the way, but if someone had been there watching them from behind the cover of the trees, they'd made their escape. She slowed to a walk and caught her breath, the thought of a killer hiding out in this isolated community a troubling possibility that made her thankful to have Dawn safely out of harm's way.

CHAPTER TWENTY-THREE

Clark met her on the path between her cabin and the main lodge. "Just coming to get you. We've found two somewhat provocative images of Rachel in a bikini on the beach in Faraday's stockpile, so the team will be going through the rest of the photos back at the station. I'll be taking Faraday with us to the station as well for further questioning. Are you comfortable handling the last two interviews with the Hydro guys or should we postpone?"

"I think it best that they're interviewed now. I'll drive into Searchmont this evening to send my notes to you."

"Good enough." He looked relieved. "Hopefully we'll be wrapping this up soon and you can get on with your life."

"And you can start getting ready for that baby."

She continued into the restaurant and didn't wait long before she heard a truck pull into the parking lot. Ian Kruger joined her; he was wearing a bright-orange shirt with yellow stripes running vertically up either side and tan work pants. He'd recently trimmed his beard and cut his hair, which was combed straight back from his forehead. Even more handsome now that he was groomed. He sat down sideways in the chair across from her and stretched out his long legs. "Blaine's gone to get some painkillers for his head and will be here soon."

"Another migraine?"

"Same one he's had all week."

"That's awful. Does he get them often?"

"Sometimes, but nothing like this one. Well, since ..." Ian paused and dropped his eyes, appearing to realize the timing of Blaine's headache coincided with Rachel's murder. He frowned. "So, what did you want to ask me?"

"Tell me about your interactions with Rachel."

"Not much to tell. She served me some meals and we chatted about the area. Blaine and I work long hours, on the road early, so we usually eat supper quickly and get to bed at a decent hour."

"The night she died ..."

"We left before she finished her shift, but she told me she had a ride coming. Sometimes Blaine or I drove her home if the weather was bad. We have two vehicles, but park the boom truck when we're not out in the bush. We'd throw her bike in the back of the pickup and it's a short jaunt up the road. I blame myself for not checking back that night."

"Did you and Blaine go directly to your cabin?"

"We did, but I went out again to fish at the end of the dock before it got dark. Blaine stayed in the cabin. I believe he was reading — and before you ask, I didn't see Rachel after we left her at the restaurant. I don't know how long she waited for her ride."

"Okay." Kala could see that he'd come prepared to distance himself from Rachel. She wasn't sure yet if this meant anything more than he was telling the truth. "Did you ever see Rachel with Thomas Faraday?" she asked.

"No. We weren't around during the day, though. We even work Saturdays."

"I understand that you and Blaine are spending less time together when you're done work."

Ian stared at her. He shook his head. "Nothing much escapes the gossip mill, I see. We've been together a lot this summer and agreed we needed more alone time. No biggie."

"You didn't have a falling out?"

"No, nothing like that."

The front screen door opened and Blaine entered; he was wearing dark sunglasses and looked a little rough around the edges.

Kala smiled at Ian. "How're the wedding plans coming?"

"Who …?"

"Blaine told me at breakfast the other morning."

"I'm letting her handle the arrangements. The date is set for December." He put both hands on the table and started pushing himself to his feet. "If that's all?"

"Thanks." She got up with him and followed him over to where Blaine was standing.

"I'll meet you at the truck," Ian said as he passed Blaine on his way outside. He let the screen door slam behind him and Blaine winced at the noise.

Kala wasn't seeing any friendliness between the two men. "Sorry to hear about your head," she said.

Blaine ran a shaky hand across his forehead. "Yeah. I'm about ready to cut it off."

"We've already spoken once about Rachel," she said. "I only have a few questions. Can you confirm where you were after you left the restaurant with Ian the last evening she worked here?"

"She served us. Ian asked her if she needed a ride home, but she said her dad was coming for her. After supper we went back to the cabin. Ian took his fishing gear down to the dock and I stayed in to read the paper. I fell asleep and didn't hear Blaine come in, but he was in bed when I woke up on the couch around midnight."

"Okay. Tell me, had you ever seen Rachel with Thomas Faraday outside the restaurant?"

"Faraday? No, not that I recall. Why?"

She didn't answer. "How much longer will you be on this job?"

"A couple of days."

"Well, that's it for now. Hope you feel better."

"You and me both."

She watched through the screen door as he walked toward the parking lot, then left the lodge and took the path back to her cabin. It was a few moments before she remembered that Dawn wouldn't be there to greet her. Dawn and Gundersund should be nearing Sudbury by now, probably pulling off the highway for lunch in a diner. Gundersund had said he might stop at a motel near Ottawa for the night. Better to have Dawn rested when she visited her mom.

They don't need me with them.

Kala broke out of the protected coolness of the woods and into the lemony August sunshine. The air was warmer than in the morning, when a crisp wind had held the promise of an early fall. Tufted cumulus clouds drifted across the pewter-coloured sky, one blocking the sun on its way past so that the earth was bathed in shadow. She waited for the shadow to pass and tilted her face heavenward to bask in the sun's warmth for a moment. This would be a perfect afternoon to be out on the water. She'd planned to take Dawn farther south to Lake Superior to explore the shoreline, but that adventure would need to wait for another visit.

She opened her eyes and took a long look at the lake before continuing across the grassy incline to her cabin. A full afternoon of typing notes on her laptop lay ahead of her before she and Taiku would go into town to send the file to Clark. She consoled herself thinking that she'd forget about all she'd given up by her decision to stay behind as she immersed herself in sorting through the evidence and getting her thoughts in a semblance of order. Thomas Faraday might very well be the killer, but God knew there were many other suspects in this secretive little community. Her mind was already cataloguing a list of possibilities as she stepped through the cabin door.

* * *

They waited until Neal saw the cop and her dog drive away from the lodge after supper to gather in the kitchen. The news that Thomas had been taken into the police station in the Soo had them on edge.

"Lots of leftovers," said Shane, turning off the stove. "The cop's niece is gone. Blaine skipped supper because he's sick, and Thomas has been taken in for questioning. No cottagers or town people tonight for supper, even."

"An early evening then," said Petra, opening the fridge. She bent at the waist so that the others had a full view of her rounded rear end. The outline of her thong was visible through the tight fabric of her skirt. She turned to look at Shane with her pointer finger between her red, glossed lips. She slowly pulled it out of her mouth and asked, "What have you got to go with whipped cream, darling?"

Shane laughed self-consciously but wasn't embarrassed enough not to play along. "I should have something in reserve."

"You always do."

"Oh, for god's sake," Martha grumbled. She'd long tired of these two. Petra was always stirring up trouble and Shane was a willing fool. She didn't like to acknowledge her own twinge of envy. "You know we have cherry and blueberry pie. Take your bloody pick."

Petra straightened and turned, holding the bowl of whipped cream. She ran her finger through the cream and popped a glob into her mouth. "I've always been partial to ripe cherries." She set the bowl on the counter and walked with exaggerated hip movement out the door into the restaurant to cut a slice of pie.

Shane made a sheepish face at Neal. "Sorry about the wife. She's been climbing the walls since being told she can't leave. She's bored, and you know how she gets." He rolled his eyes as he took off his baker's apron and went to hang it on the hook in the pantry.

Neal grunted a response without saying anything, but Martha could tell he was on a slow simmer. She wondered if it might be better for everyone if he did blow. Tell Shane and Petra — especially Petra — what he thought of them. He'd feel better and maybe forgive her for this mess of a summer. She doubted that Shane and Petra were aware of the depth of his rage. He rarely reacted when provoked, and people wrongly surmised that he was a bowl of vanilla pudding. She'd been one of the few he'd let into his inner world and she'd squandered the privilege.

She and Neal silently waited for Shane and Petra to return and drag stools over to sit around the island. The smell of onions, garlic, and turmeric lingered from Shane's earlier food preparation. He pulled out a bottle of red wine and four glasses from one of the cupboards. "Thought we might need this," he said, pouring generous amounts and handing everyone a glass.

Nobody suggested clinking glasses or making a toast. What would they toast to anyway? Martha took a big gulp and felt a rush of heat go to her head.

Neal made no move to pick up his drink. "So why'd you want us to get together?" He directed his question and sullen stare at Shane.

Shane smiled an apology as if letting Neal know that the meeting was Petra's idea. "A couple of things. We want to make sure we're all solid, you know, with the police looking to pin Rachel's murder on someone. So Petra and I thought it might be a good time to put what happened behind us — and I'm not talking about poor Rachel. It's the end of our summer and the uh … misunderstanding earlier in July was unfortunate …" he paused and looked at Petra and then Neal. "But nobody's to blame. Not really."

Petra took a drink and set down her glass. "What my husband is trying to say in his bumbling way is that there was no damage done … well, aside from your hurt ego, Neal, but believe me, what happened was inconsequential in the big scheme of life. Shane's fine with it, so why can't you get over the bit of fun? God knows, we could all use some in this boring outback."

Neal's face reddened and Martha closed her eyes. She was about to get her wish that Neal get the anger off his chest, but knew that it was not going to end well. He spoke in a deadly quiet voice. "The three of you might not care about fidelity and commitment, but I happen to. Walking in on my wife in bed having sex with … another woman is not okay with me. It will never be okay with me, and I'm more relieved than I can say that in two weeks I'll be free of the lot of you." He picked up his glass and gulped down the wine in one go before standing. He kept his gaze firmly on Shane. "I have no idea how you put up with your slut of a wife, but my advice is to get out while you can." The wineglass slipped through his fingers and smashed onto the floor. He stood for a moment looking blankly at the scattered pieces before turning and striding out of the kitchen. The slamming of the front door reverberated through the building.

Martha sat statue-still. She could feel the tears gathering in her eyes and blinked to keep them from falling. Neal had barely spoken after he found her naked with Petra in one of the cottages or in the intervening weeks, making his outburst now even more brutal.

Petra's laughter filled the kitchen, bizarre after Neal's condemnation. "He's such a fucking prude. How did you *ever* tie yourself down with such an a-hole, Martha?"

Martha flinched at her words. Shane shook his head at Petra. He reached over and grabbed on to Martha's hand. "Don't listen to her, cuz. Your marriage is none of our business."

Petra stopped laughing. Her face creased into a livid pout. "What the hell, Shane?"

Martha could barely stand being in the kitchen with the two of them any longer. She shook off his hand and got to her feet. "I'm disgusted with myself, okay? That was the poorest decision of my life, and it's no wonder Neal can barely stand to look at me. I have no idea how quickly you forgave us, Shane. You never acted like you minded at all." For a split second, she saw pain in his eyes and realized the sacrifice he'd made by choosing to overlook Petra's appetites. He had to accept her screwing around or she'd be gone, and he was addicted to her. Hot tears seeped out of the corners of her eyes. She nearly choked on her words. "You both don't seem to get that Neal is my world. I won't be able to keep Pine Hollow open without him. I have no idea what I'm going to do."

She covered her mouth with her fist and ran from the kitchen, through the restaurant, out the screen door, and into the night. She desperately wanted to chase after Neal, to beg his forgiveness, but stopped herself, knowing he'd be in no mood to hold a reasonable conversation. Instead, she forced herself to breathe deeply and calm down before she walked along the road to the path through the woods to the lake. She wasn't spooked by the deep shadows or the dark branches rustling and swaying overhead. Moonlight illuminated the path enough, and anyway, she knew the trail like the back of her hand. She reached the open stretch of beach and crossed the sand to the outcropping of large boulders, climbing across them to the large flat one that overlooked the water. She sat and hugged her knees to her chest, rocking gently from side to side. She needed to think what to do next. How to turn the clock back to the time when Neal loved her. Back to the time when the ache in her chest didn't threaten to destroy her sanity.

Shane stared silently at Petra, shaken by the exchanges with Neal and Martha. His cousin had helped them out by giving him this job, and he was fond of her. He thought Neal a solid enough guy — liked a beer and had a good sense of humour when he felt the urge to talk. Neither of them had been prepared for Petra, he knew that. He couldn't blame Martha for falling under her spell. Petra had a way of getting inside your head. She'd been a free spirit when he met her and she'd said she'd settle down, but he'd learned soon enough that it wasn't in her to be faithful. Her moods swung even when she was on medication. No amount of pharmaceutical drugs would make her believe in monogamy.

He'd slept around, too, eventually tried to make the break from her, but he always found his way back. Most of the time he was at peace with whatever the hell kept him obsessed with her. The odd time jealousy got the better of him, but it was no use letting her know. Better to keep his secrets as she kept hers.

"That went well," she said and made a face. She climbed off the stool and went over to him, linking her arms around his neck and resting her head on his shoulder. He inhaled her scent and the familiar flush of desire made him relax into her. She ran her tongue up his neck and nipped his ear. Her voice was low and cajoling. Seductive. "I can't wait to get out of this place. Promise me, baby, that you won't agree to return here next summer."

"No need to worry your head about that. I can't see us being invited back."

In one smooth motion, she swung herself sideways into his lap so that she was sitting squarely on his groin with her feet swinging above the floor, crossed at the ankles. "Who do you think killed Rachel?" she asked, sliding her hand up under his black T-shirt. She pulled back a bit so that she could see his face. He had the feeling she was looking for signs that he was lying.

"I have no idea."

Her eyes bore into his. "You can tell me if you did anything ... indelicate. I know how to keep secrets and I'm the last one to judge."

This was the closest she'd come to asking if he'd been sleeping with Rachel. She must really wonder, if she was breaking their unspoken code of silence when it came to their affairs. He liked the uncommon feeling of holding power over her. He took his time answering. "I'll let you know when you have cause to worry." He was rewarded with an uncertain look in her eyes that she covered up by leaning in to kiss him. He had questions he could ask her in return, but one hand was sliding under his shirt again and the fingers of her other were working his belt buckle. A few seconds later and he couldn't form a coherent thought, let alone figure out how to get his wife to tell him the truth.

CHAPTER TWENTY-FOUR

Clark's cellphone rang as Jordan handed him a cold beer from the fridge. He checked the caller and said before opening the line, "Give me a sec, Jordan. I gotta take this." He walked out of the kitchen into the hallway and sat on the bottom step of the stairs leading to the second floor.

"Hey, Stonechild. How did your day go?"

"It went. I'm in town having supper." He listened as she launched into her interviews with the Hydro workers. Bottom line: she hadn't uncovered anything helpful, but everyone staying at the lodge had now been questioned so they could check that off the list. He heard Valerie on the landing above him and looked up. She'd started heavily down the stairs, holding on to the banister and treading carefully with each step. He stood to let her by and kissed her cheek as she manoeuvred past him. She'd only just woken up and the right side of her face was red with spidery lines from where she'd pressed into the pillow. She continued on into the kitchen and he could hear her greet Jordan and then the scraping of a chair into position before she sat down. He tried to focus on Stonechild's voice.

"So, any breakthrough with Faraday?" she asked, he realized for the second time.

"Sorry. No, he denied doing more than photographing her that day. We found twelve photographs of her in total and all taken the same day, so maybe he told the truth. He says that he met her by accident one afternoon and she posed for him on the blanket in her bikini. He called the photos 'art.' We didn't have enough to hold him, let alone charge him with her murder."

"Do you believe his story?"

"He's a creepy, self-important old man, but that's not enough for a conviction. Hard to disprove what he said with Rachel gone."

"So back to the drawing board."

"That's about the size of it. Rachel's funeral is tomorrow afternoon at one o'clock at Father Vila's church. Can I meet you there?"

"Sure."

"We can compare notes afterward and come up with next steps. God knows we have enough suspects." He felt weary thinking about the quagmire that lay before them.

Her voice was confident. "We normally go through this despair before a breakthrough. I've just sent a file to you with my notes from today's interviews. See you tomorrow."

"Tomorrow."

He tucked his phone into his pocket and joined Valerie and Jordan in the kitchen. They both glanced at him, but neither asked about the phone call. "How're you doing, babe?" He bent and kissed Valerie before taking the seat next to her.

"Exhausted, but I slept a few hours this afternoon. Jordan set up the furniture in the baby's room."

Jordan said, "The three of you are ready to roll. My work here is done." He grinned and raised the beer bottle to his lips.

"You aren't leaving, are you?" Valerie's voice verged on desperate.

"Not until I hold my new niece or nephew in my hands. You guys never asked what you were having?"

"We like to be surprised," said Clark. Later, he'd wonder if he'd poked the gods.

At four in the morning he woke from a deep sleep, disoriented with his heart pounding. He was lying on his back, the blankets twisted around his legs. He'd been dreaming about a very-much-alive Rachel Eglan. She'd been about to tell him why somebody wanted her dead and he was searching for a pen and notebook. He kept telling her to hold on until Stonechild arrived.

He rolled onto his side and reached for Valerie, but she was gone. He could hear water running and the bathroom light shone through the gap under the ensuite door. He got out of bed and crossed the floor. It took her a few moments before she answered his knock. She was wrapped in a towel, her face rosy from the hot bathwater. "I'm going to get dressed and then it's time to go to the hospital," she said. "The contractions are twenty minutes apart and getting stronger."

Adrenalin coursed through him like a gush of cold water even as he struggled to shake the bleariness from his head. "You should have woken me."

She smiled and patted his cheek. "There was nothing you could do except worry." She walked over to the dresser and said, with her back turned, "Jordan asked to come to the hospital, too, so you should go wake him up. It's time to get this party started."

At 1:00 a.m. Kala woke for no reason she could pinpoint with images from the day running like a movie through her mind. After an hour of tossing and turning, she gave up on sleep. Out from under the blankets the air was cool, and she slipped a denim shirt over her nightgown before leaving the bedroom. Taiku followed her into the living room and stretched out on the carpet while she stood in front of the picture window watching the moonlight shimmering across the inky-black lake. A breeze had come up since she'd gone to bed, and gentle waves rolled one after the other onto the shoreline. The pine and balsam tree boughs swayed to and fro while the wind rippled the elm and birch leaves.

She thought about going outside but knew she'd never fall back to sleep if she did and would be exhausted working on the case the next day. Instead, she warmed up a mug of milk and sipped it on the couch with her head resting against the cushions so she could see the stars through the window. When she finally felt drowsy enough to give sleep another try, Taiku roused himself from the floor and padded behind her into the bedroom.

Taiku's growls startled her awake moments after she drifted off a second time. Before she could calm him, he'd leapt up from the rug and run barking from the bedroom. She threw back the covers and stumbled after him to the front of the cabin, her heart beating triple time. She skirted around the walls of the room and angled herself to look out the living-room window without being seen. Taiku stopped at the back door, his barks now a rolling growl deep in his throat. The night looked still on the other side of the glass, and after watching the shadows for several minutes she crossed the hall to stand next to Taiku. She listened at the front door before yanking it open and stepping outside. Taiku shot past her, growling and sniffing along the pathway. He stopped at the edge of the woods. She called him back, worried about porcupines and skunks that wouldn't take kindly to a dog interrupting their night prowls.

They returned to bed, but she was now too on edge to fall back to sleep. Taiku wasn't a dog that barked at shadows or stray animals. For the first time she wished that she'd packed her service revolver.

The darkness was lifting and the birds had started their morning wakeup calls when she finally fell into a deep sleep. She woke startled out of a dream with the sun filling the bedroom. Taiku jumped up to nuzzle his nose into her neck and to get his morning head rub. Kala took a moment to shake off the grogginess. She picked up her phone from the bedside table and checked the time. "Oh no." She'd slept through breakfast and had only an hour and ten minutes before she had to be at the church for Rachel's service. She threw off the covers and swung her feet onto the floor. Even without eating, she was going to cut it tight.

Kala slipped into a back pew, her entrance going largely unnoticed since the congregation was watching the choir gathered on the steps to the altar, singing a hymn, the name of which she didn't know. The closed casket was in place on a raised pedestal in front of the altar, a cascade of lilies and roses draped over the pine top. The seats were packed with townspeople including Rachel's class-mates and their parents. She scanned the congrega-tion but couldn't see Clark. Rachel's parents were sitting in the front pew with two red-headed young men who must be their sons. The other two couples with them looked to be grandparents. Darryl Kelly and his parents sat a few pews in front of her. Across the aisle, she located Reeve Judd Neilson and his wife, Elena, sitting with the Bococks. In front of them were the Pine Hollow Lodge owners, Neal and Martha Lorring, in the same pew but with an arm's length of space between them. There was no sign of Shane and Petra Patterson or the Hydro workers. She glanced up as Thomas Faraday slipped into the pew next to her. His defiant blue eyes met hers and she quickly looked away. He sat slight-ly sideways so that she was in his line of vision. She was uncomfortably aware of him next to her although she pretended not to be affected by his presence — meant, she knew, to intimidate.

Father Vila performed a full Catholic mass, beginning with readings from the Scriptures broken up with prayer. He looked pale even from where Kala sat, as if the strain of the day had worn on him. Rachel's brothers each read a passage from the Bible. Then Father Vila took Communion before offering the wafers and wine to those in attendance. Kala didn't file up the centre aisle with the others, but Faraday made his way to the altar, giving her a chance to study everyone without his intense gaze on her. She was relieved when he took a seat in Martha's pew instead of returning to sit next to her.

Father Vila waited until the last person had settled into their seat before he rose behind the pulpit. He raised both arms in a motion meant to bring stillness to the room. "We are gathered here today to celebrate the life of Rachel Eglan," he began. "A life taken from us much too soon. I was lucky enough to get to know Rachel during the time she spent here with her mother, often taking care of our youngest parishioners downstairs in the nursery." His voice faltered and he bowed his head. The silence lengthened.

Restlessness filtered through the pews as the seconds ticked by. Finally, when it felt time that someone surely must step in, Father Vila raised his face and stared over their heads. Another awkward moment and he rubbed a hand across his forehead before resuming his sermon as if nothing had transpired.

How odd. Kala sensed a puzzled relief in the pews. The tension lifted, but she noticed several heads turn with people exchanging glances. Father Vila finished the sermon and the choir sang another hymn that Kala understandably didn't recognize since none of her foster families had ever taken her to church. Afterward, he stood on the top step with his arms raised and gave the closing benediction. The organ burst into song as he walked quickly up the centre aisle with the altar boys trailing behind. Colour had returned to his face, but he kept his eyes fixed on the red carpet in front of him. The casket followed more slowly, flanked by Rachel's brothers, father, and grandfathers. Isabelle and the grandmothers kept pace a few steps back. People stood as they passed by and the murmur of voices and shuffling of feet spread in Father Vila's wake as more people joined in at the tail end of the procession.

Kala exited her pew and fell into step with Greta and Phil Bocock. They didn't notice her and she overheard Greta say, "What was *that* all about? I thought Father Vila wasn't going to be able to finish his sermon."

"He thought a lot of Rachel," answered Phil.

Greta made a noise and began to respond when Phil put a restraining hand on her arm. "Good afternoon, Officer," he said. "Such a sad day."

"It is. It looks like most of the town is here."

"Everyone knew Rachel."

"Will you be joining us for tea and sandwiches in the hall downstairs?" asked Greta.

"Thank you, but I have a phone call to make. Perhaps later."

They parted ways in the foyer and Kala stepped outside in time to see the Eglan family and Father Vila getting into two cars that would follow the hearse to the graveyard. Owen Eglan nodded at her after he helped Isabelle into the passenger seat. He got in the other side and the procession made its way slowly down the drive and onto the highway.

Kala walked down the steps and around the corner of the church where she could watch people coming and going without being noticed. She kept one eye on the church doors as she pulled her cellphone out of her pocket. She'd turned off the volume during the service and reset it. A quick glance let her know that Clark hadn't tried to reach her. "What the hell is holding you up?" she asked out loud before clicking on his phone number. The call went straight to voicemail. She left a message and scrolled through her other messages. Nothing from Dawn or Gundersund. She shoved the phone back into her pocket.

With no Clark to divvy up the surveillance, she could go downstairs for tea and mingle with the townspeople or she could wait near the main doors and catch them on their way out. Her stomach rumbled with hunger. The promise of a hot cup of tea and a sandwich made the decision easy. She took a step away from the church wall, but immediately drew back as far as she could into the shadows. Darryl Kelly was standing at the top of the stone steps next to a girl who looked the same age. Kala remembered seeing her in line for Communion. Short brown hair, a pixie face and a pear-shaped body. Average height. Her eyes were red from crying. She started down the stairs ahead of Darryl and he called for her to wait. He caught up on the walkway and grabbed on to her arm.

"You've got it all wrong," he said.

She spun around to face him. "She told me that you wouldn't leave her alone."

"I never would have hurt her."

"How do I know that?"

"Because I wouldn't. She was seeing somebody else."

"Yeah, right. Who?"

"She wouldn't tell me."

"Probably so you'd leave him alone … *if* he even existed."

Darryl was silent and the girl shoved him hard with the palm of one hand. "You're such a loser, Kelly. Leave me alone or I'll tell everyone that Rachel was scared of you."

Darryl backed away from her. His face turned blotchy red with anger. "You're the fucking loser. Rachel hated your guts." He turned and leapt up the steps, letting the church door swing shut behind him.

Kala stepped out from the wall, startling the girl, whose expression of surprise turned to one of distress, much like someone caught cheating on a test. She looked from Kala to the church doors and back again. "You're the cop," she said. "Darryl … that wasn't what it looked like."

Kala moved close enough to reach out and touch her. "What's your name?"

"Carrie Blackmore. I'm in Rachel's class. We … looked after the kids together during church service."

"Were you her best friend?"

Carrie shrugged. "Maybe once. Rachel grew away from everyone this year. Me, Darryl, everyone. She changed."

"Did something happen?"

"She never said."

"Do you know who she was seeing?"

"Someone from that lodge? I don't really know."

"Okay, thanks, Carrie. Here's my card with my cell number if you think of anything that might help me to find out what happened to Rachel."

Carrie took the card without looking at it. "Rachel wanted away from this town," she said. "We used to talk about moving to Toronto and getting a place together. I hoped we still could once she figured things out."

"When was the last time you saw her?"

"About a month ago. My parents and I went to visit Mom's family in Winnipeg for a couple of weeks, and I didn't feel like going to church last week … wait, it was July first at the town party. We were supposed to meet up, but Rachel came late and we never had a chance to talk. When the fireworks started, I turned around to say something to her, but she was gone."

"Was Darryl there?"

"Darryl was always hanging around somewhere. Like a creepy shadow you couldn't shake."

"Did you notice Rachel talking with anybody else that night?"

Carrie stood still and closed her eyes, trying to put herself back in time. "When I first saw her, she was talking to her mother and father. They were standing with Father Vila. Rachel stopped and said something to the people from the lodge after that. I can't remember who exactly. Mr. Bocock arrived, and he came over to say hi. I was standing with a few girls from school. Rachel took her sweet time coming to see us, and I was mad about that since we were supposed to be there together." Carrie's lips pushed out into a pout. "And then she left without even saying goodbye. I never saw her again."

"Well, thanks for sharing what you remember. You have my card if anything else comes to mind."

Kala left her and made a trip downstairs to the reception. The room was packed with townspeople standing in small groups, teacups and plates of finger food balanced in their hands. She located the tea urn at the back of the hall and threaded her way through the crowd. The Eglans returned from the cemetery as she was taking her first sip of sweetened tea. By the time she'd paid her respects and met the grandparents and Rachel's brothers, Martha and Neal were gone. She decided it was time to follow them back to Pine Hollow Lodge. Taiku needed a walk before she returned to town to make another attempt at reaching Clark.

CHAPTER TWENTY-FIVE

A white Ram truck that she didn't recognize was in her usual parking spot. She pulled up beside it and looked for its owner as she walked past the main lodge and took the path to her cabin. The heat of the day was fading, but the sun wouldn't set until past eight thirty. The leaves would be turning in early October. One good frost was all it would take to transform the woods into shades of red and gold. She was sorry that she wouldn't be around to see autumn in the northern woods.

She opened the front door of her cabin. Taiku had been waiting on the other side and bounded past her toward the dock. She turned and raised a hand to shield her eyes from the sun's rays. Someone — a man — was sitting on the dock, facing outward to look across the water. She started toward him and stopped when he turned his head in profile. Taiku had reached him and was jumping and bumping his head against the man's chest. He laughed and stood, swinging around to face her.

"Jordan?" She was having difficulty believing that he was truly here. A wave of joy coursed through her, followed by dismay. She quickened her steps and reached the dock, stopping at the end farthest from him. "What are you doing here?" she asked. Her mind was making connections even as she stood breathing in the sight of him. "Is it Valerie? The baby? I haven't been able to reach Clark all day."

"Hello to you, too." The boyish grin crossed his face. The same smile that used to change her knees to Jell-O. He was staring into her eyes as if erasing all the time and distance she'd put between them. "Can I hug you at least?" He opened his arms and she was suddenly in them, head against his chest, hearing his heartbeat. Inhaling his scent. Feeling at home. She broke away first. "What are you doing here?" she repeated.

"Valerie had the baby boy in the early hours, a few weeks early. The little guy had some complications and was flown to Toronto SickKids for heart surgery to fix a valve. Clark asked me to drive out here to fill you in. I've been staying with them the past few days."

"How worrying. Is the baby going to be okay?"

"The doctors say yes, but I won't kid you, this isn't a piece of cake. They should be operating about now, so we'll know soon."

"And Valerie …?"

"Clark flew with the baby to Toronto. Valerie stayed in the hospital in the Soo. I'm going to check on her as soon as I've caught you up on what's going on."

Kala studied him. "Were you planning on seeing me if this hadn't happened?"

"No. Maybe. I wasn't sure. Clark tells me you're in a relationship and living in Kingston. You've got a kid you're looking after?"

"All true. And you?"

"I'm living in Thunder Bay. I own an electrical business and it's going well. Long hours. This is my first holiday in a few years aside from the odd long-weekend canoe trip."

She felt a longing she'd thought long buried. Taiku wasn't helping. He'd wedged himself between them and glued himself to Jordan's leg, his chocolate eyes watching Jordan's every move. She and Jordan had been tight once, as tight as she'd been with anyone. But that ended after she'd left town so he'd go back to his pregnant wife. "How're your kids?" she asked to bring herself back to reality.

"Good. I see them every other weekend and holidays."

"Oh."

"Listen, I have to go, but Clark wanted me to tell you that he'll be waiting for your call at seven o'clock tonight if you can get into town."

"No problem."

"Can I meet you for a drink in town after I visit Valerie? I'd love to catch up."

She hesitated. She'd almost married this man and reconnecting was not something she'd ever considered. The wisest course of action was to say no, and she opened her mouth to say that she was too tired, but he beat her to it. "Of course, you've had a long day and you're in the middle of a case, I shouldn't …"

"I'll be at Mountainview Lodge until eight thirty. Just show up if you can make it, and if not, no worries. I have to eat anyhow."

He pulled out his phone. "Give me your number so I can text you."

Is this how it begins? she wondered as she watched him enter her cell number into his contact list.

After he left, Kala put on her workout clothes and track shoes and took Taiku for a run. They jogged past the main lodge and up the road for a couple of kilometres before turning back. Halfway home, she cut off the road onto a trail that took them to the beach. The beach where Rachel spent her breaks — where she posed for Thomas Faraday's camera.

She took off her shoes and walked the length of the shoreline, enjoying the sensation of the warm sand between her toes. Taiku bounded in and out of the water, never straying far from her. She tried not to think about Jordan, but his visit to her cabin had been a shock. When she'd left Nipigon, she'd closed that chapter in her life and never expected to see him again. His reappearance upset her equilibrium. His eyes made her remember all the intimacy they'd once shared.

She showered when she got back to the cabin and put on jeans and a washed-out denim shirt. She rolled the sleeves up to the elbows, added turquoise earrings, silver bracelets, lip gloss, and a spray of musky perfume. *This means nothing*, she thought. *I'm only catching up with an old friend over dinner.*

She left Taiku eating his supper and drove to Mountainview Lodge in the waning hours of daylight. The season was definitely changing — a coolness in the air when the sun went down that hadn't been there a week before. She preferred the crisp, frozen northern winters to Kingston's fluctuating temperatures. She hated to think about another damp, slushy winter on the horizon.

She parked and entered the rustic restaurant: knotty pine floors in a honey brown, darker stained log walls, softly glowing lamps on wooden tables. The wide-screen television was the only decor concession to the modern era, but happily the sound was muted. She took a seat with her back to the TV facing the entrance and connected her laptop to the Wi-Fi. A cheerful server took her order, eggs and bacon with a side of herbal tea. In her opinion, the all-day breakfast was the best idea since sliced bread.

She checked her watch. Close enough to seven to call Clark. She thanked the server for a fresh pot of hot water for her tea as she hit Clark's number and settled back in the chair. He answered on the first ring.

"How's the baby?" she asked after they said their hellos.

"Holding his own. They say the surgery was a success."

"I'm sending positive thoughts. Are you able to rest at all?"

"I'll try for some shut-eye after we talk. I'm sorry I missed the funeral service."

Kala took a sip of tea. "The service was interesting. I noticed a few things I want to follow up on."

"Care to share them?"

"Nothing tangible." She had to give him something. "I spoke with Rachel's girlfriend Carrie Blackmore and she told me Rachel had changed this past year. She said that Rachel was seeing somebody besides Darryl. Carrie and Darryl had a bit of an argument in front of the church after the service and neither is all that fond of the other. Based on what I overheard, Darryl had been harassing Rachel, trying to get back with her, and she wanted none of it. I believe we can safely conclude that Rachel was seeing an older man, possibly married, although he wouldn't necessarily have to be married."

"Why not?"

"He might have worried about his reputation if he was a lot older than her. Might have been a woman, for that matter."

"Cracky."

"Cracky?"

"Sorry. First word that came into my tired head. Rachel seemed to lean toward men, didn't she? There was Darryl."

"Keep an open mind, Harrison. This is the twenty-first century. Kids experiment."

He groaned. "Fatherhood is going to be a mine-field. I can see that now."

She didn't want to add to his angst and so kept from him the dark place her suspicions had gone during the service. "I'm going to keep digging," she said.

A pause on both ends of the line. He broke the impasse. "Jordan was in touch?"

"Yeah."

"Sorry about blindsiding you. He showed up a few days ago to help prepare for the baby. We thought it best that he know I'm on this case with you."

"You don't need to apologize."

"Yeah, I do. Listen, I'm dead on my feet. Is there anything I can help with on my end?"

"No, get some rest and we can talk tomorrow."

"I'll try to be back to you in a couple of days. If this goes much longer in Toronto, I'll ask HQ to send someone to work with you."

"I like working alone."

He laughed. "I seem to recall."

They signed off and she punched in Gundersund's number. The phone went straight to voicemail. She didn't leave a message, but he'd get a notice that she'd tried anyway. She ended the call and hit Rouleau on speed dial. This time, she was in luck.

"Hey, Stonechild. I was thinking of you not even a minute ago. How's the case going?"

"Slowly. It's ... complicated. The lead investigator had a family emergency so I'm alone at the moment. Have you heard from Gundersund recently?"

"He checked in a few hours ago. He and Dawn are spending one more night in Joliette at the Motel Bonsoir and plan to visit Rose again tomorrow. She's doing much better, apparently. Spirits are higher."

"That's a relief." *He didn't try to reach me.* Kala spotted Jordan in the entrance and raised an arm. "Tell him all is fine here. Say, could you do me a favour, sir?"

"Name it."

"I need to learn more about Father Alec Vila, a priest who works out of the only Catholic church in Goulais."

"I'll get someone right on it. Can you tell me what you're looking for?"

"I don't want to put ideas in your head. I'm after his life and work history and any complaints against him."

"Fair enough."

"So how are things with you?" Jordan was settling into the seat across from her. He'd changed into a black sweater and jean jacket since she last saw him.

"All is well here. Quiet for a change. How can I reach you tomorrow?"

"I'll call you. Would early afternoon give you enough time to track down the information?" She kept her eyes on Jordan.

"It should."

"I'll talk to you then."

Rouleau sat staring at the phone after he hung up. Stonechild's voice sounded odd even if she hadn't said anything unsettling.

He rolled his chair over in front of his computer and brought up the email screen. The team needed a case to bring them together again under a common purpose. Too bad they weren't up north with Stonechild. He thought for a second before assigning the background check on Father Vila to Tanya Morrison. She was adept at searches and had a way of ferreting out information from reluctant sources — and Lord knows, the Catholic Church liked burying secrets as deep as it could.

He hit send and then shut down his computer. His cellphone signalled a new message. Marci was on her way home and would meet him if he was free. He texted her back that he'd be at her place within the half hour. She was leaving for France on the weekend, and tonight he planned to give her his decision about moving with her or staying. He was still waffling.

On the way to retrieve his car from the parking lot, he replayed his earlier conversation with Gundersund and all that he'd said about his relationship with Stonechild.

Life has made her a loner, and she needs space to make up her mind about where she wants to be. Rose is coming up for early parole in a couple of months and word is that she should get it. Dawn will go back with her and Kala will be unburdened. She can slip out of our lives as easily as she appeared. She has to decide what she wants, what will make her happy in the long run.

Rouleau knew Gundersund was right. His words rang true for Stonechild and for himself. Time marched on relentlessly; there were no do-overs. They'd both come to crossroads in their lives and once decisions were made, there'd be no turning back.

CHAPTER TWENTY-SIX

The supper crowd was hardly worth cooking for tonight. Shane had roasted up a prime rib with potatoes and sautéed peppers, carrots, and mushrooms. Martha dropped by at five thirty to tell him that he'd have to handle the dinner guests on his own. Rachel's funeral had taken a lot out of her and she needed to lie down. He'd had no reason to argue and told her no worries. The Hydro workers showed up right afterward, and he served them heaping plates. They ate quickly and left while he was working in the kitchen. Thomas Faraday came in alone soon after, looking like hell. He'd blathered on about the crooked cops and their attempts to railroad him into a false confession before Shane made an excuse and left him alone to eat his supper. He was relieved to find Faraday gone when he checked back twenty minutes later but was surprised at finding his meal only half-eaten.

Petra had not made it for supper as she'd told him she would when she dropped by after lunch. He wasn't surprised anymore by her erratic comings and goings, although she'd been as stable as she'd ever been the last few weeks — since Rachel's death, actually, but he hesitated to make a connection. She could simply be settling down because they were leaving soon. This should be the last week that Pine Hollow Lodge was open for the season, but he suspected the police would keep them staying here until they knew who killed Rachel. All the planned departures would be delayed. Hopefully this wouldn't set Petra off. He'd have to speak with Martha to find out if she wanted to keep the restaurant open for the duration. If so, he'd need to get supplies.

He locked up almost an hour early and cut himself a big slab of roast, added a couple of potatoes, a scoop of vegetables, and poured brown gravy over the works. He brought his meal into the main restaurant and locked the front door before sitting down to eat. If Rachel were alive, she'd be eating with him before setting out for home. She'd been talkative and funny when they were alone, and he missed her the most this time of day. Missed her flirting. They'd had an easy banter that carried into the restaurant until Petra noticed and said something to Rachel to warn her off.

Your wife thinks I'm a threat, Rachel had said when they were eating one of their last meals together. *If she only knew.* She'd laughed before popping a French fry into her mouth and batting her eyes at him until he joined in her laughter.

Did you decide to end the threat, Petra?

He ate quickly, not letting his mind linger on Petra and what she might or might not have done.

If he went down that dark path, he'd have to make decisions, and Martha wasn't the only one worn out today. Better to keep his blinders in place, move on from this difficult summer, and begin anew with Petra in a city where she'd be happier. Where he might be able to talk her into starting a family.

And maybe I should grow a pair and face up to all the nastiness I've been ignoring.

He returned to the kitchen, which he'd cleaned during the slow supper hour. He rinsed his plate and cutlery and set them into the dishwasher; hung up his apron and turned off the lights before exiting through the back door.

An owl hooted in the spruce trees and he stopped for a moment to enjoy the night air. No wind and a clear sky overhead with stars punching through the black. He breathed in the richness of the under-growth and the earth, carpeted in pine needles. A late-summer evening to savour before the colder temperatures changed the landscape. Unlike Petra, he could quite happily live the rest of his life here.

He cut through the woods to their cabin, not-ing Petra's car in the driveway behind his truck, and relief filled him. She hadn't taken flight and left him worried and wondering where she was or whom she was with. The flutter of hope in his chest made him sad for the pathetic man he'd become. This was one of those days when he wished he'd never met her.

The lights were off and he checked the bedroom, expecting to find her asleep, or better yet, waiting for him naked under the sheets. With no sign of her, he backtracked to the kitchen, surveying the counter and sink for traces of a meal. If she'd eaten or had her nightly quota of wine, she'd cleaned up. Unusual but not outside the realm of possibility. He opened the fridge and the half-bottle of sauvignon blanc was sitting in place. Puzzled, he poured himself a glass and walked through the cabin one more time, looking for signs of her recent presence. Followed the lingering scent of her perfume.

He took his wine outside, sat in one of the Adirondack lawn chairs, and leaned back against the headrest. His eyes closed and he drifted off. The minutes ticked by while he let the night noises lull him into a dream state, content to let the day's stress and worries slip away. The crunching of tires on the gravel broke his reverie and startled him into wakefulness. He took a second to orient himself in the darkness before picking up the wineglass and ambling toward the road. He was in time to see the red taillights of a truck pull into a parking spot near the main lodge and he headed that way.

"Officer Stonechild," he said as she stepped out of the cab and slammed her truck door. "You're out late this evening."

Her eyes glinted in the soft glow from the solar lights Martha had positioned in the ground around the parking area. "Not all that late," she said. A pause. "Is everything okay?"

"Of course. Why do you ask?"

"There was something in your voice."

"I'm just waking up. I dropped off to sleep for half an hour or so waiting for Petra to come home. I think I might check the public beach. It's her favourite place to be these days. She might have fallen asleep lying on the sand. She's been known to do that after … well, after imbibing something."

"I wouldn't mind the walk if you'd like company."

He couldn't think of a polite way to refuse and shrugged, "Sure, why not?"

"Let me get my dog. He's been in the cabin a while."

He met her near the road with two flashlights that he'd gotten from the restaurant. "It's light enough once we get to the beach, but it can be hard to manoeuvre in the dark woods."

"Do the townspeople use this beach much?"

"The high school kids have parties here. Some families come for picnics, but like all wilderness areas in the North, you don't have to go far to find privacy."

She was a comfortable person to walk beside on the wide road, the dog bounding ahead and returning every so often to make certain Kala was following. "How long you been a cop?" he asked.

"Going on eight years — about as long as I've had Taiku." She whistled for the dog as they'd reached the path to the beach.

"He's in good shape."

She didn't comment, but bent to rub his side before the dog bounded down the path ahead of them. "Has Petra been upset about anything?" she asked as she followed behind him.

"She hates being forced to stay here. The wilds of Ontario aren't her thing."

"I can't say that I relate." Her voice was wistful. "I miss the woods when I'm in the city."

"I'm with you there."

The path ended and the beach and night sky opened up in front of them. He heard the gentle waves rolling onto the sand. A nearly round orb of moon cast its light on the black water with a carpet of stars as its backup. "Nice night." He turned off his flashlight and she did as well. The dog was off exploring along the shoreline, and they walked straight to the water's edge and stopped to look out at the horizon. Shane turned his flashlight back on and scanned the beach for signs of Petra. He was relieved not to see her lying in the sand, and for this moment, with the cop beside him, he let himself relax. Petra would turn up as she always did with some excuse about losing track of time.

"I'm getting a clearer picture of Rachel." He tuned in to Stonechild's words and swivelled his head to look at her. Her eyes were fixed on his profile. "Tell me if I've got this right. Her mother is extremely religious, and she worked diligently to make Rachel follow in her footsteps, bringing her to church every Sunday. She kept Rachel on a tight leash until this summer. Rachel learned to play along and be the daughter her mother wanted, but this summer she took a job that gave her freedom to become the person she wanted to be. She rebelled out of sight of her parents, pushing the boundaries by carrying on a relationship with someone whom her mother would not approve of, turned away from her high-school friends, and put distance between herself and Darryl, a classmate who'd been more of a placeholder than a real boyfriend."

He thought about his conversations with Rachel. This officer hadn't known her, but she'd somehow figured her out. He nodded, taking a moment to swallow the sadness in his throat at the certainty that he'd never see Rachel again. "I'd say you've got her right. She was frustrated by her mother's constant interference in her life and bored living in a small town. But you missed one thing about her."

"Oh, yeah, what was that?"

"Rachel was smart. Maybe not people-smart because she'd been so coddled, but she read a lot and had big ideas about where her life was going."

"Who was she sleeping with?"

The question stopped him for a second. Her searching stare made him uncomfortable and he looked out over the water. "I don't know. She flirted with everyone. It was as if she was trying to be one of those characters in the romance novels she was always reading on break. Heartbreaking in a way."

"Heartbreaking?"

"Yeah. She was trying stuff out because she finally had some freedom, but she didn't know boundaries. She was like … I don't know, a babe in the woods. I worried what would happen to her when she left home for good."

The dog rushed out of the darkness toward them, splashing through the shallow water. He barked and Stonechild called for him to heel, but the dog barked a second time and disappeared back the way he'd come. "He wants us to follow him. Do you mind a stroll along the shoreline?"

"Not at all."

The sand was hard-packed and damp, easy to walk on, and they followed the water's edge to a bend. "The beach goes on about another half kilometre," he said, "before ending in another big glacial dump of rocks."

"We should head back," she said. She cupped her hands over her mouth and called, "Taiku!" She listened for a moment before putting her fingers into her mouth and letting out a piercing whistle. "That's odd," she said. "He always comes."

"He can't be far."

Several yards on, they could see the dog's dark outline standing in the shallow water. He was facing away from them, unmoving.

"For goodness' sake," Stonechild said. She strode ahead of Shane toward the dog. "Come here, Taiku!"

Shane almost bumped into her. She'd stopped suddenly and was staring into the water. "Stay here," she said over her shoulder and began running. He froze for a few moments before ignoring her order and starting after her. His legs felt like rubber and he staggered the first few steps before gaining control. By the time he was a few metres from the dog, Stonechild had waded into the water and was dragging a body onto the sand. She got the person to higher ground and flipped them over while blocking his view. Shane stopped several feet away, choking on Petra's name as he dropped into a crouch and held his face in his hands. He took several deep breaths trying not to black out.

"It's not Petra." Stonechild was crouching next to him. She rubbed his arm. "It's not your wife."

He raised his head. "Not Petra?"

"No, not Petra."

"Who …?"

"Thomas Faraday. I need you to run back to the lodge and use the landline in the office to call the OPP detachment. Tell them to send Forensics and more police. Let them know we have another death at the beach. Can you do that?"

"My God." He got to his feet and stumbled against her. Her grip on his arm was firm and her strength transferred to him through some magic osmosis. He righted himself and took a step back. "I'll go as fast as I can. I'll give them directions."

He later couldn't remember the run down the beach to the path or his panicked scramble through the woods. He fell twice and ran into a tree but barely felt the pain. The phone was in Neal and Martha's house and he pounded on their door, barging inside without waiting for someone to answer. Neal was pushing himself up from the couch as he entered and Martha was nowhere to be seen.

"I need to use your phone," said Shane, already on his way down the hall. The office was a small room off the kitchen. His subconscious registered an empty wine bottle and one glass on the counter next to a plate with the remains of a scrambled-eggs meal. The office door was closed but the room was empty, and he placed the call while Neal leaned against the door jamb listening and watching him.

"Is Faraday dead?" Neal asked when Shane hung up the receiver.

"Drowned. That cop Stonechild and I found him on the beach. I need to get back to tell her a team will be here within the hour."

"Christ." Neal ran a hand through his hair. "What the hell is going on? Was it a suicide?"

"No idea. Where's Martha?"

"Upstairs sleeping. I'll get her."

"Have you seen Petra?"

Neal's eyes shifted from his own. "She was walking to your cabin about ten minutes ago."

"Man, if you knew what I thought when I first saw somebody in the water." He clapped a hand on Neal's shoulder as he passed by. "This summer is *not* ending well."

"That's an understatement. It's turned into a bloody nightmare. I'm not looking forward to telling Martha about this second death. She's going to think we're cursed."

CHAPTER TWENTY-SEVEN

It was going on 2:00 a.m. before Kala finally made it to bed. Every part of her body ached: her head, her shoulders, her legs. She was so tired that she lay on top of the covers fully dressed and immediately fell into a deep sleep. She woke as suddenly as she'd fallen asleep, light pouring in through the window and Taiku's head resting against her arm. She scratched his head and took a few moments to shake off the grogginess. She turned her had to look at the clock on the bedside table and Taiku licked the side of her face. She laughed. "It's seven thirty. Time for a run, boy?"

The air was bracing, but a few minutes into the jog and Kala was undoing her jacket. The day would warm to eighteen Celsius if the weather report was right. She passed the path to the beach where they'd found Thomas Faraday. Two police cars were pulled over to the side of the road at the path entrance. She didn't stop her run to speak with the officers. They'd share any findings with her, and she doubted they'd come up with anything more at the crime scene anyway. She had a lot to think about and spent the half-hour run going over the evening before. The coroner had pointed out a gash and bruising across the nape of Faraday's neck. "He was struck by something solid before he drowned."

Two murders. Both victims struck with a weapon. Both connected to Pine Hollow Lodge.

She drove her truck back to Mountainview Lodge at nine thirty after a quick shower, with Taiku riding shotgun in the passenger seat. He'd been sticking close by since finding Faraday's body, almost as if he was worried something would happen to her, too. She settled him in the locked truck with the windows open and returned to the same table where she'd sat with Jordan the night before. She ordered the breakfast special before putting in a call to Gundersund. This time, he answered on the first ring.

"Where are you?" she asked.

"Having breakfast with Dawn in Joliette. She's gone to the washroom. We're visiting Rose one last time before driving back to Kingston. What's going on there?"

Kala motioned to the server hovering nearby with a pot of coffee and mouthed the word *tea* before saying into the phone, "The case is progressing, but the lead officer is on personal leave for a few days." She didn't want to worry him with news of the second murder or spend this call talking about the case.

"So, you're on your own?"

"I have support."

She rushed to fill in the silence. "How's Dawn? Is Rose doing better?"

"Dawn has been amazingly stoic. Rose ... I'm not sure. She puts on a good face when we're there but she's still on an IV and not eating. Her lawyer has been working on early parole and looks like he's secured a hearing next month."

"That must give Rose hope."

"You'd think, but depression can be a terrible beast. Fisher's death hit her hard."

"Even though they were estranged."

"Yeah. No accounting for the human heart." His voice dropped. "I miss you."

"I miss you, too." She bit into her bottom lip. She wanted to tell him about Jordan, but not over the phone. "I have to go," she said. She didn't want him to sense that she was keeping secrets.

He took a moment before saying, "Have you changed your mind? Do you want me to bring Dawn back to you?"

"No, it's getting complicated. Could you keep her in Kingston?"

"Of course. Do you want to talk to her? She shouldn't be much longer."

"It's okay. Tell her I said hello. When I get home, I'll take her back to Joliette. I really have to go now."

"Well ... call me again soon."

"I've tried to reach you before. It's hit and miss."

"I'll try tomorrow."

She broke the connection and stared into space, putting away the feelings the brief call had evoked before focusing on her phone and checking for messages. Two waiting. She returned Rouleau's call first.

"Good morning, Stonechild. CTV reported a second death at the lodge."

"Word travels fast. Yes, Taiku found Thomas Faraday in the lake. He was a retired photographer and summer resident at the lodge. The back of his head sustained a blow before he drowned."

"Another murder?"

"Looking that way."

"Are you safe staying there?"

"I haven't felt unsafe. Taiku is with me to raise the alarm if someone tries to get into my cabin, but I'm glad Dawn is away from here."

"Any leads?"

"Not yet, although I'm getting a sense of the people and their relationships. The killer has to be one of them."

"Morrison looked into the priest's background and sent me her findings. Can I forward to you now?"

"Perfect. Thanks and thank Tanya for me."

"I'm sending it as a protected document. Password is *secretSanta*. No spaces. Capital *s* on *Santa*."

"Great."

"Anything we can do at this end?"

"Not at the moment but I'll be in touch if something else comes up."

"You take care, Kala. Call me anytime."

"I will, sir."

She hung up and opened her email. The file was in Word and contained a concise accounting of Father Vila's life and career. Kala skimmed through his childhood and school honours and focused on his years as a priest. Tanya had bolded a sentence toward the end and made a comment. *He's moved parishes four times in five years, the last placement for only eight months in Sudbury. I called the parish and they refused to speak about him. Odd, or usual Catholic stonewalling?*

Kala sipped her tea and thought about Father Vila. Young. Good-looking. Intense. Weekly access to a struggling Rachel. For this was how she saw the girl — smothered by her mother, dragged to religious services every week, obedient until this summer. Living a life of romance through books and poetry. She'd been sheltered her entire life and this bit of freedom had made her vulnerable. Kala considered the many priestly abuses and the Church's tendency toward secrecy and cover-up. A perfect storm or wrongly placed suspicion?

Kala picked up her phone and texted Morrison. *Father Vila has a sister, Sara, who lives in Sudbury. Can you get me her contact info?* She knew Clark had the information but wouldn't bother him.

The server left as if hearing some magic signal and reappeared with her meal. Kala picked up her fork and ate while she waited for the ping of Morrison's message. She checked the internet between bites. Four hours on the Trans-Canada Highway from Searchmont to Sudbury. If she set out now, she'd be in Sudbury early afternoon. The Sault police were handling the Faraday crime scene and getting alibis that they'd share with her later today. She took one last mouthful of eggs and signalled to the server for her bill.

* * *

The drive was uneventful, and she made the trip in under four hours. Memories flooded back and she felt the usual mix of good and bad as she neared the city limits. Sudbury was the largest northern Ontario city with a population topping one hundred and sixty thousand. North of the Great Lakes, its lifeblood had been nickel mining, which had terribly defaced the countryside, and the black rock formations still exhibited the effect of generations of smelting ore. Through regreening practices and improved mining techniques, the city had made great strides in beautifying the landscape and Sudbury no longer looked like the moon — an infamous description that had dogged the city for decades. Kala knew the Algonquin and Ojibwa had roamed these lands for thousands of years before the city was created around the railroad and mining in the 1800s. She herself had lived with a foster family and then on the downtown streets, making friends with the homeless population for a time. Street people she fondly remembered, but years she'd just as soon forget.

She'd punched in Sara Vila's Bayside Crescent address into her phone and followed the directions that took her to an affluent suburb adjacent to Ramsey Lake, a section of town she'd had no reason to frequent in her previous life. Sara's house was a faux-brown-brick split level with a large yard and view of the water. Kala pulled in behind a silver Subaru and shut off the truck engine. She sat for a moment and surveyed the lot. While a substantial property in a great location, Sara's home was one of the more modest houses on the street. For some reason she'd thought that Sara would live simply like her brother, but this impression came from one too many television dramas where the spinster sister lives with her priest sibling and looks after the manse. Obviously, Sara had built a full life of her own.

A Wheaten terrier with a black muzzle and ears greeted her as she stepped out of her truck. Tail wagging, the dog butted its head against her thigh. She was stooped over, rubbing its head when the front door to the house opened. Kala smiled and raised a hand to the woman. She was rewarded with a friendly smile. She started up the path with the dog leading the way.

"Are you Sara Vila?" she asked as she reached the bottom step.

The woman was in her midthirties with straight, shoulder-length black hair and deep-set eyes. She had a smooth olive-skinned complexion like her brother. When she turned her head, there was a purplish-red birthmark extending from jawline to cheekbone that marred the right side of her face. She saw Kala's eyes fixed on her face and self-consciously pulled on her hair so that strands partially covered the birthmark. Her smile was replaced by a cold gaze. "I am. Can I help you?"

"I'm Officer Kala Stonechild from the Kingston Police. I'm staying at Pine Hollow Lodge near Searchmont and helping the Sault police with the recent murders."

"Dear me, I was so sad to hear of that girl's death." Sara's frown deepened. "You said murders. Has there been another killing?"

"I'm sorry to say that a man staying at the lodge drowned as well. However I'm following up with everyone who was at the lodge for supper the night Rachel was killed."

"Of course. Please come in for tea and I can tell you what I know, which I'm afraid isn't much." She looked past Kala. "Ezra!" she called to the dog while opening the door wider to let him saunter past.

Kala followed her into a sunny kitchen with honey-coloured pine cupboards and a dated green backsplash. An oval table under a window was covered in a blue-and-white-checked tablecloth. On the hutch sat a large arrangement of yellow and orange chrysanthemums and white baby's breath next to a Bible. She took a seat at the table and looked out the window at the lake while Sara poured tea from a pot at the kitchen counter.

"You have a lovely home," Kala said as Sara set the mugs on the table before taking the chair kitty-corner to her. She'd sat so that the birthmark was angled away from her.

"It is lovely, isn't it? I've only been here a few years, but feel as if I've finally found my corner of the world."

"What do you do for a living, Sara?"

"I nurse part-time at the hospital, but I also write inspirational fiction and pamphlets. In addition, I manage several websites for various Catholic diocese in Sudbury. I'm busy."

"Do you live here alone?"

"I do now, although I've taken in foster children over the past several years. Babies, usually, before they're placed or return to their parents. I'm child-free at the moment."

"You and your brother Alec are close."

Sara's face beamed as if a ray of sunshine had struck her full on. "He's been my rock and my salvation ... well, next to the Lord, of course." She laughed and crossed herself.

Kala took a sip of tea before getting to the reason for her visit. "What can you tell me about the evening when you and Alec ate at Pine Hollow Lodge?"

"Alec had worked all day, visiting people in the hospital and sitting with a man at the end of his life. We decided that supper out would help him to relax after a long day."

"So, dinner at the lodge was your brother's idea?"

"Yes. We arrived the same time as Reeve Neilson and his wife, and two teachers, Phil and Greta Bocock, from the local high school. After Alec introduced us, they graciously asked us to join them. I knew that Alec would have preferred it be just the two of us, but he readily agreed. He's generous with his time even when he's exhausted."

Her words seemed disingenuous. Alec had easily given up a quiet meal with his sister — her last evening in Searchmont — to eat with people she didn't know. Kala was beginning to get a clearer picture of their relationship. The shy, less attractive sister who was happy to exist in her revered brother's shadow ... or was she? "Did you interact with Rachel Eglan that evening?"

"The young woman who died?"

"Yes."

"She didn't serve our table, although I did notice her. She was chatty and came over to speak with the Bococks mainly. They both taught her at one time. After she left, Greta said that Rachel was timid when it came to team sports and it was nice to see her coming out of her shell. Phil was complimentary about Rachel's writing skills. Apparently, he's been mentoring her."

"Did your brother add anything to that conversation?"

"Oh, yes. Alec said that she was a wonder with the children in the Sunday school and daycare."

"Did he interact with Rachel at the restaurant?"

Sara shifted slightly in her chair so that she was looking out the window. "Not that I saw."

"Your brother moved churches often. In fact, he stayed less than a year at Redeemer. Can you tell me why?"

Sara's head swivelled back so that she was staring at Kala. Her gaze was searching, but Kala didn't look away. Sara's shoulders dropped and she bowed her head. "A misunderstanding. That's all it was."

Kala's heart quickened. Her instincts had been right. "Tell me what happened."

"The young woman was needy and she played on Alec's kindness. He … he gave her extra attention that she misconstrued. The Church thought it best to transfer him to a new parish so that everyone would move on from her … obsession."

"Had this happened before?"

"Alec told me that she wasn't the first young woman to believe herself in love with him. He thought it was the attention he paid them when they came to him for counselling. Alec has the ability to listen and empathize. Many girls don't have that in their lives."

Kala wondered if Sara realized she'd used the word girls instead of women. "Please tell me her name."

"I never knew it. Alec said the fewer people involved, the better for the girl. He felt she'd be embarrassed later when she came to her senses."

"Did Alec speak with Rachel that last evening at Pine Hollow Lodge, even briefly?"

Sara frowned and took a moment to think. "I saw them together in the hallway when he went to the washroom, but they were only passing each other."

"And when you got back to Alec's home?"

"I went to bed to pack and read while Alec worked in his office. I didn't hear him come to bed."

"Neither of you left the house again?"

"No."

"Although is it safe to say that you wouldn't have known if he'd gone out?"

Sara lifted her chin and stared defiantly into Kala's eyes. "And he wouldn't have known if I'd left the house either."

CHAPTER TWENTY-EIGHT

S hane sat in the kitchen waiting for Petra to wake up. Her sleeping-pill container had been on the counter when he returned late from the beach the night before, and she hadn't stirred when he'd tried to shake her into wakefulness. He wondered if it was time for an intervention. She was self-medicating more and more — the prelude to her spinning out of control. She'd never accepted the doctor's bipolar diagnosis. He needed to get her back into the city where he could coax her into seeing another specialist.

There was a rap at the back door and he got to his feet. Neal was standing a few metres away from the cabin looking into the woods. He turned his head. A lit cigarette hung from between his lips and he squinted at Shane through the smoke. "Want to go for a walk?"

Shane listened for a moment to hear if Petra was up but there was no sound from the bedroom. "Let me get my jacket."

They walked down the road and through the woods to the last cabin, where the cop Stonechild was staying. Her truck was gone and she'd never know they'd trespassed. Neither of them said much, in an unspoken understanding that conversation could wait until they reached their destination.

"This is my favourite bit of land," said Neal as he eased into a sitting position on the granite rocks rising up from the lake.

Shane stood for a moment looking across at the far shore and savouring the peace. The sky was that pure, brilliant blue that made him want to get in his canoe and paddle into the endless beyond. He lowered himself next to Neal. "This is as private as it comes at Pine Hollow Lodge. Looks like a clear day ahead."

"Smoke?" Neal held out a crumpled pack.

"Sure, why not."

Neal lit Shane's cigarette with the glowing end of his own before lighting a fresh one for himself. He put the pack into his jacket pocket and pulled out a flask. He took a swig and handed it to Shane. "I'm leaving Martha when we finally get out of here," he said.

Shane paused with the flask halfway to his mouth and absorbed the statement, which shouldn't have come as a surprise. He took a long drink and handed the flask back. "You sure about this? If your decision has anything to do with her fling with Petra, I wouldn't put any stock in it. Martha loves you."

"It might have started with Martha cheating on me with Petra, but my decision's been simmering for a while. I'm restless, Shane. It's not all Martha's fault. Maybe her sleeping with Petra was a symptom of what's wrong between us. All the miscarriages have turned us into a couple I don't recognize. Martha's grieving all the time and I'm losing patience with her. I don't like the man I'm turning into when I'm with her. I've come to realize that we can't go back."

Shane wondered why he hadn't sensed the depths of the man's inner turmoil before now. Neal had gone about the place fixing what needed fixing without complaint. Even his anger at finding the two women together had appeared mild on the surface until that episode in the kitchen. Shane realized now he'd misjudged him. "Does Martha know?" he asked.

"She does, but she doesn't believe I'll follow through. We've been together too many years to count."

Shane inhaled a blast of nicotine and held it in his lungs. He welcomed the burning pain. He watched a loon and her two offspring bobbing in the waves. The young ones were big enough to fend for themselves. He exhaled.

Neal broke the silence. "I can't believe you're staying with Petra. I don't know how you put her cheating aside."

"She's complicated. We're complicated."

Neal rubbed his nose with the back of his hand and shot Shane an apologetic look. "I wasn't going to tell you, man, but I'd want to know so maybe you should, too. Petra was with one of the Hydro workers last night when you walked to the beach with the cop."

"How can you be sure?"

"I saw them … together. Standing outside, necking like a couple of teenagers. Then he took her by the hand and they went inside the boat shed down by the lake."

Anger coursed through Shane's chest and he took time to calm himself before saying, "I don't know whether to thank you for telling me or to punch you in the face."

Neal handed him the flask. "The secrets are killing all of us, man. Maybe it's time to try on the truth."

"Which one was she with?" Shane closed his eyes. "No, don't tell me. I know which one." He gulped from the flask.

Neal sucked on his cigarette and blew three perfect smoke rings before saying, "I think about telling his fiancée up in Thunder Bay, but it doesn't feel like my place."

Shane said, "I don't envy her, pinning all her hopes on a guy who'd deceive her like that." The irony was that he'd pinned his life on a woman who did the same, even if he'd initially bought into the infidelity.

Neal rubbed his temple and gave Shane a knowing half-smile. "If you decide you ever need a break, buddy, I'll be sure to get a place with a pullout couch. My door will always be open."

"I'll keep that in mind."

After Neal left him at the spot where the road split toward his cabin, Shane knew he couldn't face Petra yet. Especially not with a snoutful of rye coursing through his system. Instead of continuing to the house, he got into his car and drove toward Searchmont, knowing full well that he shouldn't be driving. Staying on the side roads, he drove slowly past the Eglans' property, spotting Owen's outfitter truck in the driveway. He made a U-turn and parked. Owen was wheeling the lawnmower out of the garage. He leaned on the handle and waited for Shane to reach him.

"I hear there's been another killing up at the lodge."

Shane nodded. "Thomas Faraday, one of our summer guests."

"Christ. I'd heard it was him but wasn't sure, knowing the way rumours go."

"It's insane."

"The cops suspected he'd killed Rachel early on, did you know that?"

"They didn't have proof to charge him." Shane wasn't sure if Owen knew about the photos of Rachel in her bikini and he didn't want to be the one to tell him if not. "I imagine the police will be looking at connections. Hard to believe we have two different killers on the loose."

"Has to be the same person. Isabelle called from town, and people are scared to bits. Reeve Neilson has called a special meeting with the police to fill everyone in and calm them down."

"What time?"

"Six o'clock at the recreation centre. I imagine somebody's on their way to Pine Hollow to tell you about it."

"I'll make sure everyone knows in any case."

"Good. I'd ask you in, but I've got a list of chores to do before the meeting."

"No problem. I only wanted to see how you're doing."

"As well as can be when your world's been torn apart."

"And Isabelle?"

"She's become a church zealot, trying to fill the void left by Rachel's passing. I feel like I've lost them both."

Shane clasped a hand on Owen's shoulder, not finding any words that wouldn't sound trite and inadequate. "I'll see you in town then. Take it easy, Owen."

Kala received a phone call about the town meeting on her way back to Searchmont. A North Bay staff sergeant would be at the mic, but her presence was requested. She checked the dashboard clock and increased the pressure on the gas pedal. With any luck, traffic would remain light … and she wouldn't be pulled over for a speeding ticket.

The parking lot was already filling up when she pulled in at quarter to six after an uneventful drive. She hurried into the recreation centre and scanned the room. Two uniformed cops were standing off to the side at the front and she crossed the floor toward them.

"Officer Stonechild?" asked the woman who identified herself as Officer Menisha Sharma. She held out her hand and Kala shook. Her dark eyes were friendly and her grip firm. The male cop didn't make any move to greet her, and it didn't take long for Kala to be reminded of Woodhouse back at the station. He looked her over before nodding. Then his eyes dismissed her and he wandered off to speak with the guy setting up the mics.

"The bane of my existence," muttered Sharma, giving Stonechild an apologetic smile. She pointed to a stocky man with his back to the room reading his cellphone. "That's Staff Sergeant Giovanni." He topped five foot six, but not by much, and had a monk fringe of hair above his ears encircling his head. "He's the one who arranged for you to help out. He's a decent man, although stuck with a lot of problems, including budget cuts and a staff shortage."

"Any word on Harrison's baby?"

"The surgery was a success and the baby's doing fine. Hopefully Harrison will be back soon. These murders have come at the worst time for our force, so we're fortunate you've been stickhandling. Come with me and I'll introduce you to the Sarge."

"Officer Stonechild." Giovanni grasped her hand in his bear paw and squeezed. "Thank you for all your work on this case ... well, cases now. Have you any idea what's going on at Pine Hollow Lodge?"

"Nothing concrete, but I'm beginning to unravel some of the relationships."

"Good. Good. I'm sending another detective to work with you while Officer Harrison is on leave. We've got Forensics sorting through the latest scene and will keep you informed. Hell of a thing about the lack of internet and cell service at that place. Like the Dark Ages."

Kala's heart dropped but she remained silent. She liked Harrison and wasn't keen to try to get along with a new case lead, especially if it was the sullen cop taking his seat at the table. Though she wouldn't mind Menisha Sharma if she had to have anybody. "We're working around the communications issues as best we can."

The mic man signalled to Giovanni that everything was ready. Kala turned and saw that the seats had filled, with media taking up the front row. CBC and CTV cameras were set to film.

"Would you like to join us at the table?" asked Giovanni. "I can defer questions to you as necessary."

"Certainly, sir."

She sat in the chair between him and Menisha Sharma, nodding to Reeve Neilson as he took his seat next to Giovanni. Looking over the crowd, she saw the Pine Hollow people — Shane, Petra, Neal, and Martha sitting in the second row; the two Hydro workers, Ian Kruger and Blaine Rogers, across the aisle, still dressed in their work clothes. Rachel's parents, Isabelle and Owen Eglan, were farther back on the same side. A group of teenagers with their parents clustered behind them, including Rachel's ex–best friend, Carrie Blackmore. Darryl stood alone at the back of the room looking like he'd rather be anywhere else. Phil and Greta Bockock arrived together and slipped into empty seats away from the kids. Father Vila was notable by his absence.

All the suspects gathered but one, thought Kala.

Her eyes scanned the audience while Sergeant Giovanni read a concise statement about the active murder cases. He looked up when he finished. "We do not believe the public to be at risk, but we advise everyone living in Searchmont and the area to take every precaution until we have an arrest. Reeve Neilson will now make a brief statement."

Judd Neilson had likely shared a beer with most of the people sitting in front of him, and Kala sensed a relaxing of the tension in the room. He was one of them, and they trusted him. His eyes made a slow sweep of the audience before he started. "As Sergeant Giovanni told you, we don't know if Rachel Eglan's death is connected to Thomas Faraday's drowning. We need to be patient and let the police do their work. I ask any of you with information, no matter how inconsequential it seems, to come forward. Your privacy will be respected. Our deep sympathies go to the families of Rachel Eglan and Thomas Faraday. The police are doing everything they can to bring the killer or killers to justice. We're a good town, a strong community, and we will get through this together." A ripple of applause cut across the room.

Giovanni fielded media questions for half an hour before wrapping up the briefing. He hadn't needed Kala's input since they were revealing little to the public. The truth was there wasn't much to reveal. This had been a public relations exercise meant to reassure the town.

Giovanni called her over before leaving with the other members of his team. "These murders are garnering national attention, so expect reporters to be circling. Officer Harrison was keeping me updated and inputting reports. I'm going to expect that of your new partner and am getting final clearance to give you access to our police database. I'd like you to make it to a quiet place with Wi-Fi late afternoons so we can update each other. Here's my card with my direct line if you feel the information warrants a phone call."

"Very good. Thank you, sir."

"I'm the one who should be thanking you."

It was going on eight thirty when she finally drove her truck out of the community centre parking lot. She hadn't eaten since morning but didn't feel like sitting in a restaurant. She had some eggs and bread back at the cabin and she'd make do with that. Time to call it a day and get home to Taiku.

CHAPTER TWENTY-NINE

Evening twilight had settled into darkness when Kala pulled into the Pine Hollow Lodge parking lot. She grabbed her flashlight from the dash before jumping from the cab and hurried down the path to her cabin, eager to be back with Taiku. Swinging the flashlight's beam toward the lake, she was at first startled and then curious when she saw the figure of a man sitting on the rocks. She tried to picture Jordan's truck in the parking lot but hadn't looked at the other vehicles in her haste. She slowed and started walking toward the lake, tired from a long day and craving time alone. The man stood and she raised the flashlight.

"What are you doing here?" she asked, unable to keep the delight from her voice.

"I had holidays coming and figured you could use a hand. Sergeant Giovanni's made me your sidekick." Jacques Rouleau bent to pick up his overnight bag.

She smiled. She wouldn't be saddled with the unfriendly Sudbury cop. "Let me get Taiku and then I'll catch you up over some eggs and toast if you're hungry."

"Famished. I'm hoping you can let me have the spare room."

"Of course. You can take Dawn's bed, although I have to warn you that it's a bunk."

"No problem. I'll manage the cooking while you take Taiku for a wander. I'm happy for some activity after sitting in the car all day."

He knows I need some space to unwind and recharge, she thought, and the day's worries eased.

A half hour later, refreshed after a walk with Taiku along the waterfront, she joined Rouleau in the small kitchen where he was scrambling eggs and toasting bread. She set out a couple of plates and cutlery, settling into the easy camaraderie that started when they first worked together on the Ottawa force.

"Who's looking after Major Crimes while you're away?" she asked.

Rouleau laughed. "Believe it or not, Woodhouse. He's become a team player over the summer, much to my relief."

"Proving that miracles really do happen."

Rouleau opened the fridge and pulled out a bottle of beer. "I brought some cranberry and soda for you, too, if you're thirsty," he said.

"That'd be great. Thanks." She lit the candles on the table and they took their places with Taiku lying at Kala's feet.

"I could get used to this life," said Rouleau looking around the room. "A simple existence near the water and wilderness."

"It is a draw."

They ate without talking. Kala got up to make tea and returned with two mugs and the steeping pot. "So how do you want to play the investigation?" she asked.

"I'm here to back you up until Clark Harrison returns. You remain lead. Tell me what's been going on."

He leaned back in the chair holding the mug of tea and listened intently while she filled him in on the two murders and the list of suspects. She ended with, "So any one of them could have killed Rachel and Thomas except the reeve and his wife, who were at Pine Hollow Lodge for supper that night, but their alibis check out. The undercurrent of strong emotions running through this community has been palpable. Rachel must have been the catalyst that brought out the rage."

"Any idea if she was involved with someone she shouldn't have been?"

"I believe she was."

"Do you know who?"

"I have a strong hunch. We'll start the day by visiting him tomorrow."

"Don't tell me. I'll sleep on all you've told me and see if I come up with the same person by morning."

She smiled and stretched. "You have lots to think about. I start the day with a jog at first light. Then we can have breakfast at the main lodge and you can meet Shane Patterson and whoever else is around." She stood. "Time for bed."

"I won't be long behind you."

She stopped at the door to her bedroom. "Thank you, sir, for coming. I already feel more hopeful that we'll get to the bottom of these murders." She didn't wait for his response before stepping into the bedroom with Taiku and closing the door softly behind her.

Rouleau took a second beer outside and returned to the rocks at the end of the property where he sat and looked out over the water dancing with sparkles of moonlight. The air had cooled since he was last sitting in this spot waiting for Stonechild and he zipped his jacket up to his chin. He stretched out his legs, drank from the bottle, and looked out at the dark horizon while he thought. Stonechild hadn't asked him anything personal or had questions about anyone else — Marci, his father, the people on the Major Crimes team. She hadn't even asked about Gundersund or Dawn. He wasn't sure what this meant, if anything at all, but he believed the absence of questions spoke to her state of mind. She was untethering herself from Kingston and her relationships. She was cutting herself loose.

He'd read her file. Her life in foster care had been a series of leavings. People had abandoned her, whether by choice or circumstance, and she'd learned not to care. To move on without looking back. He wasn't certain his presence here would make a difference because as far as he could see, she was already halfway out of their lives. Gundersund was giving her space, not wanting to let her go, but knowing he couldn't force her to stay. Was this the best strategy or was he only making her decision to leave easier?

Rouleau sighed and drained the last of the beer. There were no answers to be found looking out at the black water tonight, and sitting on this boulder in the damp was not helping anybody. He stood and turned. His eyes darted toward the forest and the path leading from the main lodge. A flash of white disappeared into the woods and his senses went from exhausted to fully alert. He sprinted up the rise of land toward the trees and stopped at the path's entrance, not seeing anything in the deeper blackness under the canopy of branches. He tilted his head and listened. Some rustling and scurrying, but nothing that sounded heavy enough to be a human. He walked a few paces down the path before deciding the dangers outweighed the risks. Without a flashlight, he couldn't see more than a couple of feet in front of him.

A few moments more and he started back toward the cabin. The long drive and fresh air had taken their toll and he wanted nothing more than to go to bed and close his eyes until morning. If somebody had been watching him from the path, they were long gone, and he wasn't foolish or young enough to give chase.

CHAPTER THIRTY

Rouleau took a seat across from Stonechild and looked around the dining room. The decor was rustic pine, warm and inviting at the same time. The wooden beams and timber were likely harvested from the forests around Searchmont. He could see the attraction to this place. Even the lack of internet and cellphone service was appealing, or would be if they hadn't been working on a case.

Two men dressed in work clothes entered and said good morning before taking a table near the window. Rouleau looked at Stonechild, but she was watching a man in a white apron coming toward them with a full pot of coffee.

"Morning, Shane," she said.

"I'll be right back with your tea, Officer. Lemon zinger okay?"

"Perfect."

He raised the pot in Rouleau's direction. "You the new cop on the cases?" he asked.

"I'm assisting, yes." Rouleau turned his cup over and pushed it across the table within reach of the pot. The two men who'd sat near the window were openly staring at him. "I'm Officer Rouleau," he added, "and you would be ...?"

"Shane Patterson. My cousin Martha and her husband, Neal, own the lodge, and I'm here with my wife, Petra, cooking for the summer season. Well, I'm cooking. Petra's playing at being the lady in waiting." He laughed. "And those two tanned specimens," he pointed to the men at the window, "are Ian Kruger and Blaine Rogers, our Hydro workers. They've been renting a cottage all summer, spending long days in the bush, and are eager to be on their way. We're only a couple of the suspects on your list, although I guess I shouldn't make light." Shane grimaced an apology before saying, "So, everyone in for waffles and sausage?"

Four heads nodded and he filled the Hydro workers' coffee mugs before disappearing into the kitchen. Rouleau waited for Stonechild to take the lead. She looked over at the two men. "You were both interviewed yesterday?" she asked.

The taller, better-looking one answered. "Yeah. Neither of us was alone when Thomas was found and we'd gone straight to supper after we finished working in the bush all day."

Stonechild nodded. "Thanks, Ian. Anything to add, Blaine?"

Blaine rubbed his forehead and took his time answering. "No, we were together the entire time. Neither of us saw Thomas that day or anything out of the ordinary."

The two men raised their coffee mugs to their mouths at the same time and Rouleau exchanged a look with Stonechild. Her eyes signalled that she'd also noticed their unease before she turned her face back toward their table. "Have you got another migraine, Blaine?"

He set down his mug and looked at her. "I think I've got it licked and it starts up again."

"That's too bad."

The kitchen door swung open and Shane reappeared with Kala's tea followed by four plates of food. He refilled coffee mugs and conversation stopped while they dug into their meals. Ian and Blaine finished quickly and they got up to leave. "Our last day on the job," said Ian, stopping at their table. "We're hoping to get your permission to go home by the weekend."

"We'll do our best," said Stonechild. Her expression was thoughtful as she watched them walk across the room and exit the front door.

"What are you thinking?" asked Rouleau.

"They aren't being truthful, but I'm not certain what they're hiding." She speared the last piece of sausage and popped it into her mouth before leaning back and pushing the plate away. "But nobody at this lodge has been truthful as far as I can determine." Her head turned toward the kitchen. "Somebody's entered by the back door. I hear them talking to Shane." She stood up. "I want to ask him a few questions anyway."

"Should I stay here?"

"No, come with me. You're my second set of eyes."

He followed her into the kitchen. Shane was face to face with a woman and they were deep in discussion, not noticing they had company until the woman touched Shane's arm and stepped around him. She was dressed for the woods in a plaid jacket, jeans, and low leather boots, her long hair tied back under a black toque. Deep lines etched into the skin around her eyes and mouth as if she hadn't slept much. Her face was pale as porcelain. "Officer Stonechild," she said.

"Martha Lorring, I'd like you to meet Sergeant Jacques Rouleau. He's driven up from Kingston and is staying with me." Stonechild turned toward him. "Martha owns the lodge and she and Shane's mothers are cousins." She turned back. "I hope we aren't interrupting."

Martha's mouth opened but Shane jumped in before she said anything. "Martha and I were discussing closing up the kitchen once Blaine and Ian leave. We're planning out meals for the next few days. Trying to clean out the pantry, as it were."

"Welcome. I'll bring new towels to your cabin this morning," said Martha shaking Rouleau's hand. She turned her gaze to Kala. "I'm sorry you haven't had a restful holiday, Officer Stonechild. I'm giving you a credit in the hopes that you'll return next year and bring back your niece."

"That's very kind of you. I won't say no. We never got around to canoeing the rivers that Shane recommended. By the way, did either of you see Thomas at the lodge after Rachel's service?"

Shane cut in before Martha. "He came for supper. Sat by himself and I served him. We didn't talk much. I was bummed about Rachel and not in a good mood. Thomas was unhappy and going on about being taken in for questioning. He said he wasn't going to take the fall for somebody else. That's about all I remember because I kind of tuned out his rant, to tell the truth. I went into the kitchen to let him eat in peace, and when I came to check on him, he was gone. He only ate half his meal, so I left the table as it was for a bit to see if he'd stepped out for a minute, but he didn't return. I locked up an hour early, ate some supper, and met you soon after, Officer Stonechild. We both know the rest."

"That's right. You were looking for Petra. Where was she in the end?" Kala asked.

"Around. She didn't really say." Shane looked back at Martha. "Sorry I cut you off. Did you see Thomas that night?"

"No. I was exhausted and went straight home to bed after I stopped by to tell you I wouldn't be working the restaurant that night." She swung her gaze toward Stonechild. "Rachel's service was so difficult. I don't know how you deal with death day in and day out."

"We don't usually know the victim before the investigation, but we also struggle from time to time once we get to know the people who love them. It helps to remember why we're involved and to keep our focus on finding the perpetrator of the crime. I've found that this is the best way to help the family heal."

Her answer was met with silence. Stonechild half-turned to look at Rouleau. "We'll be on our way but will return for supper."

Shane cleared his throat. "Good to know. I'm making hunter chicken."

"In the meantime, I'll put the fresh towels in your cabin," said Martha. "I'm also going to change the sheets today if that's okay."

"Go ahead," said Stonechild. "We'll be gone a while."

They left Taiku in the cabin and took Stonechild's truck. She seemed preoccupied and Rouleau didn't interrupt her silence. He picked up a signal on his cellphone a couple of miles away from the lodge and checked messages while she drove. She hadn't said where they were going but he knew the day would unfold as it should. This was her show and he would only assist when asked.

They'd been driving a while down a main road lined in conifer trees, and when he looked up from replying to a message, she'd slowed and was signalling to pull into a church parking lot. "I think Father Vila could be the man Rachel was seeing secretly. He had opportunity certainly and he's attractive and charismatic. I visited his sister in Sudbury yesterday and she admitted that the Church moved him because of allegations by a young parishioner's family that he'd been inappropriate with their daughter."

"What clued you in to him?"

"His distress leading Rachel's service seemed out of proportion. Also, many people said that her mother forced her to go to church every week. Rachel was quietly rebellious and romantic. Father Vila was off limits, which I believe would make him even more attractive to a girl like Rachel. Anyhow, if I'm right, the trick is going to be getting at the truth. He has a lot to lose."

"Judging from past trespasses, the Church might move him again to keep his silence. He could live with that, I imagine."

"Unless he killed her."

"You're right. Even for the Catholic Church, that would be a game-changer."

"You'd think."

She parked near the front entrance, and they entered the church. Stonechild listened for a moment before pointing toward the stairs. "He's probably in his office."

The middle-aged woman at reception let Father Vila know of their arrival before she led them into his office. Rouleau took a seat next to Stonechild, a little off to the side, leaving her the chair directly across the coffee table from the priest. He'd been typing on a laptop when they entered. He set it down next to him on the couch.

"Would you like Ethel to bring coffee or tea?" he asked.

"No, we've had our fill at the lodge, but thank you." Stonechild leaned forward.

Rouleau took a glance around the room. Sunlight streamed through the high windows and the space was pleasantly crowded with comfortable, well-worn furniture, including a scarred oak desk sitting atop a faded green carpet. Bookcases overflowed with religious works while classical music played softly from an antiquated sound system. A lit candle on the coffee table filled the room with a spicy scent that Gundersund would be choking on by now if he were here. Rouleau smiled at the thought before focusing his attention on Father Vila. Stonechild's description was accurate: thirties, strong facial features with attentive eyes, and shining dark hair that flopped across one eye. Good-looking in a Heathcliff sort of way. As Rouleau watched, the priest reached up absent-mindedly to push the strand of hair to one side, positioning himself on the couch to answer questions. Dressed entirely in black with a white collar as the only touch of colour, he seemed one with the long line of holy brothers who'd gone before him.

"I met with your sister Sara in Sudbury yesterday," began Stonechild. Rouleau could see by the resigned expression on his face that Father Vila already knew of her visit. Stonechild had been studying his face, too, but remained unflustered. "What is the name of the girl who accused you of improprieties that the Church believed serious enough to move you to this parish?"

"I can't tell you for privacy reasons."

"We will find out with or without your help, you must know that. Were her allegations true, Father Vila?"

Silence. "No."

"You appear uncertain."

Father Vila closed his eyes. "I was kind to her. She was having trouble at home and my door was always open. She came to believe that we had some kind of relationship." He opened his eyes and stared into Stonechild's. "I blame myself for giving her that impression."

"How close were you to Rachel Eglan?"

"She worked with the children downstairs during service. I'd see her sometimes after Mass on my way to my office when I stopped in to see the kids."

"Isabelle is very religious. Did Rachel share her mother's devotion to the Church?"

Father Vila laughed. "I'm afraid not." He paused. Let his mouth tighten into a straight line. "Isabelle is devout and wanted Rachel to embrace the Church as she did. She loved her daughter."

"Was this difficult for Rachel?"

"She tried to please her mother."

"Did you ever privately counsel Rachel?"

"You mean see her in my office alone?"

Stonechild nodded. "Or somewhere else. The location isn't important as much as you meeting her alone."

Vila shifted and Rouleau could see his discomfort. Stonechild said softly, "Now is the time to be honest, Father. We won't be able to ensure your privacy if you are not open with us now. I know the Church default is secrecy and evasion, but Rachel's family needs to know why she died … and believe me, we will find out."

Father Vila stared into her eyes and must have seen something that worried him. He looked down at his hands folded in his lap. "Rachel was a lamb of God and I am a shepherd. Why would I hurt one of my flock?"

"Perhaps you loved Rachel."

"I loved her as a child of God."

"Did this include physical touching?"

"Do I need a lawyer, Officer Stonechild? Are you accusing me of molesting that poor child?"

"I've accused you of nothing." Her voice remained calm. "I'm only seeking the truth."

Rouleau kept his gaze steady on the priest. A battle appeared to be raging within him. Nobody could feign the pain on his face, the sorrow in his eyes. He opened his mouth. Closed it. Rubbed a hand across his face.

"You were barely able to carry on during her service. You must have had a strong connection to her."

Father Vila pursed his lips together and gave the faintest of nods. "I failed her."

"Were you having a relationship with Rachel?" Stonechild's voice had dropped, seductive with kindness, inviting him to unburden himself.

His eyes were drawn to Stonechild's dark, intense gaze as if she held the key to his peace of mind, and he opened his mouth to speak at the same time as the door to his office banged against the wall. Their heads turned. A flustered Ethel had barged into the room. Her face was flushed and her voice was filled with urgency. "Cardinal Croquette is in the chapel. He cannot be kept waiting."

Father Vila bowed his head, whatever he was about to reveal put away. He took a deep breath. "I'm sorry, officers, but I cannot keep the cardinal waiting. He's driven from Montreal and has limited time." He stood and made the sign of the cross. "Go with God," he said before following Ethel from the room. Stonechild made no effort to stop him.

"You almost had him," said Rouleau.

"I know. He was so close to telling us the truth." She sighed and stood. "Let's go to Mountainview Lodge and call in for the results of Thomas Faraday's autopsy. We can check the case folders to find out if the interviews after his murder provide any new information. As an added incentive, they serve decent coffee that you can drink while we plan our next moves, including another approach to get the good Father to bare his soul."

CHAPTER THIRTY-ONE

Shane returned home after he finished serving breakfast and sat reading the newspaper while he waited in the kitchen for Petra to wake up. They hadn't spoken more than a few words to each other after his search for her on the beach. The search that ended with Stonechild finding Faraday's body in the lake. He continued to relive the panic of that moment. He needed to confront her about where she'd been that night and get himself out of this downward spiral.

He'd completed his distracted perusal of the news when Petra finally started moving around in the bedroom. He got up to make a fresh pot of coffee and waited while she showered and dressed. Her slow entry into the kitchen felt like stalling, but he was willing to be patient. This time, he was going to get the truth out of her.

"There you are, darling," she said. She walked over and wrapped her arms around his chest from behind, resting her head against his. He closed his eyes and inhaled the light scent of her shampoo.

She rounded the island and poured two cups of coffee. "Sorry I missed breakfast. How did it go?"

"Numbers are hardly worth cooking for. I thought you'd be by for supper last night."

She stretched so that her white T-shirt showed off the full roundness of her breasts. She smiled at him as she picked up the coffee mugs and crossed to where he sat. She pushed one mug in front of him and sat facing him across the counter. "I planned to eat with you last evening but lost track of time. Did you miss me terribly?"

"Did you lose track of time the night Thomas Faraday died, too?"

Her gaze sharpened as she looked him over. Her smile disappeared. "What is it, Shane? Are you accusing me of something nefarious?"

"Have you been getting it on with Ian Kruger?"

"Does it matter?"

"Yeah, it matters. I thought we were finally starting to get somewhere with our relationship, but you can't stay faithful to anyone, can you? All you care about is your next lay."

"You've never acted jealous before when I sleep with someone else. You know that I'll always come home to you. I've never stopped you from sleeping with other partners as long as we don't lie about them when asked. I didn't tell you about Ian because lately I've had the feeling that hearing about my trysts upsets you."

Weariness filled him. "This way of living isn't enough anymore."

"Being stuck in this bush camp is getting us both down. We'll get back to normal when we're in our own apartment in a city somewhere. This summer will become only a bad memory."

"I thought if you got your medication straightened out, you'd settle down with me. Have a few kids. Get a house."

"You can't be serious?"

"I was dreaming. You aren't capable of having a real family."

She squirmed in her seat. "I don't want to be saddled with kids. You can't say that I ever lied to you about that."

"I know." He looked into his full cup of coffee cooling in front of him. He didn't feel as if he could keep any of it down. He lifted his head. "I think we need to separate for a while when we leave here."

Her chin jutted out like it did when she was being stubborn. "Okay. If that's what you want."

He thought she'd put up a fight. Her easy acceptance made him even more miserable. Made his decision harder. They'd been together since high school and he'd always looked after her. "You can live with Martha if you need a place to stay. She and Neal are on the rocks, too."

Petra scowled. "I guess she hasn't forgiven him for sleeping with Rachel."

Shane took a moment to comprehend her words. "What are you saying?"

She dipped a finger in her coffee before putting it into her mouth. She chewed on the nail, then slowly dropped her hand to hold on to the mug handle.

"I saw them together. They'd go for walks on her afternoon breaks."

"A walk is a far cry from sex."

"He was getting revenge on Martha for sleeping with me. Classic male ego." She snorted. "What else would they be doing alone in the woods?"

"Did you tell Martha about these sightings?"

Petra hesitated. She lowered her eyes. "Why would I? I'm not vindictive."

He was thinking about living without her and answered distractedly, "No, you're not." He fiddled with the mug handle. "I'm sorry, Petra. I know that I'm shifting on you midstream, but I can't do this anymore."

"Don't worry yourself. I'll survive."

Shane couldn't tell if the bitterness in her voice came from hurt or anger. He sat silently while she got up and brushed past him. He didn't make any move to stop her from putting on her jacket and shoes and he didn't go running after her when he heard the front door slam. There were too many times he'd done just that. His world was falling apart and all he could do was stare into his coffee cup and let the wave of emptiness spread through him like so much dead air. Yet he knew that breaking free of her was his only path toward salvation. The only way to find himself again.

"I want you to meet all the players," said Stonechild when she closed her laptop. "We'll stop at Owen and Isabelle Eglan's place on our way back to Pine Hollow."

Rouleau looked up from his phone. "Great idea. I'll be better able to help you if I've met everyone."

Stonechild was standing and putting on her jacket when a man appeared in the doorway. Her entire body went still before she glanced at Rouleau and put her arm into the second sleeve. "I should go speak with this guy," she said. "Are you okay for a minute?"

"Sure," said Rouleau without giving him more than a passing glance. He lowered himself back into the chair and reopened his phone. "Take whatever time you need."

Rouleau sensed a tension between Stonechild and this man without either speaking a word. Was he the reason Stonechild seemed further out of reach than she ever had before? A message beeped on his phone and he was glad for the distraction. He opened a text from Gundersund.

Kala tried to reach me but was working in yard. Tell her all well. Dawn downtown at art studio. Hope case moving along. Sent note to Kala also to be sure one of you gets this. Trouble connecting. Will talk soon.

Rouleau tucked his phone away and waited for Stonechild to return, uncertain if he should delve into her personal life out of concern for Gundersund or let things unfold. When she called to him from the doorway ten minutes later, her face revealed nothing. She was silent during their walk to her truck. He felt the awkwardness growing and wasn't certain if she sensed the chasm as well or was too immersed in her own thoughts to notice. He put on his seat belt and looked over at her in profile. "Was that fellow part of the case?"

"No." She turned on the engine before putting her hands on the steering wheel and returning his stare. "His name's Jordan Harrison. He's Officer Clark Harrison's brother, whom you remember is the lead on this case. Clark's new baby had heart surgery, and Jordan came to tell me that Clark should be back on the job in another day or two since the baby's responded unbelievably well to the treatment. Looks like you'll be able to go home sooner than anticipated." She smiled and put the truck into gear.

Rouleau bit back more questions. She'd shared as much as she'd wanted to, and this was her story to tell … when she was ready. She was not a woman who could be pushed into confidences. He knew her well enough to understand that asking would only make her defensive.

They drove down a side road to the Eglans' home. A middle-aged man with a red beard whom Stonechild identified as Rachel's father, Owen Eglan, was working in the yard, and he walked over to greet them, leaning on his rake while Rouleau and Stonechild got out of the truck.

"How are you today, Mr. Eglan?" asked Stonechild.

He pushed his ball cap back on his head. "Getting by."

"This is my partner, Jacques Rouleau. We're here to update you and to ask a few questions."

"Come inside, then. Isabelle's home."

Owen led them into the living room where Isabelle sat next to a table with a framed photo of

Rachel surrounded by burning candles. She looked up from her knitting but didn't comment on their arrival.

"Take a seat," said Owen. "Can I get you anything? Tea? Coffee?"

"Thank you, but nothing for us."

They sat next to each other on the couch. Rouleau didn't know what Isabelle Eglan had looked like before her daughter's death, but he imagined her greyish pallor and haunted eyes were a result of the tragedy. Her shirt hung loosely on her bony frame as if grief was wasting her away. Owen cast several glances at her but didn't say anything before taking the easy chair. He took off his ball cap and twirled it around and around in his hands. His red hair was matted with sweat and an indent from the cap rimmed his forehead.

"You were both at the town meeting," began Stonechild. "An autopsy is being done on Thomas Faraday, and Forensics is going through what they found at the scene."

"Did they find any evidence of who's doing this?" asked Owen.

"I can't say yet, but they will be thorough."

The clicking of Isabelle's knitting needles stopped. "Do you think this man's death is linked to our Rachel's?" she asked.

"We're certainly considering the possibility." Stonechild paused. "Have you remembered anything about Rachel's actions during the last few months? Did she mention dating anybody new or was she talking about one person more than the others at Pine Hollow Lodge?"

Owen and Isabelle looked at each other. Owen cleared his throat. "Isabelle and I have done some soul searching since ... well, since Rachel's death. We've come to realize that she wasn't sharing everything with us about her life this summer. She lost interest in Darryl Kelly after she started working at the lodge and she began spending more time alone in her room when she was home. Rachel kept going to church with Isabelle, but she wasn't interested in religion, would you not agree, Isabelle?"

The needles resumed their steady clicking. "Yes."

He continued. "Rachel could have had a secret life going on this summer. We think she lied to us about her schedule and where she was after work. Isabelle spent a great deal of time at church and volunteering in the community, and I worked long hours, so we weren't always up to date on her timetable. However, she'd always been truthful before, and we had no reason to doubt what she told us."

Stonechild said, "Thank you for sharing this. I know from personal experience that Rachel's behaviour appears that of a normal teen trying to find her place in the world. The breaking away is as tough on them as on the family."

Isabelle lowered her knitting and raised exhausted eyes. "I saw her with Father Vila in his office. He ... they were sitting so close on the couch and he had his hand on her leg. They were both flushed and I thought ... I asked what they were doing and he stood up and said that Rachel was confiding in him about a problem she was having with Darryl. I wanted to believe him."

"But you weren't certain?"

"Her shirt was rumpled with the top two buttons undone and she fastened them when she thought I wasn't watching her. I asked her later what was going on, and she said that I should be pleased that she was taking an interest in the Church. Wasn't that what I wanted? She was angry with me and being sarcastic, so I let the matter drop. I should have made her tell me."

Owen was sitting motionless, his elbows resting on the chair arms, his hands bunched into fists. His voice was incredulous. "Father Vila was seducing our daughter and you didn't think to tell me?"

"I wasn't sure, and it seemed so horrible even to doubt him. I just … I just forgot about it."

"Horrible? You think that was horrible? What about what he was doing to Rachel? You and your damn religion. I should never have let your obsession take over our lives. It drove Rachel away from us and now it might have killed her." Owen stood and charged toward the door.

"Where are you going?" cried Isabelle.

He stopped and turned, glaring at her. "To sort out this priest. Somebody has to make him pay for what he did to our girl."

"Hold it right there," Stonechild said, and Rouleau cut off Owen's path. "We don't have proof of anything. Father Vila could in fact be innocent."

"Then I'll force the truth out of him."

"Let us handle this, Owen. Your interference could jeopardize the investigation. We will get to the bottom of what was going on, but we have to be strategic in how we go about it." Stonechild was on her feet.

"Nothing good will come of you going after Father Vila in anger," said Rouleau, and he stared down Owen until he stopped trying to push past him. Rouleau put his hand on Owen's arm. "We will find out what happened." He felt Owen's anger deflate under his touch.

Owen put his ball cap back on his head and tucked his chin into the collar of his jacket, sliding his hands into the pockets. With head lowered, he said, "Make sure you do." He tossed over his shoulder, "I'll be outside working in the yard."

"Thanks, Owen," said Rouleau, and he stepped aside to let him pass.

Stonechild met Rouleau's eyes. Hers were bottomless black and brimming with steely determination. She looked back at Isabelle. "We'll be on our way. Please don't share this information with anybody else, especially Father Vila."

Isabelle picked up the ball of wool that had fallen onto the floor. "I don't want to believe any of this. Father Vila has always been so good to us."

"Sometimes people are not what they appear."

"I don't know who to trust anymore." Isabelle returned Stonechild's stare. "You can rest assured I won't tell Father Vila anything. His fate is in God's hands now."

Stonechild nodded at Rouleau, and they turned to leave. The fierce clicking of knitting needles followed them down the hallway and out of the house.

CHAPTER THIRTY-TWO

Rouleau studied Stonechild as she put the truck into gear. "Are we returning to talk to Father Vila?"

"He's not going to admit to anything."

"Probably not. You almost had him talking though before his secretary interrupted." .

She smiled. "Are you attempting to gently lead me somewhere, sir?"

"I'm only going over options." He smiled back. "Like any decent partner would."

"It's hard to think of you as my backup." Her eyes went from amused to worried. "I feel as if whatever bad mojo is gripping this community is picking up momentum. Do you feel it, too?"

"I don't know the players as you do and I'm not as perceptive as you are. I wish I were — but if you're sensing some impending catastrophe, I know better than to doubt the veracity."

"I'm convinced that somewhere in Pine Hollow Lodge is the key to Rachel and to both murders. Rachel Eglan and Thomas Faraday stirred up strong emotion that resulted in someone lashing out. What do you say we head back to the lodge and see if we can get a better handle on the relationships? The priest isn't going anywhere ... not yet anyway."

"Lead on."

Taiku was waiting at the door and Stonechild took him for a run while Rouleau settled in at the counter with the case file and a bottle of beer. He read through Rachel's forensics report and all the witness statements, making notes as he went, looking for inconsistencies. Lies. Half-truths. Hoping he brought fresh eyes to Stonechild's and Harrison's observations. So far, he'd only spoken with Martha and Shane, Father Vila, and Rachel's parents, but he had a good picture of the other suspects from Stonechild's objective, concisely worded comments. He'd learned to read between the lines from her reports on other cases. She never wrote anything without careful consideration.

He stretched and checked his watch. An hour had passed since he started reading. Stonechild should have returned by now. He shut the folder and slipped into his shoes. There was no sign of her or Taiku along the shoreline so he hiked through the woods toward the main lodge. He glanced into the parking lot on his way to the road. Stonechild was leaning against the back of a stranger's truck with Taiku lying on the grass nearby. The same man she'd spoken with at the restaurant was standing an arm's length away from her, his back to Rouleau, and they were deep in discussion. The man moved aside when she looked over and waved in his direction. Rouleau started toward them.

"Sorry I'm so long getting back," Stonechild said. "Jordan downloaded a file that Clark sent to him and brought the material over to us. It's additional information that was unearthed from the background checks on the people who were here the night of Rachel's death."

Rouleau held out his hand and Jordan grabbed on in a firm handshake. They locked eyes for the briefest of moments, sizing each other up without needing to speak. Rouleau was sorry to admit that he liked the person he glimpsed behind the intelligent brown eyes.

"I'll be on my way then," Jordan said. "Clark should be back tomorrow, and I'll stand down. He said the Faraday autopsy is this afternoon so he should have more to share."

"Thanks for all your help," said Stonechild.

Rouleau left them and started back toward the main road. He waited for Stonechild at the path entrance. "Seems like a good guy," he said when she fell into step behind him on the path.

Her voice was low, no telltale emotion. "He is."

The wood floor was littered with rotting leaves and pine needles, and shafts of sun filtered through the boughs overhead. The shifting shadows and silence felt both embracing and ominous, and Rouleau shivered inside his cotton shirt. Taiku startled him as he bounded ahead of them, brushing past his leg. He was glad when they emerged into the bright clearing.

"I'll put on a pot of tea and we can go through this stuff," said Stonechild. "I'm hoping a few more of our band of suspects will be at supper."

She strode ahead into the cabin while he lingered outside, looking at the lake to give her a moment to herself. The water was rippling gently against the shore and reflected the satiny blue sky. Woods encircled the bay, dark treetops lining the horizon. It wouldn't take but a minute to leave the stretch of land occupied by the lodge and be in complete wilderness. Stonechild was at home in this world. He thought about the body language he'd witnessed when he'd found her with Jordan and knew instinctively that there was a deep connection between them. Stonechild was grappling with a decision not unlike the one he had to make with Marci. Yet he and Marci had not formed as strong a relationship as he'd had with his ex-wife, or even as serious as whatever was going on between Stonechild and Jordan. He'd be sad to let Marci go to Paris without him, but he wouldn't be devastated. He suspected from the couple of times he'd seen Stonechild with Jordan that she had more at stake.

When he entered the cabin five minutes later, the tea was steeping, and the files were organized on the coffee table in the living room. Stonechild's face was devoid of conflict or emotion of any kind. He took a seat on the couch next to her, added sugar to the mug of tea she'd poured for him, and began reading.

"Petra and Shane married out of high school. They both grew up in Sudbury," Stonechild said after a few minutes of silence. "They've led a nomadic life and spent the last several years out west. Shane worked in the oil fields when he wasn't cooking in restaurants."

Rouleau raised his head. "What did Petra do for work?"

"She danced in strip bars, but sporadically. Some waitressing jobs. No evidence of being in the porn industry. They moved to Sudbury a couple of years ago. Shane was working in a restaurant, but it closed."

"So, up-and-down income."

"Looks that way. You've got the info on Martha and Neal. Anything interesting?"

"They grew up in Sudbury as well and married in their early twenties. The lodge was in Martha's family and she took it over five years ago when her father died. The lodge had a few rough years when she started out, but it's made a modest profit the last three years. She and Neal own property in Cobourg, which is where they spend part of the winter. They've vacationed the last couple of Januarys and Februarys in Arizona."

"Neither couple has kids." Stonechild flipped through more papers. "No police records."

Rouleau picked up another page. "You had Phil and Greta Bocock checked out, too. Remind me again, who are they?"

"They both taught Rachel and were at Pine Hollow Lodge for supper the night she died. Phil was her English teacher and Greta taught her phys. ed. Phil appeared to fancy himself her writing mentor. The Bococks sat at supper with Father Vila and Sara, and Reeve Neilson and Elena. Clark had a preliminary report done on their work history but I asked for more depth. We already ruled out the Neilsons as they both have ironclad alibis."

"The Bococks moved from Toronto five years ago. They're both active in the community. Greta has a daughter from her first marriage who lives with the father in Toronto. A bit odd, isn't it?"

Kala shrugged. "They might not have wanted to uproot her from her friends and school."

"You're right." Rouleau skimmed the rest of the page. "Their police records are clean, too. Nothing else jumps out."

"No records, as you'd expect for teachers." She bowed her head and shuffled more papers. "The last two reports are on the Hydro workers. Ian Kruger lives in Thunder Bay. He met Blaine Rogers at trade school, as they were both attending the same years. Blaine is from Marathon, which is a small town a couple of hundred miles east on Highway 17, if memory serves. This is their first placement together. Hmm. Ian has two drunk driving charges and lost his licence for six months when he was in school. Clean since then. Blaine's record is clean. They both passed their college course with honours and were hired by Ontario Hydro straight after graduation. The rest of the information is straightforward."

Rouleau picked up his cold mug of tea and leaned against the couch back. "So nothing all that helpful. I know Father Vila is your main suspect, but a priest committing murder is difficult to contemplate. Not outside the realm of possibility, but still unusual."

Stonechild leaned back next to him and put her feet on the coffee table. "What if I've surmised incorrectly and Rachel wasn't having sex with him? Who else is a candidate?"

"Neal and Shane. The Hydro workers. Her teacher, Phil Bocock. We haven't ruled out the possibility that she was seeing a woman. Petra is overtly sexual. There's also Greta Bocock and Martha Lorring. Any one of them has a lot to lose if they were in a physical relationship with a sixteen-year-old — Rachel was fifteen at the start of the summer, making a liaison even more risky for an adult."

"We haven't ruled out the possibility that her murder wasn't about sex at all. Darryl had reason to be angry with her for ditching him."

"And her own mother was losing control of her." Stonechild rubbed her temples. "We're no closer to a solution than when all this started."

"Where do you think Thomas Faraday fits into the picture?"

"He was always in the background, taking photos and watching. His financial records indicate that he was barely scraping by." Stonechild straightened. "What if he knew who killed Rachel and was blackmailing them? He would have had to believe that he held enough cards to be safe from harm."

Rouleau considered the implications. "Quite possibly. He could have tried to weasel out some money and misjudged the person's unwillingness to kill off a threat."

Stonechild looked at her watch and tossed the file she was holding onto the table. "I feel as if we're still spinning our wheels, but maybe we're starting to get a bit of traction. In any case, I'm starving. Are you ready for supper? It's time you met more of the cast of characters now that you know all their deepest secrets."

"I could eat. Hunter chicken, was it? A good hearty meal."

"Shane's an inspired cook. His skills are underused out here in the woods. He could be working at a swanky restaurant in a major centre for a lot more patrons."

"Makes you wonder why he seems content to go from job to job without establishing himself."

Stonechild grinned. "There's a lot about these people that makes me wonder."

They chose a table at the far end of the lodge restaurant away from the kitchen and waited for the others to arrive. Blaine Rogers entered first, still in his work coveralls. He nodded at Kala before taking his usual seat near the window.

"He's alone," she said under her breath, but loud enough for Rouleau to hear. His eyes flashed agreement at this observation, but he didn't voice a response.

The kitchen door swung open and Martha stepped into the room, wiping her hands on her apron, her cheeks puffed with food. The open door released a heady smell of roast chicken, tomatoes, and spices, and Kala felt hunger rise up the back of her throat. Martha chewed as she crossed the space toward them and swallowed before reaching them. She laughed as she caught her breath. "Good evening, officers. You're in for a gourmet treat tonight. Would you like to start with salads before the main? Wine or beer?"

Kala spoke first. "Yes to the salads. Water for me. Rouleau?"

"A beer to wash it down, thanks."

"Coming right up." She smiled and flashed a mock salute before moving across the floor to Blaine's table. He was ordering a beer when the front door opened, letting in cold air and Petra, who fell laughing into the room with a sheepish-looking Ian following a few steps behind her. Petra's coat was open and her white blouse was unbuttoned, exposing her black-lace bra. Her makeup had been applied with a generous hand and a smear of red lipstick bled onto the skin surrounding her mouth.

Both Martha and Blaine turned their heads and stared motionless for the smallest fraction of time before Martha lurched forward and grabbed Petra roughly by the arm. "Are you out of your friggin' mind?" Martha hissed, loud enough for everyone to hear. She pulled Petra down the hall to the washroom while Ian took the seat across from Blaine with his back to the room.

"What's going on, man?" asked Blaine. "I thought you were done with that thaaang?"

Ian said something that Kala couldn't hear and both men laughed.

Kala saw Rouleau's shoulders stiffen and glimpsed a flash of anger when his green eyes met hers. It was gone just as quickly, but she had no doubt about his feelings. Rouleau was not a man who would sit silently by while men made a woman the butt of their jokes.

"It's okay," he said in response to her concerned look. "We're letting this play out. I gather that was Petra?"

"Yes."

They both kept an eye on the hallway, waiting for the women to emerge while straining to hear the men at the next table without appearing obvious. Kala was starting to get out of her seat to check on Petra and Martha when the kitchen door swung open. Shane poked his head into the room. He looked around, his gaze stopping on Ian and Blaine. "Anyone seen Martha?" he asked.

"Washroom," said Blaine. "Should be out in a minute." Ian hunched deeper over the table.

"Tell her she's wanted in the kitchen." The door swung shut and he was gone.

Kala relaxed back into the chair. "They're taking a long time."

"Go check. I'll keep watch here."

She met them in the hallway. Petra's coat was buttoned all the way up and her mouth had been wiped clean, although traces of red still stained her lips, bruised from rubbing, likely with a rough piece of paper towel. When she saw Stonechild, she shook off Martha's restraining hand on her arm. Her flushed face highlighted her eyes, sparkling with unnatural brilliance. Her child-like smile made her look euphoric. *Demented*.

"Offffff .... i ... cerrrrr," Petra screeched, and flung her arms wide as if to embrace Stonechild. "What's shakin'?"

Martha grabbed Petra from behind and pushed her against the wall, stepping around her to face Stonechild. "I apologize for my cousin's wife. She's had waaaay too much to drink."

"No, I haven't! I haven't had nearly enough to drink! I'm just getting started!" Petra's arms flailed, her hands scrambling to get past Martha, but Martha held firm. She shot Kala an apologetic smile and raised her voice to talk over Petra. "I'm taking her home to sleep it off. I wonder if you could let Shane know that I'll be gone a while, so he'll need to serve dinner?"

"Of course."

Martha turned and used her entire body to block and hustle Petra down the hall toward the exit. Petra tried to push past her, arms thrashing wildly and head bobbing back and forth while Martha worked to contain her. The entire scene looked like a comedy skit — as if someone were trying to put a jack-in-the-box back into its container and taking several attempts to squash the clown inside.

"I want to see Shane," Petra wailed. "I want him to know that I can make it just fine without him. The bastard."

Kala looked over her shoulder and signalled to Rouleau that she'd be gone a minute before she followed the two women out the door. Instead of rushing to help, however, she hung back, letting the failing daylight shelter her from their view. They'd reached the parking lot and all the fight had drained out of Petra. She was crying and talking loudly between sobs. "Why is he doing this to me? I've never loved anyone else. He knows that."

Martha was shushing her, looking over her shoulder to make certain they were alone. "It'll be all right," she said. "You'll survive this."

"Like you will with Neal?" asked Petra. "He's such a fool for splitting up with you. I could kill the pair of them. This place is where marriages come to die."

Kala stopped at the edge of the parking lot in the shadows and watched the women start up the path through the trees toward Shane and Petra's cabin, Petra stumbling and Martha holding on to her waist. She couldn't move any closer without revealing herself, but she didn't need to follow them any longer to know that the undercurrents she'd felt running through these people's relationships snaked deep and dangerous. She understood with certainty now that she hadn't imagined the dysfunction hidden behind their guarded interactions.

Had Rachel stumbled in over her head or had she wittingly stoked the passions for her own romantic fantasy? Which one of these people had she angered enough to want her dead? Or was the killer from the wider circle of her life in Searchmont? For now, Kala was content to let the emotions escalate while she and Rouleau watched from the wings. Her detective sixth sense told her that the truth wasn't far from the surface. It was only a matter of time.

She took one last look up the path to check that Martha and Petra had made it safely inside Petra's cabin, inhaled a full breath of the sweet late-summer air, and turned toward the restaurant and Rouleau waiting for her inside.

CHAPTER THIRTY-THREE

Clark rolled over and kissed Valerie on the forehead. She smiled in half-sleep but didn't wake completely as he slipped out of bed and stretched. The baby had been transferred to the Sault Area Hospital the evening before for a few more days of observation, and Jordan had promised to take Valerie for a visit as soon as she was up and dressed. Jordan would spend the day and bring Valerie home when she was ready.

Clark felt the familiar guilt that his long hours on the job often produced, but also a surge of excitement at the idea of being back. He wondered if having a child at home would lessen his obsession with work at all. Ever since his son was out of danger, all he could think about was the murder investigation. *Make that investigations.* He had a lot to discuss with Stonechild and Rouleau, beginning with Faraday's murder.

The morning was warmer than normal but overcast. The calendar turned a page today into September with the Labour Day holiday a few days away. Kids would be heading back to school Tuesday and summer camps would close up for the season. He was well aware that Martha and Neal were eager to shut down Pine Hollow Lodge and head south to Cobourg. He didn't think they could realistically keep them stuck in place much longer without evidence that they were involved in the murders. Even if he believed someone at the lodge had to know something.

Clark had a quick shower and dressed in his uniform. Jordan was in the kitchen with a pot of coffee on the stove when he made it downstairs. He checked the clock on the wall next to the fridge. "I'm surprised to see you up this early."

"Couldn't sleep. I thought I'd see you off before I have my shower. How's Valerie?"

"Better now that the baby's this close to home. Thanks for taking her to the hospital today."

"No worries. Have you come up with a name yet?"

"Val's superstitious and wants to wait until we have him safely home." Clark grinned. "I put it down to hormones."

"Whatever makes her feel better."

Clark filled his travel mug with coffee. "Sorry that I don't have time to chat. I'm grabbing a granola bar and I'll be on my way." He eyed his brother as he poured cream into the mug. "Is there anything I should know about you and Stonechild before I meet her today?"

Jordan rubbed the knuckles of one hand across his mouth before answering. "We've caught up on what's going on in our lives, but I haven't put the moves on her if that's what you're concerned about."

"But you plan to?"

"I'd be lying if I said no."

"She has a life down south. You should be prepared for her to turn you down."

"I know." Jordan gave a slow grin that lifted the right corner of his mouth. "But on the other hand, I might just be what she's been missing."

On the way to Pine Hollow Lodge, Clark thought about his brother and Stonechild and the chances of them rekindling their close relationship from a few years back. Stonechild had mentioned seeing somebody in Kingston, but he had no way of knowing if they were serious or not. The woman was even more closed off now than when he worked with her in Nipigon — if that was even possible. She could do worse than Jordan, who'd grown up a lot since becoming a father. He was crazy about her still, and that counted for something. The question was whether Jordan's feelings for Stonechild were enough to win her over after the mess he'd made of things the last time.

He parked and checked that Stonechild and Rouleau weren't in the restaurant before making his way through the woods to their cabin. He spotted them on the dock with the dog and thought they painted an idyllic picture with the morning sun sparkling off the water and a mama loon with her two offspring bobbing in the waves not far from shore. He walked across the uneven ground to join them while the loon's haunting call trilled and echoed off the rock face. Rouleau turned toward him first with his hand already extended when Clark reached them.

Rouleau's grip was firm and Clark gazed into his intelligent green eyes for a moment before Rouleau released his hand. He had the feeling that he'd been sized up in that one searching look.

Stonechild welcomed him back before she signalled to the dog to lead them across the dock and onto the shore. "I put the coffee on before we came outside," she said over her shoulder. "We may as well go inside where we're certain of privacy while we hash over developments."

They arranged themselves around the kitchen island and Clark listened while Stonechild concisely summarized the interviews and observations from his time away. Rouleau was attentive and added the odd observation when she asked for his input.

"I'll be heading home to Kingston today, then," said Rouleau when she finished. "I've got budget meetings that I'd hoped to miss, but should attend if I can." He directed his question to Clark. "Will you be requiring Stonechild's help much longer?"

"Hopefully not, if we can wrap this up. We appreciate that you've lent her to us."

Stonechild tapped her chest. "Hey, I'm right here, guys. No need to talk about me as if I'm a commodity."

Clark returned her smile. "Never." He drained the last of his coffee and stood. "So, based on all you've told me, I'd say Father Vila is our first stop today. We'll see if we can get him into confession … no religious reference intended."

"Go ahead," said Rouleau. "I'll get organized and be on the road within the hour." He looked at

Stonechild and appeared to hesitate. "Any messages you want me to pass along?" he asked.

Her eyes lit up for a moment before she looked past him toward the window and the view of the trees. "Nothing in particular. Just say that I'll be in touch."

Clark could tell that Rouleau wanted to ask her more questions but was holding back. Before meeting him, Clark had mistakenly thought that this might be the man she was involved with but knew now that they had a professional relationship — nothing intimate. Yet they were comfortable with each other, even if Rouleau was her sergeant. He was older than her, but a kind man who appeared to understand her. Would she give up his friendship and her position in Kingston Major Crimes to make a life with Jordan?

"Thank you again for helping out, sir," said Clark, offering his hand again. "Perhaps we'll be in a position to return the favour one day."

Rouleau's eyes danced. "I might take you up on that. Don't keep our best officer too much longer."

"We'd like to, but I understand why you want her back."

Stonechild sighed. "Guys. I'm right here."

Rouleau turned as she stood and they embraced for a moment. "Take care of yourself," he said quietly into her ear.

"I will." She patted him on the back before stepping away. A look passed between them.

"I wish I could help," he said in a low voice, barely above a whisper. "With whatever is bothering you."

She looked away. "I'm sorting it out."

Clark walked toward the front door and Stonechild joined him at the entrance. She didn't look back, even when the dog barked sharply at being left behind.

CHAPTER THIRTY-FOUR

Rouleau drained the coffee pot and called to Taiku to go for a walk. He'd planned to spend a few more days helping with the cases, and the unexpected free time had taken a bit to sink in. *Why rush back to the office when I can enjoy this gift of a day?*

Taiku disappeared into the woods on the path leading to the main lodge and the road. *I was thinking a walk along the waterfront, but okay.* Rouleau picked up his pace, slopping coffee as he hurried after the dog. The flutter of anxiety that Taiku was making a run for it eased when he reached the opening to the path and Taiku was sniffing around the underbrush, appearing to be waiting for him to catch up.

"All right, old boy," said Rouleau. "Where are you leading me?"

Taiku trotted toward the lodge but carried on past, stopping and waiting for Rouleau when he reached the parking lot. Rouleau spotted the Hydro truck still in place and remembered that Blaine and Ian were done their work for the summer and were awaiting word that they could return home. Stonechild had told him that Ian, the better-looking one, was engaged and getting married at Christmas. She'd also said that Ian and Blaine were less friendly with each other than they had been at the beginning of the summer. "Too much time in each other's company," was how she'd summarized it.

He pondered this rift as he walked at a moderate pace after Taiku. A wind had come up since breakfast but the day was warmer than the week before, and he started to enjoy being outside, alone with his thoughts. Marci had left for her new job in France with his decision about following her still up in the air. He'd have liked to see her off, but perhaps it was better this way. The sadness of their parting wouldn't overwhelm him and cloud his judgment. The dog kept darting into the woods and leaping back onto the road at intervals, always looking around for Rouleau before bounding into the bush. Rouleau was thinking about turning back when Taiku disappeared down a path leading toward the lake. Rouleau hesitated for a moment before starting after him. The trail, littered in pine needles and shaded by conifers, cut through thicker woods. He could hear the waves before he broke out from the shaded path onto the wide expanse of sand beach. Taiku was near the water being petted by someone bent over with their back to Rouleau. He straightened and turned at Rouleau's approach.

"Blaine," said Rouleau. "Sorry if we interrupted your peace. The dog's been taking me on a tour."

"No problem. I'm just killing time." Blaine pointed to a spot farther down the beach near the water. "That's where they found Thomas Faraday's body."

By silent agreement, they began walking together toward the location where he'd been pointing. "You were with Ian that entire day and evening," said Rouleau. He remembered Blaine's discomfort in the restaurant when Stonechild had asked him about his whereabouts. He'd had the sense Blaine and Ian hadn't been telling the truth.

Blaine was silent, walking with his head bowed and kicking at the sand with each step. The wind was stronger here on the open beach, the waves rolling onto the shoreline and crashing against the rocks off in the distance.

"It never helps in these investigations to keep quiet when you have information that will come out later," Rouleau said quietly. He swallowed the last of the coffee and held the mug loosely at his side. Blaine struck him as a man who had always been an outsider, probably picked on in school no matter how much he tried to fit in. His sullen demeanour would be the shell that kept him from more hurt.

The two of them stopped a metre from the water and stood side by side watching the waves roll one after the other onto the shore. A mist dampened their faces and clothes. Taiku returned from a romp in the shallow water to stand next to Rouleau. Blaine crouched and called Taiku over, ignoring his wet fur as he gave the dog a rubdown. He looked up at Rouleau.

"I wasn't allowed to bring my dogs for the summer. I have two German shepherds." He straightened. "Ian's getting married a few months after we get back to Thunder Bay, and I'm not certain if I should warn his fiancée about the kind of man she's tying herself to."

"And what kind of man is that?"

"A dishonest one."

"Can you tell me about it?"

"He's been sleeping around with Petra when her husband's working in the kitchen. That night that Faraday died —" Blaine stopped for a moment. "Yeah, that night, he went out after supper and came back an hour later with Petra. They were having sex when your officer and Shane found the body."

"You went along as his alibi. What changed your mind, Blaine?"

"We're done working together, and I don't owe him anything. Also, I liked that kid, Rachel. I could see where she was coming from. Doing anything to fit in. Thinking if she put out, she'd be popular. Problem was, she just got herself used ... and then murdered. The users never give a shit about anybody but themselves."

"Did Ian sleep with her, too?"

Blaine turned his head to stare at Rouleau. His eyes were red and watery, perhaps from the wind or from the tears that were threatening behind his eyelids. "I can't be sure, but my guess is yeah. She came by our cabin once when she thought he'd be there. She acted as if she wanted to talk to me, but I knew otherwise. I watched her walk away in the direction of the dock where he was fishing."

"How soon was that before she died?"

"A week. Five days maybe."

"Where's Ian now?"

"He took a boat out to go fishing. I expect him late afternoon."

Taiku circled them and started back the way they'd come. He stopped several metres away and returned to run around them again.

"Dog could have been a sheepherder," said Blaine. "Man, I miss my two boys."

"Will you make a statement once Officer Stonechild returns?"

Blaine took his time answering, but squared his shoulders and nodded. "If it gets me home and helps to end this mess, then I will. Like I said, I don't owe that guy one damn thing."

"I'm so glad your baby is doing well," said Kala, glancing across at Clark. He'd wanted to drive and she hadn't argued. She was overheated and tired, and the idea of being chauffeured around was appealing.

"Me, too." He shot her a sideways grin. "Valerie and Jordan will spend the day at the hospital, so my guilt level isn't through the roof being here with you instead of with them."

"Rouleau and I could have handled a few more days if you'd needed the time."

"I know." He waited for two cars going the opposite direction to pass by before turning into the church parking lot. "I'm committed to seeing this case through. I guess you know the feeling."

"Are we incapable of putting family first?" she mused aloud, not certain she wanted to know the answer. Not surprised when he changed the subject without responding.

"Is that Father Vila's car?" Clark craned his face toward the windshield to get a better look at the licence plate.

"Yes, so he's here." She breathed a sigh of relief. She'd worried that the Church would have already moved him to avoid another scandal.

Clark pulled in next to the car and rested both arms on the steering wheel when he turned to look at her. "Valerie understands that I have to work long hours. She knew it when she married me and she wants kids despite my job. We wouldn't be together otherwise."

"But what about Valerie? What about her dreams and needs?"

"If I didn't believe she wanted this life, I would never have asked her to marry me. We had many a frank discussion when we were dating, believe me. I also support her every way and chance I get."

"Like how?"

"We hired a cleaner so she doesn't have to worry about housework. We've already lined up a sitter so we can go on date night once a week and she can go to fitness classes during the day. There are ways to make busy lives work, Stonechild. You just have to stay open."

"Maybe." She got out of the car and waited for him at the front entrance. She and Gundersund had never spoken about marriage or anything long-term. He'd said once that his marriage to Fiona had taken its toll on him. Being tied down wasn't all he'd imagined when they'd moved in together. He was glad they'd never had kids because if they did he never would have left her. All of these small confessions told over the course of their friendship haunted her now.

"You should do the talking," said Clark when he reached her. "I'll stay in the background."

"Leap in if I'm getting nowhere."

"You'll do fine."

They returned to the basement. Ethel was absent from the reception desk and Kala was happy not to have to go through her to get to Father Vila. She walked ahead of Clark straight to Vila's office and rapped on the door, pushing it open at the same time. The priest had been lying on the couch with a forearm resting across his eyes, but he swung his feet onto the floor and sat up when she stepped into the room. His eyes were bleary with sleep and he blinked as he focused on her walking toward him.

"Sorry to disturb you, Father. We have more questions if you have a moment."

"I was resting. I spent the night with a parishioner who was taken to Emergency after supper. She died at dawn."

"I'm sorry." Kala didn't believe he'd told her this to make himself look good, but rather to explain why he was sleeping on the job. She could see genuine sadness in his eyes.

He ran a hand through his hair in an attempt to straighten it and yawned. He took a deep breath. Pushed back his shoulders. "Okay, then. What do you need to know?"

He seemed more resigned than upset, and Kala wondered about that. Was he ready to tell them the truth or was he unconcerned because he had been telling the truth all along? She sat in the chair across from him. Clark pulled the other chair to the side and sat down. Father Vila looked at him.

"I prayed for your son and am so happy that he's doing well. Praise God."

Clark tilted his head by way of acknowledgement but stayed silent. Kala drew Vila's attention back to her. "We've had more information come our way about an incident between you and Rachel. Is there anything that you would like to share now before we get any deeper into what went on?"

"As you know, I cannot speak about anything Rachel confessed to me."

"But she's dead, Father. Surely, this negates the vow to protect her privacy if whatever she told you leads to her killer." She wasn't certain that she'd kept the frustration out of her voice. Too many times priests had hidden behind the Church and its rules to protect themselves. Too many lives had been damaged by their silence.

"Her mother walked in on you sitting with Rachel on the couch you're resting on now. You were touching her leg and her top buttons were undone. Isabelle sensed that something was going on between you of a physical nature."

"I know how that looked, but she was wrong. Rachel assured me that she would explain everything to her mother, but I believe now that she did not."

"Explain it to me then."

"Rachel was crying in the hall when service finished. I brought her into my office and asked her what was wrong. We sat on the couch — I wasn't thinking about appearances because she was so upset, and I was trying to comfort her. She calmed down enough to tell me that Darryl had tried to kiss her and then gotten angry when she'd pushed him away. I guess her blouse came undone in the process. Her mother walked in when I patted her leg. Rachel yelled at her to get out, which she did. When Rachel calmed down, we talked over her situation, including her anger with her mom. She told me that she'd apologize and clear up any misunderstanding."

Kala watched him throughout this recital. He spoke carefully without appearing to embellish, which would have been a red flag that he was lying. His eyes didn't waver on hers. She asked, "Can you tell me more about her situation, knowing that what you say will not go any further unless it has direct relevance to her murder? To be honest, Father, we are no closer to solving her death or that of Thomas Faraday than we were at the start of all this business. We need your help."

He folded his hands in his lap and studied them while she waited. She chanced a glance at Clark, who was also sitting stock still, watching the priest mull over what he would do. Time felt suspended; an uneasy lull that built in intensity with every silent moment. When she didn't think she could wait any longer, Father Vila raised his eyes to hers.

"Rachel was troubled. She believed herself in love with a married man. She'd put on moral blinders, believing that their romantic love was pure."

In her mind Kala went through the list of married men at the lodge that last night when Rachel had served them supper. Neal Lorring, Shane Patterson, Phil Bocock, and Reeve Judd Neilson. Ian Kruger was engaged … would Rachel have thought of him as married? She asked, "Did she name him?"

Father Vila paused again and Kala resisted the urge to get up and shake him. Telling her this information went against his code, but her frustration grew with every passing second. He sighed deeply. "She said that he was her teacher. The … affair started this summer when they met up to discuss her writing."

"Did she say his name?"

"Not specifically."

"Phil Bocock was mentoring her in English. He was at the restaurant the evening Rachel was murdered."

"Then he's likely the one."

Kala knew that Vila could be lying to save his own skin, but everything he'd said held the ring of truth. Not all priests were complicit. She had to look past the fact that he was young and attractive, and past her own feelings about the Catholic Church's demand for celibacy that had resulted in so many priests violating members of their congregations. Her own parents had been abused in a residential school by priests just like this one. Yet Father Vila could be an exception. She had to remain skeptical, yet she hoped for his goodness.

"We will be following up." She didn't attempt to disguise the threat implicit in her words.

Father Vila bowed his head but said nothing.

Kala stood and looked down at him. She was honestly curious. "What did you counsel Rachel when she told you that she was seeing a married man?"

"I advised her that the married man had made a solemn vow to his wife that he would be faithful to her, and the sin was his to bear — but that she should search her heart, where she would find the truth about the relationship. I told Rachel that she would know true love one day and to be patient. I also asked her if she wanted to report Darryl to the authorities, but she said he wasn't a threat. I pray that this wasn't the wrong decision. That I didn't fail her."

"Thank you for being so candid with us, Father. I know that this wasn't easy for you."

"I have to believe that Rachel would want you to know about this man so that you can find her killer. She loved her parents even as she was trying to break free. They deserve answers so that they can find peace. I believe in my heart that Rachel would want this."

Clark didn't speak until they were on their way up the stairs that led to the main entrance. "Do you believe him?"

Kala smiled. "You're asking me this in a house of God?"

"Too sacrilegious?"

"At least wait until we get outside."

They left the church and reached the parking lot before Kala spoke again. "I think we should go speak with Phil Bocock without his wife present."

"So you believe Father Vila."

"Going against my agnostic nature, you mean?"

"On the contrary, I always think of you as the most spiritual person I know."

"But I will admit that I'm not much for organized religion. The Catholic Church has ruined many lives, including my parents'. However, in this case, yes. I tend to believe Father Vila. Everything about him spoke to a man wrestling with his conscience, but I think his dilemma was about breaking a confession rather than something he'd done. I could have leapt to the wrong conclusion initially."

"Past priest behaviour gives cause. However, I tend to agree that he appeared truthful. Based on what he said, Darryl Kelly's gone up a few spots on the suspect list, as well as Phil Bocock."

Kala opened the passenger door. "As well as Greta Bocock, but at least we're starting to get past the secrets and are coming up with a few answers. We're onto something here, Harrison. My spidey-sense is tingling."

He looked at her over the car roof as he pulled open his car door. "Then let's go spin the web, Stonechild, and see what bugs we catch in our net."

She groaned softly at his clumsy metaphor as she climbed into the car and slammed the door.

Rouleau knew he couldn't return to Kingston yet. Not with this new information that needed to be shared with Stonechild and Harrison. He left Blaine on the beach and walked Taiku back to Stonechild's cabin. Taiku seemed happy enough to go inside out of the wind, eat a few biscuits, and lie down on the couch for a snooze. "No wonder they call it a dog's life," said Rouleau, sitting down next to him. He rubbed Taiku's head and the dog's tail thumped on the seat cushion.

Rouleau thought about driving into Searchmont to call Stonechild but didn't want to leave Pine Hollow Lodge in case Ian arrived back early from his fishing trip. He got up, restless to do something to help move the case along. A day driving around with Stonechild had whetted his appetite for being in the field again and he was sorry that their time together had ended so abruptly. He'd have liked to see the case through with her. He stopped in front of the picture window and looked toward the lake. A lone figure was sitting on the dock, sideways to the shoreline. He repositioned himself to get a better view through the trees and recognized Petra's blond hair blowing around her head, brilliant in the sunshine reflecting off the water.

It all comes back to you. The idea came out of nowhere, but he realized that her drunken entrance into the restaurant the evening before had left him wondering.

Taiku didn't stir from the couch when Rouleau opened the front door, so he walked alone down the incline to the beach. The wind masked his approach and he waited on shore, watching Petra in profile. She had both hands resting on the dock behind her and was leaning back with her face turned toward the sun, positioned so that her body angled slightly toward the deeper water. She was wearing rolled-up denim jeans and her bare feet dangled above the lake. Her loose white shirt billowed around her with each gust of wind. When she swivelled her head to look at him through dark sunglasses, he jumped onto the dock and clumped across its rough surface toward her.

"Detective Rouleau," she said. "Imagine meeting you here. Please join me in enjoying the last of the summer heat."

He lowered himself next to her. "The wind is up," he said. "That doesn't bother you?" The waves weren't as large as at the open beach, but they were still a good height. The spray was a fine mist coating them with each rolling hill of water. Refreshing with the heat of the sun beating down on them.

"The best kind of tanning weather." She adjusted her shirt so that her shoulders were bared to the sky. She smiled. "What can I do for you, Officer?"

He wondered if her overt sexuality was so second nature that she wasn't aware of its effect. Was she the catalyst for the strong emotions running through the lodge?

"I'm sorry you've had to change your plans to stay here so long," he said.

"Me, too. I'm not exactly a country gal."

"Shane seems to like it here."

"He's welcome to stay then. We're separating."

He'd hoped that he could lead her into talking about her marriage and was surprised at how easily the conversation turned to this topic. The scene in the restaurant the night before had poked an opening into the wall of silence uniting the lodgers. "I can't imagine that this has been an easy decision," he said.

"Easy for Shane. He changed the rules and forgot to tell me."

"The rules?"

"I don't want to shock you."

"I promise not to be."

She stared at him through her sunglasses and flashed a crooked half-smile. "We have … had … an open marriage. I began to suspect that he wanted me to settle down with just him, but he never actually said so and I never would have agreed anyhow. I like sex. I like sex with different people." Her voice was becoming agitated. "He couldn't expect to drag me out here, work long hours, and think I'd simply sit like his trained dog in the cabin waiting for his crumbs, now could he?"

"You were having sex with Ian Kruger." Rouleau wasn't asking. He already knew.

Her laughter felt off to Rouleau — too loud and tinged with hysteria. When she stopped, her mouth feigned a pout. Her voice was meant to be flirty. "Why Officer, are you wanting me to kiss and tell? Shame on you."

Rouleau smiled so that she didn't feel foolish, but he kept speaking in the same level tone. "I'm only trying to understand the relationships at Pine Hollow Lodge and to see where Rachel Eglan and Thomas Faraday fit in."

"Neither of them fit in. They stuck their noses where they didn't belong. I didn't like either one of them, if we're being honest."

"Rachel was fifteen at the start of the summer. Little more than a child."

"Huh! You'd like to think. She was coming on to every man she came across ... well, maybe not Thomas, but only because he was old and ugly." The laugh again.

"Did anyone take Rachel up on her come-ons?"

"I couldn't say."

"Shane?"

"You'd have to ask him, but I wouldn't care if he had."

Petra's head swivelled so that she was looking past Rouleau toward the shoreline. Her body tensed but she kept her gaze focused on something. Rouleau shifted so that he could see what had caught her attention. It took two scans of the trees before he saw Neal Lorring standing in front of a clump of cedars, dressed in a green T-shirt and brown pants and blending into the foliage. When he saw them looking, Neal waved and started walking down the incline toward them.

"He was watching us until he saw that we'd spotted him," said Petra, averting her face so that Neal couldn't see her mouth moving. "If you want to know who Rachel was sleeping with, look no —" She broke off the sentence as Neal stepped onto the dock.

"There you are, Petra," he said as he got closer. His eyes were dark and hard, the set of his jaw angry. "I've been looking everywhere for you. It's time you and I have a talk." His gaze passed over Rouleau and back to her. "In private."

CHAPTER THIRTY-FIVE

Phil Bocock opened the front door. The smile on his face vanished when he saw Kala and Clark on the steps. His gaze went past them to the police cruiser in the driveway and returned to focus on them.

"What's this about then?"

"We need to speak with you," said Clark, "about Rachel Eglan."

"Then come in." Phil opened the door wider and they stepped into the foyer. He didn't invite them any deeper into the house. He was dressed in a Toronto Blue Jays T-shirt, ripped jeans, and Skechers with no socks. Kala wondered if he was trying to look like his students. "Whatever you have to tell me can be done here," he said in his stern teacher voice.

Taking Bocock's animosity in stride, Clark asked, "Greta home?"

"She's upstairs doing laundry. What's this about, Officer? We have a busy day underway."

"We've gotten information from a reliable source that you and Rachel were more than teacher and student. You were having an affair."

Clark's voice didn't leave any room for doubt, and they watched the bravado drain from Phil's eyes. He looked to be searching through images in his brain, trying to find the source of their intel, figuring out if they were bluffing. The bluster returned. "I'm denying whoever is smearing me. You're going to have to do better than a baseless accusation if you think I'm going to admit to anything untoward with Rachel. I'm insulted, in fact."

There was a noise on the landing at the top of the stairs and they all looked up. Greta's white face peered down at them. She started her descent, not taking her eyes off Phil. "What are they saying, Phil?"

"It's nothing, love. A misunderstanding, that's all."

"Tell me you weren't doing something inappropriate with that girl."

"I'm telling you. I didn't do anything inappropriate with Rachel."

Clark's glance at Kala said that this wasn't how they planned things, but he was willing to let it play out. He pressed on. "Rachel told someone in a position of authority that she was having an affair with you. She said that she was conflicted because you were married, but she believed you were the love of her life."

"She was … mistaken."

Clark's denial sounded hollow to Kala. Less assured. She looked at Greta and could see by the stare she had fixed on her husband that she also didn't believe him.

"How could you have done such a thing after what you told me was a false accusation two years ago? You *assured* me that the girl was *lying*. She's from a bad home, you said. She's starving for attention, you said. And I believed you. I was your biggest defender. I convinced everyone that the girl had to be making up a story. I made her out to be a liar and probably ruined her life. Now this? Rachel was your *student*. She was only fifteen years old when school let out." Greta put a hand over her mouth. "You corrupted a minor."

Phil reached out and grabbed Greta's arm, but she shook him off and backed onto the bottom step. "I told you what would happen if I ever caught you cheating," she said through clenched teeth. "I want you out of this house." She started up the stairs but stopped and turned half-way up. "Oh my God. Did you kill her, too?"

"No! No!" Phil spread his hands wide and looked at Clark and Kala. His expression was horrified. "All right, I admit that Rachel and I were physical a few times, but I didn't kill her. I swear to God, I'm not that kind of man."

"No, you're the kind of man who has sex with children. You disgust me."

Clark looked up at Greta. "We're taking Phil to the station for more questioning. I'd appreciate if you came as well to make a statement." His voice softened. "I'm sorry, Greta."

"Can I drive my own car? I don't want to be in the same vehicle as him."

"Of course. Phil will be coming with us."

"And you're welcome to him. I never want to speak to the lying bastard again."

Kala had no choice but to drive with Clark and Phil Bocock to the station in Sault Ste. Marie. The drive was a silent one and Phil was hustled off to an interview room upon arrival. Kala made a cup of tea in the small kitchenette and took a seat at the table to wait for her lift back to Pine Hollow. A local cop would be assisting in the interviews, and she was disappointed but happy at the same time to be done for the day. Clark entered the kitchen and tucked away his cellphone when he saw Kala.

"Everything okay at home?" she asked.

"Yeah. I was hoping to get out of here early but that's not going to happen now. Bocock is lawyering up and that'll slow the process."

"If you get the confession, you should have a better week going forward."

"One hopes. So do you think he's our killer?"

Kala decided to ignore the niggling doubt that she always had before a confession or overwhelming evidence of guilt. This case, more than others, had too many moving parts for her to stand down yet. She didn't voice any of this to Clark. "He could very well be," she said, sipping from her mug.

Clark poured a cup of coffee and leaned against the counter with his feet crossed at the ankles. "I'll be interviewing Greta first so that Phil cools his heels and has time to worry about what she's sharing with us. I'm confident from her reaction that she didn't know he was having sex with Rachel. Makes me believe that she had no reason to kill the girl."

"A good working premise."

"You don't sound convinced."

"I've learned to keep all options open until I have conclusive proof to the contrary."

"Thomas Faraday probably saw Phil and Rachel together and wanted recompense from Bocock to stay silent. Faraday was a sneaky kind of guy by all accounts. Liked taking photos. He could have a stash somewhere that we haven't found."

"It could have happened that way."

Clark laughed. "Cutting me no slack, eh, Stonechild?"

"Never." She smiled and tipped her mug in his direction before setting it down. "Looks like you won't be needing my services much longer."

"You can follow Rouleau home to Kingston."

"He should be almost there by now."

Clark's eyes studied her face, and she wondered if her voice had sounded wistful. She had a decision to make, and part of her wished that her life hadn't reached this point while another part wanted to overlook all the negatives and dream of what could be. Her phone rang and interrupted the moment.

Clark pushed himself forward from the counter. "You take that and I'll go check on your ride. I'll come out to the lodge tomorrow morning before you leave for Kingston and fill you in on the Bocock interviews."

She glanced at the caller ID and said, "Perfect. Good luck in there." She held the phone to her ear and watched Clark walk out of the room. "How are you, Dawn?"

"I'm fine but we miss you, Aunt Kala. When are you coming home?"

"I'm not sure. The case isn't over yet and I might be a while. How's your mom?"

"She's doing better. She's supposed to be out of the hospital this week."

"That's good. We can visit her when I get back."

"Gundersund said he'll take me." Dawn paused and Kala could picture her thinking, her forehead scrunched up and her lips tight together. "He seems lost these days."

Kala closed her eyes. "Tell him ... let him know that everything will settle down soon." A uniformed officer appeared in the doorway. "Look, my ride is here to take me back to Pine Hollow. I need to go. I'll call you as soon as I can."

"Okay, Aunt Kala."

The resignation in her voice stuck with Kala as she walked out of the building and across the parking lot, and a deep sadness mixed with anger welled up inside of her.

I'm not your mother, she thought. *I never wanted to be anybody's mother ... or wife. I don't know if I can do this — if I'll let everyone down because that's all I know. I should disappear and everyone will be better off.*

She climbed into the passenger seat and put on her sunglasses, turning her head to stare out the side window. She was only too aware what she should do and yet she couldn't make herself take the next step. The problem, she knew, was that while she waffled and allowed herself to contemplate a good outcome, she was running out of time.

Chapter Thirty-Six

R ouleau could have left Stonechild a note with the information he'd gleaned from Blaine and Petra, but he didn't trust that somebody would not enter her cabin and read his report. He didn't fancy driving back to Kingston through the night, but he'd made a quick trip into town to check his messages after Petra and Neal left and found that he was needed urgently back at HQ. So when Stonechild arrived at the supper hour, he'd already stowed his suitcase in his car, and he and Taiku were sitting on the rocks looking out at the choppy lake waiting for her. Taiku spotted Kala first and bounded off to greet her. Rouleau waved but waited in place until she joined him.

"Couldn't drag yourself away?" she teased, lowering herself next to him. Her voice turned serious. "Something going on?"

"I had a talk with Blaine Rogers. Seems Ian was having sex with Petra the night Thomas was killed. Blaine believes that Ian was also having sex with Rachel, but he's got no proof except that Rachel came knocking at their cabin door looking for Ian about five days before she died. I also had a chat with Petra, whom I found sitting on your dock. She admits to sleeping with Ian and says Shane is angry enough to want out of their marriage, even though it had been an open one up until then. She said that Neal and Martha's marriage is also on the rocks and implied that Neal was sleeping with Rachel, too. The betrayals are staggering when you add them up." He lightened his voice. "I had to tell you in person. Too damn unbelievable to put in a note."

Stonechild had been listening intently while scratching Taiku behind the ears. She gave his side one last pat and straightened up. "All these extra-marital shenanigans could be red herrings. Rachel confessed to Father Vila that she and her English teacher Phil Bocock were having an affair and that he was the love of her life. So we made a trip out to see Bocock and he confessed. It appears his wife Greta knew nothing about what he was up to, although she told us that another female student had put in a complaint a few years ago that had come to nothing."

"You believe her?"

"Yeah, I do. You can't feign the level of shock and anger she exhibited when she found out."

"Could Rachel have been sleeping with Neal and Ian, too?"

Stonechild's face was thoughtful. "All that I've learned about Rachel, including reading her poetry, tells me that she was a romantic. She was also a lonely, smothered sixteen-year-old girl spreading her wings this summer. She told Father Vila that the married man she was seeing was her soulmate. She might have flirted with other men, but I have a hard time accepting that she slept with them — but of course, I can't know for certain. Not yet."

"Do you and Clark Harrison believe that Phil Bocock killed Rachel and Thomas?"

"Clark leans that way."

"And you?"

"Maybe. Probably. I'm honestly not sure."

He watched her in profile. "You look exhausted," he said. "Have you been sleeping?"

She tilted her head from side to side. "Not so much." She shot him a half smile. "I have a lot on my mind."

"Anything I can help with? I'm a good listener."

She appeared to consider his offer before shaking her head. "Nothing I can't handle."

"Well, I'm always here for you."

"I know. I value your friendship, Rouleau. You've been ... well, like the father I never knew. I'll miss you when you fly off to Paris, but I understand the need to keep moving."

"Are you speaking about me or you, Kala?"

"We're birds of a feather."

He was quiet, thinking about all she was telling him with these few words. He'd known from the moment he met her that she wasn't someone who could commit easily. Her life had been lonely, devoid of trust. The friendship they shared was deep and lifelong, but not enough to keep her from leaving. She needed to continue searching for the family and the home she'd never had. He'd hoped Gundersund and Dawn and all the friends she'd made in Kingston were that place for her, and learning that they were not enough filled him with sadness — for her and for them. He'd always had trouble letting go of those he loved, but he wouldn't add to the guilt she must feel over a need that she had no control over. He slapped his hands on his legs before he stood. The wind buffeted against him, cooler than it had been earlier in the day but still pleasant enough. He cleared his throat. "I should be heading out then. Sadly, HQ is calling me back."

"I was hoping you were here another day but I'm being selfish. I'll walk with you." She stood and Taiku ran ahead of them toward the path. "What about you?" she asked. "Has Marci gone ahead to Paris?"

"Yes, she's there now."

"When will you follow her?"

"I'll visit her for Christmas if she still wants me to, but my life is in Kingston as long as my father is there. I've decided to accept the chief's job when I return. Heath handed in his resignation this week. I've yet to break the news to Marci, but I think she knows I'm not moving overseas." He turned and smiled grimly at her. "We can't risk any more acting chiefs after the last one."

"I honestly thought you'd go with Marci."

"I was tempted but I came to realize where I need to be ... for now anyway."

"The team will be relieved."

"I've asked Gundersund to apply to head up Major Crimes."

"He'll make a fine staff sergeant."

"Are you returning to the force, Stonechild?"

He wasn't sure if she'd heard his question because she'd pivoted at the same time he'd asked it and was calling to Taiku. The wind billowed around them and whistled through the trees. He was about to repeat the question, but Stonechild's closed-off face when she turned back made him think twice. Instead, he grabbed her to him in a bear hug before he got into his car.

"Take care of yourself," he said.

She settled into him for a moment before pulling back. "You, too. Safe home."

He drove slowly away from Pine Hollow Lodge, catching sight of Stonechild in the rear-view before he rounded the corner, unhappy to be leaving her behind, not convinced that he'd ever see her again.

Kala fell asleep on the couch after making a cup of herbal tea. She awoke at eight thirty, and by the time she reached the main lodge, the lights were off and the front door was locked. She kept walking toward her truck, guided by the solar lights along the pathway to the parking lot. Taiku would be fine without her for a few hours.

The wind had calmed and a thick cloud cover blanketed the sky, preventing moonlight from brightening the gloom. Those living in cities had no idea how black the darkness could be without streetlamps and the light from buildings. There was nothing quite like tilting her head way back and seeing the stars in a half globe overhead on a clear winter night. Kala felt her soul open, staring up at the wide expanse of inky blackness dotted with shimmering stars. Tonight, the overcast skies left her with a sense of desolation not improved by the first drops of rain that snaked down the windshield as she pulled into the Mountainview Lodge parking lot.

She ran for the restaurant entrance, surprised to find the room alive with the chatter of people and the clinking of dishes. Jenny, the motherly waitress who'd served her on other visits, spotted her in the doorway and motioned for her to take the table against the far wall. Kala gratefully settled in with her back to the room and opened her laptop while she waited for Jenny to deliver a tray-load of soda drinks to a table of talkative teenagers.

"What'll it be tonight, Officer?" Jenny asked, appearing at Kala's side holding a pot of coffee in one hand while sliding a menu onto the table.

Kala handed back the menu. "I know what I'm craving. The hot roast beef sandwich and seasoned fries and a glass of Clamato juice."

"Coming right up." Jenny took a step away but stopped and looked back. "If you have a minute, Ricky wants to run something past you once you're done eating."

"Ricky?"

"He helps out in the kitchen sometimes."

"Sure. Tell him to come see me when he's free."

"I'll pass along the message."

Kala read emails and had replied to the bulk of them by the time her meal arrived. Clark had sent a brief note saying that Phil Bocock had not confessed to the murders, but he believed it was only a matter of time. Greta had blasted Phil's alibi for both nights before Clark let her go home. He'd be visiting the Eglans with an update in the morning. It was time to let Pine Hollow Lodge close for the season. He'd already phoned the landline in the Lorrings' home office and spoken to Martha. Kala typed a quick acknowledgement before putting her head down and tucking in to her dinner, ravenous after the busy day. Jenny reappeared as she took her last bite. Kala leaned back and patted her stomach. She smiled up at Jenny. "I needed that."

"You were looking a little peaked when you came in. Glad we cured what was ailing ya. We have blueberry pie tonight if you have room. Wild berries picked fresh yesterday."

"I can't resist. Another cup of lemon tea to go with it, please."

"Coming right up."

Kala ate the pie slowly, savouring the sun-ripened berries, smaller than the cultivated ones sold in supermarkets but richer in flavour. She took the last bite as a man who must be Ricky walked toward her from the kitchen. She made a quick assessment: late seventies or early eighties, five foot nine, fifty pounds overweight. Bristly white stubble on his chin and thinning hair combed and gelled back from his forehead. His eyes were watery blue; his smile tentative. "Would this be a good time?" he asked.

"Sure, take a seat." Kala pushed the plate to one side and picked up her cup of tea. "Would you like a drink?"

"Nah … but thanks. My name's Ricky Fielder, by the way."

"Officer Stonechild, but you can call me Kala."

"Pleased to make your acquaintance Officer Kala."

Ricky didn't offer his hand, perhaps because both of hers were wrapped around the mug. He kicked out the chair and dropped into it with a grunt. "Been washin' dishes for my sins. Regular kid's sick with the flu or acne or whatever it is teenage boys come down with nowadays."

"What's your usual job?"

"I'm your all-around handyman. My son manages the Mountainview and I play backup when needed. I used to be a guide for American fishermen and hunters but gave that up a couple of years back."

She set down the cup and rested her elbows on the table. "So you have something to tell me?"

"Maybe. Maybe not. That fella, Thomas Faraday, word is he drowned up at Pine Hollow Lake near the lodge. That true?"

"It is."

Ricky shook his head from side to side. "Goddamn. I've been on a huntin' trip the last week and had no idea. Was it an accident?"

"We believe not. Did you know him?"

"Could say. We shared an interest in photography. He used to come in here for lunch on a regular basis and we got to talkin'. We both like using film and I have a darkroom in my basement. He'd come over and we'd develop pictures and watch a ballgame on TV. Pop a few beers." He opened his mouth and inhaled another deep breath. "Goddamn."

"Were you friends, would you say?"

"Not exactly. Small communities ain't exactly teeming with new acquaintances. Most people have their quirks, and you get along if you want to have any kind of social life. Live and let live is my motto." He paused. "Thom had a chip on his shoulder from something that happened in his photography business in Toronto. Sometimes I got the feelin' he was into things on the shady side. I didn't pry, though. Just went along and took him at face value when we got together."

"Did Thomas say anything about the people at Pine Hollow Lodge?"

"Not much except he thought they made interesting subjects for his photography."

Kala tried to assess if this information changed anything. "Did you see any of his photos?" she asked.

"Ones for the calendar that he liked. He worked alone in the darkroom usually and only showed me those he was particularly keen on. Guy had an eye, there's no doubt. He had a couple of cameras, don't you know. Digital and an old Canon with the film. Tough to get film nowadays but we order some in. Get the chemicals in special order, too, for developing the colour pictures."

"Well." Kala was at a loss. "Thomas never told you that he was involved in anything unethical?"

"Nope."

"Did he mention fighting with anybody or being upset about anything?"

"He was easy to rile up, but nothing comes to mind."

"Okay. Thanks for sharing your information with me." She raised a hand to Jenny for her bill, wanting to wrap this up and get back to Taiku for his last walk before bed.

Ricky heaved himself to his feet. "Mighty sorry about Thom and that young girl, Rachel. This has been a bad summer all around." He took a few steps toward the kitchen before stopping. "Say, I have a box of Thom's stuff at my place. Do ya think his family would want it?"

Kala blinked. If she could slap herself on the forehead and not insult him, she would have. *How the hell could you think that's not important?* "I'd like to come take that off your hands when you're done your shift," she said, keeping her voice even.

He seemed to consider her offer as if he had a choice. "I don't see why not. I'll hang up my apron and you can follow me home."

"I'd appreciate that."

Ricky lived east of town on the Whitman Dam Road in a small bungalow nestled behind a line of spruce trees. The nearest neighbour couldn't be seen from his front door. Kala parked her truck behind the chassis of a stripped-out bus parked next to a rusting trailer and walked carefully past body parts from cars and trucks strewn around the yard.

In contrast, the inside of his house was spartan, no clutter and clean as a whistle. "Sorry for the mess outside," said Ricky. "I keep my pack-rat habit contained to the outdoors. My wife, bless her soul, insisted, and I got used to humouring her. Seems respectful to her memory to keep her house spotless like she wanted it."

Kala followed him down creaky stairs into the basement and surveyed the darkroom while he retrieved a metal box from under the workbench where he had it stowed. She scanned photos hanging to dry on a clothesline and walked the length of the wall where prints of local scenes and people were displayed. The images were magazine quality. "Are these all yours?" she asked.

"Yup. Thom always put his in this box or took them with him."

"You could sell these pictures for a healthy sum. They're works of art."

"Thanks for saying that, I'm sure. My son frames some of them for the cabins at the lodge. That's enough fame for me. I don't need any more money than I got."

He insisted on carrying the box to her truck and set it on the passenger seat. He leaned on the doorframe as she got behind the wheel. "I guess I'm going to miss ol' Thom when all is said and done. He was a morose sort, but company. I hope you sort out this bad business and we can get back to normal around here."

"I'll do my best."

"See that you do, young lady." He smiled and tapped on the roof before slamming the passenger door.

She caught sight of Ricky standing motionless in his laneway in her side mirror, oblivious to the rain, watching her as she pulled onto the highway. An uncomplicated man with kind eyes and no agenda. She was sorry not to have more time to get to know him better. She had a feeling they could have become friends.

CHAPTER THIRTY-SEVEN

Kala had the strongest urge to pull over and go through the box, but the rain was picking up and the idea of the snug cabin and Taiku's warm body resting on her lap was too inviting to pass up. She drove with care through the stormy night, the road slick with rain that puddled on the shoulders and spread in snaky rivulets across the pavement. The light from her headlights pierced through the swirling fog that parted for a moment until she'd passed through and then closed in as if she'd never been.

The box was heavy enough as she carried it from her truck down the wooded path, the rain a steady downpour in the open spaces. The warmth of the day was tempered by the damp but still warm enough for the first of September. She wished she'd left a light on in the cabin. Fog hovered in wispy strands above the ground, and combined with the darkness, she could only see a few feet ahead. She stumbled once and cursed before righting herself and tightening her grip on the box made slippery by the rain.

Taiku was waiting in the hallway and she let him out, leaving the door ajar while she gratefully set the box on the floor and slipped out of her wet boots and jacket. Business done, Taiku bounded back into the cabin a minute later and Kala locked the door. She pulled the curtains and settled on the couch with the box within reach on the coffee table while Taiku ate his supper.

The first photos were close-ups of plants and foliage. Faraday had been playing with perspective and light, and she had to squint at some of the black-and-white pictures to figure out the subject. He'd taken several colour shots of Pine Hollow Lodge, and she recognized her own cabin and dock in a series that started at sunrise, getting progressively lighter as daylight brightened the landscape from soft pink and orange sorbet to the deepest rich hues. Another series of black-and-white photos featured rock cuts from a distance and close-ups of rock crystals. *Beautiful photography*, she thought, impressed with his eye for detail — Thomas Faraday had had skill and talent.

Taiku jumped up next to her on the couch and butted his wet nose against her neck. Kala laughed and set down the photos, giving him some affection for all the hours she'd left him alone. "You're so good to come home to, boy," she said rubbing his ears before picking up a photo and inspecting the image. She set the picture down and grabbed a handful more, flipping through them and setting these in a pile on the table. She repeated this action four more times before doing a double take. "What have we here?" she wondered aloud. She held the photo close to her eyes.

The shot looked to have been taken through a window into one of the cabins. Two women close. Talking. She identified Petra and Martha. So far, Thomas had kept to images of scenery and nature, and a picture with people as subjects was a novelty. Kala grabbed another handful of pictures from the box. Each photo became more erotic. Petra touching Martha's face. The two women kissing, Petra unbuttoning Martha's blouse, both women lying naked on the bed. The last image in the series had captured a different camera angle reflecting off the window. Kala held the photo closer. Rachel Eglan was ghostly but recognizable, standing off to the side, her line of vision on the photographer, her mouth open as if saying something. She might have caught Faraday in the act of photographing the two women, or more likely, Rachel and Faraday were working as a team.

Rachel could have led Faraday to the window if she'd known what was going on inside the cabin. She'd had cleaning duties in addition to working in the kitchen, so not outside the realm of possibility.

Had Shane and Neal known what their wives were up to?

Kala picked up another pile of photos. In this batch, Faraday had chosen Rachel as his model, supporting the idea that they'd had a connection. Close-ups of her face hamming it up for the camera. Pouting. Sticking her tongue out. Blowing kisses. She'd posed for several in her bathing suit, matching the photos they'd found on his camera, but also in other outfits as if doing a portfolio shoot. Faraday had taken photos of her from a distance, too, and Kala had the sense that he'd shot them without her knowledge. In some she was walking away from the camera, sometimes alone and other times with Neal Lorring. In one, Neal had his head thrown back laughing, and Rachel's face in profile looked animated ... happy. Faraday had taken a series of Rachel working in the restaurant. The word *obsessive* seemed accurate as Kala flipped through photo after photo, stopping at a string of pictures of Rachel in what looked like a heated argument with Petra.

Why had he chosen these ones to print?

Kala sat for a long time afterward, trying to make sense of all the images, wondering if these photos were the reason someone had murdered Rachel and Faraday. Faraday could have been using the prints of Petra and Martha as blackmail. Rachel had likely been in on the scheme. Kala remembered Petra saying that Rachel was sneaky, listening at doors, inserting herself where she didn't belong. *A lonely girl wanting a bigger life.* Nobody else had accused Rachel, but Petra might have had reason. The argument between her and Rachel caught on camera could have been over Faraday's photos.

Both Petra's and Martha's marriages were on the rocks after this summer, with or without their husbands knowing about their affair with each other. Could the photos do more damage, or had they been leaked to the men like slow-acting poison? Had Faraday threatened to put them on the internet? Kala paused and played the scenario out in her head. The pictures could be easily scanned and uploaded. This was a small community, and business would suffer drastically if the town believed Pine Hollow Lodge was a den of adultery. Isabelle Eglan would have pulled Rachel out of there and whipped up religious fervour against the place.

Kala leaned her head back against the couch and closed her eyes, exhausted by the possibilities. The murders might have had nothing to do with Rachel and Phil Bocock's relationship. The damning photos and underlying tensions that she'd sensed from the start pointed to the killer living at Pine Hollow Lodge. The murders spoke of desperation. *Of all-consuming anger.*

Kala thought back over the day. She pictured Petra sitting with Rouleau on her dock earlier this afternoon and replayed their conversation as retold to her by Rouleau. *If you want to know who Rachel was sleeping with …*

Her eyes snapped open. Rouleau had said that Neal Lorring had been watching him and Petra. Rouleau had found it odd that Neal didn't reveal himself until Petra noticed him camouflaged by the woods. On approach, Neal had been angry and said that he had something to discuss with Petra in private. "Never found out what he wanted," Rouleau said. Kala's heart lurched.

She pushed herself to her feet and Taiku leapt off the couch, on guard next to her. She could hear the rain pattering against the roof, see the night pressing against the window. The last thing she wanted to do was step outside into the foul weather, but Clark had sent word earlier that everyone was free to leave. The window of time in which to corner the killer was narrowing, because tomorrow the lodge would be all but empty. If she was going to press the issue, force the killer into slipping up, it had to be tonight.

CHAPTER THIRTY-EIGHT

Martha sat alone in their cabin, staring out the living room window in the direction of the lake. She couldn't see the water, with the exception of the raindrops splattering the pane, but the thought of the rolling waves and warm sand beach soothed her.

She loved this property. Land handed down from her father to her, and if things had gone as planned, to her and Neal's children. A family linked through time and space by Pine Hollow Lodge — the idea had started as a yearning that grew over the last few years into a need. She'd tried so hard to have a child with Neal but four miscarriages later she'd become weary. Worn out from grief with the need for a baby making her physically ill. She'd finally persuaded Neal to give in vitro a go when they got back to Cobourg, but that was before he'd found out about her afternoons with Petra.

What the hell was I thinking? She hadn't been thinking — that was the problem.

She hadn't seen Neal since late morning when they'd actually had a conversation and cleared the air about a few things that had been bothering her. She'd told him that Petra saw him with Rachel and that it had hurt her. Maybe it didn't make up for her own infidelity, but this proved that neither of them had been innocent this summer. She asked him to bury all their mistakes and start over. A baby would be a new beginning for all of them. She'd forgive his affair with Rachel if he could do the same for her with Petra.

Neal had sat very still while she spoke, head lowered, eyes on his folded hands. He'd waited for her to finish speaking before looking up. "Petra has not been much help to either of us," he said at last. His eyes flashed with an expression that startled her. He was angry, and maybe she should have anticipated this. After all, Petra had betrayed him twice. The first time by seducing his wife and the second by telling his wife about his own infidelity.

"We can get past all this." She reached out and grabbed one of his hands. She knew that Neal hated it when she begged, but she was willing to do whatever it took to get him back. She'd more than proven that. He was the only man she wanted to have a child with. He was her soulmate. "Please, Neal. Give me … give us another chance. I'll spend the rest of my life making up for this summer."

"I have to think," he said, pulling his hand away. He looked ill. "I need some space."

"Of course. I'll be here waiting for you."

She chewed on a fingernail and thought about pouring a glass of wine and making a sandwich. She'd been too nervous to eat all day but knew she had to get some nourishment into her or she'd become lightheaded. She stood at the same time as she heard a knock at the front door. Before she had time to cross the floor the door slammed open and banged against the wall, causing a reverberation throughout the cabin. Petra flew inside, hair sopping wet, eyes searching the room like a wild bird checking for predators. Her gaze landed on Martha.

"There you are," she said and crossed the space between them without taking off her wet shoes. They squelched on the hardwood floor with each step. She stopped a few feet from Martha. "Neal told me to come and apologize this morning. I needed time to think about it."

"Whatever for?"

Petra's eyes narrowed. "What are you doing here standing in the almost-dark?"

"Thinking. Are you okay, Petra? You seem kind of ..." she wanted to say *crazed*, but settled on "off-kilter. What did Neal send you to apologize for?"

"I'm not well. Not really. I have to get my medication sorted. It's nothing to worry about."

Martha moved past her and turned on the overhead lights. The candles she'd lit on the coffee table flickered as she passed, the melted wax nearly engulfing the wicks. She bent and blew out the feeble flames. She may as well tell Petra now, since Neal was reconsidering their future and she believed he would take her back. "The police are letting us leave tomorrow. There was a message on my phone."

Petra bobbed up and down in place. "They've arrested Rachel's English teacher. Phil Bocock was screwing her."

She knew that girl was evil. "Him, too? Seems our Rachel was having quite the summer."

Petra's face burned red. She was frowning even though laughter bubbled out of her throat. "The thing is, I was wrong about that. Neal never had anything going with Rachel. I misspoke to you, and Neal's livid."

"But you said ..." Martha's heart went cold. She spoke slowly and calmly as if to a child. "You told me that Neal and Rachel were having sex. You said that you saw them together."

"Together *walking*. Not together-together."

Martha's voice dropped to a whisper. "What have you done?"

"It was an honest mistake."

"No, it wasn't. You *made* me believe that Neal was having sex with our waitress. Our *teenage* waitress. You took great delight in telling me. In fact, you told me that he was in love with her." Martha's brain was scrambling for a toehold in the horror that cascaded down around her. "Where's Neal now?"

"He and Shane are having a drink at our place. Shane and I are going to live together if I promise to go to the doctor when we get back to Sudbury. Neal said he might come stay for a while until he finds his own place." Petra clamped a hand over her mouth. "Sorry, I wasn't supposed to say that."

Despair fuelled by rage expanded to fill Martha's chest until she screamed out her anger. One scream felt good, so she shrieked out another. The room floated in wavy lines with black dots thickening on the edges of her vision. Petra's mouth had formed into a round circle and her eyes were wide and scared, like a blow-up Betty Boop. The sight of Petra's horror made Martha stifle a giggle even though none of this was remotely funny. She rubbed her eyes and blinked hard, then took a deep breath. She felt her blood pressure lower enough so that she could see straight again. Petra's face morphed back into its normal size and shape although her eyes were large and panicked.

I'm not going down without bringing you with me, Martha thought. *Your lies are the reason I did what I did. You have single-handedly destroyed my life. You and Shane will not live happily ever after with Neal sleeping all cozy in your guest room, the three of you laughing at me as if I'm the crazy one.* She leapt the distance to the kitchen and pulled the carving knife out of the wooden block on the counter, swinging around to face Petra.

"What are you doing, Martha?" asked Petra as she started backing up toward the door. Her eyes stayed focused on the knife. She whimpered. "I need to go see Shane."

"Then let's go see him. Let's tell him and Neal that you're the reason that all our lives are ruined."

"How could our lives be ruined?"

Martha felt a small surge of power as she watched understanding cross Petra's frantic face.

Yeah, that's right. I'm the killer, not Phil Bocock or anybody else Rachel was screwing. Not anybody else who she and Faraday were blackmailing. Nobody is going to destroy what's rightfully mine. I'll kill all of you and burn this place to the fucking ground first.

A calmness stole over her. Perhaps this had been the path all along. She didn't have to bear the pain any longer — she had the power to ease the horror that her life had become. And she could make damn sure that Petra didn't live to ruin other lives or to enjoy one more wicked, self-serving second of her own debauched existence.

"Slight change of plans," she said to Petra. "We're going to take a walk over to the main lodge and see what we can cook up."

CHAPTER THIRTY-NINE

Kala and Taiku emerged from the path to the main road as a slam of thunder cracked like a gunshot overhead. Lightning lit up the landscape and Kala took the opportunity to look for anyone else out late on this stormy night. They were alone as far as she could see.

She pointed her flashlight toward the ground and walked in the direction of the main lodge. The restaurant was in darkness and she continued on past. She believed that the killer was from one of the two couples impacted by the explicit photos of Petra and Martha together in the guest cabin: Shane and Petra. Neal and Martha. She considered Neal Lorring suspect number one, but wasn't ruling any of them out. Not yet.

Shane and Petra's cabin was closest to the restaurant, set back in the woods away from the water. The lights were on. Kala stood for a moment under the shelter of a tree at the fringes of the property, watching for signs of life inside. She called to Taiku to heel and they approached the cabin together. She didn't have her service revolver and hoped that Taiku would at least make somebody think twice before attacking her … if it came to that.

She listened at the door before knocking, then gave a solid rap. Seconds later Shane swung the door open wide. She looked past him and saw Neal sitting on the couch with a glass of amber liquid in his hand. Shane held a glass as well and he drew her into the room with his free hand. She told Taiku to wait outside on the porch where he was sheltered from the rain and followed Shane inside.

"What are you doing out on such a miserable night?" Shane asked when she turned her attention back to him. "Come into the living room. Leave your boots on. I have a fire going and you can warm up." He raised his glass. "Join us in a glass of Scotch?"

"No, thank you. I'll only be a moment." She looked into the corners of the room and surveyed the kitchen. "Are Petra and Martha here?"

"Petra went over to talk to Martha at her cabin. I expect her back any minute."

She looked at Neal. "You spoke with Petra when you found her with my partner Rouleau on the dock. Would you tell me why you were angry with her today?"

Neal's eyes turned wary. "We heard you've made an arrest, so how could my anger with Petra be of any importance?"

"There's been no arrest. We're still working to put the pieces together."

Neal shrugged. "Martha told me this afternoon that Petra convinced her I was sleeping with Rachel

Eglan. It was a fabrication, and I confronted Petra. Let's say she realized how damaging her fantasy leap could be and was convinced a short while ago by me and Shane to go apologize to Martha."

"You were not having an affair with Rachel?"

"God, no. Rachel was a kid, still in high school. Petra saw normal human kindness and spun it into something ugly."

Shane had been standing next to Kala and he cleared his throat. "In her defence, Petra is manic and off her meds, and she's been known to make up shit. She's promised to see a doctor as soon as we get out of here. By the way, is there any word on when we're free to close up and leave?"

"Officer Harrison left a message with Martha, Neal. He said you can all go your separate ways tomorrow."

"I haven't been home most of the day. Did she tell you, Shane?"

"Nope."

They were silent as they pondered what Martha's silence could mean. Kala started to get a bad feeling, as if time were running out. She said, "Some photos taken by Thomas Faraday have surfaced. Some revealing photos."

Both men stared at her. Shane asked, "Can you, uh, give us any more detail?"

"Your wives were alone together in a guest cabin ..."

Neal jumped off the couch before she could finish. "Why, that prick Faraday. If he wasn't already dead I'd let him have it for being a scumbag voyeur."

Shane's expression revealed a man gobsmacked. "He was watching them? Taking pictures? Good God almighty."

Their reactions told Kala two things: they both knew about their wives' affair, and neither had known about the pictures. They might be putting on an act, but her instincts said otherwise. If she continued with the premise that Faraday had been blackmailing the killer, the only reason she could see for his murder, then only Petra and Martha remained as viable suspects.

Kala thought about the two women's opposite personalities. Martha was competent and controlled whereas Petra was manic and promiscuous. Faraday's series of photos gave evidence that Petra had initiated the sex.

Martha believed that Rachel and Neal were having an affair only because Petra had convinced her. Martha must have felt that both her marriage and Pine Hollow Lodge were under threat ... and Petra was instrumental in both. How high would Martha's anger escalate once she found out that Petra had fabricated Rachel's affair with Neal, the likely catalyst for Rachel's murder?

"I think we need to go find your wives," said Kala, making no effort to hide the urgency in her voice. "We should be prepared to stop one of them from doing something rash."

Both men stared at her with dawning horror. "Which one?" asked Shane.

Kala hesitated. "We'll find out when we speak with them."

If it's not too late.

Kala put her hand on Shane's arm when they reached the road. "Could you first run over to Ian and Blaine's cabin and ask one of them to drive into Searchmont to call 911? Then join us at Neal's cabin."

Shane nodded, his face grim, his eyes darting between her and the Lorrings' cabin farther up the road before he turned and disappeared into the veil of rain and darkness.

Martha grabbed Petra by the arm, ignoring her shriek of pain. "Walk, you bitch. Don't make me cut you."

Petra snivelled and blubbered like a baby the entire walk through the woods to the road. Martha thought about slitting her throat and being done with the irritation but that would be letting her off too easy. She prodded Petra forward in the shadows along the edge of the road in case someone happened along, although the odds were slim with the storm drenching them before they'd gone ten steps. She pulled Petra into the brush when she saw a hooded figure that looked like that woman cop going up the path toward Petra and Shane's cabin. Petra wrenched forward and tried to struggle free. "Don't even think about it," said Martha through clenched teeth. "I'll kill you here and now without thinking twice. And then I'll kill her next."

Petra froze in place. "I said I'm sorry, Martha." Her teeth were chattering from cold or fear or both. "I'll make things right." She turned to face Martha, rain streaming down her face like a steady flow of tears. She clasped both hands in front of her. "Please give me another chance. Please, Martha."

"No." Martha had never felt as certain about anything in her life. This woman needed to pay. If not for her, Neal would still want to be married and they'd be trying for another baby. *And I wouldn't have killed Rachel or Thomas.* She closed that thought down as soon as it entered her head. She had to keep herself numb and not think about what she'd done. Only madness lay on that path.

"Neal loves you. He doesn't have to know … about Rachel or Thomas and what you did. I won't tell anybody. Ow!"

Martha wrenched Petra's arm and shoved her forward. "Keep walking. I'm not listening to any more of your lies."

Petra sobbed but she stopped begging. She lurched back onto the road and resumed her weeping as she stumbled ahead of Martha while the thunder rumbled overhead and lightning lit up the sky. *How did I ever find you attractive?* thought Martha.

They reached the path to the main lodge and cut across the grass to the back entrance, which was in darkness. Martha had the key out and fumbled to open the lock. She shoved Petra inside and locked the door behind them. It didn't matter now if she turned on a light and anybody saw. Nothing mattered. She felt as if a force were propelling her toward the end.

"Sit over there," she told Petra. "Where I can see you."

"Okay, Martha." Petra used a phony, meek voice that grated on Martha's nerves. She obediently sat herself down in the corner on the stool that Shane used to reach the high cupboards, like she deserved to be punished. Martha knew that the true Petra never showed remorse or insecurity. All she ever cared about was herself. Shane would be better off without this amoral leech sucking the lifeblood out of him. In a way, she was saving his life.

Fuelled by her anger and not allowing herself to stop moving, Martha found the bucket of old cooking grease that Shane kept tucked under the counter until he had a chance to clean it out. She set the knife on the counter within reach and picked up the container, splashing oil across the counter and floor. She filled the skillet on the stove and threw the remainder of the oil in the bucket in Petra's direction, satisfied to see Petra cower as gobs of it landed on her clothes and hair. Her last task was to turn the heat up high under the pan of oil. It didn't take long for a flame to spark and send brilliant orange fire straight upward. The oil that had pooled on the counter and floor caught in seconds and spread quickly up the wall. The dry wooden structure was engulfed in flame in the blink of an eye. Martha stared through the fire and smoke at Petra shrieking in the corner and had the feeling of returning to her own body. *What have I done?*

The instinct to save herself made her frantic. *Not this way*, she thought. *Petra should die. Not me.* But she'd misjudged how fast the fire would grow, and flames had already spread to block the exit into the main restaurant. She spun back around to go out the back way, but the smoke was thick and black, and she couldn't see Petra anymore. She opened her mouth to scream and the smoke filled her lungs and stung her eyes. She dropped to her knees and began crawling toward what she believed to be the back door. Her entire body felt as if it was on fire and she realized she didn't want to die. The crackling and popping and heat were too much. Too much. Something struck her back, and she collided with a wall where she thought the doorway opening should be. "Neal!" she screamed, and more smoke choked her and the pain seared into her back and the roar of the fire consumed her as she tried with every ounce of will left inside her to crawl toward safety.

Neal and Kala approached his cabin without speaking. Taiku stayed close to Kala as if sensing trouble. Neal had his chin tucked into his rain jacket and his hands in his pockets, walking quickly and slightly ahead of her. He stopped at the edge of his property and studied the cabin. He swivelled his head to look at Kala.

"The lights are on. I don't hear any screaming." A smile flitted across his face. "You should know that Martha and I aren't together anymore," he said. "She wants to be, but I'm done."

"Can you tell me why?"

"We've tried to have a baby and she's miscarried a few times. It changed her. She started becoming obsessive and difficult to be around. Sex became a

grim chore and all she talked about. Charts, ovu-
lation windows, and body temperature — it never
ended. She'd cry for days if she got her period. It got
so bad I hated to come home. Then we came here for
the summer and she seemed a bit more like herself
until I caught her in bed with Petra and … I don't
know. Nothing feels the same for me anymore." He
wiped rain from his eyes. "Do you believe she killed
Rachel and Thomas?"

"I think you should be prepared for that eventu-
ality. She could be more troubled than you imagine.
Sometimes people struggle and do things they
wouldn't even contemplate when mentally healthy."

Neal looked at the ground. "I'll go in and try to
talk to her."

"You must be extremely careful not to make
her feel there's no hope. Don't let her know how
shocked you are by what she's done. Stay calm. I'll
be right behind you."

"Would it be better if I went in alone?"

"It might take two of us to keep both women
from harm."

"Petra could be the killer." He spoke without
conviction.

"She could be, but I believe that Martha had the
most to lose."

"I can hardly get my head around this."

They approached the house and Neal entered first.
He called Martha's name, but silence greeted them.
He walked around the living room and checked the
kitchen and bedrooms before rejoining Kala.

"They're not here."

"Then we'll have to spread out and find them. I don't think we have much time."

Taiku growled a warning as they stepped outside. He was on guard, looking toward the road. Kala reached down and grabbed on to his collar as Shane and Ian emerged from the trees. They were walking far apart, and Kala remembered that Petra had been sleeping with Ian when Shane was working in the kitchen. Thankfully the two men appeared prepared to set that aside for now.

"Blaine's driving toward town until he gets a phone signal. Have you found them yet?" asked Shane.

"They're not here," said Neal. "Could they have gone to the beach?"

"Lights are on in the main lodge," said Ian. "I thought Shane was in there working, but since he isn't, it might be them."

"The lights in the restaurant were off when I went to your cabin, Shane," said Kala. The men gathered around her. "We have to assume that this could be a hostage situation and make contact with the women while we wait for the reinforcements to arrive. Neal, are you still comfortable talking to Martha?"

"Yeah."

"Does either woman have access to a gun?"

"Shane and I don't hunt and haven't any guns, so I'd say no."

"That's good." She tried to reassure them with her eyes. "Our goal is to keep everyone safe. Stay calm and follow my lead."

Each man nodded and they hurried down the path to the road with Neal and Kala in the front. She kept Taiku at her side, wishing now that she'd left him in their cabin out of harm's way.

"Rain's letting up a bit," said Neal.

She turned her face skyward and found he was right. The rain had eased to a drizzle. That should make their wait easier if the women couldn't be coaxed out right away.

Neal stopped and Kala felt him grab her arm. "What the hell?" Neal pointed up the road toward the main lodge and her eyes followed the direction of his finger. The windows were glowing orange in the back section, and as they watched, flames began licking up the sides of the outer walls toward the roof. Kala and the others stood frozen for a second as they tried to comprehend the surreal sight unfolding before their eyes. In that split moment of hesitation, the glow from the flames lit up the sky like blowtorches.

"Hurry!" Kala cried and the men sped ahead of her toward the restaurant. By the time she and Taiku reached the parking lot, the entire kitchen was engulfed in flame with black smoke billowing skyward. The fire was crackling and popping, the noise a roar in her ears. Shane, Neal, and Ian were already circling the lodge, trying to get inside. She could hear the hiss of rain meeting fire and the rush of flames, not slowed by the precipitation that was barely making a dent. Kala pulled her jacket up over her nose and mouth to filter the acrid stench of burning wood and plastics and chemicals. As she peered into the glow of the burning building, she spotted Shane running along the side closest to her toward the front door. He yelled something before disappearing inside. Neal followed behind him through the smoke-filled door and Kala lunged forward to join them. Ian grabbed her by the arm and pulled her back.

"There's no point," he yelled above the crackling and roar of the fire. "They're insane to go in there."

She wanted to follow them inside but knew that he was right. The window of time before the entire structure was on fire was over. The men might already be too late to make it back out alive. She wouldn't risk it now. *Not now.* Taiku was huddled against her, growling and whimpering. She crouched down and wrapped her arms around his neck. The heat and smoke were blinding and her eyes burned with grit and ash. They were too far from the lake to carry buckets of water. Their only hope was that Blaine had roused Searchmont's volunteer fire brigade and they'd arrive before the forest caught fire.

"Look!" Ian shouted over the fire's roar. "They made it out."

Kala squinted toward where she'd seen the men go inside the burning building and recognized their dark shapes against the wall of flame. Ian signalled for her to stay, but he raced forward into the suffocating furnace heat. She watched until he met up with Shane and Neal who were half-carrying, half-dragging one of the women between them out of the smoke and heat. Kala ordered Taiku to stay and ran over to help. Neal and Shane dropped back and let Ian pick up the unconscious woman. He carried her at a run through the bushes to a clearing at the side of the road. Kala grabbed on to Neal who was struggling to stand and guided him after the others, calling for Taiku to heel.

Ian lowered the woman onto the sodden ground. Kala couldn't tell whether it was Petra or Martha because of the black smoke and ash coating her clothes and hair. Kala dropped down next to the woman and checked for vital signs, careful not to put pressure on her burned flesh. A sulphurous smell emanated from the woman's hair and her burnt skin smelled like charcoal. Her breathing was raspy and laboured, and Kala knew they didn't have much time. She looked up the road in the unlikely hope that she'd see the lights of an approaching emergency vehicle through the mist and tendrils of fog rising from the roadway. Ian was still next to her. She asked, "Can you watch her while I check on the others?"

He nodded and she moved over to Neal and Shane, Taiku following close at her heels. Neal was holding his stomach, bent over and vomiting into bushes, but he shook off her offer to help. She waited until he staggered back and found a spot to sit before going to Shane who was closer to the road. The intensity of the fire lit up the shadows and heated the air even this far away from the lodge. Both men were filthy with black smoke, their clothes charred. It would have been a miracle if they hadn't suffered any burns. Shane's hands were already blistering and he held them stretched out in front of him.

"We couldn't find them both." He moaned and dropped into a sitting position on the ground with his head between his knees, his arms resting on his legs so that his hands were in the air. "It's a bloody inferno."

She crouched next to him. "Did you rescue Petra or Martha?"

"Don't know." Shane hunched over and coughed while Kala steadied his back. "She's burnt so bad."

A siren sounded far off in the distance from the direction of Searchmont but gained in volume as they waited, while the fire consumed what was left of the main lodge. Kala closed her eyes and thanked Blaine for rousing help so quickly. She tried to centre herself so that she could face the long night ahead. When she opened her eyes, she looked toward the lodge. Every room was ablaze in orange flame with reams of black smoke rolling thickly across the last remains of the roof and into the night sky. If anybody was left inside they'd never make it out alive.

"I don't know which one I want her to be," Shane said, as if there'd been no break in their conversation. "Either way, both their lives are over."

CHAPTER FORTY

Kala was officially off the case as soon as the officers arrived from the Sault detachment, but they requested that she accompany them to the station anyway after the ambulance pulled away with sirens blaring. She refused to leave Taiku behind, and they agreed that he should join her in the back of the squad car. Normally she'd have preferred to drive her own truck but she was past arguing with anybody. Her energy gauge was riding close to empty.

Clark arrived sometime after she was settled with a cup of tea, giving her version of events to an officer with a tape recorder. He pulled up a chair and listened as she told of their search for Petra and Martha and the ensuing fire at the main lodge. The officer signed off when she finished talking and left them alone in the room. Taiku was sound asleep under the table.

"There was no sign of the second woman?" Clark asked Kala.

"No, but she didn't get out alive. The two of them were together and the fire spread so quickly —

like a fireball. I'm guessing Martha lit the cooking grease and the wood building went up like a torch. We couldn't identify the woman they pulled out. It could be either Petra or Martha."

"I checked the hospital in the Soo where the ambulance took her. She's being flown to the burn unit in Toronto. Still unconscious. We have a cadaver dog coming from Sudbury to go through the remains of the building."

Kala knew the answer but asked anyway. "Phil Bocock hasn't confessed to murder?"

"No, he strenuously denies being the killer of anybody, and I gotta say, I believe him despite my earlier suspicions. Greta tempered her anger somewhat and said he's too much of a spineless wimp to kill anyone. Faraday's photos that you collected certainly give someone at the lodge a motive. You said that you believe Martha Lorring murdered Rachel and Faraday?"

"I do."

"Lay out your reasoning."

"Petra had Martha convinced that Neal was having an affair with Rachel. Their marriage was in trouble because Martha had miscarried a few times and was fixated on getting pregnant. Neal shared that much. She had a fling with Petra this summer in one of the guest cabins. Neal found out and he wanted out of their marriage. Martha was desperate to get him back and she thought Rachel was a threat. As for Faraday, I believe he was blackmailing Martha with photos of her having sex with Petra, and she saw him as another threat to Pine Hollow Lodge. Rachel appears to have been Faraday's accomplice, although we'll never know that for certain. Can you imagine what would have happened to their business if the photos went online? This town would have shunned them. People like Rachel's mother would have waged war."

"Petra would have lost a lot, too."

"Not really. She and Shane have an open marriage, and he knew about her and Martha already. He'd been willing to overlook all her other affairs in any event. He had no vested interest in the lodge and they'd be moving on after this summer."

"I gather you've eliminated Neal as well."

"I suspected him, to be honest, but he certainly didn't force anyone into the restaurant and set the place on fire. He and Shane were with me."

Clark stared at her with a regretful smile on his face. "I don't like it when we haven't got concrete evidence to back up theories, but this time we might be shit out of luck."

"You still have forensics, and the woman might recover enough to talk."

"Maybe. One can dream." He slapped his thighs and stood up. "I can't thank you enough for all your help. If you're ever looking for a new challenge ..."

"I'll keep that in mind." She stood and reached out a hand. He held it in both of his.

"You take care of yourself, Stonechild, and be sure to look me up next time you're passing through."

"You can count on it. Have fun with that new baby."

His expression brightened. "Sleepless nights ahead, but I won't complain."

"Did you ever think about *not* becoming parents? I mean, the responsibility and lifestyle change could be hard on you and your marriage." She knew it was an odd question, and he studied her before answering.

"Those are considerations, but as soon as I saw our son, none of that mattered anymore. You'll feel the same if the time ever comes that you have a kid."

"I have one. Dawn, remember?" She spotted an officer standing in the hall waiting for Clark to finish up. "You're wanted."

"Going to be a busy day. Safe travels, Stonechild. Don't be a stranger." He looked at her as if he wanted to say something more, but she waved him toward the door and said, "I hate long, soppy good-byes. Get on your way, Officer Harrison, before your exit turns downright maudlin."

Kala woke up disoriented. Light was shining full bore into the living room where she lay sleeping on the couch with Taiku stretched out on the floor next to her. She glanced at the wall clock in the kitchen. She'd slept five hours since the officer dropped her off at Pine Hollow Lodge at 10:00 a.m. The police had been working the scene of the fire, but she'd stayed away, her involvement thankfully no longer required. She sat up and rubbed the back of her head where a low throb threatened to derail what was left of the day. Taiku was on his feet, his chin resting on her leg, his liquid brown eyes staring up at her.

"All right, boy. I'll get moving." She scratched behind his ears.

She stood too quickly and a wave of nausea and dizziness made her sit back down. When she'd arrived back at the cabin midmorning, she'd planned to shower, pack up her stuff, and hit the road, but exhaustion had taken over and she'd closed her eyes for a minute … or so she'd thought. Now the day was getting away from her, and she had no intention of being unwell and stuck here for the night. She breathed deeply until she felt better and stood again, but this time slowly. She took a five-minute shower and threw on yoga pants and a T-shirt in preparation for a long drive. While bread toasted and water boiled for tea, she fed Taiku and cleaned out the fridge. She ate the toast as she worked and let the tea steep in a travel mug. It took another ten minutes to throw her clothes and toiletries into a bag, and she was ready to hit the road. She checked her watch. *Quarter to four. Lots of daylight left.*

When she stepped outside, Taiku bounded ahead of her toward the lake. She called to him before she saw Jordan rise to his feet from where he'd been sitting on the rocks. He walked toward her and she met him halfway, remembering other times when they'd been together and he'd waited for her to get off shift.

"Hell of a night at Pine Hollow Lodge," he said, reaching her. Taiku was jumping excitedly around him, tail wagging at top speed. Jordan laughed and gave Taiku's head another rub before straightening and looking at her. "I've been sitting here for a few hours waiting for you to wake up and come outside. How are you?"

The sun was warm on her face, but she smelled the stench of the burned building in the air. She could hear people talking through the woods and realized that Forensics was still sifting through the building's remains. "I'm good," she said. "Eager to get out of here."

"Me too. I'm all set to head home, and I'm hoping you'll come with me." He grabbed on to her hand. "I want you to come to Thunder Bay. Make a life together."

And here it is, she thought. *The moment of truth*. She'd known without him having initiated anything since their paths crossed that this moment would come. They knew each other too well.

"Walk with me," she said, squeezing his hand before letting go, and he fell into step with her as they started up the incline toward the cabin where she'd left her bags. He took the heaviest one, and she thanked him as she'd have had difficulty juggling her mug of tea with the rest of her gear. They didn't speak and she took this moment to weigh what going west with him would mean.

The part of her that still cared for him felt his pull. They had a lot in common. Same love of the outdoors. Same easiness with each other that meant times together were good — very good. The sex had been both exciting and comfortable. She'd taken a long time to get over not waking up next to him. He was a loyal man who understood her and didn't judge. She knew that she could easily fall into life with him again. That made her next words bittersweet.

"I can't go with you, Jordan, much as I'd like to. I have commitments in Kingston, but please know that I wouldn't trade those few years with you for anything. Much as I feel the attraction to those memories and to you, I can't go back."

They'd reached her truck and turned to face each other. He was standing very close. Too close. His eyes warmed her even as she was telling him that she wouldn't be going with him. He opened his arms and she stepped into them, resting her head against his.

"I'm still in love with you, Kala Stonechild. Can I say or do anything to change your mind?"

She rested for a moment against the familiar warmth of him before pulling herself away. She had to risk hurting him or he'd keep hoping. "I've got somebody waiting for me at home. I need to give him and me a chance. I love him."

"And if it doesn't work out ...?"

"You have to forget about me," she said gently before turning and opening her truck door. Taiku leapt inside and settled on the passenger seat. She slung her bags into the back and leaned against the door, giving in to one last look at the man she was letting go. They stared at each other for a long moment before she climbed into the cab and slammed the door.

He was still standing with his hands in his pockets watching her truck drive away when she took one last glance in the rear-view mirror. She knew he was hoping that she'd stop the truck and turn around, but it was better this way. *The first cut is the deepest.* Taiku seemed to sense her sadness. He whined and got as close to her as he could. She reached over and rested her hand on his head while she blinked away the blurriness in her eyes.

"I'm all right, boy," she said. "I just need a minute."

Because if there's one thing I know how to do, it's leave people behind and never look back.

She focused her gaze on the dome of blue sky over the treeline. A hawk swooped and soared above a pine tree before disappearing from view. She rolled down the windows and let fresh air into the cab. Taiku moved away from her and stuck his nose out to catch the breeze. Kala looked back at the road and thought about the long drive ahead of them. She reached over and turned on the radio. Gordon Lightfoot's "If You Could Read My Mind" filled the silence, his deep voice rich in melodic regret for a love affair gone wrong. She smiled at the unexpected irony and glanced at Taiku as she turned up the volume. "Some fitting travel music to see us on our way, old boy. Let's hope the sad songs end and the rock and roll kicks in long before we reach Kingston."

CHAPTER FORTY-ONE

Dawn was in the kitchen helping Henri with the dishes, leaving Gundersund and Rouleau to sit with their crystal tumblers of Scotch on the balcony overlooking Kingston harbour.

"Nice night," said Rouleau, gazing out at the sprinkle of lights surrounding the shoreline casting long shafts of light on the black water. He drank from the glass and tried to find the peace that had eluded him since he'd returned from his trip to Searchmont. A battle had raged inside him on how much to tell Gundersund about Stonechild and the man from her past who'd occupied her time. So far, he'd quelled the side that wanted to warn Gundersund that she might not be coming home. Tonight, he wasn't sure that he needed to say anything. Gundersund's dark silence spoke volumes.

"Thanks for the dinner invitation," said Gundersund. "Dawn has a connection to your father, and he has a steady hand that she trusts."

"Dad's fond of her, too. They're good company for each other."

Gundersund kept his eyes focused on a boat's approaching lights. "Any regrets about Marci?"

"I miss her, but no, no regrets. She's a journalist first and foremost and always will be. My life's in Kingston."

"We can't change them." Gundersund's voice was resigned. "I thought that in staying here and letting Stonechild get whatever is bothering her out of her system, that she'd return and we could get on with things. Now I wonder if I should have chased after her. Made the grand gesture." He glanced at Rouleau and back at the water. "Some people aren't capable of settling into a relationship."

"She's had a tough life."

"It's why I can't blame her for doing what she has to do."

After Dawn and Gundersund left and Henri joined him on the balcony with his own glass of Scotch, Rouleau again wondered if he should have warned Gundersund about the man from Stonechild's past.

Henri sipped on his drink, then asked, "Mulling something over, son?"

"Only thinking how messy life can be. You belive you have the future under control and some-one throws a wrench into the mix."

"Ah, the best-laid plans. Are we talking about Marci?"

"No, I never had a future planned with her. Our relationship was centred on the present, and that suited us both. I'm more concerned with Stonechild and whether or not she'll ever find what she's looking for. She's never known stability. Gundersund wants to give her that, but she's torn between two worlds."

"Some people don't do well with commitment, especially if they've never had a secure home life."

"The odd thing is that I believe she wants a life with Gundersund, but she has this need to be off on her own. He's tried to be patient but he thinks he's lost her. I'm not certain that he hasn't."

Henri was silent. He took another sip of Scotch and stretched out his legs. When Rouleau thought it might be time to go inside and call it a night, his father stirred. "Kala is committed to Dawn and Rose. She won't desert them. Gundersund may believe he's lost her, but I've seen the two of them together and they have a bond. She's also mighty fond of you and the team. She'll find her way back, son."

"I hope you're right, Dad. She feels like the daughter I'd liked to have had."

"And that makes her my granddaughter." Henri patted Rouleau on the leg. "Trust that Kala wants her family as much as we want her here — trust that she'll find her way back to us, where she belongs."

Gundersund heard Dawn walking back and forth to the bathroom from where he sat on the couch checking emails with Minny snoozing at his feet. After three or four trips there was silence upstairs, and he imagined her in bed reading as she did every night before going to sleep. She'd been roaming the house in the early morning hours since their return from Joliette but hadn't wanted to open up to him about what was bothering her. He had a good idea anyway, since the same problems were keeping him awake.

Tonight they were both exhausted, and he hoped they'd be able to sleep through the night for the first time in a long while. At eleven o'clock, he let Minny outside for her last run around the yard, then locked up the house and climbed the stairs to bed.

Dawn was lying on her back, sound asleep, when he looked in on her. He tiptoed over to her bed and gently removed the textbook from her hand and set it on the night table. He pulled the covers up over her and turned off the light. Moonlight shone in through the open window, and he stood looking at her for a moment more before withdrawing and pulling the door closed behind him. He entered Kala's bedroom and stripped out of his clothes and got under the covers. Minny flopped down on her favourite spot on the carpet. He closed his eyes, not expecting to fall asleep without the usual tossing and turning even though every muscle in his body ached with fatigue.

His eyes snapped open and he took a moment to realize that he'd awoken from a deep sleep. He could hear Minny loping down the stairs and Dawn walking around on the main floor. He lay awake, thinking about getting up to see if she was okay, but the bed was warm and he dozed off again. When his eyes snapped open a second time, the room was still in darkness. He rolled over and looked at the clock. Quarter to three.

Minny wasn't in her usual place next to his bed. He listened for movement somewhere in the house and thought he heard a noise downstairs. Was Dawn still roaming around, unable to sleep? He couldn't ignore her insomnia any longer. He sat up and threw off the covers, grabbing his housecoat from where he'd thrown it on the chair.

He was surprised to see Dawn asleep in her bed and hesitated in the doorway, looking for Minny. The dog never strayed far from him at night, and now he worried that she was sick. He walked as quietly as he could across the landing and downstairs. Two dogs greeted him in the hallway, tails wagging and tongues out to lick his hands. Joy replaced the trepidation in his chest.

"Kala?" he called.

He found her stretched out on the couch, but she sat up when she saw him. "I didn't want to wake you," she said, holding her arms open wide. He sat down next to her and wrapped his arms around her. She kissed him and pressed her body into his.

"When did you get in?" he asked when they both came up for air.

"An hour ago. I stopped a few times en route and took a catnap in a truck stop north of Toronto. It's been a long week."

"It's been a long month." He reached to turn on a lamp so that he could see her face, but she put a restraining hand on his arm.

"Leave it off. Let's go to bed. I can fill you in tomorrow morning."

The dogs padded up the stairs ahead of them. Kala crawled into bed before him and was lying on her side snoring softly when Gundersund wrapped an arm over her hip and around her stomach. He kissed the nape of her neck and matched his breathing to hers.

When he next woke, he was alone. He could hear Dawn and Kala talking in the kitchen, and the smell of bacon frying wafted upstairs. He lay still for a while, enjoying the sound of their voices and letting himself believe that Kala had come home for good. He jumped out of bed when he couldn't stand being away from them a moment longer and threw on jeans and a sweatshirt.

He entered the kitchen and the dogs padded over to greet him. Dawn was smiling when she turned from scrambling eggs at the stove. "Take a seat, Gundersund. Breakfast is almost ready."

Kala poured him a cup of coffee and brushed against him when she set it down on the table. She poured herself a cup of herbal tea from the pot and sat next to him while Dawn served. Gundersund watched Kala's face while they ate. The bluish shadows under her eyes could be from fatigue, but he wasn't sure what caused the sadness. She caught his eye once and looked down at the table, as if trying to evade his scrutiny. She'd pushed the bacon and eggs around on her plate and had only eaten half a piece of toast.

"Is everything okay?" Dawn asked.

Kala smiled at her. "Everything is fine. I'm tired from the past few weeks."

Gundersund felt the familiar unease deep in his belly. She was with them for the moment, but was she only here to tell them that she'd be leaving again?

He finished eating without an appetite and poured a second cup of coffee while Dawn and Kala walked the dogs to the beach. He took his coffee and laptop outside onto the deck and read emails and the news, trying to keep his mind occupied while he waited for their return.

A half hour later, Kala and Dawn strolled arm in arm across the lawn with the dogs sticking close by. Kala joined him on the steps while Dawn went indoors to study. She leaned against him and wrapped an arm around his neck.

"The second woman died from her burns," he said, opening his laptop to show the news story to her.

Stonechild took the laptop and read silently. She handed the laptop back to him. "I got an email last night from Clark. The cadaver dog located the second body. Martha died in the fire, so it was Petra who got out, but she was in bad shape. Her death might be a blessing in the long run. She was in for a lifetime of pain and disfigurement. The fire was deliberately set in the kitchen."

"So one of these two women killed in the fire committed the other two murders?"

"Certainly looks that way." Stonechild pulled back and turned her body sideways on the step so that she was facing him.

"I have to tell you something," she said.

"Tell me."

She took a deep breath. "I was foolish and won't expect you to pay for my mistake. I thought about what to do for a long time …"

He groaned and cut her off. "Tell me what you're talking about, Stonechild. I can't take any more suspense."

"All right, but you might regret this when you hear." She gave a half smile and took a second deep breath, letting the air out slowly before saying, "I'm pregnant. Nearly three months." She held up a hand to stop him from talking. "Now I know you don't want kids and I'm not sure I'll be a good mother, but I've decided that I'm keeping the baby. I did a lot of soul-searching and know this is the right thing to do. Turns out, I want to have a child. You don't have to feel tied down by my —"

"What?" Her words were cut off by his shout. He picked her up off her feet and kissed her mouth. "Are you crazy, woman? I've wanted a child as long as I can remember."

She blinked. "I thought you didn't want kids."

"Whatever gave you that idea?"

"You said that you were glad Fiona never got pregnant."

"Only because she wasn't the right one and our lives would have been so messy when we split. A child with you is … perfect. I've never wanted anything more in my life." He sat down and pulled her into his lap. He rubbed a hand up and down her back. "Are you feeling okay? Is everything good with the baby? Can I do anything?"

She laughed at his joy and his worry and held his face with both her hands. She kissed his mouth, his cheeks, and his neck before lifting her head to stare into his eyes. "Everything is perfect," she said.

"Turns out my body is made for this kind of action."
She pulled back. "Are you crying?"

"No." He wiped a hand across his eyes. "But if I were, they'd be tears of happiness."

"You can't imagine how wonderful all this feels. I was so torn about even telling you and now ... now I realize how wrong I was to doubt in us."

He was silent. His finger traced the line of her jaw as his eyes held hers. "I'm in this with you for the long haul, Stonechild. Never doubt that again. And if you need to get away alone to recharge, I can keep the home fires burning." He kissed her. "Should we go tell Dawn she's about to become a babysitter?"

Kala laughed. "What every teenager wants to hear."

"She's not just any teenager. And this won't be just any baby. She'll be the best of both of us. There'll be no stopping her."

"She?"

"Okay. Or he, but I'm thinking girl. We have to go break the news to Rouleau and Henri." Gundersund started across the deck then stopped and leapt back to kiss her. The dogs were jumping around him, barking with tails wagging. He held her by both shoulders. "I'll get Dawn. You wait here." He took a step, turned. "Rest while I'm gone," he said. "I'll bring more tea."

She watched him go as she lowered herself onto the steps. "And so it begins," she said to Taiku and Minny, who were watching her from their vigil in front of the patio door. Taiku's tail thumped on the deck at the sound of her voice and he came over and rested his head on her leg. She rubbed his ears and smiled when he licked her hand. "Looks like we've come home, boy," she said. She looked out across the property, past the garden that she and Dawn had tended all summer, to the thick copse of trees and the lake beyond. Soon, her child would be playing on this stretch of grass, growing tall and strong in the sunshine. There would be no more hold from past foster homes or the aching loneliness; she could finally let go of the past and let her love for Gundersund and Dawn and this baby growing inside her fill all the hollows and cracks, until she became whole and strong and — at long last — embraced with every fibre of her being the family she'd searched so long to find.

ACKNOWLEDGEMENTS

Closing Time is the seventh and final book in the Stonechild and Rouleau series. This is both bittersweet and satisfying — Kala, Jacques, and the other main characters met every challenge I've thrown at them and developed distinct personalities and quirks with every book. I'm sad to see their stories end, having thoroughly enjoyed writing about these characters over the past several years.

The setting for *Closing Time* is closer to my own childhood neck of the woods in northern Ontario, and while Searchmont and most of the other locations in this story are real, Pine Hollow Lodge and the lake it's situated on are entirely fictional. I would also say that if you've never made the car trip from the Soo around Lake Superior to Thunder Bay, you've missed out on one beautiful stretch of scenery and should definitely put this drive on your bucket list.

I have many people to thank. First, thank you to the Dundurn team for your continued work and support: Shannon Whibbs for so capably editing the last three books in the series, Jenny McWha,

Laura Boyle, Kathryn Lane, Rachel Spence, Melissa Kawaguchi, and publicist Elham Ali. My thanks also to Dundurn president and publisher Scott Fraser, for continuing Kirk Howard's legacy of telling Canadian tales.

Since my first book was published in 2004, I've met and made friends with many people in the book industry, including authors, booksellers, bookstore owners, agents, publicists, and publishers. My life has been richer for every encounter. I've also gotten to know so many readers, both at events and through your personal notes — this continual support, feedback, and friendship mean everything. I would like to particularly acknowledge all the support I've received from my friends at the Granite Curling Club of West Ottawa.

Finally, thank you to my family: my husband, Ted, and daughters Lisa and Julia Weagle; Donna Blake and Laura Russell; Steve, Lorraine, and Dylan Chapman; and Ian and Cynthia Black.

On to the next adventure!